THE
BOOMERANG
KID

THE
BOOMERANG
KID

A NOVEL

Jay Quinn

Manufactured in the United States of America.

Published by Alyson Books
245 West 17th Street
New York, New York 10011

Distribution in the United Kingdom by Turnaround Publisher Services Ltd.
Unit 3, Olympia Trading Estate, Coburg Road, Wood Green
London N22 6TZ England

First Edition: November 2008

08 09 10 11 12 13 14 15 16 17 **a** 10 9 8 7 6 5 4 3 2 1

ISBN: 1-55583-954-1
ISBN 13: 978-1-55583-954-3
Library of Congress Cataloging-in-Publication data are on file.

Cover design by Victor Mingovits

For Jeff Auchter,
always and in every way.

Acknowledgments

I'd like to thank Mom and Dad, who have lived a different version of this story. Their constancy and abiding love have eased many sleepless nights. I'd also like to thank my friends Susan Highsmith and Joe Riddick for their support. I'm also grateful for the staff at Alyson Books for their hard work on my behalf. And Dr. Nathaniel Keller for his insight, concern, and care. And Patsy and Hailey, of course.

Finally, I'd like to acknowledge everyone living with severe bipolar disorder. Your brightness and darkness are heroic in the desperate gray world of the everyday.

Chapter One

MAURA OSTRYDER had always loved the autumn, and to her way of thinking nothing was finer than a lazy Sunday afternoon. Since it was a mellow Sunday in mid-October, she found herself expressly happy as she sat at the kitchen table listening to the coffee maker's hiss and chug as it brewed a pot of decaf. Matt, her lover and best friend, drowsed in the living room. The sounds of the football game from the flat screen television had tranquilized both of them. In the pause and deep breath before their hectic work week began, they both were content simply in each other's company. Their lives were as neatly arranged as the bowl of red apples on the dining room table.

After lunch, Maura curled up on the sofa as Matt burrowed himself into an Eero Saarinen Womb chair with his feet up on its matching ottoman. Though the iconic modern chair was very comfortable, he still joked it was the closest Maura would ever let him to a recliner. Her home was finally done now, redecorated after many years' residence. Maura had been gently urging Matt to start work on his own house in Lighthouse Point, though he could sell it as a teardown and still make a fortune. Even though at this point Matt and Maura essentially live together, they still deny this fact in many ways small and large; soon enough, that will have to change.

Just a month earlier, Maura discovered she was pregnant again, at fifty. After the initial shock wore off, she decided she was quietly pleased. Though Matt was older than she was by a few months, he'd taken her news excitedly, and now, shopping for baby furniture was more on his mind than remodeling his own house. Now, Maura looked through the Ikea catalogue, poring over the pages Matt had folded the upper corners of to mark the range of cribs, bassinets, and other items in the baby section.

It made Maura smile. She lightly dropped her hands to her still unswollen abdomen and felt the small bump growing there. "Hello, Junebug," she whispered. Soon she knew she'd have to pick a proper name, but as the baby was due in June, her private nickname would suffice until she'd had the amniocentesis that would reveal the infant's gender in addition to answering her fears about this late-in-life baby's health. Carefully, she put her fears away and studied the descriptions of cribs, reminding herself to be thankful for the surprise of the baby's advent.

When the phone rang, it startled Maura and brought an exasperated groan from Matt in the other room. Maura slid from her chair and stepped twice to catch the phone mounted to the kitchen wall. "Hello," she said cautiously.

"Hey girl," Rhett replied. "How's it going?"

Maura was surprised to hear from her ex-husband. Though they were pleasantly separated, they really didn't have anything to talk about anymore except their son. Immediately, she thought the worst. "I'm good, Rhett. Is everything up there okay? How's Kai?"

"That's what I called you about," Rhett answered, then added rather peevishly, "I'm fine by the way."

"I'm glad to hear it, Rhett," Maura said gently; the niceties had to be observed despite the fact she was now alarmed about Kai. "How's business?"

"Slack," he replied and sighed deeply. "This mortgage crisis going on right now has just about shut down the beach. I got a house going up in Duck, but after that, it looks like it's going to be a hard candy Christmas."

"I'm sorry, baby," Maura said, slipping into her natural role with Rhett. "Things down here are slow as well. We haven't done any subdivision work in ages. It's all in-fill now. We've just won a bid on some sewer rehab in Tamarac, but that's about all we have going on." Maura took a deep breath and chose her words carefully. "What's up with our son?"

Rhett laughed, but Maura could tell his heart wasn't in it. "When was the last time you talked to him?"

"About two weeks ago," Maura answered cautiously. "Why?"

"He didn't say anything to you about coming down, did he?" Rhett asked after a long pause.

"No, not a word. I thought he was coming for a visit at Christmas," Maura told him.

Rhett coughed and Maura pictured him standing by his truck in the parking lot of the Avalon Pier looking out over the waves. She could hear beach noises in the background. Whatever this was about, it was bad enough Rhett had left the cottage he shared with his girlfriend to call her in private. "Maura, he's . . . well, there isn't any other way to tell you but flat out."

"Is he alright?" Maura felt as much as heard the note of panic slip into her voice.

"Yeah, I guess. He stopped by my place with his truck packed and his dog in the cab about an hour and a half ago to tell me he was moving back down to be with you." Rhett laughed again, as if in the hope that this would in some way come as good news to Maura.

"What?" Maura pleaded. "Out of the blue? He didn't say anything to me about this."

"Well, it kinda caught me by surprise too, but I figured he'd paint himself into a corner sooner or later the way things have been going," Rhett said evenly.

"How has he painted himself into a corner, Rhett?" Maura asked, forcing herself to speak calmly.

"Well, he never came right out and said anything, but all you had to do is take one look at that boy he's been living with for the past year and you'd know he's been a lot more than a roommate," Rhett said baldly. "There's been a girlfriend in the picture too now for the past few months. Her name's Linda and she works as a home hospice nurse. She got popped last week for stealing heavy duty painkillers from her patients. Evidently, she's been doing it for awhile."

"So what's the surprise??" Maura asked. "We know he's always been bisexual, but he usually manages to keep his lovers apart."

"Oh for God's sake, Maura. Use your head. Kai ain't never been scared of a pill. My bet is he was fucking this Linda chick for the fringe benefits," Rhett said easily.

"You're probably right," Maura admitted. Her son had a history of casual drug abuse, though it had never gotten out of control, so far. "You don't think he's got a problem with painkillers, do you, Rhett?"

"Naw," Rhett said dismissively. "He's been working steady and his butt-buddy doesn't have the reputation around here as a druggie. That's more than I can say for some of the other guys Kai hangs out with up here."

"What about his real meds? Is he still taking his real meds?" Maura demanded.

"Girl, it ain't like he's still a kid," Rhett said belligerently. "I don't ask him if he's taking his medicine. That's one thing I can say nice about that boy he's been with, while he was with him, Kai's been on the up and up. Like I said, he's worked steady. God, he's done some beautiful stuff Maura, you should see the cypress paneling he did in . . ."

"Is he in any trouble with the law?" Maura demanded.

"Naw, none I imagine. They don't care about who Linda might have been getting high now they have her. My buddy with the sheriff's department says she swears she hasn't been dealing. She was just stealing the stuff for herself. But no bail. She's in bad shape," Rhett told her dismissively.

Maura's mind had moved with rapid speed past this point of the conversation to embrace the fact that Kai was on his way down I-95, quite probably in a full-blown manic episode, heading home to her. "Well, thanks for the heads up Rhett," she managed.

"No problem," her son's daddy told her easily. "Look, Maura, he's probably okay. He wasn't wild-eyed or especially amped. I think things up here just got too tight for him. Robin, that's the boy's name he's been living with, he's the one who's going to be messed up. You could tell he really loves Kai. But you know our kid, he doesn't love anybody more than himself; except maybe you and that dog of his. Anyways, Maura, he's got all his tools with him and he'll find work. He just needs a place to land right now."

"God, I hope you're right, Rhett." Maura sighed.

"Oh I know I'm right. The guy who can work with his hands will always find work," Rhett said proudly.

"That's true," Maura offered as a balm to his pride. Rhett had gone to work banging nails straight out of high school in an effort to support Maura and his first and only child. "What does a good trim carpenter make these days?"

"He can ask for thirty an hour and get it if he's working for himself. Kai's been doing that for two years now. I taught him right," Rhett assured her.

"Well, that's comforting," Maura admitted. "Still, he has to find work. Do you suppose he's coming home stone broke?"

"I don't think so," Rhett told her confidently. "I offered him some money for the road, but he told me he was all right. He would have taken it if he needed it. You know Kai."

"Yes, of course. Hopefully he's got some socked away. I'm not exactly rich," Maura said off-handedly.

"Look sweetheart, I got to go. Give me a call and let me know he got there okay, will ya?"

"How long do you think it'll take him to drive it, Rhett?" Maura asked. She had not driven that far since she'd moved down to Florida when Kai wasn't quite six years old. Twenty-one years later, she only knew it was a hell of a long drive.

"I don't know, maybe eighteen hours or less. He said he was going to drive straight through," Rhett told her gently.

"That means he's off his meds," Maura said hopelessly. "He couldn't drive straight through if he was taking his meds."

"Don't worry about him, Maura," Rhett encouraged her. "He ain't so crazy he can't drive. Probably he'll drive better in fact, if he's all manicky."

Maura laughed. When he was in a manic phase, Kai could go days without sleep.

"That's my girl, go on and laugh. You can handle him and get him straightened out. Look, his boyfriend Robin asked me for your phone number, I gave it to him. I hope that's all right," Rhett admitted.

"Sure," Maura said, eager to connect with someone who loved Kai, someone who lived with him and could give her some clue as to what was going on with her difficult son. Concerned about Kai's tendency to make some pretty poor choices in friends, she asked, "Rhett, this Robin? Is he a good kid?"

"He seems alright enough," Rhett said. "He sells real estate. He looks like he's about sixteen, but he's twenty-four. And, to tell you the truth Maura, he reminds me of you. Blond hair, green eyes, about your height. They say men look for their mothers all their lives, right?"

"Yeah, that's what they say," Maura said, flattered in an odd way.

"Babe, I got to go," Rhett repeated aimlessly and paused. Then, "You know I still love you, don't you?"

Maura glanced over her shoulder toward the living room, suddenly conscious of Matt so close by. "Yeah, I know. And I still love you too, even if you did make the strangest kid in the world with me. We really made one unique child, didn't we?"

Rhett laughed, satisfied that some bonds are only ever loosened, never broken. "You'll call me to let me know he's home safe, all right?" As complicated as his relationship was with his son, he always had genuinely loved him.

"Sure thing," Maura said and sighed. "Take care of yourself, surfer boy."

"You too, surfer girl," Rhett said and thumbed the off-button on his cell phone.

Maura heard him click off and sighed. Rhett's news came at a time when things had been going so well for her. She liked to think Kai finally had his act together. She'd never dreamed he'd pull a stunt like this. Though she would admit to being a free-spirit herself, she liked to think of herself as a practical dreamer. Her extravagances were small and it didn't take a great deal to make her happy. Now fifty, she had lived a life that forced her to consider many things ahead of herself. Finding herself pregnant for the first time, at twenty-two, she had to face hard facts early on and find a way to be happy with her choices. She'd been pretty successful overall, despite the lack of wisdom in her only experience with throwing caution to the winds.

After working her way through college, dutifully treading a path that promised every success, her world had been suddenly bordered by the reality that she would have a child to bring up with a man who was scarcely more than a child himself. It had all started happily enough. Having made good on a childhood dream to live at the beach, which she'd always loved, she'd found a promising job with an engineering firm in Nags Head, North Carolina, fresh out of East Carolina University. She'd also managed to find a year-round rental of a tiny beach cottage built high on pilings within walking distance to the beach. Her parents had reluctantly helped her move her few belongings to the long strip of sand called the Outer Banks, thinking that after a year or two of living in such a deserted lonely stretch of nowhere, she'd come to her senses and move back to Raleigh, Greensboro, or Charlotte, cities big enough to dream large dreams in and make a life that was as promising as they believed their child to be. Maura had impatiently waved them goodbye as they made their way off the beach on toward the four and a half hour drive back to her hometown. She had stood on her empty deck facing east with the sea wind blowing back the carefully blonded streaks of her shoulder length hair from her face. It was Sunday afternoon, and she didn't have to go home. She *was* home.

May hadn't even turned to June that first spring on the beach when she met Rhett at the gym. She had no way of knowing the flirting eyes of the nineteen-year-old surfer that caught and returned her admiring glances would be replicated in a baby boy's eyes within a year. Rhett and Maura's romance was epic that summer. It stretched itself in the sun and grew all out of proportion to what they thought they were about. When a stolen day in warm October found them naked on a quilt quite out of sight on a dune somewhere north of Rodanthe, Kai was conceived. Thinking back on it again and again in the years to come, a large part of what Maura could recall was how guilty she had felt about calling in sick so she could spend the glorious fall day on the beach with Rhett. There was absolutely no guilt associated with the fact they'd made a baby that day. That part of it was perfectly fine with Maura. In fact, she felt that for her first pregnancy she couldn't have planned it any better if she had given it any thought at all.

By Christmas, she'd known she was pregnant. There was never any discussion of not having the baby. Maura had been raised in a strict Catholic home and what was even more decisive was the fact that she felt what she was doing was right. On the face of it, she had a good job, she had a good-looking stud of a boy-man who seemed utterly delighted by the fact that he was going to be a father, and she had made herself a home on the beach. Maura was happier than she'd ever been in her life.

Maura and Rhett married quietly in the small Catholic church on the beach road in Kill Devil Hills in January. Rhett managed to stay employed all winter building a large house up in Corolla and Maura's office noted she was never even once late from morning sickness, and that she worked dutifully throughout her pregnancy. When she delivered a healthy grey-eyed boy the following July after an unremarkable pregnancy, she felt herself blessed. She named him Kai, which meant "sea" in Hawaiian or Japanese—she wasn't really sure which. What she was sure of was the delight she found in the tiny tangible proof of her love for Rhett and her power to make her own way in the world.

It would have been idyllic if reality hadn't set in. Pride and love aside, it was too difficult to make a twenty-year-old man out of Rhett and Maura found that being the strong one, the one who made rent and put groceries on the table consistently, to be overwhelming. She still loved Rhett, but when Kai wasn't quite three Maura finally decided it would be better to let Rhett find his own way toward becoming a man. She managed to make it two more years on the beach with Rhett walking in and out of her and Kai's lives with all the fondness of a lover and a brother and assuming no more responsibility for either of them than a casual friend.

Just before Kai turned six, a happy set of coincidences led to Maura being offered a job in Fort Lauderdale with a much bigger salary and much better prospects to grow with the firm. She took stock of her options, her meager savings and the promise of some help from her parents, and decided to make the move off the beach and on toward a better life for her and her son. The love she still felt for Rhett was as familiar and real as he was often absent. The thought of trading their tenuous yet resilient relationship for nothing held her back but she had to face facts. She packed what she had in a rented U-Haul truck driven by her brother and shot-gunned by her father. She put Kai and their yellow lab Buddy in her car and guided the little caravan of her life south on I-95.

With her parents' help, Maura was able to come up with the down payment on a small, three-bedroom, zero-lot line house in Sunrise, Florida. It was exactly twelve and a half miles straight down Oakland Park Boulevard from the beach, further than Maura wanted to be, but she contented herself with the small canal that ran behind her house. At the time, Sunrise was a rapidly growing suburb of Fort Lauderdale proper. It had the reputation of being an old folks' town as it was dominated by the tall cat-walked condos of retirees from New York and New Jersey who moved down to these two-bedroom railroad flats in droves. But there were also many others like Maura in Sunrise as well. It was a light blue-collar kind of town and neighborhood. Many residents were firemen and policemen. A few blocks away, there was a big Catholic church called All Saints that had a small school and after-school care for Kai.

While Maura's parents weren't wealthy, they did love their daughter and little grandson very much. Maura took them up on their offer to subsidize Kai's parochial school tuition, which allowed her to pay for his after-school care herself.

In the following years Maura perfected the skills of being a practical dreamer. She kept herself to herself and dated rarely. The truth was, she was still in love with Rhett with a persistence that had nothing to do with the facts of his life continuing happily up on the Outer Banks without his wife and son. Instead of investing her energy into a love life, Maura put her efforts into her job at Kellogg, Wise, and Kaplan, the civil engineering firm whose timely job offer had brought her south to Florida to begin with. What she didn't put into her work at KWK, she gave to Kai.

Kai was a different kind of child. Though he was quite pretty for a little boy, and many other children strove to be his friend, he was aloof and given to being a loner. From the time he was a baby, he loved to draw. Alone with a pad of blank paper and enough markers, pencils, and crayons to capture all the images he saw in his head, he was content. Maura, alone and often tired, encouraged his solitary pursuits, though she did enjoy being with him a great deal. She was much like him herself. Maura had never been an outgoing personality. While she was perfectly capable of being social, she really preferred her own company. In her son, she saw herself, so she reared him to be self-sufficient. While they were content to simply share the house, they both developed a closeness that was perfectly natural considering their circumstances. Maura, for want of many friends, spoke to the little fellow more as a contemporary and with a great deal of fascination and respect, enjoying his point of view and his perceptions. They got on remarkably well and didn't feel any deprivation in the small house by the canal in the subdivision way out by the Everglades.

When Kai was still quite young, Maura started noticing that Kai had trouble sleeping. He could be wild at times, dancing or running or otherwise extending himself physically until he would slump in exhaustion. These periods were followed by hollow-eyed hours of staring into nothingness. His emotions were curiously labile, shifting on a dime from a happy voluble toddler to a withdrawn child, chillingly distant and remote.

However, his pediatrician saw nothing to be alarmed about. Physically he was healthy, though he often had dark circles of exhaustion ringing his pale gray eyes. The pediatrician explained that Kai was a very imaginative child with a set of personal circadian rhythms unique to himself. The doctor told Maura not to worry about it; they'd keep an eye on him and later test him to see if he had hyperactivity and attention deficit disorder when he became older. Maura seriously doubted that Kai had ADHD. He had already demonstrated an almost preternatural absorption in whatever task was at hand. He seemed to lose himself in whatever he was doing to the point of being startled when she finally demanded his attention.

Kai had always been a precocious child. He had both walked and talked by the time he was nine months old. If he could be inexplicably irritable or moody, she just chalked it up to the transitory winds of childhood and always, if she watched and waited, he came to himself reasonably. If there was anything remarkable about him, as far as Maura was concerned, it was the degree with which he could learn. Before he was four, he had taught himself to read and Maura counted herself lucky that his most favorite treat was a trip to the public library rather than an array of expensive toys. As long as she kept him in books and drawing materials he seemed happy.

If there was anything that troubled her about Kai as a toddler, it was his extreme reaction to music. Maura herself was not musically gifted, but she loved music. What limited money she had for herself, she spent on albums and then CDs. She loved it all, rock, jazz, soul, even country music spoke to her, though her personal favorites when Kai was small were soul and R&B. Kai responded dramatically to music. On more than one occasion he had been reduced to tears by a particularly sad song of love and loss articulated by some soul diva about complicated adult emotions far from the emotional reach of a four-year-old. Likewise, Kai could be enchanted by a song and learned very early how to make the stereo play his favorite songs over and over.

Now, more than twenty years later, Maura knew all of these things about her son's uniqueness should have given her pause, but at the time, they hadn't. She never saw the shadows on the walls of their little house in Sawgrass Estates until they became impossible to ignore. Kai eventually cracked up, badly, around his ninth birthday. There was a big suicide attempt for such a skinny little boy, and ambulances, and doctors following that. Life became defined by shifting diagnoses, each grimmer than the last. Then there were the meds that ravaged her pretty son until he physically changed with each new round of pills.

When the doctors managed to agree, they defined Kai as having a rare, rapid-cycling form of Type II bipolar disorder. After that, Maura's life, more than ever, became about her son. Alone, she bent herself to shield him from the emotional winds that seemed to come like the hurricanes that threatened them each summer and fall.

Now, Kai had turned twenty-seven and Maura fifty. Two years before, he'd moved back to the Outer Banks to work with his Rhett. Despite his degree in graphic design from the Art Institute of Fort Lauderdale, Kai had chosen to become a trim carpenter, and by all accounts, he was a very good one. He specialized in custom cabinetry beyond the usual installation of baseboards and crown molding. Medicated, he was industrious and productive, but off his meds, he dissolved.

In the two years since he'd returned to his dad, Kai had been stable, and Maura was at last able to see past him and his needs. On her own for the first time in her life, she flourished. Still in the small house on the canal in Sunrise, she cautiously redecorated and brought her home to a very comfortable and pleasant state. For the first time in her life, she didn't have to support or supplement Kai's income so she was able to purchase the contemporary Italian leather sofa and slouchy modern dining room chairs to contrast with a nineteenth-century English breakfast table. She bought the Frette linens in pure white that had tempted her for years in her home design magazines. She replaced her battered Wal-Mart pots and pans with All-Clad, reveling in materialism for once.

Still employed by KWK, the same engineering firm that had brought her to South Florida, Maura had earned a respected and valued place in the upper levels of management. And, to her complete surprise, she found herself once more in love.

One of Maura's responsibilities with the firm was to be its representative member for the countywide homebuilder's association. As an allied industry member, the principals at her firm thought that it was important for Maura to participate fully in the activities of the association. For all the catered chicken or fish dinners she endured every month, she came to enjoy her membership not only for its challenges and opportunities to network, but also for its social aspect. Having been single for over twenty years, she was at last able to see herself as others saw her: an attractive career woman who'd kept her figure as assiduously as she'd kept her hair carefully blonded to preserve the girl she'd been on the beach all those years before. Maura got her share of not only second looks but also of propositions. At either she smiled confidently, but never gave anything away.

After many years in the homebuilders' association, Maura found herself on the legislative committee. This was the lobbying arm of the association and so its committee members tended to be either lawyers or the big players in the real estate development industry. Matt Jenkins was one such player. By the time he met Maura, they were both forty-eight and while she had worked her way up in a civil engineering firm, Matt had parlayed his entrepreneurial start-up home building company into a firm that employed a total of over four hundred workers, administrative and tradesmen. He eventually sold his company to a large national homebuilder with a contract that kept him on as president of the new division his own firm had become. Matt had sold out at just the right time. He made a second fortune when he sold out to the large national homebuilder. He had also made and lost a marriage with two teenaged daughters in the process.

Matt told Maura his marriage had been doomed before it began. Matt was a single-minded careerist. His wife was a Venezuelan beauty who also was as spoiled and capricious as a child. She grew into her role as a successful builder's wife with none of her flaws smoothed by maturity, motherhood, or prestige. She and Matt had divorced before he sold his company. He was not ungenerous with her or his two daughters, but he despaired of them all. Their mother was rearing the girls to be princesses and there was little Matt could do to change things.

Matt and Maura met one bright Wednesday morning in the conference room of a law firm high in an office building in the dead center of Fort Lauderdale. It was Maura's first morning as a member of the legislative committee and she impressed Matt with her intuitive questions and easy grasp of the nuances of the problems the group was trying to address. He'd seen her at general membership meetings, as Maura had seen him, but they had never spoken. For Maura's part, she knew who he was and more about his private life than he'd probably had reason to think, but the homebuilder's association was really a rather small pond and he was a large fish. Maura kept catching his eye all during that first meeting, sitting as she was, across the impressive expanse of oak conference table, but she thought little of it. As far as she was concerned, Matt Jenkins was out of her league. Matt, however, thought very differently.

As the meeting was breaking up, he made it a point to find his way across the conference room to introduce himself to Maura and exchange business cards. Maura was impressed with his ease and with the man himself. Matt wasn't conventionally handsome. Rather he was striking in his way. His long rangy form had managed to stay raw-boned even into middle age. He had reddish blond hair and warm brown eyes that were lambent behind the stylish glasses he was wearing. At six-three, he stood over Maura's five-ten and she found herself pleased to look up into his pleasantly weathered face. Matt didn't have the kind of skin meant for outdoor work in the strong South Florida sun. The harsh light had rewarded him with a fan of wrinkles around his eyes that radiated outward and deepened with his smile.

Matt actually knew as much about Maura as she did him. She was remarkable enough for being such a successful woman in what was an industry dominated by men. Besides that, she was blonde-haired and green-eyed, with a promising hint of ripeness in her trim figure. She smiled and told him she'd be delighted if he'd call.

They found themselves lovers rather quickly. For Maura, it was a sexual awakening that she had longed for but long denied. For Matt, it was an affair that excited him deeply; reawakening an adolescent longing he thought he had long grown past. With Kai recently moved north to be near his father, Maura was in her home improvement phase and Matt stepped into an area in Maura's life and home that had long been closed off, and left to the cobwebs. Though Matt still lived in an old home in Lighthouse Point he had bought and moved into after his divorce, over the following months he found himself most often at Maura's. He found himself painting her walls and changing out her kitchen with the time he had planned to redo his place in Lighthouse Point.

What surprised both of them, now, two years down the road, was the depth of their friendship. Neither Maura nor Matt had ever been in a relationship that brought companionability with passion, warm acceptance with hot embraces and an abiding respect with what they thought of as love. They never spoke of marriage. Neither of them wanted to dislodge the warm heart of what they had together with the things marriage had taught them came with the ring and the chapel.

Distracted by her concern for Kai, Maura heard the phone's alarming tone meant to remind her to hang up. She stood and replaced the phone in its cradle before she busied herself making two mugs of coffee, one for Matt and one for herself. Then, she took a deep breath, squared her shoulders and walked to the living room where she handed Matt his mug of coffee before sitting on the end of the sofa by his chair.

"I take it that was your ex," Matt said easily.

"Yes, and he had some rather interesting news," Maura said as she took a sip of her coffee. For the first time in ages she longed for a cigarette. She had only quit when she started going out with Matt.

"What did he say? He didn't upset you, did he?" Matt asked with no little concern.

"Well, he didn't upset me, but his news is a little disconcerting," Maura admitted.

"What's going on?"

"Evidently, my son is in his truck with his dog and all his personal belongings heading south on I-95 on his way home," Maura said plainly.

"Well, it'll be nice to meet him finally. He's a trim carpenter isn't he?"

"More like a master cabinet maker," Maura said proudly. "I have pictures somewhere of his high-end work. He really is very good."

"How long does he plan to visit?" Matt asked cautiously.

"I can't say, Matt. Maybe six days, six weeks, six months, hell if I know." Maura said tiredly.

"Oh boy," Matt said, and sipped his coffee.

After that, they sat quietly for awhile, drinking their coffee and Maura longing for a cigarette. Finally, Matt ventured to ask, "Well, when do you expect him?"

"If he drives straight through, by mid-morning tomorrow," Maura said and smiled.

"I guess I'd better clear out after breakfast then," Matt said.

"No!"

"Well, I do have to go into the office," Matt replied calmly.

"I'm sorry, Matt. I didn't mean to snap at you," Maura said and took his free hand in her own. "I just don't want anything to change with us just because he's here. He's got to accept there's a new man around the house."

"We'll work it out—don't freak on me, okay?" Matt told her gently.

Maura squeezed his hand before letting go and pulling her hair back with her hand. She stroked it into place well off her forehead and said, "It's only one's kids who feel like they can just barge in and expect life to have stood still while they were away."

"Mine aren't that old yet, but I'm definitely seeing the signs," Matt said and smiled.

Maura searched his face and finding his eyes, she said, "You know, it's like I'm my own ship . . . making headway against the currents on a flat calm sea and I look behind myself and there's this dingy tied up at my stern. It's just happily riding along tied to me even though it has its own motor and oar. The person who's supposed to be on that dingy is always coming back to the mothership."

"I take it this isn't the first time your son has done this," Matt said gently.

Maura shook her head. "There was the time he wanted to live with his dad when he was twelve. That was a disaster. There was the time he went to live with his dad after he graduated from high school and then came home two years later to go to the Art Institute. Now, here he is again."

"The boomerang kid, they call it," Matt said and smiled.

"What?" Maura replied.

"The boomerang kid. No matter how many times you fling them out into the world to make it on their own, they circle back to drop at your feet," Matt explained gently.

"That's my Kai," Maura said as she stood and made her way to the kitchen. She remembered she'd hidden a pack of cigarettes in the freezer in case of an emergency. One like this. She spared a guilty thought for her new baby burrowed deep inside and mumbled an apology as she opened the door to the freezer. She figured one cigarette this early in the game couldn't hurt. Her own mother had smoked continuously during her own pregnancies and everything had turned out fine for her sister and brothers. If this child was going to be anything like her first born, she'd be back to a pack a day before long.

Chapter Two

THE SKY WAS graying with dawn when Kai pulled off I-95 to gas up an hour south of Jacksonville, Florida. All of South Carolina and Georgia had disappeared under his wheels as he drove through the night. Now his eyes felt full of sand and Heidi, his Weimaraner, was growing restless in the confines of the truck's cab. The dark interior of the truck was lit only by the lights on the dash and Kai welcomed the bright fluorescent lights of the gas station as he pulled under the shelter. He was tired, but still filled with an electric energy that drove him on. For the first time in a long while he wished he hadn't gone off his meds. The charge of his mind wasn't enough to fuel his body like it had when he was younger. The mania was like an embrace he couldn't shrug off and now he knew he was tired.

After parking by a gas pump close to the road, Kai reassured Heidi he'd be back as he closed the door on her whimpering. Though the gas station was deserted, he made sure the truck was locked before he strode across the concrete in the harsh glare of greenish-white light to the door of the Mobile Mart. Inside, a bored woman behind the counter looked him over dispassionately as he made his way to the rest room. Once he was inside the stall, he locked the door behind him and drew a folded wad of cash from his jeans pocket. He was carrying the five thousand dollars he'd saved over a summer's worth of work. He'd closed his savings account in the bank in Kill Devil Hills the Friday before. Carefully he peeled off a few twenties to pay for his gas and another in the series of frozen coffee drinks sold in wayside places like this. He shoved the wad back in his left front pants pocket and stashed the twenties in his back pocket before he stepped to the urinal and relieved himself of the large frozen drink from his last stop hours before.

After he finished and zipped up, he turned to the sink and roughly washed his face with cold water. Lifting his head, he stared into his red-rimmed eyes and saw the reflection of all the on-coming headlights and red tail lights he'd chased for the past twelve hours. The tiredness in his body was like an ache. He was stiff from sitting in the driver's seat steering the truck across hundred of miles of highway, but his mind was still racing along just over the speed limit. He looked at his hands. They were curiously still, free of the fine tremor that assailed them when he was medicated. Absently, he tore off a length of paper towel and dried his face and hands.

Kai glanced at himself once more in the mirror as he considered going into the stash of painkillers he'd copped from Linda before she was arrested. He still had many miles to go, but if he treated himself to a pill now, it would go a long way to making the remaining miles more bearable. As alert as he was naturally, the little blue pill would only take the edge off his racing thoughts and ease his hurting back. His level gaze in the bathroom's mirror encouraged him to draw the little bottle from his other pocket and pluck out a pill. Anticipating the mild buzz it would bring, he popped it in his mouth and chewed it with his back molars to nullify the pill's time-release properties. He smiled at himself as the pill's bitter taste filled his mouth, and quickly stepped back out into the store.

After he served himself the frozen coffee drink he craved, he strode to the cashier's counter and offered her three twenties. The woman didn't even look at him. Sunk in her own orbit, she merely rang up his drink and told him she'd put the balance on his pump. She didn't have to ask which one he was on; he was the only customer around.

Kai nodded in reply before stepping back out into the dawn. Reaching the side of the truck, he opened the gas flap and twisted free the cap. Before he could think about it, the pump was in place and the cold handle gripped in his hand. He watched the digital counter tick off the gas as it filled his tank. The lighted numbers' dance seemed more appropriate for a Las Vegas casino than this brightly lit gas station in the middle of nowhere.

Once he'd filled his tank to the limit of the amount he'd prepaid, Kai quickly replaced the gas nozzle and capped the truck's tank. Heidi stood watching him inside the cab. He sat his frozen drink on the hood of the truck and unlocked the door to let her out. She unfolded from the interior of the cab in a fluid pour of grey hair and muscle. Patiently she waited by his side as he reached into the cab for her leash and snapped it onto her collar. Once he got her leashed, he picked up his drink and ambled along with his dog to the grassy strip alongside the gas station's pavement.

Heidi nosed her way along the trash-strewn side lot sniffing at pits of paper and discarded cups. Rather quickly she found a spot to relieve herself and took care of business without any coaxing. Kai knew the dog realized this was only a stop along the long way to somewhere else. Without as much as a look back at him, she turned and led him back to the truck. Kai glanced at his watch and stopped behind the pickup to open the door of the camper shell over the bed. He drew out Heidi's stainless steel bowl after he poured a measure of dry food into it followed by the contents of a bottle of water over the kibble. He sat the bowl on the concrete behind the truck and lit a cigarette to savor while the dog happily munched her breakfast.

While she ate, Kai looked back toward the highway. The traffic seemed to be picking up. In the east, the sky had lightened considerably since he'd stopped. He took a deep hit from his cigarette and followed it with a long pull on the straw in his frozen mochacchino. The languor of the pill's ease began to steal over him. He stretched and smiled. He knew he had to be careful with these pills. He'd seen how easily it was to get hooked. Linda had been a stone junkie before he'd ever met her. Now she was in jail and going through detox. The thought of it was a caution to him. He'd gone off his psychiatric meds long before he'd started seeing Linda, but seeing her had brought the benefit of enjoying the painkillers when she was in a generous mood.

In a way, Kai was glad Linda had gotten arrested. It saved him from having to break up with her. He'd known since Labor Day that she intended him to move in with her, but he couldn't see that happening. It would have been easy to fall into her world of partying and pills while playing at being husband and wife, but besides the seduction of trading his psych meds for painkillers, he didn't want to be anyone's husband. What he'd been to Robin came closer to being who he actually was and that had scared him too.

Heidi's nose banging the steel pan along the concrete under their feet brought him back to the present time. He gently patted her head and took the pan away from her and they walked back to the truck. The dog looked up at him expectantly and he said, "Come on girl. Time to get back on the road." With that, he led her to the truck's door and opened it for her to jump and scramble back into her place on the bench seat next to him. As she settled herself in and sank with a sigh into a tight ball, Kai climbed back into the truck and placed the cold plastic cup between his legs. He put the key in the ignition and started up the engine before he put on his safety belt and locked it in place.

Kai pulled onto the road and turned the truck toward the highway feeling good. His break from driving, walking the dog and sipping the cold drink had revived him. With a free hand he replaced the CD he'd listened to for the past few hours with a vintage Steely Dan CD he hadn't listened to in awhile. As the music swelled he merged with the current of traffic heading south into the land of oranges and sunshine. It was going on six in the morning and he still had hours to go, but every hour from now on counted. Soon he'd be home where he felt safe. Soon he'd outrun everything he'd left up on the Outer Banks. Only Robin he regretted and as he switched lanes to pass a long distance rig he wondered if he'd really left him behind at all.

Chapter Three

THE NEXT MORNING dragged as Maura tried to keep her mind on her work at the office. Though she answered her emails and returned calls dutifully, all the while she kept trying to imagine where along I-95 Kai might be at the moment. She'd driven the monotonous, straight lanes of the highway that ran in a straight line through Florida's repetitive landscape until Palm Beach County. It was seven hours of sheer monotony after the hubbub around Jacksonville to Fort Lauderdale. It would be so easy for him to fall asleep, especially if he'd driven through the night.

A low-grade anxiety gnawed at the edges of Maura's nerves. Cutting through that feeling was an ongoing struggle between anger at Kai for this sudden turning over of his world and hers and her delight at seeing him again after nearly ten months. She had to admit to a certain sad absence in her life when he was living up north.

At eleven-thirty, she tentatively dialed her own home phone number thinking he'd pick up the phone if he'd arrived. In reply, she only got her own voice mail message encouraging her to leave a message to herself. She replaced the handset in its cradle before the beep prompted any recording. Sighing, she looked at the files on her desk and then stood up abruptly, intending to go see Bill Kellogg, the partner to whom she reported. She had reached the conclusion she was useless at work and would be for the rest of the day.

Maura found Bill on the phone in his office, but he motioned for her to sit. Maura gratefully sank into one of the generous chairs in front of Bill's desk and idly looked around his familiar office rather than try to pointedly ignore him while he spoke rapidly into the phone. The framed diplomas and state board's licensure and other various framed documents of his career filled the space over a long row of bookcases lining one wall, while a large abstract canvas dominated the other. All of these things she had seen more times than she could count, so she swiveled the chair away from Bill's desk and looked out the bank of windows on the wall behind her. Bill enjoyed his view, and as it faced north, he could afford to raise his blinds as high as they could go so he could look out over the tree tops to the sky beyond without a merciless pounding from the hot South Florida sun.

After working for the man for over twenty years, Maura held him in high esteem. Bill Kellogg was kinder than either of his two partners, so it was to him that most of the staff brought their personal affairs when they conflicted with their office duties or schedules. Maura looked on him as a kind of avuncular uncle rather than as a boss. She could confide in Bill, and being a single mother with a particularly challenging child, she had always found Bill's forbearance to be as generous as his advice was sound and comforting. Though it was generally known, but never discussed, Bill was gay. He was very circumspect about his personal life, and perhaps because of that trait, he made an excellent confidant as well as being a good manager of people. His careful grooming of Maura's professional demeanor had made her into a prized employee. Bill's personal discretion had also allowed Maura to bring her quite human concerns and shortcomings to her boss without fear.

Bill finally said his goodbyes at the conclusion of his phone call and Maura swiveled her chair back to face him. He hung up the phone and brought his arms over his head, arching his back in a long, satisfying stretch. Maura smiled and said, "That sounded like it ended well."

Bill brought his arms down to rest on his desk and returned her smile. "We're working on a new bid. I don't want to talk about it yet. I don't want to jinx it. But we need the work and it's a big project."

"Sounds exciting," Maura responded happily. "When do I get involved?"

Bill shook his head and took a sip from his coffee cup. "Not for awhile now. We're at the talking point still. I'll let you know when it gets to the part where you can do your magic." Bill winced at his coffee cup and sat it aside. "What can I do for you this morning?"

"If I get you a fresh cup of coffee, can I take the rest of the day off?" Maura asked teasingly.

"I can get my own coffee," Bill said ruefully. "But you can tell me why you need the rest of the day off."

Maura's smile faded as she looked in her boss's eyes and said, "I got a call from my ex-husband yesterday warning me Kai is on his way here, to move in again."

Bill whistled and gave Maura a sympathetic look. "Let me guess, your ex-husband's call was the first news you'd had about this and you've been worried and wondering ever since when Kai is going to show up and why, by the way, he's moving in on you again."

"Pretty much," Maura told him wryly. "If he drove straight through, which he led Rhett to believe he would, he ought to be getting here by lunch today."

"Maura, how old is Kai now?" Bill asked as he pushed himself away from his desk and crossed his left leg one over the other.

"Twenty-seven last July," Maura told him, "and still not grown."

Bill picked up a pen from his desk and idly turned it end over end for several moments as he looked past Maura out the windows behind her. Finally he looked her in the face and said, "Maura, sooner or later, you've got to stop pulling him out of the holes he's stepped into. What do you intend to do with him once he gets here?"

Maura blinked once and willed herself not to cry. She had sat in this spot and talked to Bill about Kai so many times over the years, and now the frustration threatened to engulf her.

"I suppose I'll listen to him, find out what's wrong this time, and then help him work it out. Damn, Bill, that's a mother's job. I wish sometimes I'd had a puppy instead of a child. With a dog, you're on the hook for only about fourteen years. With a kid, you're obligated for life."

Bill nodded and without letting his eyes move from her face asked, "What does Matt Jenkins think about it?"

Maura was a bit taken aback. She assumed everyone knew she and Matt were together, but it wasn't really discussed. Because she never discussed her relationship with Matt at work, the last thing she expected Bill to ask her about was Matt's feelings on the subject. Still, honestly she replied, "When I told him yesterday, he didn't make any big deal about it. He told me I had a 'boomerang kid.' He kind of didn't react one way or the other."

"That's because he's a smart man," Bill told her. "Everyone knows you don't give unsolicited advice to a mother about her kids. But after all these years, I think you and I are close enough that I can put my two cents in. You have a great thing going with Matt and you deserve it. Don't let Kai waltz back into your life and interfere with that, Maura."

Maura nodded. It wasn't anything she hadn't already considered. The last thing she wanted was to let Kai move back in and upset the satisfying routine she and Matt had built together. But, Kai was her son. Besides that, there was all the guilt and emotional baggage Kai personified as an indictment against her notions of her motherhood. Even the psychiatrists had told her the genetic reality of her part in Kai's bipolar disorder. In a way, it went way beyond any pure maternal instinct she had to protect her fledgling offspring. Part of it was genetic debt for which she shouldn't be blamed, but she'd long assumed that blame.

She looked at Bill, all this considered, and said, "Bill, I like my life as it is right now. Matt and I are good. I love my job. I'm not in debt. For the first time since Kai was born, I finally have my life back. What you're telling me makes perfect sense, but the fact remains, I have to sort Kai out, *again*, in order to keep my own life running smoothly."

"Well, you're a hell of a woman, and mother, I'll give you that," Bill said as he uncrossed his legs and pulled himself up to his desk. "By now, most parents would have told Kai it was swim or sink time. I'm not sure that isn't what you should tell him when he gets here. Twenty-seven is far too old to be running home to mommy. But you're going to do what you think is best, and over all these years, you've invariably been right."

"Thanks, Bill," Maura said.

"Go on. Get out of here," Bill said as he picked up the handset of his phone. "Let me know if you need any help."

"I will," Maura said as she stood. "But I'll be fine. I'll see you tomorrow."

"Good luck," Bill said as he began pecking at the keypad on his phone.

It didn't take Maura five minutes to add an "out of office" prompt to her email and change the message on her voice mail saying she'd be out the rest of the day, but back on Tuesday. She gathered her purse and briefcase and without saying goodbye to anyone else, she walked out of the building into a beautiful October morning. On the drive home, she anxiously ticked off the landmarks of her short commute, the same one she'd been making all those years. What she noticed was the change in the light. That was really the only way you could tell autumn had arrived in South Florida. The sun was kinder, more benign than it had been only weeks before. Though it was still eighty degrees, the sky was a fall blue, not the white-hot scald it had been in August.

As she drove, Maura remembered how fall used to look on the Outer

Banks. The sea oats on the dunes had turned to gold and everything but the shadows were burnished as well. The shadows reflected the grey-green crash of the waves. It was altogether different from here, so much farther south. As a small child, Kai had hated the long stretches of windy gray up on the Banks. He'd whine, "Mama, make it warm. Mama, make it summer soon." She imagined him fleeing the impending winter up there for the warm winters he'd known from the time he was six. When he was twelve and wanted to go to live with his father, she'd packed him off as soon as school had let out. By that February, Rhett had loaded him on a plane after calling Maura and telling her Kai hadn't spoken in weeks or eaten much in the same span of time. Maura had picked him up at Fort Lauderdale International and found him to be a haunted wraith. He had grown by inches in height, but seemed awkwardly out of touch with his own body. He definitely was out of touch with the world. Still, back in the cheerful sunshine of Sunrise, she could almost watch him reclaim himself from the black depression that had hold of him. By the end of March, his psychiatrist had him restabilized on his meds, which Rhett hadn't bothered to see he took, and Maura had her son back. Those were the lithium and Ascendin years. Kai put on weight to balance his increased height and their life settled back into its comfortable routines. Now, Maura found herself wondering how he would look coming home this time. Not knowing if he was on his meds or not, she had no idea how he'd appear.

At just before eleven, Maura turned into her subdivision. From the first small bridge that passed over the canal that ran behind her house, she could see her back yard and briefly, the back of the house. It was empty. But as she turned the corner onto the street that ran in front of her house, she saw Kai's big blue Ford F-150 pickup in the drive. It sported a new camper shell over the bed, and as she pulled into the drive she noted he had respected the rule of leaving the side of the drive closest to the front door reserved for her car. He was home!

Knowing Kai was home, safe and sound, Maura found the excitement over his arrival she'd been holding back fill her with a visceral rush. She quickly gathered her purse and briefcase, shut off her car and made her way into the house. Before she could put down her purse and keys on the shelf in the bookcase Kai had built many years ago along one wall of the foyer, she was greeted by a large, lean hound who appeared from the hall leading to Kai's bedroom. The dog stopped abruptly it the nexus of the foyer, hall, and great room and barked at her with enthusiasm.

"Kai?" She called out. "I'm home. Where are you?"

"Hush Heidi!" he said before she saw him. In an instant he appeared next to his dog, who he soothingly stroked on the back of the neck. He lifted his eyes guiltily and with a ghost of a smile on his face said, "Hi, Mom."

He was taller than she remembered, and his shoulders, leanly muscled, stretched out on either side of the tight white tank undershirt he wore. From his narrow waist, a pair of camouflage cargo shorts hung, revealing a long stretch of thin calve to his slender bare feet. He'd buzzed off most of his hair, except for a short curling bit of ash blond thatch on top of his head. While he didn't look as emaciated as she expected, he was still on the thin side. But for the slight swell of his stomach under the ribbed T-shirt, he looked much as he had when she'd seen him last Christmas.

Without another word, he stepped to her, reaching out his long arms to hug her close. Maura felt his arms enfold her and she rested her head on his shoulder to breathe in his clean singular scent. "Oh my baby," Maura said tearfully. "What am I going to do with you?"

Kai gave her an answering squeeze and then pushed her away gently to reach down to calm Heidi, who was anxiously jumping up on them. "This is Heidi," he said simply as the dog calmed under his touch. "You'd better say hello or she'll knock you down. She doesn't like to be ignored."

Maura cautiously offered the dog her hands to sniff before she too stroked her big head and said, "Well, hello Heidi. What kind of dog are you?"

"She's a Weimaraner," Kai told her proudly. "She's got papers and everything. I got her when she was just a puppy, about two years ago."

Heidi backed away from Maura's touch and shook herself all over, ending with her head, which she then shook fiercely, making her beautiful long ears flap loudly. When she had finished this little display, she gave a low growl and then bounded, seemingly sideways into the hall and on into Kai's bedroom. "She's a good girl, Mom," Kai said earnestly. "I promise you she won't be any trouble. You have no idea how much I love that dog."

"It's no problem," Maura said a bit doubtfully. It had been a long time since the last of Kai's dogs, a Doberman named Mack, had passed away while Kai was studying at the Art Institute and living at home. She'd encouraged Kai's love of dogs from the time he was a baby and Rhett had brought the yellow lab, Buddy, home for him as an unexpected gift. After Buddy had died at fifteen, Kai had been inconsolable and had begged until she relented and got him Mack.

"I'll take care of her, Mom. You know I'm responsible with my dogs," Kai assured her.

At that moment, Heidi bounded back to where they remained standing, with what was left of a stuffed animal in her mouth. The thing was eviscerated, nothing but the flimsy cloth of its shape suggesting that it had once been a sheep. Heidi nudged Maura with the remains of her toy and Maura tried to take it from her. Heidi's response was to fiercely begin a game of tug of war with the thing. She was strong and nearly pulled Maura off balance. Maura let go of the toy and Heidi turned, lifted her stubbed tail proudly and marched with the toy back to Kai's room.

"She likes you," Kai assured his mom.

"I'm glad," Maura said and gave him a smile. "When did you get in?"

Kai rubbed his head and shrugged eloquently. "Long enough ago to take a shower and feed and walk Heidi." He looked around and said, "I wondered if I was in the right house. I really like what you've done in here, Mom."

"Well, after you left, I thought the place needed changing out. A new start for the old house," Maura said, pleased.

"Are these Cassina Cab chairs? You didn't have these the last time I was home," Kai said as he stepped backwards into the dining area of the great room and pulled one away from the table to inspect.

"Yes, they are," Maura replied proudly. "I got a rather generous bonus last spring and I went a little wild."

Kai looked around the open space of the large room. "I'll say. It looks like *Elle Décor* blew up in here."

"And what do you know about *Elle Décor*?" Maura teased.

"This friend of mine, Robin, *Elle Décor* is his bible. That and *Met Home*," Kai told her.

"Yes, Robin," Maura said evenly. "You've been living with him for over a year—I understand he's a bit more than just a friend."

Kai gave her a lazy grin in reply. "You've been talking to Dad."

"Let's just say I had some warning you were on the way," Maura countered.

"What else did Dad fill you in on?" Kai asked cautiously.

"Enough that I have some questions for you and some things I need to get straight before I can just let you move back in and take up residence," Maura said firmly.

Kai carefully slid the Cab chair back into its place at the table and nodded his head. "Why don't I make a pot of coffee and we'll talk. Unless you have to rush right back to the office?"

Maura looked at him and shook her head. She hugged him once more briefly before she made her way to her own bedroom. Along the way she told him, "I've taken the rest of the day off. I'm going to get out of these work clothes and into a pair of shorts and T-shirt then we can talk."

"I'll start the coffee. Can I still smoke in your house?" Kai asked hopefully.

"Yes, there's an ashtray in the sink. Your father's news yesterday made me want a cigarette after two years off them. You can smoke in the house today, but after that, you'll have to go out on the back porch," Maura told him firmly.

"That's cool," Kai agreed.

"Do me a favor and call your father to let him know you got here in one piece, will you?" Maura asked gently.

"He doesn't give a shit, why should I?" Kai responded with some heat.

"He asked me to let him know, Kai." Maura said firmly. "He cares a great deal about you and you know it."

"Okay, whatever," Kai said as he made his way past her to the kitchen.

"Thanks," Maura said as she turned and closed her bedroom door behind her. As she walked toward her closet, she saw Heidi stretched out, lying on her back in the middle of her bed. She stepped up to the bed's edge and lightly gave the dog's breastbone a few gentle rubs and said, "Well, you've certainly made yourself at home, Miss Girl." In response, the dog yawned hugely and rolled over on her side away from Maura. Ruefully, Maura shook her head as she slipped off her shoes, then opened the closet door.

She placed her shoes on the shoe rack and hung up her jacket, blouse and skirt. From another hanger, she took a fresh Calvin Klein T-shirt and slipped it over her head. From a stack of khaki shorts, she selected a clean pair and stepped into them. In her off-work outfit, she sighed in relaxation. For many years now, she had developed a uniform consisting of the T-shirts and khaki shorts. Whenever the

T-shirts went on sale, she bought several and when she found the shorts, she did the same. With her blonde hair and trim figure, the colorless outfit suited her, but even more, it comforted her. Choosing what to wear was one hassle she could avoid by sticking to this simplicity. In the rare days when a cold snap settled over Broward County, she had heather-colored V-necked cashmere sweaters she ordered from Land's End to keep her warm. Thus she dressed as she lived, simply and predictably.

As she dressed, she thought about Kai's outfit. It too was a sort of uniform. He'd worn what she discouraged him from calling Guinea T's since adolescence. And, invariably, he had on a pair of shorts. She remembered the onset of the cargo shorts trend. He'd taken his own funds, gone to the Gap and bought two of every color that suited him. It wouldn't have surprised her to find he'd owned the pair he had on now since then. It struck her as funny how they shared such a casual regard for what they put on their backs. But then, they both had valued other things.

In a way, this similarity comforted her. To her eyes, Kai hadn't changed, despite the brutal haircut. He seemed stable emotionally, as far as she could tell from their short interaction so far. There were no circles of fatigue under his eyes as the result of prolonged periods of sleeplessness. He wasn't skinny as a rail, so he must be eating. Outwardly, he appeared okay. However, she thought as she closed the mirrored closet door and looked at herself for a moment, something was wrong or he wouldn't have decided to come home. And what that something was she intended on finding out immediately.

Reflected in the mirror, she could still see Heidi comfortably stretched out on her bed. That would have to stop. It was an easy fix; she would just have to remember to keep her bedroom door closed. Not a hard adjustment to make if Kai intended to set up residence again. But that all remained to be seen. "Come on girl," Maura said animatedly. "Off the bed!"

Heidi responded by furiously wagging the docked stump of her tail against the mattress.

A sly smile stole over Maura's lips as a memory came to her unbidden. "Cookie!" She said happily. "Good girl wants a cookie!"

Heidi responded by immediately standing and jumping off the bed. Like a fluid gray streak she moved, stopped at the closed bedroom door and looked back at Maura expectantly. Maura's smile turned into a grin. Kids or dogs, it all came down to the same training. She'd used the same enticement with Buddy, then Mack. It pleased her that Kai had kept up with the same method of dog training once he'd had a puppy of his own.

She walked to her bedroom door and opened it. Heidi bolted out and turned the sharp left into the kitchen from Maura's bedroom. Maura followed her and decided a cracker from the box of stale Triscuits she had would serve as the promised cookie as she followed the dog, remembering to close her door behind her.

Kai stood at the kitchen table, his back to her as he stared out the bay window with a cell phone at his ear. As he glanced over his shoulder at her, he began to speak. "Hey, Dad. Sorry for calling the house, I forgot your cell number. I just want to let you know I got to Mom's safe and sound. My truck drinks gas. I had to stop to fill up four times. I didn't get pulled or anything, just stayed in the flow. Everything's good. I'll talk to you later. Bye."

That said, he dropped his arm and peered at the dial face on his cell phone as he shut it off and snapped it closed. He looked at his mom and shrugged.

"Thanks, Kai," Maura said quietly as she fed Heidi her promised treat and put away the box of crackers. As Heidi chewed she laid down on the kitchen floor, quite at home. Kai sat down to the place he'd always claimed as his own at the table. Maura noted it was also the same spot as Matt had claimed. She busied herself by pulling two mugs from the cabinet and selecting two spoons from their drawer.

With her free hand she opened the refrigerator to retrieve the carton of half-and-half from the door, then closed it with her hip. In the small kitchen, it was only two steps to the table. She set out the coffee things and glanced at the coffeemaker, hissing its way through its cycle. "Are you hungry?" she asked Kai.

"No thanks, I'm good," he replied and kicked out her chair gently. "Sit down, don't hover."

Maura sat and watched him as he opened his box of Marlboro Lights and drew one out. "Can I bum one?" she asked.

Kai handed her the cigarette with a grin. "I should say no, since you quit, but what the hell, right?"

"Yeah, what the hell," Maura answered and put the cigarette between her lips and leaned forward to accept a light from her son.

Kai lit a cigarette of his own and looked out the bay window, sighing as he exhaled a long stream of smoke. "It's good to be home," he said happily.

"It's good to see you," Maura said as she wrapped her fingers around his wrist and squeezed. "But we have to talk, Kai. What on earth made you drop everything and come home, and why didn't you let me know you were coming?"

Kai gave her an open look and said simply, "I was afraid you'd say no, not to come. And Mom, I . . . , I had to get off the beach. It was closing in on me."

Maura squeezed his wrist once more and let it go. She took a careful drag off her cigarette, welcoming its burning rush into her lungs and the slight dizziness that accompanied it. It gave her a moment to ask the first hard question. Finally, she looked at him and asked firmly, "Have you gone off your meds?"

Kai nodded wordlessly and flicked his cigarette into the ashtray they shared.

"When?" Maura asked angrily.

Kai lifted his chin defensively and answered, "Six months ago. I got into something I thought I could handle that was better, but I know I've fucked up, Mom."

Maura willed herself into calmness then simply said, "Painkillers."

Kai laughed harshly, and said "You better go on and tell me everything Dad's told you. We can cut right to the chase."

"Fair enough," Maura said as she stood and walked to the counter at the coffeemaker's beeping. Actually, she felt it would be easier to talk if she was doing something; then her urge to smack her son's smirk off his face wouldn't be so close to the forefront of her thoughts. Calmly, she began, "It seems you've been living with a boy named Robin, who was 'good for you,' was how your Dad put it," she said as she returned to the table and filled her own mug, then Kai's. "Then you started dating a girl named Linda, I think he said, who was stealing her patients' pain medication. Evidently, she shared with you and then she got busted and put in jail. Now you've hurt Robin, you're addicted to painkillers and your source is in jail. Sounds to me like you have fucked up. Do I have the gist of it?"

Kai took a package of Splenda from the sugar bowl on the table and carefully tore a square section out of the upper left hand corner before dumping the packet's entire contents into his coffee. As he reached for the carton of half-and-half, he said quietly, "You pretty much have it all neatly wrapped up, except I'm not addicted to the painkillers. I'm not that stupid, Mom. You just don't know about my plan to get it together."

"You know how easy it would be to believe you," Maura said sarcastically. "You're a walking DSM-IV and PDR after all these years. You know more about medicating yourself than is probably good for you."

Kai laughed and took another cigarette from his pack, then lit it with the one he had in his hand before stubbing the old one out. After exhaling a long stream of smoke, he said, " Mom, I've been crazy my whole life. I know how to live with being me."

"What made you start on the painkillers in the first place?" Maura demanded. "This poor Linda, she didn't force it down your throat or stick a needle in your arm," Maura said as her eyes strayed to look at the skin of Kai's long arms. Relieved, she saw only the taunt stretch of clean flesh interrupted by the vertical razor scars from long ago. There were no tracks.

"I've never shot up, Mom. Give me some credit," Kai told her as she looked back to his face.

"Well, thank God for that," Maura sighed. "But why, Kai? Why did you start in the first place?"

Kai took a long hit off his cigarette, exhaled, and sipped his coffee. "Because it's beautiful, Mom. Being buzzed on painkillers is what I imagine normal people must feel like when they're happy. I can sleep. I'm not anxious and scared all the time. I feel like I have a million ideas and they're all possible. For the first time in my life I don't feel like I'm on one side of a wall and everyone else is on the other. Life is so easy when I'm high." Kai said quietly. He took another sip of coffee and looked Maura in the eye. "You wanted to know why. I told you." He said simply. "It made me feel comfortable for the first time in my life."

Maura nodded and hung her head. She did understand. "Still, that's no excuse for going off your psych meds. Why don't you answer that question?"

"Because I don't want to go into why I decided to quit. I needed a break, that's why. I haven't gone overboard on the painkillers, they're just a sometimey thing. I don't want to end up a junkie and I don't want to go to jail," Kai said evenly. "Besides, it's insanely expensive and I can't make enough money to keep it up and not end up losing every-thing. I already lost . . ." Kai said and abruptly stopped. "Mom, look. Take my word for it. This is me being real, okay? Besides the fact that Linda got popped, I'd decided to quit anyway. I'm going to see Dr. Roth and get back on the plain crazy meds and be as close to normal as I'll ever be. I promise you that."

"What have you lost?" Maura prodded. She had him in a vulnerable position and she needed to know everything.

"I lost Robin," Kai said finally. "I had to say goodbye so I could break it off clean and come home to start over."

"Tell me about Robin," Maura urged him.

Kai dropped his forehead in his hand and rubbed it between his fingers before rubbing his hair roughly under his palm and smoothing it back. "What time is it?" He asked.

Maura glanced over her shoulder to the digital clock on the microwave. "It's just before noon. Why?"

Kai stood in one fluid unfolding of his long frame. "I have to run to the bathroom, I'll be right back," he said as he stood and headed out of the kitchen.

"The question is still going to be here when you get back," Maura said.

"Thanks for the warning," Kai shot back from the dining room.

Maura sighed and stamped out what was left of her cigarette. She had to admit she was curious about this boy named Robin. To her knowledge, Kai had never sustained a relationship—with either a boy or a girl—for as long as a year. She had long ago dealt with the reality of Kai's sexual fluidity. She had surprised him, *in flagrante delecto,* with another boy when he was fifteen and she'd come home from work early. That utterly embarrassing episode led to a long and frank conversation with Kai about his predilections then and there. She couldn't get him to see how complicated life was with a sexual partner, nevermind the consequences of unwanted pregnancy or HIV. Worse, over the years she had really come to think he had no capacity to love anyone in the way she had loved his father in the past, and certainly not in the way she loved Matt now, in the present.

"It's apples and oranges, Mom," Kai had explained earnestly. "Sometimes you want an apple, sometimes you want an orange. It's no big deal." That was Kai's point of view at fifteen and now after twelve years of various apples and oranges, he'd never shown any particular commitment to either. This Robin, however, had managed to hang on to her son's affection for a year and he'd even admitted to feeling he'd "lost" something by leaving him. That alone made Robin interesting to her.

Searching her memory of Kai's various relationships to which she'd been witness, all of them were attractive in their way. But Kai was very careful to keep her outside of and apart from his emotional attachments, or at least his sexual partners. He never encouraged them to become a part of the family. When she'd noted that a current favorite was no longer a topic of conversation, Kai had easily dismissed him or her without much explanation. Maura was convinced her son had never really been in love, but most generally only in lust. By nature, Kai was a loner, and Maura understood that.

She had also come to cope with her son's bisexuality, though the homosexual part of it had disturbed her. Her upbringing had been sufficiently orthodox when it came to the subject. She had always felt it to be innately wrong, if not sinful. A frank discussion with Kai's psychiatrist had done much to change her way of thinking. Dr. Roth had explained to her that bisexuality was just symptomatic of the hypersexuality that came as a part of Kai's manic episodes. Even in a depressed state, hypersexuality was symptomatic. Combined with Kai's poor impulse control, he would have sex with anyone if it offered some release. With his fetching looks and the outlaw, nonconformist personality he was already aggressively exhibiting by age fifteen, he was more than capable of finding sexual partners. The kind doctor told her it was more important to try and work on his impulse control than to worry about his morality. He encouraged her to be frank and open with Kai, especially in regards to protecting himself from AIDS and other diseases.

Maura found herself buying condoms for her son before she had to pay for driving lessons. As a result, her aversion to Kai's sexual proclivities when it came to other boys was outweighed by the realities of keeping him healthy in every way she could. While she never encouraged him in one direction or the other, she simply held her tongue and came to accept his choices of sexual partners as a product of his larger mental health issues. After awhile, she found she could cope with whomever Kai was sleeping with as long as he assured her he was being sexually responsible.

Now she remembered Rhett telling her that Robin had asked for her phone number. She wondered how long it would be before that call came. She suspected Robin wouldn't be as easily left as any of Kai's other relationships.

Kai returned to the kitchen with one of his black, hardbound sketchbooks which he laid on the table before stepping to the coffee pot and bringing it to the table for a heat-up. He held the pot over her cup and Maura nodded. As he poured a thin stream of coffee into her mug, Maura opened the sketch book and looked at the first page. Kai's practiced and accomplished hand had caught a young man asleep on what looked to be a lounge chair on a deck. The following page was filled with a drawing of the young man's face, eyes closed, lips slightly parted. The nose was slightly aquiline, the cheekbones pronounced and the chin dented slightly. If this was Robin, he was fey, and more cute than handsome. He had a look of somehow not being quite finished, stuck in a state between teenager and man. Maura flipped through the pages rapidly, scared of what she might see, rather than curious now. All of the drawings were too intimate for her to bear. She closed the book on a drawing of the boy nude. There were some things she didn't need to see.

"Robin, I guess," She said simply as she slid the sketchbook across the table to rest in front of her son.

"Yeah, that's him," Kai said flatly. "The fascinating little fucker. I did all those drawings within the past month," Kai added and sighed.

"He's young, isn't he?" Maura stated calmly.

"He's only three years younger than me, Mom. He's legal. I'm not a pedophile for God's sake," Kai said with some exasperation. He took a sip of his coffee and sat the mug down with a quiet determination that flowed into his own pushing of the sketchbook away toward the center of the table.

"Of course you're not a pedophile," Maura said calmly, "I never meant to give you the impression I thought so. He's just young-looking, that's all."

"He may look young," Kai told her, "But he's more mature and wiser than I ever will be." Kai sighed and looked out the window. "I fucked up bad this time," he reflected.

"How?" Maura asked him, her bluntness and language carefully gauged to measure her son's. "How did you fuck up with Robin?"

Kai turned his attention from the backyard to meet his mother's eyes and said, "I fell in love with him, that's how. I don't usually do that. I mean sex is one thing, but it's messed up when you fall in love."

"Oh." Maura replied simply and sipped her own coffee. After the silence became noticeable, she said, "If you were in love with Robin, then why Linda?"

"It was because I was in love with Robin that I started seeing Linda," Kai told her evenly. "I'm not gay. Have you seen the way the world looks at gay people? The hell with that. I thought if I started sleeping with a girl again, I'd get over Robin and, you know ..."

"No, I don't know," Maura said truthfully. "I don't understand that part of you. I never have. But, I've never been the kind of person who had sex just to scratch an itch."

Kai chuckled at that. "I wish I was more like you. Life would be a lot easier."

"What does Robin think about you and Linda and the painkillers," Maura prodded.

Kai shook his head and looked away again, "He's in love with me, still. Go figure that out," Kai told her.

"What do you think he's going to do now?" Maura asked her son. "I mean, he's not going to stop loving you just because you packed up and left."

"Hell, I don't know," Kai said miserably. "I just know I have to get my own shit together before I'll be any good for anybody."

"Don't you think you have some responsibility for Robin—or for Linda for that matter," Maura asked him directly.

"Linda can take care of herself," Kai said harshly. "She wasn't ever that big a deal to begin with. It was about the painkillers mostly. She put herself where she is. I didn't ask her where she got the stuff. I just got it from her, then it was about the money. She made enough money off me by the time it was all said and done. I don't give a shit about Linda."

"But what about Robin?" Maura pressed.

Kai threw up his hands and rolled his eyes. "What about Robin, Mom? What about him? The truth is he's hurting right now and there's not much I can do about it. I have to deal with hurting too, and getting off fucking Oxycontin, and finding work. What do you want me to say?" Kai demanded.

Maura shook her head at Kai's outburst and paused, waiting for the air to clear before she softly said, "Are you still in love with him?"

"Yes," Kai answered without hesitation.

"How did you leave it with him then?" Maura asked. "Did you tell him it was over?"

Kai looked at her and hesitated before he said, "I told him to give me some time to get it together and we'd talk. I didn't make any promises. I just told him we'd find some way to work it out."

Maura nodded. It was as she'd begun to think. She felt relieved in a way that Kai had finally fallen in love. At least he had the capacity to fall in love after all. She reached across the table and took Kai's hand in her own, squeezing it lightly. "Then you did make a promise, son. You'll just have to find a way to work it out."

"Like you did with Dad?" Kai demanded sullenly. "You left him, still loving him. For all those years I was growing up, you never stopped loving him. I can't live like that."

Stung, Maura let go of Kai's hand and reached for his cigarettes and lighter. As she drew one from the pack, she said, "Then don't. Take my advice and find a way to be with him." She lit the cigarette and exhaled. "You can, you know."

Kai rubbed his eyes for what seemed a long time before he muttered, "Whatever."

Maura smoked in silence while she studied her son's face. He looked fatigued now in a way that he hadn't when they'd first begun talking. His hands trembled when he took his pack of cigarettes and lit one as well. There was resolve there. There always had been, especially when he'd hit rock bottom in one way or another. He certainly was in a complicated set of circumstances, but it wasn't hopeless. She'd seen him through worse. She'd see him through this.

Chapter Four

KAI TURNED DOWN the opportunity to meet his mother's boyfriend when she invited him to have dinner with them at Pebbles. He was beat. What he wanted more than anything else was to be able to sleep, but he knew if he crashed so early in the evening he'd never be able to sleep through the night. He'd hit a period of sleeplessness again. He'd wake up every night between two-thirty and three and that would be it for the night. He'd be alone in the loneliest time of the entire day when the normal world slept peacefully. He hated that more than anything. So he sat in his mother's kitchen and stared out the bay window as night drew down over the old neighborhood.

For a moment, he closed his eyes and saw himself clearly in the dawn light in that gas station parking lot off I-95. He'd been up for the dawn and the sunset the day before. Now he craved sleep but his mind was still going ninety-five miles an hour. Heidi didn't have his problems. She had her dinner and a long walk around the perimeter of the neighborhood and now she was fast asleep on the carpet just outside the kitchen door. Her paws moved as she galloped deep in some doggy dream. Kai smiled watching her.

He sipped at his Diet Coke and for a few long minutes considered taking another painkiller. The ease it proffered tugged at him, but that tug was exactly what he feared. He didn't want the tug to turn into an insistent pull. Besides, he knew the pills should be saved for special occasions or times when he was feeling particularly bleak. And the way his mood was descending, a bleak time seemed inevitable. He knew it was normal to crash after he'd been in a manic phase, and he'd been manic since the Thursday before, when he'd reasoned his sudden departure from the Outer Banks. Usually he cycled more rapidly from low to high to low. Often his moods could swing dramatically within the same day rather than days or weeks.

This sudden burst of mania had been awhile coming on. The more he felt trapped by the way things were going, the more he felt the mania stealing through him as cold and quickening as a chilled IV drip. It was like a fight or flight response in ordinary people, but in him, the rush of adrenaline seemed to go on for days, infusing him with a physical dread of staying still, staying stagnant, staying sane.

It had all started when he and Robin had run into a group of guys he knew at the lunch place every local on the beach frequented. This one jerk had decided to make a comment about—Robin and about Kai being with him—that made the other guys snigger. The shame and anger it caused in him had grown into a full-fledged panic attack. He couldn't finish his lunch, and his heart felt like it would bang out of his chest. His feet tapped out his confined urge to jump up and grab the guy by the throat and smack the shit out of him. But he didn't do that. Instead he swallowed his rage and acted like nothing was wrong at all.

Still, Robin had known he was upset. He did a good job of trying to hide his concern from Kai, and hated the fact that Robin loved him and that he loved Robin in return. It was so damned inconvenient and unfair.

Sitting in his mother's kitchen Kai helplessly listened and watched as the scene in the lunch place played over and over in his head while he stared vacantly out the bay window across the table. Each time the scene played again he felt all the rage and shame anew. It was like he couldn't erase the tape, and its endless loop tormented him afresh with every repetition. Finally, to break the cycle he pushed back from the table abruptly and stepped over Heidi to go to his room. He found the little bottle of painkillers still in the pocket of his jeans where he'd kicked them off once he'd gotten home. He actually got the bottle out of his pocket and opened it before he got control of himself.

Instead of taking one of the damn pills, he stepped over to the dresser that sat under his bedroom window and opened his underwear drawer. Though he had been gone for two years, he found the drawer still held the stack of clean boxer shorts he'd left there when he'd moved back up to the Outer Banks. He shoved the bottle under some boxers at the back of the drawer and was surprised when another brown medicine bottle appeared. He picked it up and looked at the label. It was what was left from a prescription for Valium he'd gotten from Dr. Roth back then, the last time he was home. Kai shook the bottle and felt the heavy clunk of the pills inside. He opened the bottle and saw it contained perhaps half a month's worth of a script. He must have put them away in case he needed them.

Quickly, he popped two of the ten-milligram tranquilizers in his mouth and dry-swallowed them. The Valium was *really* what he needed, as hyper as he was. He laughed as he screwed the cap back on the bottle and put it back in its hiding place. He sighed, and shook his head. As glad as he was that he'd found this old prescription, he knew it was no substitute for what he really needed to break this cycle of mania and depression. He needed to get back on his real meds, and sooner rather than later. He decided then and there to call Dr. Roth's office as soon as it opened in the morning. He knew that if he was in a crisis, his old psychiatrist would see him as soon as he could—and if he wasn't in a crisis now, he didn't know what one was.

Feeling better on the promise of relief the Valium offered before it even kicked in, he made his way back to the kitchen and sank once more into his chair at the table. He lit a cigarette and took a long drink of his soda. There was nothing to do now but wait for the pills to take hold. Maybe then he could find some rest. As it was, the pills hit his empty stomach like lead fishing weights and he grew nauseated. The back of his head was gripped in a vise of dull ache. As he rubbed his neck he thought about how long it had been since he's eaten.

The day before, when he'd finished packing the truck, Robin had made him a sandwich, and Kai had only eaten half of it then. When he was manic he lost all taste for food. He ate part of the sandwich then, more as a gesture acknowledging Robin's consideration than because of any real hunger. That was over thirty hours ago. Now, his body was starting to override his brain in its demand for sustenance.

Kai finished his cigarette before he stood and glanced around his mother's kitchen for something to eat. On the counter was a loaf of fresh sunflower bread from Publix, an old favorite. The refrigerator offered all kinds of options including some tasty frozen entrees, but Kai didn't want to wait even for the time it would take to microwave them. Besides, his nausea was growing and the thought of meat or sauce made him queasier still. He decided on a carton of banana-flavored yogurt and a couple of slices of bread.

Returning to the table, Kai ate methodically, not really enjoying the flavor or texture of his dinner. He ate because his body demanded it. He took no pleasure in the food itself. Still, by the time he'd finished, threw away the empty yogurt carton and wiped the tabletop free of bread crumbs, he began to feel better. The tight grip at the back of his head started to ease and his nausea miraculously disappeared.

Kai sat back in his chair and tried to concentrate on the music coming from the radio on top of the refrigerator. It was tuned, as always, to Love 94, the local smooth jazz station. For years he'd tuned into that station and the calm, sophisticated melodies and downbeat heavy rhythm tracks never failed to soothe him. He felt the chemical charms of the Valium begin to seduce him and the food begin to quiet his stomach and aching head. For a few minutes, he thought he could relax a bit now, let down his guard. Then he thought of Robin.

At this time, between the end of the work day and early evening,

Robin would be at the gym. With a flinch, Kai remembered waiting at Robin's house, which had really become his own home, waiting for Robin to appear at the front door up a flight of stairs from the dirt driveway. Once he'd come in, Kai would hug him briefly and wait for him to ask what he'd cooked for dinner. Whatever Kai had made, Robin would be happy.

That's the way their days had spooled out in the year they'd been living together. It was the most contented time Kai could recall. His happiness living with Robin was what had made him quit his meds. For the first time in his life he felt sane and calm. Now he had fucked it all up, for sure.

There was no doubt Robin was hurt now, worse than in any of the ways Kai had hurt him before. If the raw ache Kai felt as a result of his decision to leave Robin behind on the Outer Banks was real to him, he knew Robin was hurting in the same way. The responsibility he felt in causing Robin that hurt was crushing his mind. His brain ached with it and he couldn't get away from the feelings of regret and shame that he felt.

After these thoughts had intruded on his appreciation of the jazz blowing sweetly from the radio for some time, Kai glanced at the clock. If he called the house now he'd be sure to miss Robin, who was still a half hour or so away from finishing his routine at the gym. Kai wanted to communicate that he'd arrived safe and sound, but he didn't want to actually talk to Robin himself. Kai felt too fragile for that. He knew if Robin said the least little thing to make him question his actions any more, he'd fall into a million little pieces. And he couldn't risk that, not now.

So he stood and walked once more into his bedroom, which was lit by the last rays of the sun in its west-facing window. He found his cell phone and quickly punched in the number for Robin's house. It rang several times as Kai prayed that Robin wouldn't be home. At last, Robin's home voice mail kicked in. Kai felt bathed by the sound of his familiar voice on the recorded greeting. When he at last got the beep preceding his message he said, "Hey, baby. I just wanted to tell you I got here safe and sound. The drive was a beast, but Heidi and I made it fine. My mom's happy to see me, so that's good." Kai paused and licked his lips nervously before he said, "I miss you, you know that. And I love you. I'll talk to you soon, I swear. Bye."

Once he'd managed to get that out he quickly pressed his thumb on the button to sever the call. Guiltily, he imagined Robin returning home and checking his messages. He knew it wasn't enough, not after all they'd shared, but it was the best he could do for the time being. Kai closed his phone and put it on his dresser to hook it up to its charger, and then he left his room and returned to the kitchen's solitary comfort.

Chapter Five

PEBBLES IN PLANTATION was Maura's favorite restaurant. It was there she'd agreed to meet Matt for dinner when he'd called that afternoon to see if Kai had arrived. He'd insinuated that it was perfectly okay if Kai wanted to join them, so Maura had asked, but Kai declined. By three that afternoon he was showing his fatigue from the long drive and claimed he'd rather meet his mother's boyfriend when he was in better shape. Maura agreed. She wanted them to like each other and she was really rather relieved that meeting wasn't going to occur immediately.

When Maura left the house, Kai was still awake and voluble, though he had been drinking coffee all afternoon. He was running on a sort of manic adrenaline rush that she recognized for what it was, and it did concern her. However, she was far more interested in how Kai was thinking of earning a living and how long he planned to stay with her. She left to meet Matt for dinner feeling cautiously better after hearing of his plans and looking at a portfolio of his recent trim work on his laptop.

Matt was waiting for her at the bar when she walked into the restaurant. He waved at her and mimed a drinking motion. In answer she nodded her head vigorously before she answered the hostess's query as to whether or not she'd like to be seated. After telling her she was meeting someone at the bar, she made her way to where Matt was sitting and sat on the stool beside him. Almost immediately, the bartender sat a Stoli Strawberry on the rocks in front of her and Matt leaned toward her for a quick kiss.

Maura responded first to Matt's kiss and then took a nice long sip of her vodka. Matt's reassuring presence and the sweetish astringent taste of alcohol had a good effect. She felt a slackening of the tension she didn't know she was holding between her shoulder blades.

"Thanks, Matt. I don't know which I needed more, you or the drink," she sighed.

"So it's going to be just you and me, then?" Matt asked.

Maura nodded and said, "Kai's looking forward to meeting you, but he said after driving all night and talking all afternoon, he really would rather crash," Maura explained.

"That's understandable," Matt agreed. "To tell you the truth, I'm sort of relieved myself."

"Really?" Maura asked. "Whatever for?"

Matt grinned but answered carefully, "Well, he is your son and I am sleeping with his mother. I don't know if it would be more or less awkward if he wasn't an adult himself."

Maura smiled and slipped her hand in his as it rested on the bar. "You don't have anything to worry about. For one, I think he's pleased I've found someone after all these years, and secondly, he's so self-absorbed as a rule that he'd never give you a hassle," Maura admitted.

"So, is he in any kind of trouble? What's brought him boomeranging home this time?" Matt asked as he nursed his own drink.

Maura thoughtfully gathered up the paper napkin her glass rested on around the sides of the glass and took another sip of vodka. Carefully, she weighed exactly what and how much to tell Matt. Part of her wanted to be completely honest with him and explain Kai's complicated reasons for coming home, but part of her warned that Matt was a potential work resource for Kai, and she knew the facts of his homosexual love interest and current mental state weren't promising references for her son.

"He's been off his meds," she replied honestly enough. She had long ago explained Kai's bipolar condition to Matt. It was an inextricable fact of her past and present, far too important a detail to keep from this man she'd fallen in love with. "And winters are really hard on him," she said. "Then too, this current housing crash has hit the beach up there as hard as it has here. It didn't look to be a great winter for a trim carpenter."

Matt tilted back his glass and drained it. Before he could set it down on the bar in front of him, the bartender appeared with a questioning look. It was a slow night, so he was particularly attentive. Matt held his hand over the top of his glass and shook his head at the barman before giving Maura a quick glance and saying, "It doesn't look too promising down here either. I've laid off staff and have cut sub-contractors loose left and right."

"Kai understands that," Maura told him. "But he's not any regular trim carpenter. Do you know what his last job was?"

"I have no idea," Matt replied reservedly.

"He was hired simply to frame and hang fifteen solid walnut interior doors. They were going in a multi-million-dollar house, and because there was absolutely no room for error because the doors themselves were so expensive, they hired Kai to do it," Maura explained with a note of pride in her voice.

Matt nodded, impressed but still told her, "That's pretty rarified work. It takes a while to build up that kind of reputation down here. Does he have any pictures of his work?"

Maura paused, her glass on its way to her lips, and said, "He has a whole portfolio prepared on his laptop that he's going to print out and bind for presentations. He plans to make appointments with only custom home builders, interior designers and architects. He has a whole self-marketing plan."

"Pretty ambitious," Matt commented. "Does he have any money to live on until this work starts coming in?"

Maura set her glass down, feeling the liquor soothe her anxiety over Kai's prospects. Matt had not laughed out loud at his plans, and that was encouraging. "He has a few thousand in savings. He's even offered to pay me rent and give me money for groceries for as long as he stays home," she told him earnestly, aware that she was painting the best possible picture of her son.

"I hope you accepted his offer," Matt told her. "After all, he is an adult."

"I did," Maura assured him, not elaborating on the meager amount she'd countered with. The truth was she'd rather give Kai free room and board if it meant she wouldn't eventually have to come up with his truck and car insurance payments, not to mention pay for his visits to Dr. Roth and the medications that would come as a result. Kai had been off her own health care plan since he'd ceased being a full-time student. She knew how much he'd need to resume treatment under Dr. Roth's care, and it wasn't a trifling amount.

"Well, I look forward to seeing his work," Matt said encouragingly. "I might know of some people to refer him to if his work is as good as you say."

Maura gave him a warm smile and said, "I couldn't ask you for more than that."

Matt nodded and then asked if she was hungry. Maura told him she was and he caught the bartender's eye and asked for the check. Maura only watched as he left some bills on the bar to cover the tab and stood as he took her elbow in his palm, urged her up from her bar stool and on toward the hostess. In a matter of moments they were settled at a familiar table under the supervision of a favored waiter. As regulars, they were treated promptly and well. It was turning out to be exactly the kind of evening Maura needed.

Their conversation switched to other, lighter, topics as they ate. It was only after Maura refused an after-dinner coffee that Matt looked at her and asked, "So, does Kai plan on going back on his meds? I mean, knowing what I do of his circumstances; that has to be in his best interest, don't you think?"

Maura wiped her lips primly with the cloth napkin, then said, "He's already assured me he plans to go to see Dr. Roth, his old psychiatrist. I'm urging him to do exactly that."

"Why did he go off his meds in the first place?" Matt asked curiously. "From what you've told me, I understand he's been on one kind or medication or another since he was nine years old. It's like being a diabetic, it seems. Why go off the medication if you know you'll get sick?"

Maura sighed. It was difficult to explain the effects of the medication to someone who'd never known anyone bipolar. For someone who cycled as rapidly as Kai did, "normal" meant feeling electrically alive. Even the deep and paralyzing sadness had a certain beauty to it to Kai, though it was a really harsh and private beauty. Maura thought for a moment to try to find a way to explain this to Matt. Finally, she said, "Matt, have you ever taken as much as a Valium?"

Matt laughed at this, then replied, "Not since I was in college, and that was thirty years ago. I did Quaaludes once and that was enough for me. I don't like feeling so out of it. Hell, I don't even drink that much."

Maura knew this was true. While he wasn't a teetotaler, she had never seen Matt as much as tipsy in their nearly two years together. "It's hard to explain why Kai goes off his meds sometimes, but from what I understand, being medicated all the time has its drawbacks. He's always been high-functioning, despite his personal challenges. It's just that sometimes I think he rebels against the notion that he needs to be drugged for the world's benefit. For him, his feelings are genuine, though they can become debilitating if things get bad."

"So what you're saying is Kai doesn't see himself as crazy," Matt said gently.

"Essentially, no. He's never had a history of violence against anyone but himself. Kai says he knows how to deal with being himself by now," Maura told him.

"So why go back to see this Dr. Roth, then?" Matt asked, honestly confused.

"I'm not doing a very good job of explaining this," Maura said sadly. "It's just, you have to understand, his mental illness is like a fire— sometimes it's all flames and smoke, other times it's just embers, glowing hot under the surface. The trouble comes when something—anything makes those embers flare up again." Maura shook her head and looked Matt in the eye, "The worst thing is it never gets any better. The fact is it'll get worse as he grows older. He knows this. He accepts the fact he'll need to be medicated as long as he lives, if he wants to have what you or I would call a normal life."

Matt nodded sympathetically and said, "As if we know what's normal anymore." He reached across the table and took her hand in his and said, "I just know my life is better and more normal since I've been with you."

Maura squeezed his hand and whispered, "Thanks."

"No. I mean it. I'm not just trying to flatter you," Matt replied. "My marriage was a nightmare. I never knew it could be so easy loving someone. Now I know, thanks to you." With that, he leaned across the table to lift and kiss the back of her hand.

Unashamed in the very public space of the uncrowded dining room, Maura lifted her other hand to reach across the table and stroke Matt's cheek. "I feel the same way, Matt. My record before you isn't the best. But you're easy to love," she told him.

Matt let go of her hand after gently squeezing it in reply, and settled back into the comfort of his side of the booth. "I hope you still think so when I tell you I'm going back to my place for a couple of days," he said quietly.

Maura withdrew her hand and let it rest in her lap. In a way, his announcement wasn't unexpected, but it still stung a bit. She had grown used to his presence in her home and in her bed. For a moment she started to protest, but caught herself before she could respond with the resounding *no* that filled her thoughts at the moment.

"I want to give Kai a few days to get used to being back home before I barge in. I'm so used to being the alpha dog that I don't want to make him feel like I'm a bastard," Matt admitted honestly.

"Matt, it really doesn't matter," Maura responded quickly. "Kai is not that fragile. In fact, he's anxious to meet you. He told me you must be something pretty special to make me so happy."

"That's good to hear," Matt replied with a reassuring smile. "Still, it's been weeks since I spent more than a night at home. Let's take a couple of nights off and plan on me coming back to your place on Wednesday night for dinner. I'll come over and I just won't leave. We'll treat it as something perfectly natural. We might as well start the way we intend to continue if he's going to be around for awhile," he told her reasonably.

Maura nodded. She saw the good sense in what he was saying, but she still felt some pangs of both jealousy and regret. Still, she brightened and forced herself to smile. "We'll see each other tomorrow night anyway. That is, if you're planning to go to the general meeting of the builders' association."

"I was planning on skipping it," Matt admitted. "But I'll go if you want me to."

Maura wanted him to, though she didn't want to admit it. "No. If you were planning on skipping out, I might too. I really need to get back to the office tomorrow and if I don't go to the general meeting, I'll have some more time with Kai alone before you come back Wednesday night."

Matt nodded, then said, "Sounds like a plan, then. Will you miss me a little?"

Maura smiled at him and said, "I'll miss you a lot actually. I'm not used to sleeping alone anymore."

"Well, we can rough it for a couple of nights," Matt assured her, then added, "Don't worry. I'll call."

That said, Matt managed to catch their waiter's eye and motioned for the check. The young man appeared quickly with the check in its leatherette-bound book. Matt glanced at it perfunctorily, then reached for his wallet and drew out a credit card. He placed the card in the book and handed it back to the waiter who disappeared as unobtrusively as he'd appeared.

"Thanks for dinner," Maura said warmly. "Thanks too for being so wonderful about Kai."

Matt made a masculine motion of dismissal with his right hand and said, "Nothing to thank me for yet, my dear. I just want you to know I'm not going to let that son of yours turn our lives upside down. For the first time in years, I'm happy. I intend to stay happy and keep you happy too."

Maura sighed in simple pleasure tinged with relief. "So we're good?"

"Absolutely," Matt told her, and she felt he meant it.

Maura was tired as she drove the familiar route home. For her, it had been an unusually fraught day. Though she hadn't really expected Matt to follow her home in his car, she couldn't help but feel some disappointment that he didn't. However, her recognition of her emotional fatigue made her realize she was relieved as well. She was glad she wasn't going to have to introduce Kai to her boyfriend after the day she'd had already. There was time enough now for her to fully explain the extent to which her life was intertwined with Matt's. She honestly didn't believe he'd make a big deal of it, but there was a nagging sense that it wasn't going to be as easy as she hoped.

She drove through the busy streets between Plantation and Sunrise thinking she certainly couldn't fault Matt for her reservations about integrating Kai into their lives. Matt had made it very clear, in word and deed, that she shouldn't be concerned on his account. She felt a pang of guilt about not being totally forthcoming about the details of Kai's sudden relocation, but in a way, she had protected his privacy. Her son was an adult, though his immediate actions impinged on her life as they had when he was a child. As an adult, he deserved to have his privacy. Still, Maura wondered how he was going to resolve his relationship with Robin and go about rebuilding his life in this world of his childhood.

Turning from Pine Island Drive onto Oakland Park Boulevard and nearing home, Maura decided the best thing she could do was to try and remember Kai's larger sense of self-preservation. No matter his mental state, he'd always landed on his feet. He had as many lives as a cat, though he'd never tested the farthest limit of self-destruction since he had slit his wrists as a child. Maura shuddered, recalling dressing the stitched insides of his forearms as he stood before her with a complete air of detachment. It had been as if he had reached a place where he had so disassociated himself from what was really happening to him that it was as if he was watching his life like one does a television show. Ever since that time so long ago, she'd seen Kai's detachment from himself and others grow in exact proportion to the nearness of catastrophe he stood.

Dropping everything, packing his truck and dog to come home to her was a signal to Maura of exactly how desperate Kai was. He'd seen how close he was to the edge and had suddenly and severely cut himself off from everything that was threatening him. That unfortunately included Robin, to whom he'd vocalized a real connection that he'd never demonstrated before to anyone.

Maura found the window control on her arm rest and lowered her car window to the reassuring rush of air outside. She drove confidently, steering with one hand, while she pushed her hair away from her face as she let the wind dispel her discomfort over Kai. She assured herself he'd be okay, that everything would be okay. She could get through this and so could he.

By the time she returned home, Maura found herself glad of the company of her son waiting for her. She found him sitting on the sofa with a bottle of water carefully placed on a coaster on the table beside him, watching television. The ashtray by his bottle of water was nearly full, but other than that, everything seemed fine. Heidi didn't even stir from his side where she lay on the sofa next to him as Maura walked into the great room. "I'm back," she said when he didn't break his long stare at the television's screen.

Slowly, Kai looked away from the television and gave her a polite smile. "How was your dinner?" He asked perfunctorily.

"Delicious. We went to Pebbles. I had the duck with wild mushrooms," Maura told him cheerfully.

"Excellent," Kai replied as he stroked Heidi's long side. "Matt didn't come home with you? I thought you guys were practically living together."

Maura strode past her son and sat down at the other end of the sofa, the place she normally called her own. As she made herself comfortable and tucked a small pillow at the small of her back, she said, "No. Not tonight. Matt wanted to give you some time to get acclimated before he comes back."

Kai drew a cigarette from his pack and looked questioningly at his mother. "Cigarette?"

Maura shook her head and gave him a rueful smile.

"He really didn't have to do that," Kai said evenly. "I certainly don't want to get in the way any more than I have to. I don't want you both to break your routine because of me. I'm a big boy. I can handle you having a boyfriend."

"Thanks," Maura told him. "But we agreed it was a good idea to let you get settled. Matt's coming over for dinner on Wednesday night and won't be going home. This really is his home now."

Kai lit his cigarette and replaced the lighter by his box of cigarettes carefully. "Where is his place? I mean, when he's not here?"

"He has an older home in Lighthouse Point, where he's lived since his divorce," Maura told him. "He's been so busy helping me fix up this place in the past year that he really hasn't had time to focus on doing any remodeling there."

Kai looked around the small house's great room which included both the sitting area and the dining area and smiled. "Sawgrass Estates is a comedown from Lighthouse Point," he said. "You should sell this place and move in with him."

"That's something to think about," Maura admitted. "But I've been on my own a long time. Moving in with somebody or getting married again is a big deal at my age. Besides, neither of us is in any big rush. If it happens, it happens. If not, I'm happy here in my own little house that's nearly paid for."

Kai looked at his mother with sympathy and said, "You've always had to be the one who thought about safety and security, haven't you?"

Maura nodded her head and thought before she spoke. Finally, she replied, "I've been the breadwinner since I was twenty-three years old. Your father did his best, God love him, but he still isn't grown. I had to grow up fast in order to take care of you and him. My mom and dad helped with you, of course, but when it comes right down to the fine point, you're totally correct. I've always been the one to think about our security. I can't get out of the habit."

"But Matt is well-off, isn't he?" Kai countered. "You should feel a bit more secure now that you two are together. Unless you don't trust him. Do you trust him?"

Maura envied Kai his cigarette, but she had made a promise to herself not to start smoking again, as tempting as the thought was and as convenient as Kai's near chain-smoking habit was. She gave herself a moment to carefully consider answering his last question without the comfort of a cigarette to occupy her fingers and figure in her body language. At last, she said, "Kai, I don't know the answer to that question yet. In many real ways, I trust Matt absolutely. But I don't think

I'm ready to lean on him, if that's what you're asking. Leaving your father so long ago taught me to stand on my own two feet. I can't unlearn something that was so hard to adjust to so long ago."

"I knew Dad really fucked you up," Kai told her quietly. "But I don't think it would be so bad now if you had been able to quit loving him long before you did."

Maura sighed. "That's all said and done, Kai. No use in looking back. I don't think I gave up believing Rhett would come for us until you'd graduated from high school. Somehow, I always thought he'd love me or you enough to put us all back together."

"You're still in love with him aren't you?" Kai asked her as he thumped his ash from his cigarette into the crowded ashtray.

Maura chuckled. "A little part of me will love your father for as long as I live. There's no use saying anything different. Part of it is, I know he still loves me a little. What we had was pretty intense."

"God damn, Mom. That was so long ago," Kai said tiredly. "I gave up on Dad by the time I was seven and we were settled right here in this house. After living here for a year, I knew he wasn't coming to get us or live with us. I realized I couldn't count on him for anything."

"I know, and I'm sorry about that, son," Maura replied sadly.

"Don't be sorry," Kai told her calmly. "I'm not sorry."

"No reason for you to be," Maura assured him. "None of it was your fault."

"Jeez, Dad was my age when we'd been here a year," Kai mused. "I thank Christ I don't have kids. No way."

Maura was tired of the subject. It was familiar territory, after all. Kai's relationship with his father was his own affair these days, and she knew what she knew. There were hot nights spent in that first little house in Avalon Beach that would stay with her as long as she lived. They were hers, those memories of Rhett before they became parents. She'd never felt that way with anyone else. It was a fundamental part of her now, inextricable from who she was. Maura wasn't sorry either. Not for any of it, including her years alone rearing this strange boy-man sitting beside her on the sofa. She knew she could never convince Kai of that, or communicate what she felt for his father. Instead, she asked, "Did you eat anything?"

Kai took a long hit off his cigarette and nodded. "I ate a couple of slices of bread and a banana yogurt. I'm fine."

Maura shook her head without saying anything. She knew he could have made a sandwich, or heated up any of a variety of microwave meals in the freezer. But from long knowledge of her son, she knew if all he wanted was bread and yogurt, he was sated and fine. "What are we watching?" she asked, turning her attention to the television.

"The History Channel. Nostradamus." Kai said idly. "I don't really watch TV anymore. Robin and I used to get all these movies from Netflix. TV sucks."

"What kind of movies did you and Robin watch?" Maura was curious.

"All kinds. New stuff, old stuff. Robin likes British movies, Merchant Ivory, stuff like that." Kai answered without animation.

"Did you enjoy British movies as well?" Maura asked.

"Yeah, kind of. They're well made. I like the history part of it," Kai admitted.

"You always did like history," Maura commented. "When you were small you read all of those books by Will and Ariel Durant. What was it?"

"The History of Civilization series," Kai told her automatically. "I'd forgotten about that set of books. Do you still have them?"

Maura motioned toward the foyer. "Of course, they're in the bookcase you built by the front door."

"Funny," Kai commented as he put out his cigarette and stood. He leaned over his sleeping dog and lifted her head. "Come on Heidi. Wanna walk? Let's go walk!"

"Want some company?" Maura asked hopefully.

"No need. We're not going anywhere but the backyard so she can pee. I've got to crash," Kai said tiredly. "I took two Valium about an hour ago and I'm finally starting to feel sleepy."

Alarmed, Maura asked before she thought, "You've got Valium? How?"

Kai laughed as Heidi got to her feet and looked up at him expectantly. "The Valium is legal, Mom. I have a script for it."

"If you have a script for the Valium, what about your regular meds?" Maura pressed. "Can't you just get them refilled like you do the tranquilizer?"

"Don't worry about it, Mom," Kai said defensively her as he led Heidi to the back sliding glass doors that led from the great room to the backyard. "Those scripts are too far out of date. I need to see Dr. Roth to get new ones." With that, he opened the door and followed Heidi outside.

Maura watched until they faded into the darkness of the small yard beyond. She cautioned herself not to press or pry. Kai had told her he was going back on his meds and he seemed determined. She picked up the control for the cable TV and pressed the information button. It was now nearly nine o'clock.

Snorting to herself in exasperation, she switched off the information panel from the TV screen. Compared to some of the meds he'd been on, two Valiums for him was the equivalent of her taking two antihistamine tablets. He'd get sleepy for only a little while, then it would soon pass. How many nights had she awakened to find him sitting at the kitchen table in the middle of the night, staring out into the darkness outside the bay window? For him, it was going to be a long night, but she had to get up and go to work the following day. She decided she might as well go to bed herself.

When Kai returned a few minutes later, he walked Heidi to the dining room table and unsnapped her leash. Freed, the big dog made her way toward his room, as if she knew it was bedtime herself. Kai looked at his mother tiredly and said, "Thanks, Mom, for putting up with me. I promise I'll get it together soon."

"No problem, sweetheart," Maura said as she reached once more for the cable remote and switched off the TV. "Everything's going to be alright."

Kai smiled at her gently. "Somehow, when you say that, I can find a way to believe it."

Maura switched off the lamp by the end of the sofa as she passed on the way to her son. Once she reached him, she lifted her arms to place her hands on his shoulders and drew him near. As he embraced her she said, "You better believe it. When have I ever let you down?"

"Never," Kai said as he returned her embrace and quickly stepped away. "That's why I'm back."

"Goodnight," she said simply.

He nodded and turned to take the few steps toward his bedroom door. Maura watched as he walked into his room and carefully shut the door behind him. Suddenly she felt very old and very tired. She turned and stepped into the kitchen to turn on the light over the stove in case Kai got up in the middle of the night, before she headed into her own room and closed the door behind her.

Chapter Six

KAI WAS BACK HOME by eleven. He let himself into the house and greeted Heidi, who was very excited to see him. She had grown accustomed to not being alone. Though it was only a couple of hours since he'd been gone, Heidi acted as if she'd been alone for a week. Kai took the CVS drugstore shopping bag into his bedroom and opened the stapled-shut paper bag inside. He let the four bottles of pills fall onto his bed as Heidi promptly jumped up onto the bed to nose them curiously. Kai smiled as he joined the dog on the bed as well. One by one he picked up the pill bottles and looked at the names: Risperdal, the antipsychotic; Strattera, the attention deficit disorder drug; Sertraline, the generic form of Zoloft, an antidepressant; and the last bottle held lorazepam, an anti-anxiety drug. Dr. Roth had approved of the same regimen he'd been on before he'd stopped taking his medicine months before.

All in all, his appointment with Dr. Roth had gone well. Kai liked his old psychiatrist and could almost claim that Dr. Roth had seemed happy to see him again after the two years he'd been back up on the Outer Banks. He'd been honest with Dr. Roth about everything that was going on with him, except for taking the painkillers. Dr. Roth had known him a long time, and Kai knew that he'd have reacted very negatively about that and the vacation from his legitimate meds.

He'd been more interested in Kai's quandary about Robin. Kai guessed that the doctor, like his mother, found the fact that he'd fallen in love at last to be pretty significant. Dr. Roth had strongly suggested Kai go into counseling with one of his staff clinical social workers, but Kai had told him no, he couldn't afford therapy. With no job and no health insurance, there was no way he could get into therapy. Dr. Roth understood, but rather than schedule Kai for a routine meds renewal in three months, he'd insisted that Kai come back in three weeks so he could evaluate how he was doing once he'd resumed taking his prescription medicine.

Kai had agreed to those terms, of course. But he knew already what he would have to report. The Risperdal would wipe away not only the demons, but a great deal of the affect in his personality. The Strattera would allow him to concentrate and actually get work done. The Zoloft would minimalize his insecurities around other people and keep the blackness at bay. And, the lorazepam would keep him from crawling out of his own skin. What he wouldn't be able to tell Dr. Roth was how detached, remote and divorced from himself he would feel. The drugs worked, but who they left him as was not really who he was.

Kai picked up each bottle in turn and placed them in a row on the nightstand by his bed. He stared at them briefly and sighed. He couldn't help but feel he was back in the game once more. He stood and walked over to his chest of drawers under the window and opened the top drawer. In the back, tucked under a layer of boxers, was a brown prescription bottle that held the painkillers. He twisted the cap off and shook the blue pills into his hand. There were fewer than thirty left. He knew how many were left to the last quarter of a pill. It was time now to quit them.

Kai glanced at the clock. He decided he wasn't hungry and he needed this drug worse right now. He needed some clear space to relax and think about things. There was plenty he should be doing, but for the next three hours, all he wanted to do was float and think. He carefully tipped all the pills but one back into the bottle and screwed on the lid. He thoughtfully raised the pill in his palm to his mouth and let it fall in. With his tongue, he guided the pill to his back right molars and crushed it there, before the bitter taste could flood his mouth. That done, he placed the bottle back underneath the boxers in the corner of the top drawer and slid it closed.

"Want to go pee-pee?" Kai asked his dog. She stood on the bed and leapt to the floor in reply, her paws never slowing down as she headed out the bedroom door and toward the foyer where she knew her leash waited. Kai picked up the empty plastic CVS bag and stuffed it in his back pocket in case his dog produced more than urine, and followed her to the foyer. Heidi stood by the door looking up at the shelf that held her leash. Kai took the leash from its perch and snapped the business end onto the D-ring on Heidi's collar. The big dog waited patiently after he let them out the front door and then turned to lock it behind them. At last, he said, "Let's go, pretty girl," and the dog took off, happily given permission at last to stretch her legs.

Kai walked Heidi down the street to the corner and turned right to leave the neighborhood for a quick stroll around its high-walled perimeter. Heidi pulled him along, anxious to get to the sidewalk that ran between the subdivision's walls and a line of live oaks that arched overhead. Already the dog was familiar with this same walk Kai had made with his other dogs as he grew up. He and his mother had moved to Sawgrass Estates before it was completely built out. The neighborhood had changed from being made up of mostly Italian and Irish transplants from New York and New Jersey to now being home to more Latins and West Indians, and it had remained neat and prosperous. Kai remembered the days when the walls had been only shadow box fencing the back boundary of the neighborhood's perimeter lots, but in the late nineties, the city of Sunrise had built the concrete block and stucco wall to replace the wooden fencing when it had widened and reconfigured the intersection of Oakland Park Boulevard and Flamingo Road.

Kai still felt remarkably at home and at ease on this walk, though Flamingo Road was now a very busy highway, and what had been a vacant lot across its seven lanes of traffic had sprouted a tight cluster of high-rise condos. He could have felt stalled being back to the same sidewalk he had first walked at six years old, but instead he felt safe. He let Heidi lead him as she walked, sniffed and left her own scent to mark their passage. However, when the sidewalk brought them to the Flamingo Road entrance to the neighborhood, he turned Heidi around to retrace their steps back home. His dog gave him a disappointed look; no doubt she had anticipated walking the full boundary of Sawgrass Estates, but she good naturedly turned and trotted ahead of Kai in the direction of home.

As he walked under the spreading arms of the live oaks, Kai began to feel the insistent tug of the drug. Soon he would have the full effect of the painkiller rushing to his brain. He was eager to be home, sitting comfortably at the kitchen table with his cigarettes and something to drink close at hand, and the radio playing jazz for company. Within a few minutes, that's exactly where he found himself as the rush of the drug began to take effect.

Kai felt his body relax and his mind begin to drift on a slow current. He felt euphoric and happy. The demons that deviled him disappeared, only to be replaced by pleasant thoughts. For the first time since he'd gotten up at six, he felt sane and centered. His normal anxiety was a bit more pronounced as the time lengthened between the morning's events and the last time he'd swallowed the tranquilizers the night before. He'd slept only fitfully, waking every hour and a half or so. Kai had fought the urge to get up and sit in the kitchen rather than toss and turn on his bed. He had rightly figured that his hellish night spent thinking of all the things he'd fucked up so badly would give him the proper haggard look to present to Dr. Roth.

Kai still rose before his mother and started a full pot of coffee before feeding and walking Heidi. As she had slept next to him since she was a puppy, the dog was used to being awakened by Kai's gentle strokes on her side as he soothed her in the middle of the night. Somehow the dog understood he was trying to soothe himself as he softly ran his palm over her side. She was accustomed to rising early as well. Kai rarely could tolerate remaining in bed past six in the morning, especially if the night had been a sleepless one.

Once Maura was up and about, Kai took his coffee outside to the porch off the great room. He chain-smoked when he got up as he fought to leave the images that had kept him awake in the night.

Now, with Heidi occupied with a new bone, Kai sat smoking in the kitchen and let his mind wander. Once he was high, his mind could take off on the most wonderful, confident course of plans and ideas. Starting with his plans for the afternoon, he mentally organized himself at the dining room table with his list of interior designers and custom home builders he had put together in the days he'd been back in South Florida. He had limited his search to areas he didn't mind driving to. He'd immediately canceled out any firm or person in Dade County. There was no way he wanted to work south of Hollywood for any amount of money. That still left him all of Broward and Palm Beach County to draw from.

One by one, he was calling to try to get appointments to see these designers, architects, and homebuilders so he could introduce himself and leave them with his brochure. Kai was proud of his brochure. It was a nice little presentation piece that was substantial enough to show the full range of the fine cabinetwork, trim and boiseries he could create. He'd been very good about documenting his work with digital photographs as he'd finished each project. So far, he'd been successful in setting up a few meetings beginning the following week.

The thought of the upcoming meetings reminded him of another fact and that was exactly how urgently he needed to stop taking the painkillers altogether. When he was high, as he was now, he could see the sense of it.

Kai sat back in his seat at the table and lit another cigarette. Immediately, he thought of Robin. He saw his perfect skin stretched taut over his bare chest and the ridges of his abdominal muscles. Robin had such flawless skin, not a hair, blemish, freckle or mole on him. His skin looked like it would taste of cream and honey and it always surprised him to find Robin had no taste at all. That was what he always thought of when Robin stole into the stark empty loft of his buzz. Then Kai recalled his face, his green eyes and the fringe of blond hair that fell over his forehead. When Kai was high, he felt as if he could look at Robin's face forever. That was another reason he wanted to be off the painkillers. If being high all the time meant he couldn't see Robin clearly, there was no way he could know if he loved Robin himself or just the idea of Robin.

That conundrum was what was always foremost in his mind. The aesthetic and physical attraction he felt for Robin had been insistent from the first time they had met. Kai had been hanging crown molding in a spec house being built by a realtor-builder he'd been doing work for ever since he'd moved back to the beach. Thanks to his dad, Kai had been hired by the company as a trim carpenter in his own right, not as part of Rhett's regular crew. Though he was living with his dad at the time, Rhett had made it clear he wanted him to move out on his own as soon as possible. By the time he had found himself working on that particular house in Southern Shores, Kai knew he had overstayed his welcome. It was at that precise time and place that Robin appeared to show the house to a middle-aged couple looking for a new vacation home.

Kai had studiously ignored Robin and the couple as they made their way around the large house, yet he listened carefully as Robin talked with the couple and tried to sell them the house. When they all returned to the dining room where Kai was working, Robin had introduced himself and the couple in order to ask if Kai would be available to do some custom work the potential buyers were interested in. Kai had climbed down from his ladder and discussed what they had in mind, simple work really, just some California-style cabinetry in the bedroom closets and a wall of shelves to be built around their planned plasma-screened television and stereo system. It ended with them all exchanging business cards.

Robin had given himself away in some subtle but discrete ways. Kai had caught and held some questioning looks Robin had extended, and he'd reciprocated with some of his own. Robin fascinated him. Not only was he drawn to the younger man's fey features and lightly-muscled form, but Robin also had a certain shy way of putting himself forward that Kai found exciting. Yet, Robin so quietly made his interest in Kai known that the couple he was trying to sell to probably never noticed the current of attraction that ran between Kai and Robin. By the time business cards were exchanged and Robin took his leave to escort the couple along on their tour of other beach houses, Kai knew he had made a conquest. He looked at Robin's card for a few minutes and wondered who would make the first move. He decided to give it a few days, and if Robin didn't call him first, he would definitely call Robin.

In the week that followed, it seemed Robin was everywhere he looked: drawing gas at the 7-Eleven in Kill Devil Hills, buying groceries at the Food Lion, emerging sweaty and bleary-eyed from the sauna at the gym. In a place where locals clung in tight little groups to the people they knew, Robin stood out by being always alone. Kai asked around, but none of the buddies Kai had that he got high with, or worked with, or surfed with knew anything about him. Kai tried hard not to show too much interest as he made his inquiries; he made it a rule to keep his gay activities well separated from his friends. In a community as small as the one he navigated, he didn't want to be labeled as being gay. If he was, he knew he wouldn't be shunned outright, but he'd be let known he was suspect and no longer trustworthy among "the guys."

In the year he'd been back on the beach, Kai had avoided all the local men who were known to be gay in the string of beach towns. He'd limited his sexual activities to hookups on line and that only when there were plenty of tourists around. In the winter, he laid low. Occasionally, he dated and slept with a few different girls, but Kai carefully avoided getting too close to any of them. The girls he met were either very young or if closer to his age, were looking to settle down or on the rebound from some guy he inevitably knew. While the Northern Banks swelled to well over one hundred and fifty thousand people spread over the many miles from Corolla to the Oregon Inlet, off-season the local population was hardly more than thirty thousand in the same area. Whole neighborhoods resembled ghost towns in the off-season.

Most of the guys Kai knew and hung out with were either married or hooked up with some girl or another over the winter. Those who were hooked up used it only as shelter from the cold. By the time Memorial Day rolled around, they ditched their girlfriends in order to troll the shoals of bikini-clad tourist girls who flocked to the beach in the summer, either to relax in the sun or to work summer jobs before going back to college in the fall. Kai knew this—it was part of life on the beach. He dated women often enough to keep up his street credibility, but he could plausibly lay low in the winter, unattached and free of suspicion.

This suited Kai well. Though he would never admit it, the older he got, the more he found himself more likely to connect emotionally with other guys. Women, he had come to believe, were satisfactory for diversion and sexual pleasure, but were far too needy emotionally, and Kai didn't want to be needed, not by anyone. He had a full-time job keeping himself together and felt far too vulnerable himself to be able to support anyone else emotionally. One of the main things that drew Kai to men was the impossibility of them ever needing him for security or for love. That's what he had thought from the time he became aware of sex—until he ran into Robin again one day in September the year before, when he had gone to the realtor-builder to pick up a check.

Robin had an office in a warren of small offices in the building that housed the company on the 158 By-Pass in Nags Head. Kai noticed him sitting at his desk as he passed by him in the corridor that led to the bookkeeper's offices. Startled at the sight of him, Kai had jerked up his chin abruptly by way of a greeting and swiftly walked on to pick up his check. But, as he passed on, Kai kept count of the doors between Robin's office and the bookkeeper's. After he got his check, he made up his mind to stop and speak. So, in only a couple of minutes, he found himself standing in the doorway of Robin's office waiting for him to look up from the magazine he had open on his desk. "Hey," he said simply, and Robin looked up and straight into his eyes with a look that betrayed absolute pleasure and desire.

Now, sitting in front of the bay window in his mother's kitchen nine hundred miles away and thirteen months later, Kai could replay every detail of what they had said, and every nuance of how Robin had looked. Though the conversation was just brief enough to make a movie date, Kai knew he'd found a lover. He couldn't have known what else he'd found.

Now, Kai stretched in his chair and sighed. Even though he was high, he couldn't escape the sting of loneliness and loss he felt. The familiar confines of his childhood and adolescence comforted him, but seemed too small to accommodate the larger emotional life he had grown into during his time in Robin's trim beach house in Wrights Shores in Kill Devil Hills. It was a neat little place that sat high up on pilings, west of the bypass on a lot that bordered the Wright Brothers' Memorial tract. From Robin's back deck, he could look south to an unobstructed view of the small museum and the large dune that had been stabilized with grass to hold the monument, an Art Deco white marble wing. With no neighbors near, they had slept naked on that deck after making love under the black velvet sky seeded with stars. The empty vastness of the acreage of the memorial was surrounded by the beach town, but the constant wind that fueled the first flight of Wilbur and Orville still smoothed the undeveloped dunescape there.

Kai looked at the clock on the face of the microwave over the stove. An hour had passed as he'd sat there, smoking and wandering through the range of his memories. His last cigarette had burned down to a long cylindrical ash in the ashtray by his left hand. Kai picked up the butt and ground the grey cylinder into flat dust. Then, with steady hands, he lit another cigarette and returned to the first evening he'd spent in that house.

Robin hadn't invited him in when he'd driven them back after the movie. Instead, they had sat in his truck for many long minutes without saying anything. Finally, Kai had spoken bluntly. "I want to have sex with you," he said evenly. "But I think you know that already."

Robin only nodded in reply.

Kai reached across the seat of his truck's cab and gently laid his large hand on the part of Robin's thigh just below his shorts' hem. When that wasn't rebuffed, Kai had slid his hand up under the loose leg of the shorts and reached even higher with his little finger, which he used to lightly caress the inside of Robin's thigh. "Why don't we go inside?" Kai whispered huskily.

Robin looked away, outside his window and said, "You scare me."

Kai withdrew his hand from underneath Robin's pant leg and instead reached across to gently take Robin's chin in his hand. He firmly pulled Robin's face to look at him and whispered once more, "You don't have anything to be afraid of."

"God, I hope that's true," Robin whispered back. Then, quite clearly he said, "Just remember, you wanted me once this badly. Okay?"

With Robin's chin still in his grasp, Kai had pulled Robin's mouth to his own and kissed him hard and long. Then he said, "I won't forget it, will you?"

In reply, Robin looked at him and shook his head before pulling away, opening his car door and getting out of Kai's truck. Once he closed the door, he walked to the front of the truck, pulled his keys from his pocket and waited until Kai got out of the truck as well and closed his door. Robin waited for Kai to join him before, together, they walked up the steep wooden steps to the front door and went inside.

The memories of the events that followed were still enough to make Kai hard, despite the control the painkiller was exerting over his body. Kai reached between his legs and readjusted himself in his shorts to accommodate the sudden swell of recall. Robin wasn't sexually inexperienced, and he was more than a match for Kai's hunger and need. With more than a year's experience of Robin and of what he himself was capable of feeling, Kai told himself he should have been the one to be scared that night, not Robin. Robin threatened everything he thought he knew about himself and what he wanted.

Within a week of that first night, Robin gave him a key to his house. Within three weeks, Kai had moved in. It all seemed to fall into place. Heidi fell in love with Robin, just as Kai had, and while she continued to be Kai's dog, she made it known in ways small and large that she'd accorded Robin a proper place in her pack. It was so logical, so easy, Kai thought now. His father was glad to see him move out and none of his friends knew Robin, so no one asked any awkward questions, at first. But Kai began to change from the moment he walked into Robin's house.

The Italians have an old saying: "Love and a cough cannot be hid." Like anyone else in the first blush of love, Kai had little time for anyone other than Robin. Kai came to work on houses when they were near completion, still he had ample occasion to see other tradesmen. It wasn't long before the people at Robin's office noted how often he and Kai were together and from the office, word began to trickle out to the job sites speculating as to the reason why the usually laconic and withdrawn Kai was so suddenly full of banter and good humor.

By Christmas, Kai started getting thinly veiled comments from the buddies he got high with about his long absences and sudden interests in Wrights Shores. Others started asking him about "that little faggot realtor." Kai just blustered past all of it, thinking Christmas would soon come and by the time he got back from visiting his mother in Florida they would all have something else to talk about. Invariably, somebody would get in a fight, or get pulled for DUI, or popped for possession. Besides, work slowed to a crawl during the cold winter months and most of the people who were being nosy would hibernate, get high, or go surfing in Tortolla. He thought he wouldn't have to deal with any issues about his sexuality that would lead to anything more than some pointed teasing.

Christmas did come, but it came with the realization that he was in love with Robin. On the long drive to Fort Lauderdale down I-95, he missed him with an ache that only grew over the days he spent back home with his mother. Of course, he didn't discuss anything about Robin with his her. In fact, he kept waiting for the subject to come up, as his father had squarely hit him between the eyes with the question as to whether or not he was sleeping with his roommate before Thanksgiving. Kai had answered his father honestly. As with many other topics between him and Rhett, Kai's attitude was generally that none of it was his father's business. As far as Kai was concerned, Rhett had long abrogated any say in Kai's behavior or life at all.

Still, his father had surprised him. Rhett had let him know, rather kindly, that he knew it was none of his business, but that he approved of Robin and his son's relationship with him. While Rhett was mainly concerned with Kai's reliability as a tradesman he recommended and supported and how that reflected back on him, he was loyal when it came to other things. Rhett had long accepted responsibility for essentially abandoning his son, but he still loved him. After all the years that had spun by so quickly in Rhett's life, he had sired no other children. Nor had he married again. Rhett had been serially monogamous with an array of increasingly younger women, but he was of the age and generation that liked to be married in the winter and single in the summer. A lifetime on that beach hadn't cured him of his old habits, one of which had been Maura. He'd fallen in love with her when he was still a boy and lost her when he was just becoming a man. No other woman had ever held on to his imagination the way she had, and his only child was the living proof of that.

As old-school as his father was about so many things, Kai was surprised by his attitude concerning his relationship with Robin. He had expected his father to be belittling or condescending about his gay side. While Kai would tell anyone, especially his father, that he didn't care what they thought, the truth was, he did care. Kai knew all about labels. He'd grown up being labeled as mentally ill. He'd had to cope with getting special permission to miss school for psychiatrist appointments. Each year he was in school, he noticed how his teachers had treated him differently than they had the other children. In the small Catholic school he'd attended through eighth grade, there was no way he could escape being labeled as special, different, and often, odd.

This was where he didn't give his father enough credit for loving him or for the responsibility he felt for Kai's emotional troubles. Rhett blamed himself, just as Maura did, for Kai's mental illness. Rhett secretly thought his own drug use had poisoned his sperm. Then, when he added on his own guilt over his failures as a husband and father, he had promised himself to be as accepting of Kai's peculiarities as he could be. When Maura had called him late one night to tell him she'd caught Kai in the dominant role of anal intercourse with another boy when Kai was only fifteen, Rhett did his best to console her, telling her boys would be boys, and that all of them "experimented." He even admitted to experimenting some on his own when he was a kid.

Maura was somewhat mollified by his confession and Rhett himself was consoled by the fact that Kai was at least the fucker and not the fuckee. Again, he blamed himself. His son was growing up without any male influence. Rhett carried his shame deeply, but couldn't see any way to make things right. He'd already failed when Kai had chosen to live with him when he was twelve. Those months with his silent, tormented son were seared into his memory.

Rhett had tried to make up for the fact he'd packed Kai off on a plane back to his mother when he was obviously so hurting and ill. He had first welcomed Kai back when he'd returned when he graduated from high school. He'd taken his son under his wing and taught him to surf and how to make a living as a trim carpenter. From the time he was eighteen until he was nearly twenty-one, he'd kept Kai as close as Kai would allow. In those years, Kai had thrived. He'd stayed on his medication and thrilled Rhett with his talent at the craft that Rhett had made a living off of since he, himself was Kai's age.

When Kai had decided he wanted to go to the Art Institute back down in Fort Lauderdale, Rhett had been supportive. He knew Kai was too talented to become just someone who banged nails on the beach for a living. He'd sent him back to his mother and also sent along any spare cash he could to help Kai out once he was back in school. And, after Kai had finished his degree in graphic design and had failed in his early career in advertising, Rhett had once again welcomed him back to his home on the beach. But by then, Kai had turned twenty-five and Rhett's patience had grown thinner. He began to realize having a son meant he'd always be a father and, in that sense, Kai would never fully get grown to adulthood. He seemed to Rhett to be perpetually eighteen years old and forever starting over. He wouldn't settle down and seemed to have no interest in having any sort of abiding relationship with anyone. When Rhett recognized the tell-tale signs of being in love from his son's behavior toward Robin, he felt no shame that it was a gay relationship. He just wanted

Kai off his hands. If a boy like Robin could do it for his son, Rhett really didn't give a damn. He just wanted an end to his own feelings of guilt and responsibility.

Rhett had even gone so far as to cultivate Robin's friendship. In the year Kai had lived with Robin, Rhett would appear every couple of weeks or so with some small gift: deer meat from a hunting trip down in Tyrrel County, a case of beer when his current girlfriend had him drive her to Sam's Club up in Virginia Beach, and occasionally a quarter bag of good sensimilla when the opportunity presented itself. Kai appreciated his father's attention and grew confident enough in it to treat Robin as his de facto partner in his presence, though only once did he admit he was sleeping with him.

Kai knew his mother and father still communicated and more specifically, they communicated about him. He fully expected to be greeted by some embarrassing questions from his mother when he came home for Christmas, but she never brought the subject up and neither did he. Kai made it through the ten days' separation from Robin with the help of a score of painkillers he'd gotten from one of his buddies. It wasn't his first experience with the painkillers, but it was the first time he considered going off his medication and using the pain medication exclusively.

Arriving back to the trim little cottage in Wrights Shores, he found himself profoundly glad to be coming home to Robin. In the winter months that followed, their relationship deepened. For the first time in his life, Kai began to see some other place than his mother's house as home. Buttressed by Robin's unconditional love and support, he found himself drawing again after more than a year's disinterest in his artistic pursuits. In love for the first time in his life, and in a kind of love that was returned rather than only reflected, his brain chemistry was flooded by the endorphin, dopamine, and serotonin rush that is a physical fact of the state. He began to skip his meds until by late spring, he wasn't taking them anymore at all. Of course, his naturally-elevated brain chemicals were enhanced by a particular abundance of painkillers on the drug scene. Stealthily, his indulgence turned into a habit. By summer, he was an addict.

Kai's work had begun to pick up long before Memorial Day. The large, expensive houses that he specialized in trimming and fitting out had begun construction in the fall of the year before. The small, routine work he did for the company Robin worked for picked up as the builder rushed houses to completion for sale or rental for the tourist season. Robin's work picked up as well. While they had spent from Christmas to Easter comfortably cocooned in their own little world, both of them had to get up and back to work as the days grew longer and the sun hotter.

With the warmth came the return of the increasingly pointed taunts and jests from the guys Kai knew. Suddenly, he found "that little faggot realtor" to be more of an issue than he had before. Summer season was on and the opportunities to delve into the sexual surfeit of tourists became a constant topic of conversation. As Kai found himself defending his comfortable and deepening relationship with Robin, he also found himself staying high on painkillers. The drug took away a lot of his old inhibitions and also gave him a false feeling of safety. These factors grew together to the point where they intersected with a girl named Linda.

Linda was the best friend of Kai's dealer buddy's girlfriend. In Linda, Kai found a way to kill two problems with one stone. By starting to publicly date Linda, most of Kai's harshest tormentors about Robin were silenced. As a bonus, Linda had a steady supply of heavy pain medication and she was delighted to share with Kai, as long as he fucked her first. Linda was a local, born and bred. She knew who Kai was, and truth be told, she had her eye on him for a long time. She wasn't deaf to the rumors that he slept with Robin, but that just made the game more interesting to her. She was an addict herself and she knew what she was looking at when she saw Kai. Not only was he good-looking enough to be gay himself, but he was also known to be a hard worker and quite a catch for a girl who had a good job and wanted to settle down. As far as she was concerned, her pain-killers were more than a trump for any gay boy, no matter how cute he might be.

What neither Linda nor Kai took into consideration was the fact that Robin genuinely loved Kai. Robin knew Kai's whole story, the demons in the night, the years on medication and treatment for the bipolar disorder. Robin was also astute enough to see clearly his place as the little faggot realtor. No one knew better than Robin how that colored everybody's perception of him. Robin also knew how many painkillers Kai was taking. Kai's legal medication sat in un-touched bottles on Robin's bathroom vanity. It didn't take a rocket sci-entist to read the refill dates on the bottle and know Kai had gone off his meds. Then too, it was usually his bed that Kai lay sleepless in and his kitchen where Kai chain smoked, uncommunicative in the three a.m. darkness. All of this Robin saw as he tolerated Linda and waited and watched.

Kai didn't fight. When Linda or Robin began asking questions that hit too close to home, he simply got up and left. Robin wanted him badly enough to stop asking questions he knew Kai wouldn't or couldn't answer. Linda pushed and as the summer dragged on, she pushed harder. Winter was coming and Linda had every intention of bringing Kai to live with her by fall.

On Labor Day, the traffic on the bypass and the beach road didn't trickle off, it simply stopped. The summer, usually a riot of excess and sunburned faces, hadn't quite been as frenetic as usual. High gas prices, high real estate prices and high living stopped the party as swiftly as a pulled plug. Robin and Kai felt it first. Housing sales and starts dried up. While the fact that there would always be a class of people who could want and afford second or third homes assured Robin he'd have a job for the winter, it wasn't enough of a population to warrant Kai's employment. All around them, the loose talk turned to the coming of a tough winter.

Rhett stopped by Robin's house and found Kai there alone one day. Kai invited his father in for a beer and a bong hit. Rhett accepted both, then he followed Kai out onto Robin's back deck and looked south to the Wright Brothers' Memorial. "Son, I know it ain't none of my business . . ." he began.

"Oh hell," Kai groaned. "Whenever you start out a sentence by calling me *Son*, and telling me it ain't none of your business, I know some real bullshit is about to follow."

Rhett took a long hit off his beer before looking Kai in the eye and saying, "What I've got to tell you ain't bullshit, and if you got any sense you'll listen to what I have to say."

Something in his father's tone warned Kai not to be flippant, but to listen. He reached in the side pocket of his cargo pants, pulled out his cigarettes and lighter and lit up. Blowing smoke through his nostrils, he looked out, following his father's gaze, and studied the marble monument in front of them. "Go ahead, then. I'm listening."

Rhett sighed and said quietly, "Robin's company is going to lay off all sub-contractors at the end of the week. I don't know about Robin, but they're laying off sales people too."

Kai nodded and took a hit off his cigarette, "I heard. Robin's safe. He's, like, their number two seller. I've got a house up in Duck that'll see me through mid-October. Other than that, the phone hasn't exactly been ringing off the hook, but I've got some money stuck back. We should be okay."

Rhett shook his head and turned to face his son, "That money won't last long the way you're going with your pill problem."

"Oh yeah?" Kai asked rhetorically. "And what makes you think I've got a problem? Has Robin been whining about me to you?"

"No. I haven't seen Robin lately," his father said truthfully. "I got other ways of hearing things. Like I happened to hear that girl you've been dating is looking mighty interesting to the Dade County Sheriff's Department. You better watch your ass, son. You've been playing both ends against the middle all summer."

"And that means what?" Kai asked defiantly as he took another hit off his cigarette before turning to put it out in an ashtray on the picnic table behind them.

"All I'm saying is you better open your eyes and take a look around. If Robin kicks you out you may not have any holes to hide you," Rhett told him bluntly.

Kai nodded finally before he turned to look at his dad and said, "I appreciate the advice, but there's always one place I can go no matter what."

"You can't get there if your ass is in jail," Rhett said hotly. "And what makes you think your mama wants you back? She's been dating someone pretty seriously since you've been gone. She don't want you coming home with your tail between your legs."

"Mama said I've always got a home if I need one," Kai replied with the same amount of heat. "She's never told me I've worn out my welcome."

Stung by that, Rhett pushed himself away from the deck's railing and turned to leave. Before he did, he said, "Take it from somebody who fucked up every good thing in his life, don't make the same mistakes I did. Figure out who loves you and just hold on to that."

"Yeah? Well, the apple never falls too far from the tree, does it?" Kai replied.

Rhett shook his head and stepped through the sliding glass doors back into the house. Kai stood on the back deck and waited for the sound of the front door to close behind his father before he left the deck and went into the house himself. He walked to the bookshelf he'd built for Robin over the winter and reached high to the books on the top shelf. Standing on his tip toes, he pulled out the first three books and reached into the blind space behind them and pulled out the empty Valium bottle that held his stash.

The bottle was full. There was another one hidden in the laundry closet as well that was only half-full. For the past few weeks, he'd been helping himself to Linda's stash whenever he had the chance. So far, she hadn't called him on it, but he figured she knew. If she didn't she was either over-confident or didn't care, he didn't know which. Kai took a single pill from the full bottle and promptly chewed it up and swallowed it before he replaced the bottle and books. Then he went back out on the deck and eased himself into a lounge chair. He lit a cigarette and began to think.

Now, Kai sat at the end of the trail those thoughts had led him down. He looked behind him once more and checked the microwave's clock. Another hour had passed while he was sunk in memory. Heidi lay in the doorway between the kitchen and the dining room with her chin on her crossed paws, asleep and dreaming. The radio hummed with a jaunty sax figure that sounded like Kirk Whalum to Kai. In his glass, the ice had melted to small bits which hung in the watery remains of his tea. The ashtray in front of him was full. From what he could tell, his buzz was still strong, despite the fact of his dredging up the past to chew on once more. He stood, and emptied his ashtray and glass before opening the bay windows to let out some of the smoke in the house. Then he concentrated on making himself another glass of iced papaya tea before he resumed his place at the table, once more picking up the threads of the past.

The night following his father's visit he fucked Robin like he'd never fucked him before, desperately, lovingly until they both were spent and the moonlight coming through the skylight over their bed showed tear tracks creeping out the corners of Robin's eyes. Kai had licked the tears from the sides of his face down to his hairline before kissing him gently and turning on his side to try and sleep.

Two days later, Linda was arrested. Today was six weeks gone by.

Kai hesitated a moment, then stood and walked over Heidi's sleeping form on his way to his bedroom. Once he was inside, he took another pill from his stash and chewed it up before swallowing it. Then, he found his cell phone plugged into its charger on his chest of draw-ers. He unplugged it and flipped the top open. He found Robin's num-ber in memory and pressed the digit to dial the number. After three rings, Robin answered. "Hey," Kai said gently. "What are you doing?"

"I'm on the beach road between Kitty Hawk and Kill Devil Hills," Robin said with a quick throb of happiness in his voice. "What are you doing?"

"I just wanted to hear your voice," Kai said helplessly.

For a moment, Robin didn't reply. Kai heard his car's radio in the background for a moment before Robin said, "Please don't do this to me, Kai. I miss you so much. This doesn't make it any easier."

Kai felt a stab of regret as sharp as if he'd cut himself on broken glass. There was a searing then a profound sense of separation where there shouldn't be any. "I'm actually calling you to tell you something," Kai said beseechingly.

"Okay," Robin replied tentatively.

"I talked to Mom. I've been thinking . . . could you consider coming down here for Thanksgiving? Mom's looking forward to meeting you and I miss you a lot. I thought it would be easier on us both if we had something to look forward to," Kai said in a rush.

Again, Robin answered him with a pregnant pause before he said, "Kai, won't this make it worse?"

"I have something else to tell you," Kai said quickly before Robin could continue.

Robin sighed, then asked, "What else?"

"I'm quitting. Cold turkey. Tomorrow, I've set the day. I saw my psychiatrist today. He's put me back on my psych meds. I start tonight," Kai told him urgently.

"What did your psychiatrist say, Kai?" Robin asked with concern.

Kai laughed. "He mainly wanted to talk about you. Everybody

wants to talk about you. You're the only person I've ever been in love with. Nobody thinks you're real."

"Oh, I'm real enough," Robin said ironically. "Are you really going to quit, Kai?"

"Yes. Spit swear. Double dog swear," Kai said easily.

"And you're going back on your meds?" Robin pressed.

"I'm looking at them," Kai said as he turned to see the brown bottles lined up on the table by his bed.

"Kai, what difference is it going to make if I come down there for Thanksgiving?" Robin asked him genuinely, without a trace of frustration or bitterness.

"A lot," Kai answered honestly. "I'll be thinking straight for the first time in over a year. I'll be clean and not crazy." He took a deep breath and let it go slowly before he continued. "I'll be back to the me I was when we met."

"Let me see what I can work out," Robin told him. "I have clients who may be coming Thanksgiving weekend."

"Then come the week before," Kai said without realizing how needy he sounded. "Just get down here, please."

"Okay. Look, let me get back to the office and make some calls. Can you call me tonight?" Robin asked.

"Nine o'clock. Sharp," Kai said happily.

"Okay, cool," Robin said and laughed. "You are crazy, you know that?"

"I know I still love you," Kai told him seriously.

"Kai, don't," Robin told him in reply. "It's not enough to tell me that anymore. You only say it because you know I want to hear it."

"Then I'll show you, you little brat. Just get your ass down here, I promise," Kai said and laughed.

"I'll let you know tonight," Robin said firmly. The he said, "I love you too," and disconnected his phone.

Kai looked at the screen of his phone and noted how long they had spoken. Just a minute and a few seconds, but it had been enough. He turned his phone off and sat it down on his dresser. Suddenly he felt his buzz intensify. He felt as if he stood on a cushion of air and he stayed, swaying there for a moment before he moved once more to his spot in the kitchen. There was so much to plan and do as soon as this buzz wore off. He would get through tomorrow somehow, but right now he just wanted to be happy for just a little while.

Kai returned to the kitchen and refilled his drink and collected a fresh pack of cigarettes from the carton he kept in the cabinet with his mother's canned food. All that accomplished, he sat once more and lit a cigarette. Heidi stood, shook herself all over, then trotted over to him and nudged his forearm with her nose. Kai put his cigarette in the ashtray and shifted in his seat so that he could take his dog's head in his hands. Gently, he smoothed back Heidi's long ears and scratched her neck. "Robin's coming, girl," he said softly.

The dog took two steps away from him and turned to look toward the foyer. "Yes!" Kai said happily. "Robin!" Heidi barked and began to run for the front door, her claws scrabbling on the kitchen's tile floor. Kai watched her dash away, her sharp barks echoing in the still house in Sawgrass Estates. He felt guilty for getting Heidi all jazzed up, but he felt much the way she did. He only wished he could follow her and open the door to find Robin on the other side.

"I might as well go on and admit it," he said aloud miserably. "I'm a fag, a drug addict and a mentally ill person." He listened to Heidi scratching at the tiles at the front door and put his forehead in one hand and picked up his cigarette with the other. He sat up, squared his shoulders and stiffened his spine. "At least by this time next week I'll just be another crazy queer." That said, he took a long hit off his cigarette and savored his deepening high, knowing all too well what he'd committed to accomplishing.

Chapter Seven

CONSIDERING THE DAY Maura had at the office, she was grateful that Kai had insisted on cooking dinner for Matt. With her Wednesday spent putting out administrative fires and assorted other minor crises, Maura didn't even take time to eat lunch. She'd had only a can of V-8 juice at her desk, and breakfast was no more than a half an English muffin and a quick cup of coffee. In a way, she was glad her day had been so hectic; it left her no time to think about Matt's return to her house and his first meeting with Kai. She knew she didn't really have anything to worry about; Kai wasn't socially inept, no matter what his mood, and Matt was clear that he was looking forward to the event. When he called at about three, he told Maura he'd be there by seven that night, so she'd called Kai in turn to let him know.

When she called, Kai sounded upbeat and cheerful. He'd been to the grocery store for dog food and dog cookies and he told her he'd come across the Cuban Mojo marinade for pork that he'd always loved. It had been a long time since he'd tasted those flavors unique to South Florida and he told her to expect a pork roast marinated in the Mojo sauce with rice and black beans and *maduros*, the sweet fried plantains. Maura had responded that the dinner would please Matt, who had a fondness for Cuban food as well. Relieved after the call, she'd plunged back into work and hardly had a chance to lift her head from her computer screen until it was time to leave for the day.

Arriving back home to an enthusiastic greeting from Heidi, she found Kai sitting at the kitchen table in the midst of rich drifts of roasting pork and simmering black beans. A pan already holding a half-inch of oil for frying the plantains sat on the stove along with a pot of water waiting to be heated for the rice.

"Hey, Mom," Kai said as he stood to greet her.

Maura noted he'd shaved, showered and had on a fresh navy blue T-shirt and clean pair of khaki cargo shorts. As she gave him a brief hug, she caught the scent of cologne from his neck. In every way he knew how, he'd cleaned up, as if to show her he understood how important this dinner was to her. The Kai of the past might or might not have made the effort. He was normally unconcerned with superficial appearances. Maura gave him a smile and said, "Dinner smells delicious. How long has it been since you've cooked a meal?"

Kai shrugged and then stepped to the counter to retrieve the corkscrew and pick up a bottle of Rosemount Shiraz. He presented the label to her proudly before turning to open the bottle of red wine.

"Nice choice," she commented. "When did you learn to appreciate wine?"

"Robin," Kai replied as he uncorked the bottle. "Who called here today, by the way," he added coolly.

"I was wondering when he would call. Your father gave him the number," Maura explained.

"Fucking Dad," Kai muttered. He set the bottle of wine on the counter by three wine glasses already retrieved from the cabinet over the dishwasher, ready for the night to begin. As he twisted the cork free of the cork screw, he said, "I really wish Dad hadn't done that."

"Why?" Maura asked carefully.

"Because now Robin can ambush me here at the house," Kai said peevishly. "I'd a whole lot rather be the one who does the calling. He can call me on my cell phone and leave a message anytime he wants, but I don't like having to talk to people just because they want to talk to me," he explained irritably.

"Well, you have talked to Robin since you got here, haven't you?" Maura asked calmly.

"I left him a message on his voice mail on Monday afternoon," Kai told her. "I let him know I got here safe and sound, don't worry. I just didn't want to talk to him this afternoon, that's all."

Maura patted Heidi absently as the dog milled around her legs demanding attention. Deciding she didn't want to pursue the subject of Robin just now, Maura instead turned her full attention to the dog, who danced under her hands. Finally she calmed the dog into sitting before she said, "Did you buy treats for Heidi?"

Kai walked past them both and gestured toward the cabinet between the stove and the refrigerator. Sitting there was the old Willow ware lidded dish that Maura had bought at a yard sale in Nags Head before Kai was born. From the advent of Buddy the lab, Maura had always kept it on the counter of her home filled with dog cookies. Kai had managed to find it where Maura had put it away after his Doberman died and he'd moved away. She was happy to see the old Blue Willow bowl again. It was a familiar presence that communicated much about the sense of continuity Kai valued.

Maura said, "It's good to have this back out." With that, she lifted the bowl's lid and extracted a dog cookie for Heidi.

"I was happy I could find it," Kai said gently. "It brings back a lot of memories."

"Good ones, I hope," Maura told him as he returned to the table and sat down.

Kai lit a cigarette and settled back into his chair contentedly, only giving her a smile in reply.

"I thought we agreed you'd smoke on the back porch after Monday," Maura scolded him.

Kai looked at her unchagrined and said, "I totally forgot. I'll start that, I promise."

"Matt doesn't smoke," Maura told him easily. "He's not a Nazi about it, but it bothers him, okay?"

In reply, Kai leaned to reach the short space to the window nearest him in the bay, unlocked it and raised the lower window. Immediately, the southeast breeze flooded the small kitchen with fresh air. "I'll try to respect that, Mom. It's really not a big deal to go outside to the porch to smoke. At least I shouldn't get wet if it's raining."

Maura granted him a tolerant nod and then sighed tiredly. "I'm going to get changed, and maybe then you'll pour me a glass of that wine before Matt gets here," she said.

Kai nodded and flicked his cigarette into the full ashtray in front of him. "No problem. I'll join you. I'm feeling a little weird about meeting this guy."

"Don't," Maura said quickly. "He's not at all what you'd expect. He's . . ."

"It's okay, Mom. I'm not freaking or anything." Kai replied quickly. "You know how I am about meeting strangers. I'm always wondering if I have this bright blinking light over my head flashing 'Big bipolar, bisexual boy'. It's my issue, not his. I'm sure he's a nice guy, I'm just always wondering how I'll come off. Okay?" Kai responded anxiously.

"There's no sign I can see," Maura teased.

"Exactly how much does your Matt know about me?" Kai asked cautiously.

"Bipolar, everything. Bisexual, nothing," Maura told him. "I've been as scrupulous as I could be about protecting your privacy."

"Okay, Mom." Kai sounded relieved. "Thanks."

"Just remember, it's up to you to discuss what you think is relevant. You don't have anything to be ashamed of, even Robin. Got it?" Maura said firmly.

Kai nodded in reply before taking a long drag off his cigarette and dismissing her by turning to face the window.

Maura glanced at his hand holding the cigarette by the ashtray and noted he was trembling. The lithium from long ago had always made the trembling worse. Now, it was only a fine tremor, but Kai was anxious, she knew. Kai had always been agonizingly wary when meeting people for the first time. Without wanting to, he often came off as either aloof or downright cold as a result. She knew how hard this dinner was going to be for him, which was one reason she'd agreed to let him cook. It was a degree of control, demonstrable on his part, but anxiety-ridden all on its own.

Suddenly, Kai stubbed out his cigarette and asked her what time it was. Consulting the clock on the microwave oven mounted over the stove she told him it was not quite six-fifteen. Kai nodded, slid his chair back from the table, and stood, saying, "Excuse me, I need to run to the bathroom."

"What? Are you going to take a tranquilizer?" Maura asked him bluntly as he passed her in the small kitchen.

Kai didn't answer her as he made his way out of the kitchen. She turned to watch him as he passed the dining room table and turned past it to go towards his room. "Don't ask, don't tell," Maura muttered to herself as she walked to her bedroom just off the kitchen.

Heidi followed her and immediately jumped on the bed and made herself comfortable as Maura closed her bedroom door and began to change into her nightly uniform. "Heidi, what are we going to do with your Daddy?" she queried the dog as she hung up her day clothes.

Heidi nonchalantly extended her rear leg *en pointe* and began to groom her hip and haunch. "You're no help," Maura commented as she slipped on her khaki shorts. When she had pulled her clean T-shirt over her head, she walked to the side of her bed and sat down to stroke the dog. Heidi responded with a wary sniff of her hand, which Maura stilled. Heidi, deciding she was okay, tentatively licked her hand gratefully, before resuming her grooming.

Maura rubbed under the hound's luxuriant ears for a moment before standing and making her way into her bath. Methodically, she washed her hands and face. She decided she looked presentable enough for a few quick strokes of her brush against her hair to complete her presentation of herself for dinner. After one final glance in the large mirror, she turned and switched off the bathroom's light before walking back into her bedroom.

Heidi sat with her long chin drooping over the edge of the bed and watched her switch on the lamp beside the bed with a worried look. "Why is your brow all wrinkled, girl? Are you anxious too?" Maura asked the dog, who only continued her doleful watch as Maura moved away toward the door. "Cookie?" Maura asked, getting far more response. Heidi was off the bed and waiting at the door before Maura reached it herself.

Maura and Heidi returned to the kitchen to find Kai pouring the wine. As Maura got a cookie for the obedient dog, Kai extended her glass, waiting for her to take it. When she accepted it with a small nod of her head, Kai lifted his glass and said, "To new beginnings."

Maura clinked the rim of her glass against the base of his and repeated, "To new beginnings." They both sipped their wine and Maura was surprised by how good it was. "So. how's Robin?" Maura asked easily as Kai sat down at the table once more.

Kai gave his mother a sharp look before defiantly lighting another cigarette. That accomplished, he twisted in his seat to empty the ashtray into the trash bin behind him. "Robin believes in happily-ever-afters," he commented dryly.

"I take it you don't," Maura commented just as dryly as she sat down opposite her son.

"I've never had any proof they exist," Kai replied sullenly.

Not wanting to encourage this line of reasoning, Maura skillfully redirected her question by asking, "Is he doing okay?"

"Mom, the only way Robin is going to be okay right now is if I tell him I've made up my mind to be gay and he's the one I want to be with," Kai told her candidly.

"And you haven't decided that yet, right?" Maura asked casually.

"It's a good thing he called after all," Kai admitted grudgingly. "I forgot Heidi's flea and tick medicine. He's going to mail it to me here," Kai answered, dodging her question entirely.

"Well, that's good news," Maura said as she sat down next to her son and rested her glass of wine on the table so she could pat the dog. "We don't want a houseful of fleas, do we, girl?"

Kai sipped his wine and watched his mother and his dog approvingly. "She's so good," he commented. "She's never had fleas or ticks, but she's mostly been an indoor dog, except when I took her to the beach." He sighed as he set his glass down beside his mother's and reached to extend his hands toward the dog, "Why can't people be as easy to love as dogs are?"

"Dogs don't ask as much of you, that's for sure," Maura said as Heidi moved from under her hands to Kai with a panting smile on her face. "Not to probe you too deeply, Kai. But why are you so conflicted about Robin? If you love him, you shouldn't push him away."

Kai scratched under Heidi's chin, and looked up at his mother's face. "What do you want me to do? Ask him to move down here too?"

"It's an option," Maura offered. "Do you think he would?"

Kai rubbed the top of his dog's head gently before shifting back to reach for his wineglass and snorted, "In a fucking heartbeat, he would."

Maura watched as he sipped his wine thoughtfully. "He cares for you that much?"

Kai nodded and swirled the wine in his glass absently. He gave his mother an abrupt look before setting his wineglass down once more and then replied, "Yes. Without a doubt. And, to tell you the truth, we've talked about it. But Mom, I've still got to get myself together. I need to find some work. I need to get back on my meds to make sure I'm thinking straight."

Maura nodded expectantly in reply. To her, nothing was more important than Kai getting back on his medication. From what she could tell, the painkillers had no visible effect on him. She hadn't known what to expect when he'd admitted taking them, but to her observation, he wasn't as nearly affected as he'd been when he was a pot smoker. Back then she could tell if he was high. From what she'd observed of him in only the few days he'd been home, she had no idea he was even taking anything, other than an odd sort of lassitude that came over him at times. That, in combination with his willingness to talk, was the only difference she saw in him.

Before Maura could respond, they heard a knock at the front door. Heidi gave a deep bark as she roused herself from the kitchen floor between Maura and Kai's seats and ran toward the foyer. Both Maura and Kai pushed their chairs back from the table and stood. They eyed each other anxiously for a moment before Maura said, "I'll get it. It's Matt. You and I will finish this conversation later."

Kai nodded as he stubbed out his cigarette and looked away. Maura realized she was so angry at him that she could shake him. In fact she wished she could shake him as she had when he was small and misbehaved. Back then she had always been so cautious not to take her anger or frustration out on him fearing she would hurt the little boy. Now, she looked at the man and wished she could shake him until his teeth rattled.

All the while, Heidi was barking from the foyer. Maura shook her head and turned to walk toward the door. As she did, another tentative knock sounded. As she struggled to compose herself, she shouted, "Hold on, I'm coming," and stepped quickly from the kitchen to the foyer. She shushed Heidi and took a deep breath, hoping the rest of the evening wouldn't be so difficult.

Maura managed to open the front door with a smile on her face and one hand holding Heidi's collar as she fought against the re-straint. She looked up into Matt's amused smile and immediately felt better. If nothing else, his familiar lean form promised some stability and strength. He held up his arms in surrender, one hand clutching a CVS bag and the other a bottle of wine. "Does it bite?" He asked in-nocently.

Maura stepped back, pulling Heidi along with her, whimpering now in excitement over this new unfamiliar presence. "C'mon in," Maura said. "She's just excited you're here. She doesn't bite."

Matt came inside, handed Maura the bottle of wine and closed the door behind him. Cautiously, he extended his hand toward the big dog, who reached Matt's outstretched hand with her nose. Once Heidi had sniffed, Maura let go of her collar and reached up to give Matt a quick hug saying, "You'd better pet her or she'll jump up. She'll settle down once you're in the house."

Matt handed her his CVS bag and sank down on his haunches to take Heidi in hand. The dog responded by fluidly circling him in the small space of the foyer as he rubbed and patted whatever part of her was closest. "You're a happy girl," Matt said with a laugh.

As Heidi responded by licking his face, Maura curiously peeked into the CVS bag and found a new pack of razors, a can of shaving cream and antiperspirant. Matt stood as she closed the bag and said, "My supply here was running low, so I thought I'd restock."

Happily, Maura stretched to give him a quick kiss before saying, "Well, you've met Kai's better half, you should come to the kitchen and meet Kai."

Matt followed her to the kitchen, noting she left the CVS bag on the dining room table as she passed. As Matt, Heidi, and Maura all entered the small kitchen, they found Kai peeling a plantain at the chopping board on the counter next to the stove. He ignored them until he had the fruit removed from its skin, and then he turned and smiled. Quickly, he placed the fruit on the cutting board and the peel on the counter before extending his hand for Matt to shake. "I'm the prodigal son," he said shyly.

Matt took his proffered hand, shook it firmly and said, "I'm the boyfriend."

Everyone laughed as they let go of each other's hands. Kai stepped to the edge of the table and quickly shifted his glass of wine and ashtray to the place at the table closest to the stove, and gestured for Matt to take his place. "Please sit down, Mr. Jenkins. Can I get you a glass of wine?"

Matt sank into his preferred seat, and looking up at Kai said, "Please call me Matt, and I'll take that glass of wine with pleasure."

"Okay, Matt," Kai said as he reached for the bottle and the remaining glass. He poured Matt a half glass of wine and handed it to him before seating himself between his mother and her boyfriend. Maura, aware of the awkward seating arrangement, sat down in her own preferred spot and watched as Kai lifted his glass and said, "To new friends."

Matt clinked his glass against Kai's and then followed suit with Maura's glass as well. "To new friends," he echoed pleasantly before he took a sip of his wine and watched as Maura and Kai completed the toast. "Dinner smells great," he commented warmly. "And I'm starved."

"I hope it'll be okay," Kai said as he glanced over his shoulder at the stove. "It'll still be about a half hour away. I need to cook the rice and fry the plantains."

"No problem," Matt responded. "I'm sure it'll be worth the wait."

"Kai's a great cook," Maura said quickly, betraying her anxiousness. "He's been helping out in the kitchen since he was a little boy. By the time he was ten, he was a better cook than I was," she admitted.

"I can burn a pot of water," Matt countered. "If it wasn't for your mother, I'd have starved in the past two years."

"Mom's a good cook," Kai answered. "I had a good teacher."

"I never thought I was teaching him," Maura admitted. "It all just started as a way to spend time together after work and school. Before I knew it, Kai had picked up how to prepare whole meals, hadn't you?"

Kai nodded and instinctively reached for his cigarettes. He had one extricated and on the way to his mouth, before he caught his mother's eye and stopped. He looked Matt in the eye and said, "I'm sorry about the cigarettes in the house. Mom told me you don't like smoke so much. But, if it's okay with you, and you don't mind, could I smoke in the house just for tonight? I've promised Mom I'll start smoking outside."

Matt met his eyes with a kind look and said, "You shouldn't have to ask permission to smoke in your own home. It's not a problem."

Kai nodded gratefully and lit his cigarette, then said, "But I understand this is kinda your home too, so I just want you to know I'm not an assho . . . , a *jerk*."

"I appreciate that, Kai. But I certainly don't think you're an asshole because you smoke. Have you thought about quitting?" Matt asked gently. "It's not so much rude as it's not good for you."

Kai sighed and examined his cigarette thoughtfully. "I know, I know," he said resignedly. "But I love it so much. Because I'm crazy, I guess."

"You're not crazy," Maura corrected him automatically.

"Mom told me she'd explained to you about me being bipolar," Kai told Matt, ignoring his mother. "Well, my psychiatrist says we're the hardest type of patient to get to quit. Smoking does something good to our brain chemistry. It increases the dopamine or something. I know that's not a great excuse, but it's the best one I have for not quitting," Kai told Matt honestly.

Matt nodded understandingly and said, "You'll quit when you're ready. I wouldn't worry about it."

Kai gave him a grateful smile and proceeded to take a deep drag off his cigarette, then exhaled it pointedly overhead so as not to blow smoke in Matt's direction.

"Just remember, you promised outside from now on," Maura told him quietly. "So, how was your day?" she asked Matt directly.

"Not so terrible," Matt replied agreeably. "No worse than usual, in any event. How about yours?"

"Long," Maura replied without hesitation. "I felt like I was in a pinball machine. But, I'm home now and whatever's not done will be waiting for me tomorrow."

"How about you, Kai?" Matt asked curiously. "Have you started looking for any work? Your Mom tells me you have a whole marketing plan and presentation piece to go along with it. I'd like to see it when you get a chance."

Kai gave him a sheepish glance and then admitted, "I haven't started looking yet. I worked today on the layout of my brochure. I plan to go to Kinko's in the next couple of days and get some printed out and bound. Otherwise, I'd show you the piece right now. Of course, maybe you could look at it on my laptop before I do and give me some input. Having a degree in graphic design, I think I might have gone a little overboard."

"I'd be happy to do that for you," Matt offered. "But as a leave-behind, I think having as many pictures of your work as you can afford to show is a good idea."

"That's what I think," Maura interjected. "Maybe you could take a look at Kai's work after dinner," she suggested lightly.

"Aw, Mom," Kai chided her. "Give the guy a break. Maybe Matt can take a look at it tomorrow night. I should be finished tweaking it by then."

"Whatever's good for you," Matt replied and gave Maura the ghost of a wink. "I'd rather you got dinner ready just now."

"Right," Kai said and stubbed out his cigarette. He took a quick sip of wine and stood. "I'll get the show on the road and you guys talk."

With that, he stood, went to the sink and washed his hands before resuming the task of preparing the plantains for cooking.

Maura smiled inwardly. So far, things seemed to feel natural and right. As a result of either the wine, or the relative ease with which the evening seemed to be going, she relaxed and listened as Matt and Kai resumed their friendly banter while Kai started the rice and fried the plantains. Kai, she noted, seemed self-assured and remarkably open to conversation. Matt responded with intelligent, but not probing questions, and offered more information about himself. To Maura it seemed like an elaborate game of staking out territory, some to be shared and others to be held inviolate. However, both her adult son and her boyfriend seemed to be getting on well.

The tenor of conversation remained gracious throughout the meal, which was delicious. Kai had really outdone himself. Maura and Matt ate heartily, but Maura noticed Kai only ate sparingly from his own plate and didn't reach for seconds of anything. All the while, Heidi lay in the doorway between the kitchen and dining room area of the great room beyond. Kai had trained her well. She never came to the table to beg once, but when Kai stood with the remains of his dinner on his plate, Heidi stood as well. Taking her bowl from the floor behind Matt's seat, Kai placed it on the counter and scraped his leftovers into her bowl. The big dog watched his movements with great concentration until he returned the bowl to its spot on the floor when she skipped to it and noisily began to eat.

"Do you always feed her table scraps?" Matt asked as he carefully pushed himself away from the kitchen table and crossed his leg to let his right ankle rest over his left knee.

Taking Matt's plate to the sink, Kai said, "Yes and no. She has her own dog food which she gets twice a day. But on special occasions, or if there's anything left from dinner, she gets that as well. Robin says I deliberately . . ." Kai caught himself and turned abruptly and began rinsing the Matt's plate under the tap.

"Robin says what?" Maura urged him.

"He says I make a point of saving half my meals for Heidi," Kai said from the sink without turning around.

"And who's Robin?" Matt asked innocently.

Kai and his mother both began to speak at once. Both realized what they were doing and stopped talking within a syllable of each other.

Matt looked from Maura to Kai questioningly until Kai finally spoke saying, "Robin is my housemate on the beach back on the Outer Banks."

"Kai and Robin have been living together for the past year," Maura elaborated.

Matt raised his eyebrows at her questioningly as Kai turned back to the table and took her plate. "That's right, Mother," he replied stiffly without looking at Matt. "Would you guys like some coffee?" he asked in an obvious attempt to change the conversation.

"None for me," Matt answered heartily. "I usually only drink coffee in the mornings."

"Nor me," Maura declined.

"Blame it on my fucked up brain chemistry," Kai said. "But it calms me down rather than giving me any kind of caffeine buzz. I'm going to make a little pot. If you guys change your minds, you're welcome to share."

"Since you cooked, why don't you let your mother and me load the dishwasher," Matt offered.

Matt looked at him gratefully and said, "I think I'll take you up on that." As he began to prepare the coffee, he looked at his mother questioningly once more.

"I think I will have a cup, if you're going to make some anyway," Maura told him.

Kai nodded and gave her a ghost of a smile to show her he wasn't angry with her about discussing Robin.

Matt watched Kai move around, combining the leftover black

beans with the rice into a single bowl and covering it along with the remains of the pork roast as the coffee brewed. What was left of the plantains, he tossed to Heidi who deftly caught the three pieces one after the other. Once the coffee had brewed, Kai moved in the lengthening stillness in the room, rattling his and his mother's coffee mugs as he set them on the counter and poured their coffee. The spoon's tiny ringing complaint against the sides of the mugs as he stirred in the sweetener and cream were the only sounds in the room. At last, Kai brought the mugs of steaming coffee to the table. Before he could sit down, Matt asked, "Is there any more wine left in that bottle, Kai?"

Kai stepped back to the counter and held the bottle up to the light revealing perhaps a third of the wine left. Once more he stepped to the table and poured the remainder of the bottle into Matt's glass before placing the bottle back on the counter and sitting down.

Matt took a sip of his wine and nodded once in appreciation before saying, "I take it when your mother said you were living with Robin, that you were involved on a deeper level than just as roommates."

Kai gave him a hard, sharp look, but instead of answering right away, he defiantly lit a cigarette. After he got it lit, he took a sip of his coffee, then replied, "The answer to your question is kind of complicated. I did have a sexual relationship with Robin, if that's what you're asking. But I don't consider myself to be exclusively gay. That's a good part of the reason I left the beach and came home. I need to sort out exactly how much I can commit to Robin, knowing he's prepared to commit completely to me."

Matt again merely nodded before he took another sip of his wine and then said, "That is complicated. I didn't mean to put you on the spot, but I'm a fairly direct man and I like to know what's going on." He stopped and put his hand on Kai's wrist, gripped it gently once, then took his hand away. "You know, I'm in love with your mother. Because of that, I also wanted to know more about what was going on with you and your sudden reappearance. I hope you understand. I don't mean to pry, but I find I have."

Kai chuckled slightly and said, "It's no worse than I deserve. At least the subject isn't hanging there in the air like a big balloon."

"I want you to know I don't have a problem with it," Matt said quickly. "It really is none of my business."

"You're right. It isn't," Kai said bluntly. "But I made it your business when I came home the way I did. I'll be perfectly honest with you. I have no idea what in the hell I'm going to do about Robin. I just know I'm going to concentrate on not disturbing your life with my Mom any more than I have."

"I appreciate that," Matt said evenly. "For my part, I want to be honest with you and say I intend to respect your place in your Mom's home. No matter what, everybody deserves the right to be able to go home if they can."

Kai gave Matt a smile and said, "Thanks. Now if you two don't mind, I'm going to take my coffee and my dog and head back to my room. I've got a call I promised to return." With that, he stood, took his coffee and headed toward the opposite side of the house with Heidi following along happily behind him.

Maura listened for the sound of his door closing and when she heard it, she finally felt like something held tight inside her relaxed and let go. She reached across the table to Matt, who extended his hand to take hers. For a moment they both just looked at each other, then they smiled with relief. Maura shook her head and said, "Whew. I wish I could tell you it's not always going to be this intense, but Kai is . . ."

"Pretty intense." Matt finished for her. "Poor guy. Hell of a night for him. Meeting me, getting outed about his boyfriend. Pissing out territory. I'm just glad we don't do this every Wednesday night," he finished, giving her hand a final squeeze and letting it go.

Maura took a sip of her coffee and said, "The thing about Robin, well, Kai and Robin . . . that really doesn't bother you?"

Matt glanced at her and gave her an exasperated look. "Of course not. What have I ever done to give you the idea I was so narrow minded?"

"Nothing really," Maura said. "But then again, the subject of gay people has never really come up. I mean, I know gay people, but you and I . . ."

"I know gay people too," Matt interrupted her. "I have two gay guys and a lesbian who work for me, but they're not exactly family, or even close friends for that matter."

"Well, I'm used to it. Kai has been sexually active since he was fifteen, and he's never stated a preference of girls over boys or vice-versa," Maura admitted. "As a matter of fact, there was also a girlfriend, who's now out of the picture, who he was seeing while he was living with Robin."

"Damn," Matt sighed. "I don't know if he's a lucky little shit or really fucked up. In any event, I can't handle more than one woman at a time. I can't imagine a girlfriend and a boyfriend simultaneously."

"I think Kai has grown to the point that he can't either," Maura confided. "This Robin is someone special. I can tell. Kai's never been so emotionally involved in any of his relationships before. In fact, he even admitted he loved Robin."

"So what's the problem?" Matt asked genuinely.

"Kai doesn't like to be thought of as being gay. For some reason, he has a real problem with that," Maura told him.

"Do you have a problem with it?" Matt asked her carefully.

"Not at all," Mura answered promptly. "I just want him to be happy. If he can get past this hang up about being seen to be gay, I'm all for Robin, or any guy, if he's in love."

"Well, working in the world Kai does, being known as gay can have its drawbacks," Matt told her honestly. "Construction sites aren't the most accepting of places."

"I can imagine," Maura told him. "But by the time it gets to the point where Kai would come in, the house is basically done. How much does he actually interact with a framing crew or roofers?"

"Down here, none. Unless he speaks Spanish," Matt told her. "That's not it though. It's the culture. Guys who wear tool belts for a living don't usually have much to do with gay people. At least, not that they know of."

"Where he's been working, it's a much smaller world too," Maura admitted. "His dad has been banging nails since he graduated from high school. They all know each other up there. But, for what it's worth, he got involved with Robin up there so . . ."

"Don't worry about it, Maura. He'll figure it out one way or another," Matt assured her. "If he is crazy, he's crazy like a fox." `

"Maybe you're right," Maura said as she stood, leaving most of her coffee unfinished. "You want to give me a hand with these dishes?"

"Of course," Matt said and stood as well. "If we work together we'll be done in ten minutes. Kai's already done half of it."

Working as a team, Matt and Maura made short work of the kitchen chores. At last, when the table and counters had been wiped down and the dishwasher turned on, Maura glanced at the clock on the microwave and noted it was nearly nine-thirty. "Would you like to watch TV for awhile?" she asked Matt tentatively. In truth, what she wanted more than anything else was to go to bed. Her day had been tiring and her evening riddled with minefields.

Matt carefully folded the damp dish towel he held in his hand and laid it next to the chopping block on the counter. He looked at Maura with his own weariness evident on his face. "To tell you the truth, what I really want to do is brush my teeth and go to bed," he told her honestly.

"You read my mind," Maura confessed. "Why don't you go ahead and get in our bathroom. I'm going to knock on Kai's door to let him know we're off to sleep."

Matt nodded and moved past her, lightly kissing the side of her neck as her passed. "Please bring in my CVS bag when you come in," he reminded her as he passed into the bedroom door.

"Sure thing," Maura said. Then she gave the kitchen a final glance and switched off all the lights except for the one over the stove. As she made her way past the dining room table, she lifted Matt's bag of grooming products and carried it with her down the small hall to Kai's closed door. From the other side she heard murmuring. She lifted her hand to knock on the door and was answered by Heidi's bark, plus she distinctly heard Kai tell Robin to hold on.

In a moment, Kai opened his door with his cell phone in one hand and the other gripping Heidi's collar. "What's up?" he asked her brightly.

"I just wanted to say good night," Maura told him. "Matt and I are turning in. Do you want me to turn off the lights in the great room?"

"No, I'll do it a little later," Kai told her. "I'll need to take Heidi out before we go to bed."

In the background from Kai's room, Maura could hear the jazz station playing on the radio by his bed. The room reeked of cigarette smoke, dog, and Kai's own scent. It seemed almost like the nights she had come to say good night in many years past. In its way, this comforted her. She reached up and stroked his smooth face as she said, "Sleep well. Don't worry about us, we'll both be sawing logs within a half hour or so. You won't disturb us."

Kai allowed his cheek to be stroked and gave her a small smile. He said, "Your Matt is a pretty good guy. Tonight wasn't so bad was it?"

"I'll let him know you approve," Maura said lightly, then added, "Tonight was fine. And it'll get easier, I promise."

"Good night then," Kai told her glancing at his cell phone idling in his hand.

Maura nodded and turned as Kai closed his door once more. She heard him apologize for the interruption during his call, then he was silent once more as Robin responded. Maura hoped his call was going well, but she knew there was little she could do about it. As she made her way back to her room, she looked forward to letting it all go and surrendering to sleep. For the past few days, the only time she'd truly had to herself was spent in sleep. When she was awake she had work, Matt, and Kai to worry about.

When she entered her room, she found Matt already in bed, the covers pulled up to his bare chest and his eyes closed. She shut the door behind her as quietly as she could, but when she turned she found Matt looking at her with a tired smile. "Everything okay?" he asked with concern.

"Kai thinks you're a pretty good guy," she told him as she ducked into the bathroom to place Matt's bag on the vanity. That done, she walked back into the bedroom and pulled her T-shirt over her head as she walked into her closet. "And I think you're fantastic on an international scale," she added as she unbuttoned her shorts and eased them over her hips to let them fall.

"Well, thanks," Matt answered sleepily. "You're world class yourself."

Maura unhooked her bra and removed it before slipping another outsized T-shirt over her head. A men's extra large and sporting a logo from a fishing pier up on the Outer Banks, it was special in its own way. It had been Rhett's at one time. It was a keepsake of a night stolen together not ten years ago. Though they had formally divorced, she and Kai's father had continued to sleep together on her infrequent trips up to the Kill Devil Hills over the years. Matt of course knew nothing of the T-shirt's provenance. Maura hadn't appropriated any of his T-shirts to wear as night dresses. She had outgrown the habit after Rhett, but this particular T-shirt was her favorite sleep garment still, after so many years.

Comforted by the T-shirt's soft fall to her mid-thighs, she slipped from the closet to brush her teeth quickly before going to the bed and getting in. As she burrowed beneath the covers, Matt lifted his head and leaned across the small space between them for a good night kiss. Maura kissed him not once, but three times in quick succession, emphasizing both her gladness that he was back in her bed and her gratitude for his being so easy on this difficult night.

"Tonight didn't go so badly, did it?" Matt asked as she switched off the lamp by the bed.

Maura turned to face him after she lay down and said, "Kai asked me the same thing. I think tonight went very well. Everything's going to be all right. Just wait, you'll see."

"I think you're right," Matt whispered in return. He reached across the bed and patted her hip gently. "Good night, sweetheart," he said as he drew his hand back to his side of the bed and let it fall near his chin.

Maura looked at him lovingly in the meager light from the dark night outside the drawn blinds. Her eyes adapted to the darkness and she could make out the contours of his face as he lay next to her. "Good night," she echoed and sighed in comfort before closing her eyes.

Chapter Eight

IN WHAT SEEMED no time at all, she heard something in the kitchen and smelled coffee stealing in from the room on the opposite side of the wall. Startled, she turned to glance at the clock and saw it was nearly three-thirty in the morning. Though she knew instantly what was going on and could have just as easily rolled over and gone back to sleep, she gently drew off the bed covers and got up quietly so as not to disturb Matt.

Matt snored on. Grateful for his deep sleep, Maura let herself silently out of the bedroom and turned into the kitchen. As she expected, Kai sat calmly where he had for dinner, staring out the middle of the bay window into the night. On the counter, the coffee machine groaned and hissed as it brewed fresh coffee. Kai hadn't turned at the sound of her bedroom door opening, nor did he turn now. Instead, he just sat, smoking a cigarette as Maura crept to her seat at the table, pulled out her chair and sat down. "Can't sleep?" she whispered.

"Not tonight," Kai said in his lowest, calmest voice. "Too many demons. Too many bad dreams."

"What did you dream?" Maura asked him gently. Over the years, she'd heard of the convoluted and dead-ended scenarios of his subconscious on many other nights like this, shrouded with a fog of cigarette smoke and scented with drifts of coffee, from the time he was a teenager. Before then, he was just a little boy sitting alone without any comforts, in the darkest part of the night.

"It doesn't matter, Mom. I couldn't explain it if I tried. It's an amalgam of places, here but not here, the beach, but not the beach. It's all the noise in my head, like twenty radios playing at once. I can't concentrate, much less sleep. They won't leave me alone," he tried to explain.

The indescribable *they*. Maura knew them well. *They*, those unnamable things that came into Kai's overactive brain and tormented him with thoughts and scenes he couldn't relate, but robbed him of sleep and solace day and night. "Can you hang on until you see Dr. Roth again?" Maura asked him.

Kai nodded. "I did half a painkiller. I'll be high in about twenty minutes and they'll all go away. I'll be able to concentrate then." He reached in his pack of cigarettes and lit the new one off the butt of the old one. After a moment, he looked at his mother and said, "You should go back to bed. You can't be used to this any more and you have to work tomorrow."

Maura noticed he was trembling; it was more pronounced now than it had been earlier. She laid her hand over the one Kai rested on the table and squeezed it in the vain hope the trembling would stop. After a moment, he opened his hand and took hers in his own and returned the squeeze before letting it go. "I'll be fine, Mom. Go back to bed. You know this is nothing new. I'll be okay."

Maura felt her fatigue gather in close to her bones. She was tired and sleepy, but her child was awake and filled with fears that had no name. There was no way to soothe him. She knew he was doing his best to soothe himself. There was the drug, the cigarettes, and the coffee dripping into the pot. He would wait alone until daylight crept across the eastern sky outside the bay window across from him.

Maura watched as he took a drag on his cigarette and stared out the dark window. Under the moon and the ambient light of the city that sprawled out in front of them toward the ocean, she could make out the canal and the house across the way. They were familiar comforting shapes in the night. Kai turned slowly to look at her and said, "This is stupid after all these years, to still be doing this."

"It's not stupid, and it's not your fault," Maura said as she'd said so many times before. "I wish I could fix it."

"Nothing can," Kai said hopelessly. "They can even break through the Risperdal. I was on Risperdal before I quit taking my meds."

"What's Risperdal?" Maura asked him with concern.

"It's an antipsychotic, Mom," Kai told her simply.

Maura wasn't surprised. Kai had been on a variety of drugs over the years as the technology and research had developed. She remembered the years on Haldol. Kai could stumble on a pattern in a rug when he was on that. Still, there had been the sleeplessness, the racing thoughts. Nothing held or lasted.

"Don't focus on that," Maura reassured him. "No matter what a drug is for, if it helps, don't worry about it."

Kai nodded but said, "Still, if you're on antipsychotics, you must be psychotic. Especially if they work."

"Does the Risperdal work?" Maura asked him in turn, refusing to give him room to retreat.

"Ninety percent of the time," Kai told her.

"What about the pain medication?" Maura pressed him.

"Oh, that . . ." Kai said and smiled around his cigarette. "It just makes me feel like it's all going to be okay."

"Then I understand why you got hooked," Maura said soothingly.

Kai only shrugged in reply and calmly twisted the bright hot tip of his cigarette on the side of his ashtray. Finally he looked back out the window and said despairingly, "But I can't keep doing it. I've got to stop. I need to quit so I can have some for emergencies, like tonight. It's too good to waste dealing it out in dribbles and drabs like I've been doing. I need to just stop. Then I'll have some for when things get really bad."

Maura had nothing to say to this line of reasoning. She didn't approve of him taking an opiate painkiller to begin with, but there was also the rationalization any port in a storm that gave him shelter was worth it. She reached for Kai once more, but he got up abruptly and made himself a cup of coffee. Maura watched his clean, deft movements and admired their economy. She knew he was concentrating on the details of his task so its mundane aspects would focus his attention and keep him from spinning out into a world where his thoughts danced out of control.

Kai returned to the table with his coffee, his cigarette held between his teeth contorting his face into a rictus of a smile. He sat down and put out his cigarette before taking a sip of his hot coffee. Then, setting the mug on the table, he dropped his head in his hands and rubbed his temples remorsefully. When he stopped, he looked at his mother again and said, "You really should get back in bed, Mom. I'll be up the rest of the night. There's no use in both of us going without sleep. Go back to bed."

"Where's Heidi?" Maura asked, to turn his attention away from her.

"Sacked out on my bed. She doesn't have demons, but she does have those doggy dreams where she whimpers and growls and moves her paws," Kai told her. He smiled in the darkness and said, "She's a good girl, my Heidi."

"Yes. She is," Maura said evenly as Kai lit a cigarette once more. She thought his lungs must be black by now. He had started smoking when he was barely in his teens. It was something she'd let him get away with, knowing what other problems he faced; smoking seemed like a minor problem and it did seem to calm him. Now she could kick herself for not taking a firmer stand against the habit.

Kai sighed deeply and a shiver ran down his spine as she watched him. He dropped his head and then rolled his neck, stretching unseen muscles. "I'm starting to drop," he murmured.

"The pill is kicking in?" Maura asked.

"Ummm, yeah," Kai said contentedly. "Pretty soon, I'll be all right. They won't bother me anymore and I can just sit here and enjoy the quiet and dark."

"Will you feel like talking?" Maura asked him gently.

"Probably. The pain meds make me chatty as hell," Kai said and smiled. "Not that you haven't noticed."

Maura smiled back across the dimly lit table. "Well, I admit, you've talked more in the past three days than you did when you were home for a week at Christmas."

Kai nodded and took a deep hit off his cigarette, "Christmas was tough."

"You seemed okay," Maura told him. "Why was Christmas tough?"

"Christmas was when I realized I was in love with Robin," Kai told her directly. "That messed me up pretty bad."

"Kai, being in love is not supposed to mess you up," Maura whispered harshly. "Being in love is perfectly natural and good for you. I won't say it doesn't hurt sometimes, but you have to give it a chance."

Kai flicked the ash from his cigarette contemptuously and said, "Not if you're me. I don't ever want to depend on any one that much for my happiness, what little of it I can find. Besides, I'm not gay."

"Kai, why do you keep saying that?" Maura asked as she tried to keep her voice down. "No one cares whether you're gay or not. The important thing is to be happy with someone. Does Robin make you happy?"

Kai rubbed his eyes this time before answering, "Why are you so interested in Robin all the time? Robin. Robin. Robin. You'd think it was somebody I was married to."

"Robin is the first person you've ever said you loved," Maura explained gently. "You're twenty-seven years old and you've never loved anyone else. That alone is fact enough to make me curious about Robin."

"Okay. Fair enough, Mom," Kai said agreeably. "Ask me what you want to. I'll tell you."

Maura stood and walked to the coffeemaker. She reached overhead and got a mug from the cabinet and nearly filled the mug before she went to the refrigerator for the half-and-half. As she prepared her coffee and doctored it with the requisite packet of Splenda, she thought about what exactly to ask. There were a lot of obvious questions that came to mind, but she did know what Robin did for a living, how old he was, and roughly what he looked like. Rhett had told her he looked like her, so she pictured a shortish blond with green eyes. Other than that there was a great deal she wanted to know.

Finally Maura returned to the table and sat down before she asked Kai, "Why him? What is there about him that made you fall in love with him?"

Kai snorted, then said, "If I knew that, maybe I could stop loving him and get over him." He stubbed out his cigarette and then immediately lit another one before taking a sip of his coffee. "I don't know, Mom. He just has this sexy little way about him and he makes me laugh. That and he *gets* me. Nobody else quite gets me. He does. I know he does and that's why he's so hard to get free of. Like, like . . ." Kai stalled and smoked in silence for a moment.

Maura tried to understand what he'd told her so far. In many ways, it was exactly the same way she felt about Matt. She thought he was sexy, certainly. But it was in that larger sense she knew Kai was correct. Matt got her. He understood her little ways and moods and feelings. That feeling that she was understood and still accepted and cared for was what bound her to Matt. And at long last, here was her son finally saying he felt the same way about a human being and not a dog. In a way, it was funny. She had waited all through his childhood and adolescence for him to confess to being in love. Now, here he was finally suffering through what was really an adolescent emotion mixed with an adult's needs.

"Like what?" she prompted.

"Like when I told him I was going to move back down here," Kai said. "He told me it would hurt him to let me go, but because he really loved me, he'd let me leave and do what was best for me."

"Then he really does love you," Maura said and took a moment to sip her coffee. It was warm and comforting in the near darkness and it allowed her to think before she added, "And I mean a whole lot, not just a little. If he's willing not to manipulate you into staying for his own benefit, he's really in love with you. That kind of selflessness can't be faked."

"Yeah, I know. I've thought about it," Kai admitted. "What I can't deal with is realizing it makes me love him even more. But it's still fucked up. I just don't think I'm ready to be full on, full-time gay."

Maura sipped her coffee and said, "I don't understand. Is what you're scared of never sleeping with women again or thinking you're going to have your own float in the gay pride parade?"

"Maybe a little of both," Kai said abruptly. "Though it's not the sex thing so much as it's all about the gay thing. I don't see myself marching in any gay pride parades. No way."

"Is Robin that kind of gay person?" Maura asked.

"You mean, all radical and shit? No. He's not like that. He's just like a regular guy except he sounds gay when he talks. I mean, all you have to do is be around him a little while and you know. It's nothing obvious, it's just . . . well, you know. He's gay," Kai struggled to explain.

"At work, did you get any grief about Robin?" Maura asked.

"Oh hell yeah," Kai told her loudly.

Maura shushed him and listened to hear if they'd startled Matt awake. In the quiet house, she could detect the sound of his soft snoring still. Finally satisfied he was still asleep, she quietly asked Kai, "Did you really give a damn? I mean you still lived with the boy for a year."

"Well, no. Not really. It wasn't anything more than being teased a lot. But I gave back just as good as I got, and finally nobody made a big deal about it any more," Kai told her in a near whisper. "Of course, I started seeing Linda and that shut a lot of them up."

"Did Linda know about Robin?" Maura asked .

"I suppose she did. I would never talk about it with her. I told her

Robin was none of her business, and she pretty much dropped it after that. But I could tell she was jealous," Kai admitted.

"And Robin knew about Linda," Maura stated obviously. "You've said he did."

Kai put his face in his hands and rubbed until Maura wanted to stop him. Finally he looked up at her and said, "He was hurt and I knew it. I'm not proud about what I did, sleeping with Linda while I was sleeping with him, but to me it was about getting the pain pills. I think Robin understood that's all it was. He knew he came first in other ways."

Maura sipped her cooling coffee and tried to imagine the sad little triangle playing itself out along the familiar sights of the beach road and bypass between Nags Head and Kitty Hawk. She knew, she'd lived there too and had her own dramas there on that long spit of sand and sea oats. It was a place where the sun came right down and touched the ground. Nothing there came easy or soft. It was a place that actively aided and abetted personal drama. No wonder Kai had felt that it was all closing in on him.

"Mom?" Kai asked gently, bringing her back from her reverie.

"What Kai?" She responded in the same tone.

"Would you mind if Robin came down for Thanksgiving?" Kai asked her out of the blue.

Maura smiled. It seemed like a reasonable request. In fact, she rather liked the idea of Robin altogether. Getting to meet him and talk to him would give her some real insight into her son at the moment. She touched Kai's hand and said, "I think that's a good idea, if you do."

Kai nodded and said, "In four weeks, I'm back on my real meds again. My head should be straightened out, and maybe seeing him here will help me make up my mind about him."

"Do you miss him?" Maura asked Kai bluntly.

Kai nervously smoked for a moment before he blew out a long

stream of smoke and said, "I think I do. I just want to have some stuff accomplished before I see him again. But if I have that to look forward to, and he does too, I think it'll make things easier."

"Then by all means, ask him," Maura said and yawned. Glancing at the clock she saw it was nearing half past four. Kai seemed to be less lost and desperate now than when she'd come into the kitchen. While she knew he'd undoubtedly be up the rest of the night, she also knew she'd managed to shift the rails his mind was running on to a different, more positive direction. Now at least, *they* wouldn't bother him anymore tonight. She'd given him something to think about. "Are you feeling better now?" she asked him.

Kai nodded and said, "For sure." He stubbed out his cigarette and stretched before he again slumped protectively over his coffee mug and ashtray and lit another cigarette.

"Kai, you know it's a whole different big world down here. It's a place where you and Robin can live any kind of life you might want to make. Think about that. I'm going back to bed," she said as she stood and walked over to the sink. She poured what was left of her coffee down the sink and congratulated herself on not giving in to the urge to bum a cigarette. Now she felt like she could go back and get another couple of hours of sleep before she had to get up.

She turned from the sink and stood directly behind Kai's chair. She put her arms around his shoulders and rested her cheek on top of his head. Kai reached up and patted her arm saying, "Thanks, Mom."

"Any time," she said and gave his shoulders a quick squeeze before turning to go back to her room and bed. She noiselessly let herself back into her room and quickly got back into bed. Matt sighed and turned to his other side in his sleep. Maura waited until she heard his breathing resume its slow, deep rhythm. Satisfied he was undisturbed, she closed her eyes and willed herself to go back to sleep. It was difficult, knowing Kai was awake and alone on the other side of the wall. She hoped whatever peace he'd get from the pill would come soon and fully. Other than accepting him for what he was, demons and all, there was nothing she could do.

There had been many other nights when he'd been small when she'd sat up with him, just so he wouldn't be alone, but ultimately, the periods of his sleeplessness came so frequently that she had to leave him on his own. There was the fact of Kai's self-imposed isolation during these times as well. Even if she had sat up with him, he'd never been as communicative as he was tonight. She'd forgotten, since he'd been gone, how much it robbed her of her own sleep. Maura allowed herself a quiet sigh, then turned on her side and tried to mend the torn seams of her sleep once more.

Chapter Nine

AS SHE DROVE into the subdivision on her way home from work, Maura saw Kai walking Heidi. Knowing he'd be back soon with his dog, she changed quickly into her after work clothes and went into the kitchen to start a pot of coffee. If she was lucky, she'd have a couple of hours before Matt came home, and she wanted to use the time to talk to Kai alone. Since he'd come home, she could never seem to find the right time to tell him she was pregnant. Once he'd slid so quickly into a dark period, the last thing she wanted to do was trip him into falling any further. But now that he seemed to be feeling better, she knew she'd better give him the news.

She sat at her place at the kitchen table and listened to the coffee brew and stream into the glass carafe. Kai had left the radio on and it played a nice song from its spot on top of the refrigerator. She was grateful for the distraction. She didn't want to entertain any fantasies of Kai's reaction being negative. She couldn't stand the thought he might be angry or hurt. She honestly didn't know how he would take the news, but take it he must.

She thought about the time she broke the news to him that his father was moving out of their little house in Avalon Beach. He was only three years old at the time, but he'd taken the news stoically. He seemed more concerned about whether Buddy, his dog, would be staying. She thought it was funny that even as a child his ideas of what would most bitterly affect him were so different than her own. Rhett's moving out he seemed to take in stride. It would have been a major catastrophe if he'd lost Buddy, his confidant and living teddy bear.

As she was lost in these memories, Kai came in the front door. She heard him release Heidi from her leash and then her claws scrabbled over the tile floor on her way into the kitchen for a treat. Kai walked into the kitchen right behind her.

"Coffee smells good. You read my mind, Mom," he said cheerfully.

"It seemed like that time of day," Maura answered obliquely. "Take a seat, Kai. I need to talk with you."

Kai gave her a concerned look before pulling out his chair. "What's up, Mom? Why so serious all of a sudden?"

Maura watched as he pulled a pack of Marlboro Lights and his lighter from the pocket on his left thigh of his cargo shorts. When he got one extracted, Maura reached across the table and took it from his fingers and put it between her lips.

"Oh boy," Kai groaned. "This is going to be intense if you have to have a cigarette to get it out." He shook his head and pulled another cigarette from the pack for himself. He lit Maura's first, then his own before crossing his arms on the table in front of him and looking at her with open-faced curiosity.

Maura took a shallow hit off her cigarette and blew the smoke out immediately without inhaling it. She met his gaze and said, "Son, there's something I've been putting off telling you. It's kind of a big deal for Matt and me, and I want you to be happy for us."

Kai's face lit up and he said "You're getting married? That's great, Mom. Matt seems like a really nice guy."

Maura smiled and thumped her cigarette against the side of the ashtray. She studied the round bit of grey ash for just a beat too long before she said, "Well, that's only part of it. Matt and me getting married, I mean."

Kai raised his eyebrows and leveled a long look into her eyes, waiting for her to go on.

"Kai, I'm pregnant. You're going to have a baby brother," she said evenly.

Kai nodded and quickly moved his eyes from her face. He took a deep hit off his cigarette and hung his head for a moment in silence before he began to snicker. When he looked up at her once more, his eyes were genuinely lit up in a way she hadn't seen them since he'd come home. "You crazy heifer," he said as he shook his head. "You mean having me wasn't bad enough? You had to sign up for round two? And at your age?"

Maura nervously took a hit off her cigarette, inhaling this time. She tilted her head back haughtily and blew the smoke out through her nose before she said, "Well, for your information, I didn't exactly plan this, but I'm not displeased. In fact, I've decided I'm pretty happy about it. Matt is happy. In fact, he's ecstatic. I was hoping you'd be happy as well."

Kai laid his cigarette in the ashtray before he slid out of his seat and knelt by his mother's side. He took her in his arms and hugged her tight saying, "Oh Mama, my crazy, wonderful Mama."

Maura found tears welling up in her eyes as he held her and rocked her gently from side to side. When she could trust her voice, she said, "You don't mind?"

Kai placed his hands on her shoulders and pushed her gently away saying, "Of course I don't mind. I think it's cool as shit. I'm serious." With that he kissed her forehead and returned to his seat.

Maura sobbed and put her face in her hands.

"Ah, c'mon Mom. No crying, okay?" Kai said gently. "Everything's good. You're going to have a baby, how cool is that, huh?"

Maura's sob turned into a snort and she laughed as she wiped at her eyes and put out her cigarette. "I certainly didn't expect you to react like that, Kai."

"Ah Mom, how did you think I was going to react?" Kai said with genuine consternation.

"I don't know . . . I thought you might feel, I thought it might make you sad or something," Maura admitted.

Kai took a hit off his cigarette and then blew the smoke straight up toward the ceiling in a show of nonchalance. He said, "Actually, it makes me kind of excited. In a way, it's better than having a kid of my own. I get to play with yours. I've always wanted a kid, especially a little boy, but considering everything, I decided a long time ago that I'd never have kids."

"Really, Kai? Why not?" Maura asked with genuine concern.

Kai snorted and shook his head. "You know as well as I do."

"No. What are you talking about?" Maura pressed him.

Kai sighed, put out his cigarette and took his time lighting another one before he said calmly, "I'd never bring a child into this world and pass along this head shit I've got. You know as well as I do it's hereditary. The bipolar thing is genetic, and what's worse is it gets worse with every generation." He shook his head emphatically and said, "No. No kind of way. No babies for Kai. Forget about it."

Maura reached across the table and took his forearm in her hand. "I had no idea you felt that way, Kai. But you have to understand, so much of things like that are in God's hands. It's not for us to decide."

Kai gave her a kind, but firm look and said, "Bullshit. I will not make any crazy kids. This shit ends with me." Then he laughed and said, "Maybe God does have a hand in it, after all. The only person I've ever loved enough to think about making a kid with is Robin and that's not going to happen. Last I heard, spit doesn't make babies."

Maura let go of his arm, vaguely repulsed by the image he'd proffered. She had nothing to say. In a way, it gave her pause. For a moment she was confronted with the thought that God was making her carry the baby Kai would never have. The thought of it made her feel somehow betrayed. She shook her head and looked out the window.

Kai sat beside her smoking in silence for many long moments before he said, "When are you due?"

Maura pulled herself back from her disturbed thoughts and answered absently, "June."

Kai nodded his head and put out his cigarette. Leaning in his forearms, he looked at her and said, "Do you know if he'll be messed up like me? I mean what are the chances, right? I'd just hate to see you get stuck with another fucked up kid. I mean, I'm punishment enough, right? God wouldn't put you through all the shit I have again would he?"

Maura felt a wave of tenderness move through her as she once again placed her hand gently on Kai's forearm and said, "I'd be a lucky woman if God gave me another little boy like you. I don't think you're fucked up. You're my son and I love you. Don't ever forget that, okay?"

Kai nodded and patted his mother's hand awkwardly. He said, "Thanks, Mom. Still, I'm going to light a candle in church and pray God gives you a kid who's normal this time. A kid who can sleep and who isn't in outer space half the time. I'm gonna do that, okay?"

Maura nodded and looked out the window once more. She didn't have any answers to the large questions like the ones Kai posed. She just knew whatever this child was going to be, he'd be just fine, and so would her grown son. For whatever he was, he was never predictable or boring, and somehow he always said the right thing.

Chapter Ten

BY FRIDAY MORNING, Kai's depression had subsided enough for him to join his mother and Matt in the kitchen for breakfast, though the thought of food nauseated him. Ignoring Maura's concerned look, he poured himself a cup of coffee and doctored it up so that it was creamy and sweet. Once Kai sat down, Matt closed the business section of the *Sun-Sentinel* and studied Kai's slumped form and haggard face. "You look like death warmed over," he said with some pity.

Kai rubbed the three-day-old stubble on his chin and said, "I actually feel a little better this morning. I need to shower and shave, and maybe then I'll look a little better."

Maura said gently, "Don't you think you should eat a piece of dry toast, just to have something in your stomach?"

Matt managed a broken grin for his mother and said, "I'll have a piece of toast before I take my Strattera. If I don't I'll be sick."

"So the Strattera is the only one of your pills you take in the morning?" Matt asked as he folded his paper and sat it aside. Matt was new to this whole notion of bipolar disorder and so was prone to exhibit a keen interest in Kai's medications and his illness as a whole.

"Yes, it's like an up. You don't want to take it before bed. It's better to have it kick in as you start the day," Kai told him.

"So the other ones you take at bedtime, right?" Matt asked again.

Kai nodded and again attempted a smile. "The Risperdal and Zoloft make me sleepy, and that's a good thing. The lorazepam I can take whenever I need it," Kai explained.

"It's like being a diabetic, right? These medicines fix something in your brain that's out of whack," Matt responded.

Kai nodded and took a sip of his coffee. He didn't really feel like talking, but for the past two mornings when he'd been going through the worst of this bout of depression, he had completely ignored his mother and Matt as much as he could. Right now, he wanted nothing more than a cigarette and some quiet, but he knew Matt was trying to be nice and didn't deserve to be treated rudely. "I'm sorry if I've been difficult over the past couple of days, you guys," Kai said. "I've felt like hell."

Maura stood and rested her hand on Kai's shoulder for a moment. "We could tell how sick you were, don't worry about it. I'm going to pop a piece of bread in the toaster for you," she said as she moved past him and on toward the counter.

"How much of your being sick do you think is because of the pills?" Matt asked innocently.

Kai tried hard not to laugh. To him it was funny for everyone to be talking as if he had a bad cold or the flu. He wasn't sick physically, but a depression this bad was like being sick in that it had a physical component. He looked sick, he acted sick, so everyone just acted like it would pass on its own. He managed to look Matt in the eye and say, "Actually, none of it. Going on the meds doesn't make me sick. I just had the bad luck of getting sick when I started back on them," Kai told him. In itself, it wasn't a lie.

"How're the interviews coming?" Matt asked. "Have you been able to set any more up, or have you been too sick?"

As thin and raw-edged as Kai's nerves were at the moment, he almost told Matt to go to hell, but instead he swallowed hard. He took a sip of his coffee and tried not to call attention to his trembling hands by placing them under the table before he responded, "I did make a few calls yesterday. I got an appointment with an architect and an interior designer for week after next. They were very nice over the phone."

"Who was the architect?" Matt asked.

"Raul Valdez," Matt answered calmly. "According to the AIA Directory online, he does residential work. High-end residential."

"I've never heard of him," Matt replied. "He's not a member of the home builder's association that I know of."

"Oh! That reminds me of something," Maura said as she stood waiting by the toaster. "Kai, you remember my boss, Bill Kellogg?"

"Yeah, nice guy," Kai responded automatically.

"Well, I showed him a copy of your brochure and he'd like you to give him a call about some work. He wants to redo a bedroom in his house to turn it into a library. I told him you were under the weather, but he said if you felt up to it, maybe you could run by his place on Sunday and listen to his ideas, maybe give him a quote."

"That sounds great," Matt said heartily. "Even if it's a small job, it'll get you started."

"Sounds good," Kai said with feigned enthusiasm as the toaster popped up his piece of bread. He watched as his mother picked up the hot toast gingerly and laid it on a paper napkin that she set in front of him. "Thanks," he told her, giving her another attempt at a smile.

"He's in all day today if you want to give him a call. Just dial the main office number and Sheila will put you through," Maura told him.

"I'll do that later this morning," Kai promised as he looked at his toast. The sight and smell of it made him vaguely nauseated, but he knew his mother was watching him, so he lifted it and took a bite. Surprisingly, it tasted rather good and he found himself suddenly ravenous.

As Kai wolfed down his toast, Matt stood and carefully slid his chair back under the table. He quickly embraced Maura and gave her a peck on her cheek. "I got to dash. I'm going to be late," he said happily.

"Have a great day," Kai managed to say around a mouthful of dry toast.

"Yes, have a great day, and drive safely, okay?" Maura said as she escorted Matt out of the kitchen.

There was a pause, which his own experience informed him was filled by another embrace and kiss out of his sight before he heard Matt call out, "Feel better, Kai!" Kai shook his head and swallowed the dry toast. "Thanks!" he called back. Try as he might, Kai couldn't find it in himself to dislike the man his mother had decided to fall in love with. At first, he'd been prepared to tolerate the man politely, but he found himself liking him, despite his obvious "master of the house and universe" demeanor. Kai knew that successful men like Matt were often assholes. He was profoundly glad Matt wasn't. Besides the fact that he obviously adored Kai's mother, he was more than polite to Kai. He was honestly trying to make a friend of him and his dog. Kai knew his sometimes awkward questions were just his way of trying to get to know him. Matt wasn't the kind of guy who had any unexpressed thoughts.

It had been a little over a week since they'd met, and in that time they had established an easy relationship, but Kai was well aware that Matt was watching him to see if he was really going to get off his ass and get to work. That did put up a wall that was hard to negotiate. Kai knew that Matt was the kind of man who judged others by their actions, their prowess and accomplishments. Kai's laid back approach was totally alien to Matt, but then Matt never had to live in Kai's head.

He heard the front door close and his mother chase Heidi out of the Womb chair in the great room before she reappeared with Heidi trotting along beside her into the kitchen. Maura glanced at him before she reached into the old Blue Willow bowl that held Heidi's dog cookies. She held the treat out to the dog, but wouldn't give it to her until she sat. In a short battle of wills communicated only by his mother's sternly pointed finger and his dog's intent stare at her treat, Heidi finally sat and Maura not only gave her the cookie but bent down and kissed the top of the dog's head. "How are you doing, baby?" She asked Kai as she sat at her place at the table.

"Imagine if you're driving a stick shift, going seventy miles an hour, and you throw the gear into reverse without pushing down the clutch," Kai responded bleakly. "The bottom end of the depression cycle was pretty bad this time."

"Oh boy," Maura said sympathetically.

"It's okay, Mom. I'll be fine, don't worry," Kai said as he lit a cigarette.

Maura reached for his pack of cigarettes as well and didn't say anything until she'd extracted one and got it lit. "You're going to kill me one of these days, Kai. I swear, if you don't stop pulling shit like this and not telling me about it, you're going to break my heart."

"Oh Mom, don't be so melodramatic. It's not that big of a deal. I'll survive," Kai said consolingly.

"But I don't know whether to be happy you're coming out of it or mad because I can't do anything to help you. You should see yourself. You look like hell," Maura told him.

"Believe me," Kai said firmly, "it'll all be okay. I'll shave and get cleaned up and I'll look a thousand percent better. I'm feeling better, I really am."

"You're living on Gatorade, Hershey bars, and cigarettes," Maura said despairingly. "Can't you at least begin to eat? That toast is the first real food I've seen you put in your mouth since Tuesday."

"I've been eating and drinking the right things, Mom. The Gatorade is keeping me from getting dehydrated and the chocolate helps too. It has endorphins or something," Kai explained patiently. "The toast was actually pretty good. I might have another piece in a little while. I swear."

Maura just shook her head and put her hand over his wrist. "What you will never understand is how much it hurts me to see you suffering. Really, Kai, I can't stand to watch you like this. Please tell me you'll be better soon."

"I'm already better," Kai said to reassure her. "I didn't talk about it because I didn't want you worrying. Now you don't have anything to worry about."

Maura searched his sunken eyes for any hint he might be lying just to make her feel better. She found nothing dishonest in his returned gaze. She took a long drag off her cigarette and thumped its ash into Kai's ashtray. "Is there anything I can do? Do you need anything?"

Kai patted her hand and shook his head.

Maura sighed, started to speak, and then abruptly cut herself off.

"What is it Mom," Kai asked tiredly.

"Nothing, not really," Maura said and hesitated. At last, she said, "I was just wondering how much of this depression cycle has to do with me telling you I'm pregnant again. I mean, you have to be shocked, and it does affect you in some very real ways."

Kai laughed and shook his head. "Mom, as hard as it is for you to believe you're not responsible for my mental problems, the truth is, you're really not. I think it's great you're having another kid. I really do. If I'm worried about anything it's your health. I want you to be worried about yourself for a change, okay?"

Maura lifted her hand and patted his scratchy cheek. "How are you doing going back on the real meds?" she asked with concern.

"I'm fine, Mom. I'm taking them just like I'm supposed to. I won't lie and tell you I don't feel like the gears in my head are stripped, but don't worry about it. It's okay," Kai told her once more.

"Have you spoken with Robin since you've been going through this?" Maura asked him carefully.

Kai nodded and smoked a moment in silence before he said, "That's good news I've been saving to tell you. Robin's coming down the week of Thanksgiving. He's flying in on the Sunday before and has to fly out

the Friday after, but he's going to come down. That's what I'm holding onto."

"Oh baby, that is good news," Maura said as she visibly brightened.
"So you're feeling a little less conflicted about your relationship, then."

Kai shrugged, but betrayed his nonchalance by saying, "All this is
going to be easier for him and for me if we have something to look forward to. We'll see what happens."

"He'll be here in only three weeks or so. Maybe I should buy some
new linens for the guest room and clear up some of the clutter in there.
I've just been tossing stuff in while Matt and I were fixing up the
house. The guestroom is a mess," Maura said eager to have something
she could control and put her hand to.

"Mom," Kai said gently, "Robin will be sleeping with me and staying in my room. I don't think you need to worry about the state of the
guest room."

"Yes, of course," Maura said briskly. "What am I thinking? Of
course, you'll want him with you. I just never—"

Kai laughed at her sudden embarrassment. "Mom, we lived together for a year. And we might end up together in the long run. Just
be cool, everything will be fine."

"I've got to go to work," Maura said as she stood and ground out her
cigarette in the ashtray. "I never thought I'd say this, but I'm actually
looking forward to it. You're enough to make me want to run out
screaming with my hair on fire, this morning."

Kai laughed once more as he stood up as well. "C'mere," he said as
he opened his arms. Maura stepped into his embrace and he hugged
her long and hard. "It's okay, Mom."

Maura was surprised to find the easy tears coming as she clung to
her son. He was rawboned and rangy, but the strength in his enfold-
ing arms was real. She always forgot how strong he was when he was
in the center of the storm he created all around him. She furtively let
him go so she could wipe at her eyes.

"Are you crying?" Kai asked as he grasped her shoulders and pushed her away gently. "No crying is allowed," he told her.

She sniffled and looked at his hollowed eyes and his sunken cheeks bristling with his unshaven beard. Her child was undeniably a fully grown man for all he could lapse thoughtlessly into childhood occasionally. "Okay," she said finally. "No crying." With that she slipped from his grasp and walked to her bedroom to finish getting ready for work.

Kai poured out what was left of his coffee and refilled his mug. Once he had it doctored the way he liked it, he left the kitchen and went into his room for his Strattera. He eyed the chest of drawers, but instead of getting what he craved with every screaming nerve, he turned instead and picked up the bottle of Strattera and fished out his morning dose. He also opened his bottle of lorazepam and hesitated before he took only one from the bottle. Quickly, he tossed both pills in his mouth and dry-swallowed them before he turned and left his bedroom without another glance for the chest of drawers under the window.

In the kitchen, he found his mother standing over the toaster once more. He knew she wouldn't be satisfied until she watched him eat another piece of toast before she left. The scent of toast actually smelled good to him now. He sat at his place at the table and took two hot sips of his coffee before he ground out the remains of the cigarette he'd left burning in the ashtray and lit another. He heard the toast pop up and as he'd expected, his mother placed it on another paper napkin and set it in front of him before crossing her arms and leaning back against the kitchen counter.

"Eat that while it's warm," Maura told him.

Sighing, Kai laid his cigarette in the ashtray, picked up the piece of toast and by folding it in half, managed to get half of it in his mouth. He chewed for a moment, then asked his mother if she felt better.

"Yes, I do," she replied, and smiled as she reached for her purse waiting in its spot under the wall-mounted phone. "You'll call Bill this morning?"

"As soon as I get showered and shaved," Kai promised.

"Okay then," Maura said as she bent and kissed the top of his sweaty head. "I'm off."

"Have a great day, and don't worry about me, okay?" Kai admonished her.

"I've worried about you every day for the past twenty-seven years," his mother said as she shouldered her bag and made her way out of the kitchen. "Why should today be any different?"

Kai chuckled as he heard the front door open and then close behind her; he then heard her key turning the lock home. Obediently, he finished his toast before he settled back to enjoy the solace of the lorazepam unknitting the muscles in his shoulders. Bringing his mother to tears what not something he wanted or needed that morning. He had enough on his plate as it was. The sight of her tears on his behalf always shamed him and made him feel hopeless and small.

Kai almost never cried. Considering the amount of time in his life he had been clinically, if not suicidally, depressed, that was a remarkable fact. The last time he had cried was when Mack the Doberman had to be put to sleep. Even then, he had taken the big dog alone to the vet's office and stayed with him as the doctor gave him that last merciful shot. The dog had been nearly twelve years old and was covered in the fatty tumors that Dobermans are prone to; still, losing the dog made him cry when he could never cry for himself.

For most of his life, really until he'd met Robin, Kai always looked at his own life from a remote, detached perspective. The only way he could deal with his mental torment was to view it as dispassionately as he could, as though it were happening to someone else. Now, he looked down at the long thin razor scars that ran up the insides of his forearms and remembered watching the doctor take out the stitches when he was nine years old. His mother had had tears trickling down her face as the doctor clipped the sutures and extracted them with a pair of tweezers. He remembered the doctor asking him how he could do that to himself. Quite honestly, Kai told him he didn't think he was cutting himself, he was just killing that other little boy. The doctor had looked at his mother significantly and said, "Can you tell me how he knew to make vertical cuts, not horizontal ones?" His mother had shaken her head without answering. The doctor gently rubbed Neosporin into his forearms and said, "If you ever want to hurt that other little boy do you promise you'll tell your Mommy first?"

Kai always remembered what he'd told the doctor. He'd said, "It wouldn't matter. She can't help him." Even then, there had been a part of him that dwelled utterly separate and alone.

Kai calmly finished his cigarette and fought the temptation to remember anything more about being a small child. It hurt too much. He mentally just drew a curtain on that little scene as he always did if he went further back in his memory than the past four or five years. He made a conscious effort to block any memories of his life before he was eighteen and left once again, to try to live with his father. Of his mother, he tried to remember her separate and apart from him. There were a few happy times he liked to recall from when he was small, but instead of focusing on his experience, he tried to concentrate on his perception of his mother's experience of the same time. It was from this remove that he retrieved his past and much of his present experiences. But that remove had cost him dearly.

Viewing himself from his remove was what allowed him to act so abominably toward Robin by cheating on him with Linda for drugs and social status as a straight man. Realizing he was in love with Robin had forced him to integrate his life view for the first time. Kai wanted to be in love with Robin, he wanted to experience every tender, passionate touch and taste for himself, but realizing that in doing so he was admitting he was gay scared the hell out of him.

Sitting in his mother's cheerful kitchen, Kai saw for himself how deluded he had been for so long. For a moment, he knew he'd trade anything to be sitting out in the chill morning air of Robin's back deck gazing at the Wright Brothers' Memorial, rather than sitting in Sunrise, Florida, trying to make it all right. He'd done what came natural to his old self—he'd run away to try and start over. But Kai realized he never should have left Robin in the first place. Unfortunately, his life had progressed to a point where his do-overs came at a high price.

Kai knew Robin loved him. He had known it all along and with that knowledge, he'd opened up to Robin. He'd told him painful truths about his past. He'd admitted to his personal demons and his mental illness. There was no ugly fact about himself he didn't show Robin, and Kai had dared him to keep on loving him. Every flaming hoop he'd set up for Robin to jump through he'd passed with flying colors. Now that he saw this, he wondered what in the hell he was going to do.

Robin's life was set up on the Outer Banks. He had a good job he was good at. He had a secure lease on that little house in Wrights Shores. Would or could he really give all that up in order to move to Florida to be with Kai? In his way, Kai knew how selfish it would be to ask that of him after everything else he'd put Robin through. But Kai also knew he didn't want to leave South Florida for the beach again. It was too easy to fuck up there. He'd set his patterns and engraved them in stone. He knew too many druggie people and too many people who made it easy to just get by, watching the summers turn until he'd find himself like his dad. He didn't want his dad's life, with a bitch of a girlfriend half his age, a bad back, and a rental cottage in Avalon Beach for a home.

Down here in South Florida, there was an opportunity to start clean. No drugs. New work to fuel the new reputation he'd begin to build. Here Kai felt like he could get it right before he turned thirty. The bitch of it was there was no Robin, and Kai knew he might never allow himself to love anybody else like that ever again. Kai was a loner by nature, yet in Robin he'd found someone who respected all his boundaries and gave him the space around himself he needed. Besides that, Robin was strong on his own. He never sapped Kai's strength or clung to him needlessly. Robin had loved him enough to let him walk away.

Now Kai had to convince Robin he was worth the risk of staking his whole life and future on. Even as he thought this, Kai felt the pull of that brown bottle of painkillers in his chest of drawers. He knew all he had to do to make all of these swirling thoughts calm down and make sense was to get up, walk to that back bedroom, and just cut one pill into quarters. A quarter bump would take the physical need and emotional doubt away. It would be as easy as what fifteen steps could lead him to.

Kai stood up and walked into the living room and then to Heidi's curious gaze, back into the kitchen to stand gripping the corners of the sink as if it would anchor him to the spot and force him to fight the great urge to swallow just a quarter of a piece of a pill.

The only thing that stopped him was the realization that within a couple of weeks, or even days, all those little blue pills would be gone. Down here in South Florida, Kai didn't know where to get more. They were definitely out there. The whole nation was full of people who secretly lived through those little blue pills. Somewhere in Sunrise there was a cancer patient who was filling a thirty-day script and selling two-thirds of them to afford the one-third they couldn't live without. Somewhere in Broward County there was some guy or girl who had a stash from a car accident that left them with nerve damage. Somewhere there was a doctor who could be as free and loose with his prescription pad as a stack of Benjamins could pass from hand to hand. Oh hell yeah, there were pain pills to be had. Kai knew it. But he also knew there was a jail downtown, just like there was a brother or *chulo* with a gun who thought one white boy with a habit was an easy target.

Kai let go of the kitchen sink and sat down at the table once more. He sipped his cold coffee and lit a cigarette with the glowing butt end of the one before. Kai knew all these things and he knew he didn't want to risk anything—no, damn it, he didn't want to risk *Robin* anymore.

So he sat and smoked and brooded alone, waiting for the jangling of his nerves to pass. He knew he could make a whole day of sitting in that same spot, chain smoking and going over and over his troubles in his head. That would be easy. The hard thing to do would be to fight his depression by getting up, getting showered, shaved, and dressed before taking Heidi for a nice long walk in the warmth of the early November morning. He also knew he'd promised his mother he would call Bill Kellogg about his home library project. Just following through on that little detail would mean he'd made some progress toward getting better. But Kai knew what a great effort just that small task would take.

"What I want," he said aloud, "is to be left alone." There, he'd said it. That was one of the things the pain medication gave him, the pleasure and delight in his own company, free of nagging doubt and depression. More than anything else, he just wanted to get high and postpone moving forward for awhile longer, because moving forward meant accepting responsibility for his life and what he was going to make of it. Kai liked talking of starting a new career as a custom carpenter of fine, detailed work, but he liked the idea of it better than actually doing it. Doing it meant he had to get out and deal with people, and people were all rough edges and thin slicing actions that cut him in odd hurtful ways. Interacting with people was too threatening for him. He felt as soft and defenseless as a baby right then.

No one knew what an effort it took for him to even get out of the house to go to the grocery store or the post office. Ever since he'd come back home, he'd seen no one but his mother and Matt, and that was fine with him. The visit to Dr. Roth's office was something that had taken days for him to emotionally prepare for. Kai had been surprised by how easy it was once he'd actually done it, but the thin skin of dread preceding the event was remarkably resilient. It lay over all his actions.

Now he tried to calm himself in preparation for his call to his mother's boss. Kai knew he had no reason to dread the call so much; after all, the man wanted him, or at least the skill he could provide to make something nice. With his mind and hands he could make something tangible and lasting that would not only serve a utilitarian purpose, but would give Bill Kellogg something in his home to admire whenever he saw it. Kai liked that part of what he did. It was solid and real. He even liked the physical act of figuring out the project and actually constructing it. From selecting the wood to making the carefully measured cuts to assembling the thing with screws and his nail gun, to rubbing it with either paint or stain. There was pleasure in that. The hard part of the process was the interaction with other people it took.

Kai sighed and stretched. "I can do this," he said once more aloud. Then he took a final hit off his cigarette and stubbed it out in the ashtray. He stood and mechanically began to tidy up the kitchen from the small mess the morning's breakfast routine had created. He put the coffee mugs and dishes into the dishwasher and wiped down the kitchen counters and table. After only a few moments, he looked around the sunny kitchen filled with morning light and liked what he saw. With everything neat and tidy, it would be easier to move forward, even if his next step was only to get himself cleaned up and ready for the long empty day ahead. He promised himself he'd just take it all one step at a time.

Clinging to that thought, he walked to his bedroom and found Heidi asleep on his bed. Kai felt a rush of affection for her, with her sleek gray body curled around so that her chin lay on her rear paws. Kai affectionately ran his hand over her back, and Heidi responded by wagging her stump of a tail rapidly, but she didn't open her eyes or stretch languorously under his hand. Kai smiled and turned to his chest of drawers. He took a deep breath and opened the top drawer, willing himself to only pick out a clean pair of boxer shorts. He chose a pair and closed the drawer immediately. Then he stepped to his closet and stripped, throwing his dirty clothes into a heap on the closet floor. From the neatly hung row of T-shirts, he selected a navy blue one to go with his white boxers before he closed the door and walked naked to the bathroom just outside his bedroom door.

Briefly, he took stock of the familiar contours of his body. Over the past two days, his stomach had visibly tightened as a result of his nausea and diarrhea. His smooth chest was broken into even planes. He had a broad-shouldered, rangy frame, naturally muscled and well defined for someone who did little more than expend energy with long walks and slight physical labor. His genitals were substantial enough to save him any concern in that department, for which he supposed he had to thank his father. Overall, he had his father's body, made tall and kept slender by his mother's metabolism, which was high enough to have kept her from the thickening common in other women her age.

As he reached to turn on the faucet on the sink, he caught a flash of his ribs descending from his pectoral muscles like long, broad fingers holding his torso. Kai had no spare flesh and that pleased him. He let the water run until it was hot, then he wet his face and smoothed shaving cream over it and his neck. As he shaved, he examined his reflection. As familiar as it was, it still seemed at times to belong to someone else. He caught sight of his gray eyes ringed on the outer rim of his iris with a circle of dark blue that mimicked the dark circles of fatigue under his eyes.

"I do look like death warmed over," he thought as he finished shaving and eyed himself critically once more. He stared into the mirror vainly hoping to see himself as Robin saw him. Robin had loved to watch him shave. Many mornings Robin had sat on the closed lid of the commode and silently took in the sight of Kai before they'd shower together, sharing the head of the shower in turn, often bathing each other and washing each other's hair. In the first few months, this had often led to sex, and later became a time of quiet tender ministration each for the other.

Kai remembered all this now, alone in the bathroom of his mother's house. Again, he sighed and stepped over to the tub to turn on the shower and let the water get hot. Alone, he methodically washed himself before he stood under the shower head letting the water drum the top of his head and flow down over him comfortingly. The rush of water felt good as it soothed away his morning anxiety. Kai stood there until the water began to run cold.

At last, he toweled himself off and dressed quickly in his boxers and T-shirt. As he ran his fingers over his cropped hair and coaxed the longer bit on top into curls, he admitted to himself that he did feel better. The problem was that the space in his clearer mind felt as sharp and brittle as broken glass. There were too many memories there to plague him. There was a sense of emptiness that threatened to claim him. As tall and sturdy as his body looked in the mirror, his mind was not right and he knew it. It was working well enough for him to function, but any capacity for joy or happiness couldn't be found there. He looked into his light eyes and knew the familiar ache that resided there wasn't going to go away. Not today. It would still be some weeks before the meds worked their trick and the demons went to sleep.

Kai shook his head sadly, turned from the mirror and reached for the wall by the door to turn off the lights. The physical fact of him was ready for the day, but his mind was still far, far away.

Chapter Eleven

MAURA STILL attended All Saints Church regularly. She had been a parishioner there from the very beginning and stayed even after the beloved parish priest had moved on and the archdiocese had brought in another, very different priest to replace him. Still, the parish was a part of Maura's life. Kai had attended school and after-school care there until he was finished with eighth grade. Thanks to Maura's parents' ongoing generosity, Kai had attended the co-ed Catholic high school closest to them after that, but Maura continued attending mass at All Saints, along with Kai as long as he lived at home.

Kai noted Maura's surprise when she found him waiting in the kitchen for her quick cup of coffee before they needed to leave for the eight a.m. mass, but he could tell she was pleased. They left Matt sleeping still at seven-forty and were in their usual pew by ten of eight. Kai followed his mother's lead and knelt for a moment once they sat down, but he didn't actually pray. Instead, he only searched for the comfort of long habit in the spacious sanctuary. It hadn't changed in the time he was away; it was a rock of familiarity for him. And he did find comfort in that. He followed along with the lector for the morning's readings and even took Communion, though it had been more than two years since he'd gone to confession or even to church, with the exceptions of the Christmas Eve masses he'd attended with his mother. He never went when he lived on the beach, only when he was home, at All Saints.

After mass, Maura and Kai waited for the priest and his attendants to reach the back of the church before leaving their pew. When they joined the throng leaving the mass, Maura touched him lightly on the shoulder to get his attention. When he looked down at her, she was smiling. "It's good to have you back," she said happily.

Kai looked around him at all the unfamiliar faces in the familiar place and said, "It's good to be back. This place never changes, at least."

Maura nodded as she reached in her purse for her car keys and said, "It has changed, though. So many of these people I don't recognize, though I come every week. A whole new group is here now, running things. The people who have been here from the start, like you and I, are now few and far between. Churches are dynamic places, I guess."

Kai strode alongside his mother to their spot at the far end of the parking lot, closest to the exit. Beside them, cars nosed their way into the flow of traffic coming in for the next mass, while the crowd from their mass was trying to leave. "The neighborhood has changed as well. You must be one of the last original owners in Sawgrass Estates," Kai remarked.

Maura pressed the button on her key that automatically unlocked their doors as they reached the car and said, "There are a few others left, but most of the original owners sold out when the big real estate boom tripled the house values." With that, she opened her car door and got inside as Kai did the same. Once they were in the car, she started the engine.

"Why didn't you sell out and move somewhere nicer?" Kai asked her as she finally managed to steer the back end of the car past a family walking in the middle of the space behind her.

"I could have, I suppose," Maura said as she headed for the exit. "But where would I have gone? I thought of those patio homes in Jacaranda and Plantation, but then I'd have had higher taxes and maintenance fees each month. I decided it was better to stay put and try to pay the place off. I've had fun fixing it up since you went back up to the Banks. But, you know, I've had a happy life in Sunrise. I just decided to stay."

Kai nodded and held on to the arm rest by his side as his mother quickly broke out of the church's exit and across three lanes of oncoming traffic to head back west to their neighborhood. "It's not a place I imagine Matt wanting to live forever," he said.

"Well, maybe you're right," Maura told him easily. "We'll just have to wait and see. We've been staying at my place ever since we started seeing each other, so I suppose he's comfortable enough."

"Didn't you guys ever talk about getting married?" Kai asked her.

"Not until recently, when I found out about the pregnancy," Maura admitted. "Neither of us has a great track record when it comes to marriage. For the past couple of years, we had reached a sort of understanding and that was good enough. There seemed like plenty of time to wait before we started to think about marriage. Of course, now we have to think about it. Matt feels fully responsible for me and the baby."

"So what are you going to do? You can't get married in the church, can you?" Kai asked.

Maura shook her head. "You know we can't. Your dad is still very much alive and we don't have the time or patience it would take to get my marriage to him annulled. Besides, Matt's not Catholic. A civil ceremony will be just fine this time around," Maura said confidently.

"Don't you ever feel guilty about being shacked up?" Kai asked her candidly. "I mean, the church and everything . . . don't you ever feel guilty?"

Maura put her left turn signal on and moved into the turning lane to head back into the neighborhood. "Not really. Don't you ever feel guilty about shacking up with Robin?"

"It's not the same thing, Mom," Kai said and laughed. "We couldn't exactly get married. Besides that, it's different if you're in your twenties, but you guys are middle-aged."

"Oh, I know that," Maura said as she managed the two quick turns that brought them home. "But it is the same in that you care for each other, you have sex. What's so different, really? It doesn't matter how old you are."

Kai didn't really have an answer for that. Instead of responding, he simply sat as his mother pulled into the drive and turned off the car. When she unbuckled her seatbelt and got out, he followed her.

Heidi greeted them excitedly at the door. Matt called out a hello from the kitchen as Maura and Kai walked in to join him. "There's fresh coffee for you holy people," Matt teased from his spot at the table.

First Maura, then Matt claimed their mugs from earlier that morning and poured themselves a cup of coffee before joining Matt at the table. As they sat, Matt reached behind himself and lifted the window saying, "Kai, I know you must be dying for a cigarette about now. Instead of exiling you out back, why don't you just smoke in here?"

"Wow, thanks!" Kai replied happily as he stood once more to retrieve his cigarettes and ashtray from on top of the refrigerator.

"So, how was church?" Matt asked him pointedly as he sat once more and got a cigarette lit.

Kai looked at him and said truthfully, "It was nice. It's only when I go that I realize how much I've missed it."

"It was nice having him back," Maura added.

Matt nodded and leaned back in his chair. "It must be like going home to you guys, considering how long you've been parishioners."

"Yeah, something like that," Kai said. "It's comforting. It just shows you some things never really change."

"I guess I never looked at religion like that," Matt said easily. "I wasn't really brought up in church. We went on Christmas and Easter when I was a kid."

"What religion were you brought up in?" Kai asked him.

"Episcopalian," Matt replied then added, "Whiskey-palian. My parents believed the golf course was a spiritual place on Sunday mornings. They took Communion at the nineteenth hole. I guess that's why I'm the way I am. I don't give religion that much thought."

"Yeah, but I know your heart's good," Maura told him with a warm smile. "It's what you do that matters."

"Like letting me smoke in the house," Kai teased. "You've got a good heart, Matt."

Matt laughed and stretched. "What time are you meeting Bill Kellogg to talk about his project?" he asked Kai.

"Eleven o'clock," Kai said and glanced at his watch. "I need to leave here about ten-thirty or so, right Mom?"

Maura took a sip of her coffee thoughtfully before she replied, "If that early. He just lives over in Jacaranda Lakes. Fifteen minutes should give you enough time on a Sunday morning. You've been there once. Do you have directions to his house?"

Kai nodded and said, "Yeah, he gave them to me when we talked Friday morning. Is he partners with the same guy? I guess I'll be meeting with him too."

"I didn't know Bill Kellogg was gay," Matt interjected.

"Not a lot of people do," Maura answered Matt first. "Bill has always been very discreet about his personal life. The only reason Kai knows is that he escorted me to a small Christmas get-together Bill hosted at his home a few years ago." Maura then turned her attention to her son and said sadly, "No, Kai. Paul was a diabetic. He had a stroke, and died about a year ago. As far as I know, Bill is alone."

"Jeez, I'm sorry to hear that," Kai said sincerely. "He seemed like a nice guy."

"How long were they together?" Matt asked.

"Nearly thirty years," Maura told him. "Bill was pretty torn up for awhile. You see, Paul lived for about six weeks after his stroke. Bill looked after him at home until he died."

"And not a word got around," Matt mused quietly. "I saw Bill not too long ago; he didn't say anything to let on about what he'd been through."

"Well, like I said, he was always very discreet," Maura answered crisply. "Things weren't always as open as they are now. I suppose Bill thought his relationship with Paul would have held him back professionally if it was common knowledge."

"Thirty years ago, you'd be right," Matt said thoughtfully.

"It depends on where you are," Kai said quietly. "Some places haven't changed. I caught a lot of shit about Robin back up on the beach."

"I imagine you did," Matt said sympathetically. "But down here, it's not a big deal anymore."

Kai shrugged and stubbed out his cigarette without answering.

"Robin is coming down for Thanksgiving," Maura told Matt brightly.

Matt caught Kai's momentary look of dismay as Kai shot his mother a glance. "That's great," he said heartily. "I look forward to meeting your friend," he said to Kai.

Kai gave him a searching look before he replied, "I'm looking forward to it too."

"Has Robin ever been to Fort Lauderdale before?" Matt asked him gently.

"Um . . . no," Kai said uneasily. "This'll be his first trip down and meeting Mom and everything."

Matt leaned forward and rested his forearms on the table saying, "Well, you know he's welcome. We'll have to make sure he has a nice time. How long is he going to be staying?"

Kai lit another cigarette before he answered, "He's flying down on the Sunday before and leaving the day after Thanksgiving. He has some people coming to the beach for the holiday that want to look at houses, so he has to get back."

"Still, he'll have five days down here. That's plenty of time for you to show him around. I'll plan on taking us all out to dinner one night while he's here," Matt offered.

Kai looked at him and smiled. "That would be great, thanks."

"No problem," Matt told him, and glanced at Maura, who returned his look with a grateful smile.

"Who feels like some breakfast? I could cook," Maura asked.

"Or I could go for bagels," Kai offered. At the moment, he wanted to flee the kitchen. Matt had made it a point to let him know he had no problem with Robin and Kai appreciated it, but he didn't want to talk about I his relationship with Robin anymore. Enough had been communicated already.

"Either way, I'm happy," Matt said expansively.

"Bagels sound great," Maura told Kai with relief in her voice. "The deli by Publix is still open, so you won't have to go far."

"Sesame? Plain? What?" Kai asked.

Both Maura and Matt exclaimed, "Sesame!"

"Done," Kai said and stood. "I'll be right back."

"Drive safely," Maura cautioned him. Kai didn't answer, but the sound of the front door opening and closing punctuated his departure. Maura looked at Matt and smiled. "He seems better today, doesn't he?"

Matt nodded and returned her smile. "You think it's the medicine kicking in?"

Maura sighed and said, "It's a little too soon for that. It takes up to six weeks for the meds to really have a full effect. I think he's just moving out of this depressive cycle with his usual speed. He cycles very quickly. He always has, but as bad as the depression was these last few days, I was concerned it would take him a while to get better."

"What happens next?" Matt asked.

Maura shrugged. "I don't know. I'm going to be watching him to see if he gets too happy and self-confident. If he does, it just means he's ricocheted off the bottom and will be heading back for another full-blown manic episode."

"Christ, how do you stand it? It's like living with a Jack in the Box. I mean, you have to wonder how many turns of the crank it'll take before the clown jumps out of the box," Matt asked seriously.

Maura laughed. "Oh it's not all that bad. It's worse for him. It has to be exhausting having your head jerk you around like that. God, you have no idea. When he was little, he could cycle four times in a day. It makes me tired just to think about it."

Matt leaned back in his chair and stretched his legs out under the table. "We're going to have to think about what we're going to do with him, Maura," he said calmly.

"What do you mean?" she asked, feeling suddenly defensive.

"Look, I have no problem with him being here in the short term," Matt began cautiously. "But we have a baby to get ready for. I want to paint that bedroom and get new carpet put in."

"Matt, the baby's not going to be here for another seven months," Maura interrupted.

Matt held up his hands to block her sudden exasperation. "I know that, sweetheart. But those seven months also need to be filled with calm and peace for you. Besides, Kai's a grown man. He needs his own space. With his boyfriend coming down here and everything, I don't know. It's just a little awkward."

Maura nodded and stood. She walked to the kitchen sink and poured out what was left of her coffee and rinsed her mug. Forcing herself to sound casual and nonconfrontational, she said, "Do you have any suggestions?"

As she turned and took a glass from the cabinet, then reached into the refrigerator to pull out the gallon jug of milk, Matt said, "Actually, I do. Tell me, do you think Kai is stable enough to live on his own? I mean, he won't harm himself or anything, right?"

Maura poured milk into her glass before carefully replacing the jug of milk back into the refrigerator and sitting down at the table once more. As she sat her glass of milk before her, she lifted her eyes to

Matt's face and said hesitantly, "No. I don't think there's any risk of that. I think he can handle himself alright. He just needs our support right now."

Matt leaned forward and rested his weight on his forearms. His look told her he was being serious when he said, "You're absolutely right. He does need our support. But I think he needs some sense of self determination responsibility as well. It's all too easy to just come home like a college student, but we're kidding ourselves if we think that's what best for him. I've talked with a friend of mine whose daughter came home after a bad marriage with her two-year-old daughter. He told me the best thing that helped her get back on her feet was to get her back out of the house as soon as possible."

Maura cut him a hard look, but took a long swallow of her cold milk before she said, "Tough love? I've never treated Kai like that. He's sick the same as if he—"

"I'm not disputing that, Maura. And I'm not saying you should kick him out into the street. Just wait a minute and hear me out, okay?" Matt demanded quietly.

Maura nodded, but wouldn't look at him.

"I say we give Kai a couple of weeks to let his medicine get in his system and then we offer him my place in Lighthouse Point," Matt told her.

Maura looked up at him in surprise, "Are you serious? You'd do that?"

Matt reached across the table and grasped Maura's upper arm gently, "Of course I would. I don't think he'd trash the place, and actually he could be doing me a favor."

"In what way?" Maura asked as she took his wrist gently to signal she wasn't angry with him before letting it go.

"I don't like the house standing vacant," Matt said decisively. "There're too many teenaged kids in the neighborhood. I'm surprised the place hasn't been broken into before now. Also, in this market, I don't think it's a great time to sell. I'm willing to let Kai move in if he's willing to maybe do a little painting inside and out and keep an eye on the place. You know I don't want to let you out of my sight, especially now, when you're carrying this baby. I'll be here with you and Kai'll have some independence and still be close enough to keep an eye on. What do you think?"

"I think you're the most wonderful man in the world," Maura said. "That's a great idea!"

"Do you think Kai'll go for it?" Matt asked.

"He'd be crazy not to," Maura said without thinking. When the realization of what she'd said hit her, she laughed.

Matt allowed himself a chuckle as well, then said, "Let's watch Kai over the next couple of weeks to see how he handles himself and we'll maybe bring the idea up to him weekend after next. How's that sound?"

"It sounds like a plan," Maura said. "But the idea has to come from you. I don't want him to think I've put you up to it."

"That makes sense," Matt said agreeably.

Maura took another long swallow of her milk and sighed.

"What is it?" Matt asked.

"I don't know . . . , I was just thinking I wish I'd had you around before now. My life and my relationship with Kai would have been so much easier if you'd been in our lives," Maura stated bluntly. "I've always had to do all this thinking and looking out for him on my own. I think he would be in better shape today if he'd had somebody other than his mother running interference for him."

"I don't know about that," Matt said reassuringly. "I think you've done a hell of a good job. Kai's a good kid. He just needs to learn to stand on his own two feet."

Maura nodded. In some ways she knew Matt was right. But she also knew Kai worked awfully hard to stand on his own under some difficult pressures. But she couldn't communicate that to Matt without seeming like she was making excuses for her son. Matt was being more than generous, considering he didn't owe Kai anything. "Thanks, Matt." Maura said and reached across the table to take his hand.

"No problem," Matt assured her as he returned the pressure of her clasp.

Chapter Twelve

THE TIME IT TOOK to run to the deli and then have breakfast with his mother and Matt quickly used up the time Kai had before he needed to get across town to see Bill Kellogg. It wasn't very far, just a couple of miles down Nob Hill Road, and he spent the short time it took to get there giving himself a pep talk about how professionally he wanted to come across to this client who'd appeared out of the blue. Kai knew the money wouldn't be great, but the work was what he really needed in order to feel like he was moving forward with his new life. He deserved a good job for a good price, but he didn't want to take advantage of his mother's boss.

Bill Kellogg's house sat on a pie-shaped lot at the end of a cul-de-sac in the Jacaranda Lakes subdivision. Built in the late 1970s, it had a typical look to it that all houses built by South Florida developers possessed. It was easy to tell they had looked to design trends from Southern California to emulate. Still, it was a good-sized house in what had been an expensive and favored area. Kai noted that the neighborhood had aged well. The houses were all kept up and the landscaping was lush and well-tended. Still, the number of toys, bicycles, and Big Wheels scattered in the driveways and open garages of the neighborhood testified to the fact that the neighborhood had turned over more than once as the original owners aged, their children grew up and left home, and younger families moved in. It was obvious that Bill Kellogg, like Kai's mother, had resisted the urge to capitalize on the real estate boom and move else-where.

Kai parked his truck on the driveway made of brick pavers and locked it behind him. Though the neighborhood appeared safe, Kai remembered he was back in South Florida and not up on the beach in North Carolina. Down here, someone would steal your car in the blink of an eye. It was prudent to help keep people honest. Kai, clutch-ing a pen to sketch with and a legal pad to take notes on, made his way past the low, trimmed ixora and ficus hedge that led to the home's front door and rang the bell. No familiar sounds of music or television made it outside to the small stoop. Kai checked his watch to make sure he was on time before he rang the bell once more.

No sooner had he rang the bell for the second time than Bill Kel-logg himself opened the door. He looked Kai over quickly, before he stuck out his hand and said, "Kai. You're right on time. Come in."

Kai stepped into the home's living room, shook Bill's outstretched hand firmly, and said, "I appreciate a chance to look at your job."

"I was sitting out by the pool," Bill said as he released Kai's hand and took a step back. "Can I offer you coffee or a soft drink?"

"Um, no thanks," Kai answered awkwardly. "I've been drinking coffee all morning. I'm fine."

Bill nodded and said, "In that case, why don't you follow me and I'll show you the room. I also have some photos from a couple of maga-zines to give you an idea of what I'm thinking about."

"Excellent," Kai replied. He followed Bill through the living room to a hall that ran toward the rear of the house. As he followed along behind him, Kai noticed that Bill was dressed in a bathing suit and a polo shirt. The few times Kai had ever met him, he'd always been dressed for the office or for a party. It seemed strange to see him re-laxed and casual at home on a Sunday morning.

Bill arrived at a door at the end of the hall and opened it before strid-ing in. Kai followed him inside. The carpet had been ripped out along with its padding, leaving bare concrete. The room was painted a sage green and was devoid of any trim save for the inexpensive three-inch baseboards builders were prone to put in. A set of French doors was along one wall that opened onto a corner of the lanai and pool area. On the rear wall, a bare double window gave a view out onto the lushly planted back yard. The wall opposite the French doors was blank. The remainder of the wall that held the door they'd just entered through also held a smaller door that led to a walk-in closet, then a bathroom. It was a good-sized room. Kai estimated it to be about fourteen by sixteen feet. Considering its placement at the rear of the house and its adjoining bath, Kai asked, "Isn't this the master bedroom?"

Bill nodded and looked around before he looked at Kai and said, "It was. When my partner was ill, I moved to one of the other bedrooms and put a hospital bed and a cot in here. As you can imagine, there are some sad memories in this room. That's why I've decided to keep the other bedroom and completely change the function of this one. As sad as some of those memories are, I still love this room, and I want to enjoy it. I just don't ever want to sleep in here again."

Kai nodded sympathetically and said, "My mom told me you lost your partner a few months ago. I'm sorry to hear it. I know I only met him that one time at your Christmas party, what was it? About three years ago? He was a very nice guy."

"Thank you, Kai. I appreciate that," Bill said quietly. Then, stepping to the French doors, he opened them and said, "Why don't we sit out by the pool and talk about what I'd like done?"

Kai glanced around the room once more to try and fix it in his mind before he said, "Sure," and followed Bill out to a glass-topped table by the pool. He waited for Bill to sit first, then sank into a cushioned chair opposite him and laid his legal pad and pen on the table top.

"First, I wanted to ask if you did painting. I want to change the color of the room and I'd prefer to have it painted before you start adding in bookshelves and trim work," Bill said.

Kai thought a moment. He didn't usually do painting, but he had nothing but time and it would mean a few more bucks for the job. He gave Bill a level look and said, "I don't do painting as a rule, but it looks to be a relatively straightforward job. I think I could do it for you. It looks like one day, maybe two days, depending on what color you want to paint over that green."

Bill smiled. "I was rather hoping you'd say that. I hate painting and I'm willing to pay somebody to do it rather than do it myself. I'm also going to ask you if you'll paint the bookcases and trim once you have them in."

Kai gave him a sly smile and said, "You are looking to spend some money, aren't you?"

Bill laughed in reply with genuine good humor. "Well, before we talk about how much, why don't you take a look at what I have in mind," he said as he slid a manila folder across the table's glass surface to rest by Kai's legal pad.

Kai opened it to find pages torn from home design magazines that featured different versions of classically appointed libraries. The photos of the rooms differed in degrees of complexity and color, but all of them featured ceiling-to-floor bookcases and elegant dadoes and moldings. Nothing he saw was beyond his capabilities, but he was a little dismayed by the range of finishes represented on the carefully-torn magazine pages. The rooms varied in style from a beachy, all-white scheme to a dark walnut-stained Edwardian look, with some dark red and dark blue lacquered looks thrown in as well. Finally he shuffled the pages neatly back together, placed them back in the folder and said, "I can do any of these looks. But what you want determines a great deal about time and materials."

Bill nodded, but asked in complete innocence, "So what you're saying is, what look I choose will ultimately determine the cost."

"That's right," Kai explained patiently. "For instance, if you choose the deep lacquered and painted look, I can choose cheaper wood because it will be painted, but what you'll save in wood costs will be eaten up by the extra time to paint and achieve the high-gloss lacquered finish."

Bill reached across the table and took the folder of photos from Kai. Opening it, he thumbed through the pages to find the photo he was looking for. At last, he pulled out a page and handed it to Kai. "I really like this dark blue room. Can you do this and achieve the same effect?"

Kai examined the photo closely. The bookcases and everything on the walls was lacquered a deep royal blue. "Yes, I can do this. In fact, it would be easier because I can build the bookcases directly onto the walls rather than having to create a case first and then affix the individual units to the walls like cabinetry. I'd recommend doing that if you want to showcase the wood grain. I'd also have to buy higher grade wood to work with."

Bill leaned back in his chair and smiled. "Good man. That's exactly what I would do if I wanted to do this myself. As it happens, I really want the dark blue. The exact color name is printed on the page. The paint is Benjamin Moore. Now let me ask you, how would you handle the wall with the window on it?"

Kai said, "Hold on, let me sketch this out in plain view and ask you some questions and we'll rough it out." Working from memory, Kai drew an accurate floor plan of the room and showed it first to Bill, who nodded approval of his sketch. Then Kai asked "Do you plan to put a small sofa or anything under the window, a desk maybe?"

"Actually, I have a loveseat I was going to have recovered and put under that window," Bill replied.

"Okay," Kai said. "Now, do you want a knee-hole desk anywhere or is it all to be bookshelves?"

"I have an antique pedestal table I'm going to set in the middle of the room," Bill answered, and watched as Kai sketched in place both the loveseat and the table.

"Do you plan to put any stereo or video components on any of the shelves?" he asked.

Bill thought a moment and said, "I'm only going to put a nice CD player and radio on one of the shelves. No TV or anything."

"Do you plan to shelve any CDs in this room? If so, how many?" Kai probed.

"I must have a couple hundred CDs, and I'd like shelf space to store more," Bill replied. "Listening to music is kind of a hobby of mine. I'll be doing a lot of it in this room."

Kai nodded and asked, "What about your books? Are they mostly novels, or do you have a lot of large art and photography or design books?"

"Mostly novels and biographies," Bill said. "Why?"

"Art books require deeper shelves," Kai explained. "If you had a large collection of art books, I might suggest making some of the shelves sixteen or eighteen inches deep."

"Oh no, I don't need anything deeper than twelve inches," Bill said. "I don't want to eat up my floor space with a lot of deep shelves."

"Good," Kai responded. He bent his head over the sketch and quickly drew in the shelves, then turned the page of the legal pad and began to sketch each wall to show how it would look with the shelves in place. He drew the eight-inch plinth the bookshelves would rest on, and also included a bit of extra molding at chair rail height and topped them off with a neat six-inch crown. The effect was elegant and restrained. At last, he finished the pages and handed them to Bill.

Kai watched as Bill studied each sketch in turn. At last he looked up with a grin. "It's like you read my mind," he said. "Everything has a place. I love how you've put in a bookcase for CDs on the wall between the room's door and the door to the closet and bath. I suppose that's why the shelves there are so narrow. I won't have to move a stack to see what's behind them. Excellent."

"And you like the proportions of the design and the extra trim?" Kai asked cautiously.

"Yes! It's classical, very nice," Bill responded. "When can you get to work?"

Kai laughed and shook his head, "You *are* eager. Fortunately, I have nothing else going on but some appointments to show my work. I could get started as early as tomorrow. But we need to talk about cost."

"What are you thinking?" Bill asked.

Kai reached for his pad and quickly ran some numbers, separating labor from materials. At last he finished and handed the pad back to Bill.

Bill looked over his estimate and asked, "You didn't mark up the paint, or lumber or anything else, I see."

Kai shook his head and said, "For anyone else, I would mark it up twenty percent. But you're a friend of my family from way back. I just warn you the materials might be more than I've estimated. I'm used to thinking in North Carolina prices, not South Florida."

"I can understand that," Bill said evenly.

"I'll give you receipts for all the materials on the day I buy them, and you just reimburse me at cost then and there," Kai told him.

"I want to do right by you, Kai," Bill said sincerely. "Are you sure you can live with your labor costs?"

"Absolutely," Kai told him.

"Then I think we have a deal," Bill said and offered his hand. "If you really can start tomorrow, that would be great."

"I'll need a key and your alarm code," Kai said. "Plus, if you don't mind, I'll be leaving my tools here while I'm working. It's a bitch to pack and unpack my table saw and compound miter saw everyday. I promise I keep a neat work site," he said as he took Bill's hand firmly.

"Of course," Bill said agreeably. "Let me get you a key now." With that, he stood and left the lanai by way of the kitchen door.

Kai sighed, closed his eyes, and turned his face up to catch the sun.

It was a nice little job. He had given a lot of thought to how long it would actually take, considering not only the construction of so many bookcases, but the degree of high finish Bill was looking for. The walls alone would take two coats of high-gloss paint, and the wood for the shelves would have to be primed with a tinted primer and one coat of paint before he even began to cut it up and assemble the shelving. After it was all built, he'd have to caulk and lightly sand all the nail and screw holes, touch them up and then give it another coat of high gloss paint before he applied two coats of clear varnish. There was no doubt about it, it would look rich and expensive. Kai had calculated it would take nearly two weeks to finish. He wanted to be done, and he wanted to be paid for it, before Robin flew down. For the time Robin would be in Sunrise, Kai didn't intend to work at all.

"Here's a key and a note with the alarm code," Bill said, interrupting Kai's reverie.

As Bill sat down, Kai opened his eyes and watched him as he came into focus through the sun's glare that had permeated his closed eyelids. He took the key and note from Bill's outstretched hand and said, "Thanks."

"How long do you think it will take in terms of days for you to finish the work?" Bill asked. "I'm just wondering when I can schedule getting in the guys to lay the new hardwood floor I'm going to put in."

"I plan to be finished in two weeks, maybe less if the lacquer dries well," Kai told him confidently. "Would it bother you if I need to work next weekend?"

"Not at all," Bill replied. "But I don't want you to feel like I'm rushing you. I want it done right. You can take all the time you need."

Kai smiled and said, "Oh, I don't think more than two weeks will be necessary. Like I said, I'm pretty free right now, though I will have some appointments during the time I'll be working on it. But considering how long it'll take for all the coats of paint and lacquer to dry, I should still have plenty of time. And to tell you the truth, I won't be working the week of Thanksgiving. I have a friend coming down from the Outer Banks for the holiday."

"Someone special?" Bill asked carefully.

"Yes," Kai responded quietly. "Pretty special, actually." He watched Bill's eyes flicker with interest and hold his with both empathy and a shade of envy.

Bill nodded his head and leaned forward to rest with his forearms on the table top. "Then you must take that week off. Take it from me, if you have someone really special, every moment is a treasure. You don't realize it until they're gone."

Kai looked down and picked up his pad. "I'll type up this proposal and bring you a copy tomorrow when I come to start painting. I should be here as soon as I can get the paint and supplies. If you want to check in at lunch, I should be here," he said and stood to leave.

"I'll do that," Bill said and stood as well. "Thanks for taking this on, Kai. I appreciate it."

"I'm looking forward to it," Kai said confidently. "It'll be good to get working again." With that, he held out his hand for Bill to shake once more. As Bill took his hand and clasped it briefly, Kai thought about what Bill had told him. He realized he had heard exactly what he needed to hear.

Kai had surprised himself by agreeing to get started so fast, but he knew if he had to sit in his mom's kitchen chain smoking and listening to the radio he would go crazy. He needed to be working in order to jump the rails his mind was running on. As he said goodbye to Bill Kellogg and got in his truck, he allowed himself to smile. It looked as if things were starting to turn around.

Chapter Thirteen

THE MEETING broke up just before five, and Bill followed Maura to her office as they left the conference room chatting about the project. Once Maura sat by her desk, Bill leaned against the door jamb and looked at her with concern. "How are you feeling these days, Maura?"

Maura sighed and clasped her hands over her stomach. "I'm good, for the most part. I seem to get tired more easily. I thought I was going to fall asleep in that meeting. Emerson does drone on and on, doesn't he? Why do you ask?"

Bill crossed his arms over his chest and regarded her with a concerned smile. "I don't know. You and I have been friends for a long time and I like to think I'm a caring boss. I just want to make sure you're up to your work load while you're carrying this baby."

Maura felt a tug of insecurity but quickly dismissed it. While she had always prided herself on playing her angle without any excuses that might come off as particularly "female" in her male-dominated office, she did know Bill was sincerely concerned about her. He wasn't looking for an excuse to get rid of her. She gave him a quiet smile and said, "Bill, I appreciate your concern, but I'm going to be fine. My doctor says I'm healthy as a horse. While I am a little old to be carrying a baby, I feel great, and I don't foresee any problems with working."

Bill nodded and thought a minute before he said, "How much sick leave do you have built up?"

Maura offered him a level gaze and said, "After all these years with the firm? Are you kidding? I have over six months of sick leave and five weeks of vacation I've never taken."

"I see," Bill said as he shifted his weight to his feet and shoved his hands in his pockets. "Well, I want you to take it as you see fit. If you need to take it easy in the middle of the week, do it. Okay?"

Maura nodded and smiled once more. "I will, I promise. But you still need to be able to depend on me. I plan to work as long as the doctor tells me I'm okay. If anything changes, you'll be the first to know."

Bill nodded and said, "I want you to know I've been impressed with the work your son is doing at my house. He's gotten a lot done in the past two days. He's pretty conscientious, but I suppose the apple doesn't fall too far from the tree."

"I'm glad you're pleased," Maura said confidently. "I think finding a job like yours is just what he needs right now. He was pretty depressed for the first week after he got home, but he's come out of it surprisingly quickly now that he has a reason to."

"He mentioned he was going to have a visitor over Thanksgiving. He wasn't very forthcoming, but I could tell he's looking forward to it," Bill mentioned off-handedly.

Maura motioned for him to step into her office and said softly, "Close the door."

Bill stepped into her small office and closed the door behind him before settling into one of the chairs across from Maura's desk. Once he'd crossed one leg over the other he looked at her expectantly.

"His visitor is his housemate from up on the Banks," Maura said. "You're the only one besides Matt I can talk to about this," she said and looked away. After a moment she shook her head and said, "My son has finally fallen in love. With another boy . . . well, man. Named Robin. Though he looks like he's about sixteen. It's not like I care, as long as he's happy, but . . ."

"But you have your reservations," Bill concluded for her. "That's understandable."

"Not for the reasons you might think," Maura said seriously. "I really don't care about the gay aspect of it. God knows, I'm just happy he has the capacity to love anyone. My reservations have to do with how fragile he seems right now. I don't know how far he intends to pursue this relationship. It's problematic just in distance, much less anything else."

"You think he's that serious about this kid?" Bill asked calmly.

Maura nodded. "You see, I don't think Kai's ever really been in love before. He's never gone through the knocks most of us go through as teenagers. You know, first love gone bad, that sort of thing. From the little I've gotten him to talk about it, he's still conflicted about being known as gay, but he freely admits he loves Robin. I don't know. It just seems problematic for so many reasons," she concluded sadly.

Bill chuckled and said, "I don't think you really have anything to worry about. It'll either work out for Kai or it won't. Either way, he's twenty-seven years old. Sooner or later, he's going to have to come to terms with his attractions."

"That's true," Maura admitted. "Of course, I'm probably worrying for nothing. I've just never met Robin. I have no idea what kind of person he is, or whether or not he's really prepared to deal with Kai and his challenges."

"You're just acting like a mother, Maura," Bill said consolingly. "Sooner or later you're going to have to trust someone to come along and love and look after your boy like you always have. It's the way life goes. It's just taken you an extremely long time to get to this point."

Maura sighed and gave Bill a brittle smile. "You're absolutely right, of course. I find myself hoping this Robin is a good kid and capable of taking Kai off my hands, in a way."

"For your sake, I hope so too," Bill told her. "You're going to have your hands full with a baby, Maura. The little one is going to need your full attention. Hopefully, Robin loves Kai as much as Kai loves him. If he does, you'd be looking at a pretty healthy scenario for both of them, despite Kai's challenges."

"God, I hope you're right," Maura said. Bill had made her feel better. She looked across at him and noted the lines on his face that hadn't been there before his partner had died. "How about you, Bill? Are you seeing anyone these days?"

Bill gave her a wan smile and shook his head no. "I'm still grieving, if you want to know the truth. I don't want to have anyone come into our home, even though it's just mine now. Besides, I'm not good-looking anymore and most of the guys my age are looking for a twenty-year-old for arm candy. The last thing I want or need is some kid who's never heard of Aretha Franklin. I'm just fine on my own."

Maura nodded. "Well, I beg to disagree about your looks, but I understand exactly where you're coming from. I feel so lucky to have found Matt. I was where you are a couple of years ago, so I understand exactly where you're coming from. But hey, if I can find somebody, and even my disturbed child can find somebody, it's got to be just a matter of time for you."

Bill glanced at his watch and stood. "Maybe you're right, Maura. Hell, I don't know. What I do know is it's now past five o'clock and we should be getting out of here. I'm ready to get home and see what your son accomplished today."

Maura stood as well and said, "Thanks, Bill."

"For what?" he asked blankly.

"For being so concerned about me for one thing. And for giving Kai some work. It's made a real difference to him, I know. I can tell," Maura said sincerely.

Bill waved her off as he turned and opened the door. "Forget about it," he said. "I'll see you tomorrow."

Maura nodded and watched as he turned and walked down the hall toward his office. When he went inside, she looked at her computer resentfully. Knowing she should really check her email one last time, she instead crouched down and retrieved her purse from her lower desk drawer. It had been a long day and she was tired. After one last look around her office, she shouldered her purse and left without shutting her computer down for the night.

When she got home, she spied Kai lying on a lounge chair in the dying light outside. Heidi lay by the chair in the grass grooming her paws. Maura looked at Kai's half-naked form appreciatively. It gave her a certain amount of satisfaction that she had borne a baby that had grown into such a well-knit man. With his hair still damp from the shower, curling on the crown of his head, Kai looked substantial soaking up what was left of the sun. It made Maura disbelieve his less substantial grip on the world he strode through it at war with the demons in his own mind.

She set her purse on the dining room table and eased her feet from her dress shoes before she walked to the sliding glass door and pulled it open. "Hey, surfer boy," she said. "How long have you been home?"

Kai lifted his arm to shield his eyes from the low sun's brightness. "Not long. How was your day?"

Maura lingered in the door frame and said, "Not too bad, just long. You haven't started any supper, have you?"

Kai sat up and gave her an apologetic look. "No, Mom. I'm sorry. I haven't even thought about eating. But I can get up and check out what's in the refrigerator if you don't feel like cooking."

"Screw it," Maura said easily. "Matt's not going to get in until late. He went to Orlando today. Maybe we'll order Chinese. How does that sound?"

"Sounds good," Kai admitted, obviously relieved he wouldn't have to cook.

Heidi stood and shook herself all over before ambling to stand before Maura expectantly. Wordlessly, Maura took a step back and the dog came into the house and pushed her hand with her nose. "Have you fed Heidi?" Maura asked Kai.

"When I got home. She's just looking for some attention," Kai said.

Maura absently patted the dog's head and said, "I'm going to go get changed."

"Cool," Kai responded before sinking back against the lounge chair's frame.

Heidi looked up at Maura expectantly. "Come on, girl. We'll get you a cookie," Maura said as she turned and made her way toward the kitchen. The big dog trotted happily ahead of her and waited by the counter until Maura could retrieve a cookie from the old Blue Willow bowl. Maura tossed the cookie and Heidi caught it deftly. Maura gave her another quick stroke before she made her way to her bedroom to change.

Once she had changed into her after-work uniform, Maura went into the kitchen and poured herself a Diet Coke. She decided she wanted to join Kai outside and share the onset of evening. Now that it was getting near the end of daylight savings time, the day was drawing to a close more rapidly every day. The weather remained gorgeous, a gift of South Florida's stubborn reluctance to show the seasons as they changed. She took her soft drink and stepped over Heidi who had sprawled out on the kitchen floor with a sizeable bone Kai had brought her from Publix.

Once Maura was outside, she dragged the other lounge chair close to her son's and settled into it with a sigh. Lying down felt good. Her feet had swollen in her shoes during the day and they ached slightly. She stretched them and extended her toes, trying to squeeze the hurt out. "How's Bill's library coming?" she asked Kai easily.

Kai didn't open his eyes as he replied sleepily, "It's going good. I have only a few more shelves to cut and place, then it'll be down to the final painting and lacquering. It's looking really sharp."

"I spoke with Bill today," Maura said as she closed her own eyes and rested her head against the lounge's taunt fabric. "He is really pleased with the job you're doing."

"That's good," Kai answered. "I didn't overcharge him, but he's still spending some bucks to get it done. I want him to be good with it so he'll refer me to his friends."

"I'm sure he's pleased," Maura responded. "And if I know Bill, he'll be happy to pass your name along. In his clique, someone is always renovating or redoing something in their houses."

"Gay guys are like that," Kai said off-handedly. "They like things to be just so. I guess I could get into it if I had the money and my own place."

Maura let the comment pass, though she noted Kai had spoken of himself and "gay guys" in the same sentence without making any disparaging comments. She let it float away in the warm air between them for many long minutes as she sipped her Coke and enjoyed the breeze. After a few minutes, she carefully asked, "How's Robin?"

Kai opened his eyes and turned his head to give her a wary look. When she met his gaze with an open expression of simple interest he sighed, scratched his side, and said, "He's good. Looking forward to coming down, I think. I know I'm looking forward to seeing him."

"So you're a little less conflicted about the situation between you two, I take it," Maura answered casually.

Kai sat up and turned so that he was sitting on the side of the lounge chair with his feet resting on the ground and looked at his mother. "I've had some time to think things through. Now that my meds have kicked in, I haven't been too panicky to deal with it. I think the answer to the whole deal is pretty clear."

Maura nodded encouragingly for him to continue and took a long swallow from her glass.

Kai leaned down and plucked a blade of grass from the lawn and then, placing it between his thumb and forefinger, began to spool it into a tight cylinder with his other hand. "I'm going to ask him to move down here to be with me," he announced confidently.

"Do you think he will? Really?" Maura asked gently.

Kai answered first with an elaborate shrug before finally admitting, "I hope so, but it's complicated. He's got a great job and he makes a lot of money. And he has a chance to buy the house we live in for a pretty good price. The owners moved to bumfuck Texas or somewhere and they're willing to finance the deal since the economy has gone to shit. There's plenty to tempt him to stay put."

"I can see that," Maura said thoughtfully. "But if he loves you, what good is having a house if there's nobody to love in it?"

Kai shrugged once more as he studied the tight cylinder of grass between his fingers. "I don't know. You did it when you were still in love with Dad."

"Ah, but I had you," Maura answered with certainty. "It's not as if I was alone."

Kai nodded, but didn't reply. Instead he stretched and went back to playing with his blade of grass.

"Would it kill you to move back up to the Banks if he doesn't want to move down here?" Maura asked him sincerely.

Again, Kai shrugged, but the force of his response belied his interest. He said, "I hate that place now. I feel like I'm under surveillance all the time when I'm there. Somebody is always watching and somebody's always got something to say about your business. Down here is totally not like that. You know what I'm talking about, Mom. C'mon."

"Does it really matter what people say, Kai? You and I both know they always find something else to talk about after a while," Maura replied rationally.

"Yeah, you're right," Kai said dejectedly. "But even so, it's so easy to fuck up there. In the winters I get so into myself and everything's so fucking bleak. I don't think I can live like that anymore."

"Was last winter so bad, when you were with Robin, I mean?" Maura asked him gently.

Kai tossed the blade of grass away and promptly plucked another one and began the process of rolling it up all over again. After a few minutes he said, "No, Mom. It was pretty good with Robin, actually. We get along so well. I was never bored and we never fought. It was actually pretty fucking great now that I think about it. Not working, watching movies, hanging out . . . all the time really enjoying being around him." Unexpectedly, he flung away his blade of grass and slumped back into the lounge chair. "Oh man, I don't know if I've really fucked everything up or if everything's really going to work out. I hate this not knowing."

Maura reached across the space between them and laid her hand on his bare shoulder. Consolingly she said, "I don't think you've broken anything past fixing. Robin will come down, you'll talk and work something out I'm sure. I just don't want to see you bouncing off the walls like you were when you came home."

Kai ignored her hand and looked away in the opposite direction. "I'm back to being properly doped, Mom. No matter what, I probably won't be in too bad shape thanks to the miracles of modern pharmacology. I'll just be medicated into not really caring, I guess."

"Is that the way you feel now?" Maura asked solicitously. "Do you feel numb?"

"Sort of," Kai admitted. "It's better than hurting all the time, I guess. I just wish I could feel shit like normal people. I get sick of being crazy sometimes. Especially now. I'm always policing myself to make sure I'm acting appropriately. There's nothing natural about how I am. I'm just here," he concluded sadly.

Maura patted his shoulder awkwardly and started to say something encouraging, but Kai suddenly stood up and looked down at her before she could speak.

"It's okay, Mom. Don't worry about me or anything. I'm good. This is just some shit to get through. No matter what, I've made my mind up to focus on my work and getting my shit together down here. I was thinking, I need my own place, with a garage to keep my tools and shit in. I know I'm in the way around here with you and Matt and everything. Jeez, there's going to be a baby too. I know I need to clear out so you can get the place ready for that. Just give me a little more time, okay?"

Maura nodded and said, "No one's pushing you out the door but you. Settle down. Everything is going to fall into place, just wait and see. Who knows? You may be house hunting with Robin in a month's time. Try to look at it like that, okay?"

Kai nodded and started away, but he hesitated and said, "Would you like some more Diet Coke or anything?"

"No, I'm good," Maura told him. "Where are you off to?"

"I'm just going to make myself something to drink and get my cigarettes," Kai told her as he started away once more.

Maura watched him enter the house and waited to sigh until after he had made it inside. She rattled the ice in her glass and took another sip of the now-watery Coke. She knew he was going to be okay. She just hated that his way had to be so fraught. But, there was nothing she could do about it. Her days of making sure every step he took, from here to there, was free and clear of obstacles was long gone. She understood there was nothing she could do about the obstacles he put in his own way. Still, she wondered and a small part of her still worried. Idly she hoped he would stay inside and wouldn't rejoin her in the back yard. Her feet were finally starting to feel better and the evening sun made the air seem like pink-tinged gold. Selfishly, she wanted to be free of Kai's anxieties while the sun set. Later she would feed him take-out Chinese food and find something else to talk about. For right now she just craved solitude.

Chapter Fourteen

THE MORNING'S meeting with the interior designer went well. Rachel Weiss had a small shop that held some nice accessories, a few select pieces of furniture and her fabric swatches. Between two rows of hanging swatch books stacked from ceiling to floor there was an antique French farm table with contemporary Knoll office chairs that rolled underneath its worn plank top. That's where Kai sat with the designer and showed her his presentation piece. Rachel Weiss was a nice lady, well into her sixties, who had the brisk manner of a no-nonsense business woman about her, but Kai could tell she had warmed to him personally. Like all of the business owners he'd met on the round of appointments he'd set up in the weeks since he'd been home, she had no immediate work for him, but she kept his portfolio piece and promised to call him the next time she needed custom cabinetry or trim work. Kai felt that she would; he just couldn't help but wonder when.

He thought about this as he changed from the neat khaki slacks and polo shirt he'd worn for his meeting to a pair of old shorts and a plain white T-shirt in the master bath at Bill Kellogg's house. He folded the dressy clothes and neatly tucked them into the paper shopping bag he'd packed his lunch and work clothes in. It was now ten-thirty and he had the final coat of varnish to apply to Bill Kellogg's bookcases. Barefoot, he walked from the master bath past the walk-in closet and closed his eyes as he took the last steps into the master bedroom he'd converted into a library. Once he felt the cool, bare concrete floor under his naked feet, he opened his eyes and looked at his work.

A pleased smile broke over his face as he stood in the deeply toned room. The sunlight coming in through the bare window and French doors highlighted the sheen of the walls and of the bookcases that now marched across the walls. Except for the space under the window where Bill planned to place the loveseat, rows of shelves rhythmically lined every wall, even over the window and doors. Kai had first painted the popcorn ceiling with a clean, bright white, and then he'd covered the sage-colored walls with two coats of the deep blue high-gloss paint that Bill had selected. Before he began to cut and assemble the inexpensive pine shelving, he'd given the boards and trim work two coats of blue-tinted, thick primer that smoothed their imperfections.

The cutting of the wood into the trim upright components and shelves went smoothly. Kai had paid particular care to cutting the various stock moldings that defined the details of the shelving. Rather than simply banging the trim onto the assembled shelves with his nail gun, he'd glued and tacked and set the trim nails in by hand. With everything assembled, he'd caulked and spackled all the nail holes and tiny imperfections, like where the crown molding didn't quite meet the crooked ceiling. Only when everything was perfectly smooth did he begin to lay on two coats of high-gloss enamel blue paint. Fortunately, the weeks between his beginning the work and getting to this day had remained fair and warm. The paint had dried evenly and after two days, even the first coat of clear varnish had dried. The work was ready for its final coat of varnish.

Kai left off admiring his work and turned on his work radio to the jazz station he listened to all day and all night. In the weeks he'd been home, he'd become so familiar with its playlist and daily format that he could almost tell the time by which song was playing. Rather than becoming monotonous, the music kept him company as he did the concentrated handwork the job required. It also kept him distracted him from the complex thoughts that could plague him as his mind fit itself to the rhythms of the skill it took to do the work. Kai's mind had always worked on various channels simultaneously. The thought it took to work to exact measurements and care it took as he operated dangerous power saws and a nail gun took up perhaps two channels. The ambient music took up a distracting third channel and on the fourth, he tried to think of only pleasant things.

Kai felt much better now that he was back on his meds. The Strattera helped with his concentration and the Risperdal kept his mind broadcasting only four or five channels of thought rather than a score at once. He could feel the Zoloft anchoring him like a taut rope from the abyss of despair he felt about his life in general, and the lorazepam kept the jitteriness at bay. All he had to do was look around the room he stood in to see that the orchestration of his brain chemicals was back in tune. It was a satisfying feeling to work long and well, alone in that room.

Now, he checked the surfaces of the shelves to make sure no dust had settled that might spoil the integrity of his work. With everything clean and ready, he stepped to the middle of the room and picked up the ladder and walked with it to the door from the hall. Once he was satisfied with its position, he walked back to the middle of the floor where he'd left his cleaned brush and gallon can of varnish. He eased the lid off with a screwdriver and gently stirred the contents with a clean piece of molding until he was satisfied that it looked right. Then, with great care, he took the gallon tin of varnish and his brush to the ladder, mounted it to reach the uppermost corner and began.

The new Chris Botti song started on the radio as he dipped his brush and began work. Taking great care to avoid leaving any drips or visible brush strokes, he began to apply the varnish to the crown molding. It was only then, with the rhythm of the work begun, that he allowed himself to think about his phone call to Robin the night before. It had been one of those nights when he'd slept fitfully until three in the morning and then awakened with the full knowledge he wouldn't be able to go back to sleep. He'd gone into his bathroom to relieve himself and then debated whether or not to make himself some coffee or just return to his room where Heidi slept on peacefully. Even as he considered his options, the thought of the brown bottle in his chest of drawers popped into his mind. It was now three weeks since he'd taken any pills from that bottle. The physical cravings were gone, but the psychological need hadn't lessened one bit. Peace lay in that bottle. He knew it and he wanted it as badly as ever. But instead of giving in, he walked in the dark to the kitchen and made a short pot of coffee instead.

As Kai sat at the kitchen table waiting for the coffee to finish brewing, he lit a cigarette and stared out over the familiar view of the canal to the back of the house beyond. The waning moon was still bright enough to leave glimmers of silver on the inky canal. Staring at the moon's rippling reflection on the water, his mind took him to the darkened kitchen of Robin's house in Wrights Shores. He could wander that house unlit just as easily from his seat in his mother's kitchen in Sunrise as he could if he were there. Only there, Robin slept, while he was awake no matter what.

He could imagine himself climbing the stairs to the loft where Robin's big mattress and box springs sat on the floor under the sloping roof. He could feel the textures of Robin's cheap Turkish prayer rugs under his feet as he walked from the stairs to the bed. He could see Robin curled on his side breathing the deep slow breaths of the dreamless.

Kai missed Robin with an ache that none of the drugs he took to keep himself sane seemed to touch. He felt a physical longing for him that made him actually hurt inside. It was like no other feeling he'd ever experienced. At first, it had been easy to dismiss. Then it had been easy to blame the feeling on withdrawal. Now, there were no excuses. Kai knew he was deeply in love with another man and there seemed to be no way to avoid it. Moving eight hundred miles away from Robin hadn't cured him of it any more than quitting the painkillers cold turkey had. As the coffee's steady stream into the glass carafe slowed to mere drips, Kai fought against the idea of what he knew he was about to do.

Finally, he gave up fighting. He stood from his seat and put his cigarette out with water from the tap before dropping it into the kitchen's garbage can. He calmly made himself a cup of coffee, collected his cigarettes and lighter and returned to his room as quietly as he could. Once he was back inside with his door closed, he opened his blinds to let in the light from the streetlamp outside his bedroom window. He settled himself on the bed, his coffee and ashtray on the table next to his bed and reached for his cell phone. While he was waiting for it to power up, he lit a cigarette and took a sip of coffee. The smoke and hot liquid soothed him as he picked up his phone and punched in the digit to speed dial Robin.

The number rang only twice before Robin sleepily mumbled "Hello?"

"It's me, baby," Kai said softly. "I'm sorry I woke you up. I just needed to hear your voice right now, that's all."

"It's . . . ." Kai could imagine Robin stretching to read the clock on the floor by the bed, ". . . three-seventeen, Kai. You can't sleep can you?" Robin said, clearly becoming more awake by the second.

"No. I woke up at three, but I know it's no good trying to go back to sleep. I made some coffee and while it was brewing, I had you on my mind. I miss you so much, Robin," Kai whispered heavily into the phone.

Robin chuckled softly and said, "You just want to make sure I haven't changed my mind about getting on that plane."

"That's part of it," Kai said as softly as he could. He didn't want to wake his mother or Matt, or rouse Heidi for that matter. She resented it when he talked on the phone and would whine at him until he either paid attention to her or took her outside. "I've been living for this visit for the past three weeks. It's been really tough. I really want to be with you."

"Are the meds helping?" Robin asked gently.

"With everything but missing you," Kai replied honestly. "I've stayed clean, Robin. It's been three weeks today."

"I'm proud of you, Kai. I know that's been tough, but tell me, are your meds helping you?" Robin insisted.

Kai sighed and mumbled, "Yeah. My moods are okay. I've been working. Everything's alright, I just really miss you, you know?"

"I miss you too, Kai. It seems like you should be here with me right now, not down there. What are we going to do about this mess?" Robin asked. Kai could hear the emptiness in his voice. "I don't know if coming down there is such a great idea. I can't get used to missing you, but I don't know what good coming to visit is going to do."

"It'll be all good. Baby, I swear," Kai pleaded. "I want to touch you so much. I want to *be* with you."

"Don't get me started," Robin said hungrily. "Or did you call me so we could talk dirty while you beat off?"

"No!" Kai answered in his normal speaking voice. In the dark room, with the light coming in from the streetlight outside, it seemed like a scream. After a moment, he lowered his voice and said, "That's not what this is about and you know it, Robin. I'm fucking hurting here."

After a pause, Robin said, "No. I know it's not just about the sex. I'm hurting too. Do you think I haven't been counting the days until you and I are looking at each other again? I don't know what I'm doing anymore."

"You're coming here to be with me," Kai said firmly. "While you're here, there're things we have to talk about. Things we have to discuss about the future. I can't see my life without you in it. I mean full on, all the time. Since I got back on my meds, I've been thinking straight for the first time since . . . since . . . ."

"Since you met me," Robin said candidly. "You and I, we were living a dream this time last year. Now I don't know . . . have you woken up?"

"I don't want to wake up anymore if you're not there," Kai said honestly. "It's not a dream. What we have is real. If it wasn't we wouldn't be talking this way in the middle of the night, would we?"

"No," Robin replied sadly. "No, we wouldn't. I'm on my way to you. I'll be there, and we'll talk seriously, okay?"

"Yes, we will. One way or another, we're going to work this out, Robin," Kai said firmly.

"Okay, let me go now." Robin said. "We both have to work tomorrow. Try to get some sleep okay?"

"Okay," Kai said gently in reply. "I love you, okay?"

"I know. I love you back," Robin said. "We'll talk again before Sunday. I promise."

"Go back to sleep, baby," Kai said softly. "I love you," he said once more before pressing his thumb on the off button. He sighed and looked at the little screen on his cell phone to make sure he'd terminated the call. Satisfied he had, Kai closed his phone and laid it back on the table by his bed. He took a final hit off the cigarette he had burning and stubbed it out before taking another sip of his coffee. Then he sat replaying the conversation he'd just had with Robin over and over in his mind, trying to memorize its nuances in tone and content.

He had finally fallen asleep again at about five only to have the alarm wake him at six-thirty.

Now, as he layered the last coat of varnish over his work he thought over the old deliberations in his head when he'd argued against admitting he was gay. In the twelve years since he'd had his first sexual experience with another boy, he'd gone from being frightened of what the fact of his attractions meant to trying to live two kinds of lives to finally admitting he was gay. By his own reasoning, the limitless need he felt for Robin meant he was gay, and he was simply tired of fighting the idea of it any more. In the years he'd lived on the Outer Banks, he'd been frightened of being known as gay. He was afraid of being ostracized by the groups of friends and co-workers that had filled his world. Now, distanced from that whole scene, he realized how little those other people mattered.

Since he'd left Robin and the beach to move back to Sunrise and the security of his mother's house, he had thought about being gay night and day. What he had discovered in all his racing or rambling thoughts was the fact that he wasn't any different for admitting to himself that he was gay. No big tone of doom had echoed in his head when he'd admitted it to himself; in fact, he had felt relieved. In being cut off from Robin and all the love and companionship he provided, Kai realized he couldn't step back into his childhood anymore; he had out grown it. Kai realized life inexorably moved on and he was standing still. Everything had changed. His mother's house had even changed in her own relentless drive to make things over and keep her life in flow as opposed to being static and unresolved.

Kai wasn't so deluded that he couldn't see the destruction he'd brought on himself by refusing to confront a central reality of his life. In the past three weeks, he'd given up fighting it. What he wanted more than anything else was a life that held some love, the kind of love Robin embodied. He was tired of being alone all the time, isolated from a kind of happiness that seemed so available to other people that he had never been able to grasp.

When he'd come back to Sunrise and found his mother so happy and so involved with Matt Jenkins, it had thrown him for a loop. All of his life, his mother had seemed so strong and so *single*. He had always taken it for granted that she was still in love with his father and that one day Rhett would come to his senses and get her back. It was something he'd taken as fact ever since he could perceive his parents as people. Then, he'd reappeared in South Florida a month ago and found his mother busily moving on with her own life, deeply committed to another man. While his mother had remained single for so many years, he had been able to see himself as single as well, a lone wolf who could always come home again. He'd walked instead into the very real fact that he needed to make his own home.

The fact was, he had made a home with Robin in the past year. In the little house on pilings in Wrights Shores, he'd learned how secure and happy his life could be if he allowed himself to feel deeply about someone else. Still, he'd rebelled against the notion he could be so happy with Robin. He'd gone out of his way to numb that idea with drugs and actively attack it by casually starting a relationship with Linda.

As he thoughtfully applied varnish to the shelves of the bookcases, he allowed himself to think of her. He knew Linda had wanted a stable relationship as much as he did. She had tried everything she could think of to lure him into living with her instead of with Robin. The problem was Kai watched every move she made with a knowing, cynical eye. Deep inside, he knew he already had the kind of relationship with Robin that Linda wanted with him. Kai knew, but couldn't admit that he'd already made a choice between Linda and Robin. It would have been so easy to step from Robin's house into Linda's and pick up the thread of security—except for the fact he loved Robin and he didn't love her. That certainty deep inside is what freaked him out. Then, Linda got arrested, and that ended her ability to offer him anything other than becoming further enmeshed in her life.

Now, Kai realized he'd panicked. He saw Linda implicating him in an effort to ease her own case, though Kai had never sold any of the painkillers she made available so readily. He had, however, enjoyed the painkillers himself to the point that he knew he was an addict. Through that trauma, Robin had remained steadfast and solidly in his corner, despite the fact that Kai had treated Robin so callously. When

Kai realized what he really wanted could be had so easily if only he'd admit to his true feelings, his panic had doubled. The only way out he could see was to pack up and head south to his mother to get things sorted out.

Three weeks sober and back on his medication, Kai realized what a mess he'd created for himself and for the people he cared about the most, his mother and Robin. Coming out of the fog, he'd had to ask himself what he really wanted. With Robin only days away from arriving in South Florida, Kai found himself actively planning on getting Robin to leave the Outer Banks to move south and live with him. In his mind, he had it all worked out. His mother would understand how much they needed to be together, so she'd move in with Matt into his house in Lighthouse Point, leaving him and Robin to live in her house in Sunrise. It was the answer to everything. Now he had to convince not only Robin, but also his mother that his plan would work out with everyone left a winner.

This is what he fantasized about as he worked his way around the room, shelf by shelf, leaving a glossy hard finish to set in his wake. He was so absorbed in both his work and his daydream that he worked without hunger through the lunch hour and on into the afternoon. The shifting light coming through the window and French doors barely registered in his mind as he varnished and dreamed about the life he'd make with Robin once he was safely settled down in the house in Sawgrass Estates. So, when he found himself back at his starting place by the room's door leading to the hall, he was surprised. His watch told him it was half-past five. He smoothed away the last of his brush strokes and climbed down from the ladder.

There was a familiar ache in the small of Kai's back, but he welcomed it as he moved the ladder to the center of the room and banged the lid home on the gallon can of clear varnish. The ache was a way of knowing the job was finished. It was a good, manly ache he could claim as his own. Smiling to himself he calculated that there was perhaps a quarter inch of varnish left in the can. He congratulated himself on accurately gauging how much of the finish it would take to do the job. He put the now-worn brush in a Ziplock bag and sealed it inside. There was nothing to do now but return the ladder and what was left of the varnish to Bill Kellogg's garage. The job was finished and it looked beautiful to his practiced eye.

Once he'd tidied up, he fished in the pockets of his shorts for his cigarettes and lighter. He found the Diet Coke he'd brought to have with his lunch and stepped outside the French doors to the patio to celebrate finishing the job with a cigarette and a drink. He'd run a bit over his estimate, time-wise, but it wasn't enough to adjust his quote. Kai stretched and sighed with contentment. He planned on finishing his cigarette and leaving before Bill got home. He thought it would be good enough to call from his truck to tell the man he'd finished and he'd stop by the following day to pick up his check. However, as he stood smoking on the patio, he heard Bill's familiar voice ring out in the house.

"I'm out back," Kai called back in reply. In a moment, he saw Bill enter his new library and look around in awe. He stood in the center of the room and turned to take in the finished job. At last, his eyes fell on Kai's lanky form standing just outside the French doors and he smiled. "So, what do you think?" Kai asked with a grin.

"It's beautiful!" Bill said as he looked around once more. "So you're finished then?"

"Yes, just a few minutes ago. A little behind schedule, but it's all done," Kai told him.

"How long would you give it to dry?" Bill asked as he stepped outside to stand by Kai and look back into the deep blue of the room.

Kai drained the last of the warm Coke, then neatly took a final hit off his cigarette and deposited the butt into the empty can. "It should be dry to the touch by this time on Sunday," he said. "But I'd give it a week to cure before I started putting anything on the shelves. When are your floor guys coming in?"

"Tuesday morning," Bill said happily. "They say it should only take them a day to do it. I've had the wood acclimatizing in the living room for the past week. I decided to go with laminate rather than real wood. Same look, but cheaper and less hassle."

"Some of those laminates are very good looking," Kai responded. "You can spend Thanksgiving moving into your new library."

"I can't get over how beautiful your finish is," Bill said happily. "It's better looking than the picture I gave you to go by. I love the detailing you've added. I love the dentil molding under the crown."

"I won't lie and say that was easy to paint or varnish," Kai admitted. "But I'm pretty sure there are no drops or drips anywhere. I took my time doing it."

Bill stepped back into the room and walked around the bookcases, peering up at the molding to confirm Kai's claim. "It's perfect," he announced with a grin. "You've done an amazing job. Your mother said you were good, but you have more than earned your money. You're a real craftsman."

Kai smiled, but only shrugged in reply before nervously lighting another cigarette. It was obvious he was enjoying the praise, but his natural shyness and reserve wouldn't let him respond. Kai didn't know how to accept compliments; he didn't trust them.

Bill stepped back outside to join him, reaching in his rear pocket as he did so. He took out his wallet and said, "I know guys like you might appreciate being paid in cash, so I stopped by the bank at lunch. I left work a little early so I could catch you here."

"Wow, man! Thanks," Kai said as Bill drew out a wad of notes from his wallet, then stretched out his hand to hold them as Bill slowly counted out twenty-four hundred dollar bills. "Hold up," Kai said as he reached the twenty-fourth bill, "That's too much. The quote was for only twenty-three hundred."

"That's a hundred dollar bonus for getting it done when you said you would and for being so reliable," Bill said dismissively. "Frankly, there hasn't been a workman in this house for all the years I've lived here who showed up when they said they would, got the job done right the first time, and kept the place so clean."

"I can't take this, Bill," Kai told him as he urged a single hundred dollar bill back toward his client's hand. "Your recommendation is bonus enough. Just mention me if you know of anyone else who is looking to have some work done."

"No, that's yours," Bill said as he took Kai's hand and folded his fingers over the bill. "You said you had someone special coming. Take them out to dinner on me."

Kai watched as Bill gave his hand a friendly squeeze over the crumbled bill in his hand before letting go. "Jeez, thanks. I appreciate this," he said.

"You can count on me to send some clients your way," Bill added. "I have several friends who are thinking about updating their houses."

Kai looked up into Bill's smiling face and decided to offer something back for the kind man's generosity. He hadn't been blind to the older man's secret looks of admiration and subtle appreciation of his youth and looks, though Bill had never said anything to betray his interest. Kai knew Bill had to wonder about him, having essentially known of him since he was a small boy. He decided he could be honest with Bill as an offering to the new sense of freedom he felt in dealing with his feelings. He said, "Robin, that someone special. His name is Robin."

Bill lifted his eyebrows and gave Kai a look of interested connection. "I *was* wondering," he admitted.

Kai grinned and said, "'Someone' is pretty vague. I just wanted you to know—well, I guess I just felt like it would be okay to tell you."

"Your mother and Matt Jenkins know, of course?" Bill asked with an expression of amused reserve.

"Yes. They're cool with it," Kai told him. "Robin and I lived together all last year. It's only since I left the Outer Banks that I realized how special he is. I'll definitely take him out somewhere nice while he's here, thanks to you."

Bill nodded shyly and looked back into the dark blue library as if he could see other times and other faces there. He said, "Son, take my advice. If he is someone special, don't waste any time letting him know. Time is more precious than you think when you run out of it."

"You must miss your partner a great deal," Kai said gently. "I'm sorry he's not here to see your library."

"Oh!" Bill said and laughed quietly. "Don't say that. If he was still around there'd be no library. But yes, I do miss him very much. That's why I can tell you not to waste one minute being with your Robin. I hope you have a great visit."

"Thanks," Kai said quietly. "I'll take your advice."

Bill nodded and stepped back into the library and began to look around. Kai gave him a moment there alone as he folded the pay for the job and stuffed the bills into his front pocket. He smoked alone on the patio while Bill collected his thoughts. It was time to be heading home. Now, while he was feeling so good. All in all, it had been his best day since he'd returned to South Florida. He felt the fleeting self-assurance of confidence without any panic gnawing at its edges.

It took nearly twenty minutes to go the three miles back home in the Friday evening traffic. It was after six when he pulled up in the drive behind Matt's Porsche Cayenne. He left the space nearest the front door open for his mother out of long habit. The little considera-tion was his mother's due; he never for a moment forgot it was her house. He eased himself out of the truck and walked toward the sounds of Heidi's barking behind the front door. "I'm home, girl. Your daddy's home," he called out and the barking gave way to a scramble of claws on tile as he opened the front door and let himself into the foyer.

Heidi circled his legs and began barking again as he got the door closed behind him and knelt to receive her sloppy kisses. "Hey, Matt!" he called out.

"Hey, yourself," Matt said from his chair in the living room. "I let Heidi out back when I got in. The poor dog was dying to pee."

"She's hungry, too," Kai said as he stood and walked into the living room. He made his way to the sofa and perched on the edge of a cushion to stroke the hyper dog into relative calm. "Thanks for taking Heidi out. It took me a little longer than I expected to finish."

"No problem," Matt said easily. "She knew it was you just now. She's either psychic or she knows the sound of your truck, but she was just lying on the sofa and all of a sudden she lifted her head, looked around and then got up, trotted into the foyer and started barking. It was the damnedest thing."

"Robin says she did that all the time," Kai said before he thought about it. For a moment, he was stunned at having so casually brought him up in conversation. He was a little uncomfortable for a moment.

Then Matt said, "Do you think Heidi'll be happy to see him?"

"She'll freak out," Kai told him. "She was big buddies with Robin."

Matt laughed and said, "Where will she sleep while he's here? In bed with you guys?"

That said so easily and naturally made Kai relax. He snorted resignedly and said, "Of course. She always did before."

"Isn't that a bit awkward sometimes?" Matt asked candidly.

"Well," Kai said slyly, "There were times when she got locked up in the guest room downstairs. If you turn the Luther Vandross up loud enough you don't hear the whining," he said and gave Matt a wink.

Matt laughed at that, then said, "Your mother is at the beauty shop. She won't be home until about seven. We were thinking about getting a bite at Pebbles. Would you like to come with?"

Kai shook his head and stood saying, "No thanks. It's been a long day and I really just want to take a shower after I feed and walk Heidi and then maybe watch a little TV. I've been up since three this morning. I hope I'll sleep through the night tonight."

"What will you do for dinner?" Matt asked. "There's not much in the refrigerator until your mom makes a grocery run."

Kai straightened his shoulders and moved his chin to crack the tension in the muscles there that he'd worked applying varnish all day. He sighed and said, "I don't know, maybe I'll just eat my lunch. I got so into working I didn't stop to eat. I'll either do that or order a pizza or something."

Matt gave him a sympathetic look and said, "You haven't eaten all day? Damn. No wonder you're beat. You really should come with us and have a nice dinner."

Kai smiled but again, shook his head no. "Thanks just the same. Heidi's been cooped up all day by herself. I don't want to leave her alone, she'll get spiteful and chew something up. Can I get a rain check?"

"Suit yourself," Matt said affably. "If you've been up since three, you probably want to crash fairly early."

"Yeah, I probably will," Kai said and turned to walk into the kitchen.

Matt stood and followed him into the kitchen. "Kai, if you don't mind me asking, doesn't your medicine help you sleep?"

Kai leaned down to retrieve Heidi's bowl from the floor and then took it to the counter while he filled it from the large bag of dog food stored under the sink. "I don't mind you asking," he said evenly, wondering why Matt even cared about his sleep. He was just mildly annoyed at having to explain something that was so normal for him, but so unusual for everyone else. "The medicine sort of works. I mean, I can get to sleep, but it doesn't hold. I have bad dreams and my mind starts racing and I can't go back to sleep. It's fairly normal for me. I've been that way since I was a little kid. Something broke in me a long time ago, and I don't think it'll ever be fixed. It's just the way I am."

As he took the bowl from the counter and set it on the floor for Heidi, Matt pulled a chair out from the kitchen table and sat down.

He looked up at Kai and said, "I'm sorry if I sound like I'm prying, I'm just trying to understand. What makes you feel as if you're broken? You seem to have it pretty together to me. You're working. You're going out to find work. You're back on your meds. Is this as good as it gets for you, or are you ever happy?"

Kai fished in his pocket for his cigarettes and then laid them on the table. He took his ashtray from the top of the refrigerator and sat down, joining Matt at the table. He thought how best to answer as he lit a cigarette and looked Matt in the eye. "This is about as good as it gets, Matt. I realize I was happy when I lived with Robin, but even then, I still had times when I didn't sleep. It's just me. I'm not happy like other people. I'm kind of dead inside if you want to know the truth, just empty. That's mostly how I feel if I'm not hurting. It's fucked up, but that's the hand I got in the gene poker game."

Matt nodded slowly and didn't flinch from Kai's unbroken gaze or bare self-admission. He said, "Do you plan to get back with Robin? I mean if the only time you're happy is when you're with him, it seems like you'd want to never be apart."

Kai nodded and took a long hit off his cigarette before he responded guardedly, "I hope to work things out with Robin when he visits. I don't know. We'll see, I guess."

"I hope you guys work it out," Matt said sympathetically. "I really do."

Kai nodded and peered at the ashtray for a moment before he said, "Now can I ask you something? I'm not trying to pry, I'm just curious."

"Of course," Matt told him as he relaxed into his chair and crossed his leg to rest an ankle on his knee.

Kai thumped his cigarette into the ashtray and looked into Matt's eyes once more. "You and my mom . . . are you guys going to get married someday or what?"

Matt laughed and uncrossed his legs anxiously. "You're pretty intense, you know that?"

Kai let a ghost of a smile flicker across his lips before he answered. He was enjoying making Matt as uncomfortable with personal questions as he felt being asked them. "I don't have much of a bullshit filter," Kai admitted. "I can't make small talk, sorry."

"No, that's okay," Matt protested. "Of course you're bound to be curious about our relationship, your mother's and mine, I mean."

"Well sure," Kai said and again took a drag off his cigarette.

For a moment the only sound in the room was the hollow ring of the dog's bowl as Heidi nosed it across the tile floor as she ate. After a moment, Matt said, "Kai, I'll be honest with you. Your mother and I are in a good place right now. We're just happy being together. We haven't really discussed marriage and I haven't given it much thought. We've both had difficult first marriages. We'll be getting married before our baby comes, that's certain."

"So you're happy here, in this crappy little zero-lot line house in West Broward," Kai asked earnestly.

"Of course, I'm very happy," Matt responded vehemently. "Your mother has worked hard to make this feel like home for me. Why do you ask?"

"Just curious," Kai told him lightly. "I mean you being who you are, a big deal in a lot of ways, you drive a Porsche for god's sake. I don't know, I'm just wondering if maybe you're just slumming a little."

"I'm not slumming," Matt said earnestly. "I'm here because your mother is here and she makes me very happy. Being successful or rich or driving a Porsche doesn't make you happy," he concluded dismissively.

Kai nodded slowly before he said, "It isn't easy for anyone, being happy, is it?"

Matt sighed and looked away, "No," he said. "When you think of all the bullshit everyone drags along behind them, it never is."

Kai watched as Heidi finished licking her bowl and turned to him expectantly. He stubbed out his cigarette and stood, saying, "Don't hurt her, Matt. Just try not to hurt her is all I'm asking."

"That's the last thing I would ever want to do, Kai. You must believe me," Matt pleaded.

"Oh, I do believe you," Kai said as he looked down on his mother's boyfriend. "I just know how easy it is to fuck something really good up."

Matt looked up to meet his eyes and felt a real connection with Kai for the first time. "I hear you," he answered.

"I've got to take Heidi for her walk," Kai said as he turned away. "We'll be back in a little while."

"Before seven?" Matt called out as Kai left the room with his dog trotting after him. From the foyer, Matt could hear the scrabble of Heidi's claws and the click of her leash meeting with her collar's D-ring.

"Sure," Kai called back. "We'll make it back before then." With that, he opened the front door and eased outside with Heidi leading the way. As she led him along at a fast pace, Kai suddenly felt very tired and sad. He believed Matt was being honest with him. Still, thinking of his mother and Matt he could only think that even things that seemed to be so strong could turn out to be built on sand. At least he'd planted the idea of marriage in Matt's head. Kai really wanted the house. He wondered what else he was going to build a future on with Robin as he walked with Heidi to the sidewalk outside the walls, under the trees. For Kai, nothing came easily or for free.

Chapter Fifteen

HER OFFICE PHONE rang just as Maura was coming back from the ladies' room. After weeks of feeling just fine, she was struck by a sudden wave of nausea. She'd tried to stave it off by slowly eating some soda crackers she'd brought to the office when she'd first discovered she was pregnant. Ultimately, she was unsuccessful. Fortunately, the episode was brief. After she'd thrown up, she felt better quickly. Now, coming into her office to a ringing phone, she was sorry she wasn't sitting in her familiar living room with a magazine as she recovered. She picked up the phone and answered it in one fluid motion as she sat down.

As she scrolled through the morning's emails, Maura was struck by a sudden wave of nausea. She reached into her desk drawer for the stash of soda crackers she was keeping for such an event, but even they didn't help this time, and soon she was bolting toward the ladies' room.

On her way back, she groaned as she heard the phone ringing; if only she were home in her familiar living room with a magazine. But she wasn't, and she had no choice but to deal with whatever the person on the phone would demand. She picked up the phone and answered.

"I hope I'm not catching you at a busy time," a gentle young male voice greeted her. "Is this Maura Ostryder?"

"Yes, it is. Who am I speaking to please?" Maura responded as civilly as she could. She was taken off guard by the caller's tentative tone and expression of concern.

"My name is Robin. Robin Taylor. I'm a friend of your son's. I'm sorry for bothering you at work, but I thought I should give you a call," he said cautiously.

Maura sat in her desk chair in surprise. For a moment, she couldn't reply as she tried to assimilate the circumstances. Finally she said, "Of course, Robin. Kai's spoken of you often. How can I help you?"

"God, this is so awkward," Robin answered and took an audible breath. "I really just wanted to check in with you before I came down to visit soon. I'm a little concerned that Kai might have—well, I just don't want this visit to be uncomfortable for you. I know he's said you're fine with me coming down, but I wanted to offer you an opportunity to let me know if there's any problem or anything."

Maura smiled. She found the young man's obvious discomfort charming.

"There's no problem at all, Robin," she said. "We're all anxious to meet you. I know you mean a great deal to my son, and I want you to know you're welcome."

"Thanks. Thanks, Mrs Ostryder. I appreciate that. I don't know what I was thinking, calling you and everything. I found this number on your company website and thought, here I am, sort of just showing up at this lady's house for Thanksgiving . . ." Robin offered as an explanation.

"Robin, it's perfectly all right," Maura said consolingly. "I think I understand your apprehension. Don't worry about it. Like I said, I look forward to meeting someone who means so much to Kai."

"I look forward to meeting you as well," Robin said, obviously relieved, but still nervous. "I also wanted to call you to ask how Kai's doing. I mean, he says he's doing okay, but you know how he is. He was in pretty rough shape when he left here. I suppose I just need to know he's really okay."

Maura wondered what Kai might have said to fill the young man with such concern. She said confidently, "Robin, Kai's doing fine.

Since he's been home he's been doing a lot better. I know you two talk. Has he said anything that concerns you?"

"No, not in so many words. It's just a feeling I have. He seems kind of fragile and I don't know if it's because he's having trouble or if he's just—"

"Whining?" Maura said, interrupting him. "Robin, without going into a lot of detail, I can tell you he misses you a great deal and he's anxious that you two come to some understanding with each other. Now, beyond that, the specifics are really between you and my son."

"As long as he's okay," Robin answered shyly. "I, um, I'll be down there soon and I want you to know I really care a lot about him. I know he's your son and everything, but I'm in love with him. I think you should know that."

Maura smiled once more and shook her head. "It's okay, Robin. I understand your relationship completely. You should relax. We're going to have a lovely Thanksgiving."

"I appreciate your being so understanding," Robin said. "Please, could we keep this between us? I don't want Kai to think I'm bothering you or checking up on him."

"No problem, Robin. I won't mention your call. Now I have to get back to work. You relax. Everything's going to be fine, okay?" Maura told him sincerely.

"Okay, thanks!" Robin said with obvious relief. "You have a great day."

"You too," Maura said and quickly hung up the phone. She sat back in her chair and leaned it as far as the spring would let her. The boy sounded charming. Obviously he was well brought up to be so concerned about his reception and to want so much to avoid any awkwardness. A southerner herself, Maura appreciated the cultural propensity to layer pleasant social pretense over such things as out-of-town visits. She knew if Robin were to come down and find he was the cause of a familial tempest, he'd be deeply embarrassed as well as emotionally hurt. Whether or not his call was entirely self-serving, Maura wasn't completely sure. What she was sure of was that her interest in Robin was once again piqued. She really wanted to meet this young man who had so captivated her difficult son. With that thought, she turned back to her emails and reluctantly opened the next one in the queue. It wouldn't be too long now before Robin himself appeared and all her questions and curiosity would be satisfied. For now, she had work to do.

And work she did, through a long, busy day. When she got home, she was somewhat relieved to see only Matt's car in the driveway and no sign of Kai's truck. It occurred to her that Matt was home unusually early and Kai was unusually absent. She dismissed her sudden anxiety at the thought and let herself into the house, calling out for Matt.

"I'm in here," he called from the bedroom.

Maura lay her purse on the dining room table and continued into her bedroom to find Matt undressed to his boxers, curled up under the covers of their bed. "What's wrong, sweetheart?" she asked him as she perched on her side of the bed and removed her shoes.

"Not anything really bad, I just came home with a headache, that's all," Matt answered. "How was your day?"

Maura leaned across the bed and kissed his forehead. "Pretty good, except I've hit a milestone with this pregnancy. This morning was my first bout of morning sickness. Cool, huh?"

Matt took one arm from under the covers and patted her hip gently. "I'm sorry. Were you terribly sick?"

Maura shook her head and smiled. "Not so bad. As I recall, I seem to do pretty well with it. Or I did twenty-eight years ago. With me, it doesn't last forever. How about you? What gave you this headache?"

Matt rubbed his face with his hand and then stared up at the ceiling. "Just stress. I'm smart enough to go home and pull the covers over my head rather than have a heart attack. I actually feel a lot better now."

"How long have you been home?" Maura asked solicitously.

"What time is it?"

"About quarter of six."

"I got home around three-thirty. Your son was on the way out the door with Heidi. He said he was taking her to the beach. I have no idea which one. I didn't think they allowed dogs on the beach these days," Matt said and yawned.

"I don't know either," Maura said as she stood and began to undress on her way to the closet.

"Anything else happen today that was interesting?" Matt asked.

"Now that you mention it," Maura said as she unhooked her bra and placed it neatly on a shelf. As she pulled a clean white T-shirt over her head, she said, "Kai's boyfriend called me this morning, out of the clear blue sky."

"Oh God, what did he want?" Matt asked.

Maura stepped into her khaki shorts and pulled them up over her hips. Buttoning them, she said, "He said he just wanted to make sure it was cool if he came for Thanksgiving. I told him it was fine. I think he just wanted to be sure we weren't going to fag bash him or anything. Poor kid."

"If I were him I'd be a little anxious," Matt offered reasonably. "First time meeting the folks. A reunion after a month's separation. You know what's going to be first on their minds, don't you?" Matt said and chuckled.

Maura emerged from the closet and lay down on the bed with her head on Matt's chest. "Please, don't draw me any graphic images. I can imagine what I'd want to do and it wouldn't be playing cards with the old folks." She sighed and closed her eyes. "I don't know if I can stand the throes of young love in a fifteen-hundred square foot zero-lot line house. Maybe we should rent them a hotel room so they can have some privacy."

"That would make us responsible for Heidi," Matt said as he

stroked her hair off her face. "Have you forgotten my idea about let-ting Kai stay at my place in Lighthouse Point?"

Matt's hands on her hair felt good. Maura could feel herself relax-ing. She said, "To tell you the truth, I had forgotten. But that would solve several problems, wouldn't it?"

"Yes, it would," Matt said agreeably. "I think we should tell Kai about it sooner rather than later. That'll give him a few days to get settled in over there before Robin comes. Of course they're welcome here as long as they want to hang out with us, but this way they'll have a place all to themselves."

"You're absolutely right, Matt. Today's Thursday. Matt has a shrink appointment tomorrow. I think we should tell him about it to-morrow night and then we can take him over there on Saturday morn-ing. Does that sound good to you?"

"Absolutely," Matt said. "As far as I'm concerned, the sooner we get him settled in over there the better. I'm looking forward to having the house for just the two of us again."

"It hasn't been that bad having him here, has it?" Maura asked earnestly.

"No, not at all. To tell you the truth, I'm going to miss Heidi as much as I'll miss Kai. I really like having a dog. Did you know that?"

Maura sat up and looked at her lover. "No. I never knew you were a big dog fan. You never said anything."

Matt nodded. "I had dogs the whole time I was growing up. It was my ex-wife that couldn't abide them. The selfish bitch wanted every ounce of my attention. It wouldn't have been fair to the dog to bring one into our house."

"God, I hate to hear you say that," Maura said gently. "Tell you what, if you want a dog we can get one. I always had one while Kai was growing up. I'm used to having them around. My only re-quest is that we go ahead and get one now. I don't want to be house-breaking a puppy and changing diapers simultaneously."

"Would you really do that for me?" Matt asked incredulously.

Maura tossed her hair and gave him a smile. "Hey, I'm the earth mother, didn't you know that? I was born to raise a house full of dogs and boys. It's who I am."

"My earth mother, huh? Lady Madonna, babies at your breast . . . remember that Beatles song?" Matt teased.

"Well, you can forget the breast feeding bit. I only will go so far. But I'm serious about the dog. Christmas is coming. Be thinking about what kind of dog you want," Maura said seriously.

"Nothing yippy," Matt countered.

"Hell no! The bigger the better," Maura countered.

Great Dane? Wolfhound?" Matt teased.

"I wouldn't say no," Maura said with a smile. "I think dogs are great for kids. Kai's dogs saved his life. He could relate to them when the larger world was a fun house ride for him. I think our son deserves a dog, too, don't you?"

Matt leaned across the bed to kiss her quickly. "'Our son.' It sounds nice doesn't it? 'Our son?'"

"Better get used to it, buddy," Maura advised. "You're on the hook for the rest of your life now."

"Don't I know it," Matt said ruefully. "But I'm pretty happy about it, Maura. Are you, still?"

Maura nodded and looked down at the mattress for a bit before she raised her head and said, "Yes. I'm very happy. The panic is gone now. And one good thing Kai's coming home has done is letting me know I can handle this. I feel confident I can handle anything but the baby being born sick or damaged in some way. That I don't think I could take. But to be honest, I don't think that's going to be the case with this one. He's going to be a happy baby. You and me, and him, we're going to be just fine. Don't you think?"

Matt reached across the covers and took her hand. "I believe that's the way it's going to be. I'm old, but I'm in a great place to really enjoy this kid and be a part of his life, unlike I was with my girls. To tell you the truth, Maura, I feel like you've given me a huge prize. I'm only worried it might be too much for you."

Maura squeezed his hand and gave him a meaningful look comprised of modesty and confidence as well as a good portion of resolve and said, "I'm pretty tough, Matt. I'm not a leaner, but I am going to need your help, okay?"

"What makes you think I wouldn't give you all the help you need?" Matt asked with concern.

Maura let go of his hand and gathered her legs under her. She said, "I don't think you won't, not really. Just don't forget my first husband let me go rather than step up and be a man. That memory's like a scar. Sometimes it aches a little. But I know you're nothing like Rhett. You're an adult and he still isn't even after all this time. I just want you to know I'm counting on you to step up."

Matt nodded. He didn't necessarily feel bad being compared to Maura's first husband. He knew comparisons came with the territory of second loves. But he was determined to show her he would step up, as she put it. He was a man of action, not a lot for glib promises. He looked at her and nodded sincerely.

Maura took in his suddenly serious expression and it touched her. She decided to let any further discussion slide and said instead, "Are you getting hungry?"

"I could eat," Matt admitted.

"How about some roasted Italian sweet sausage, roasted butter-browned potatoes, and fava beans?" Maura suggested.

"You could do that? Just pull that out of your ass on a Thursday night?" Matt asked incredulously.

"Actually, I planned it last weekend when I went to Doris's Italian Market," Maura confessed.

"You're pretty wonderful, Maura," Matt said quietly.

"So are you," She answered him steadily. "So are you."

Chapter Sixteen

THE FOLLOWING morning, Kai sat in Dr. Roth's waiting room idly thumbing through a copy of *People* magazine looking for pictures of Hollywood movie stars with their shirts off. There was always at least one good shot of a movie star's chest in every issue. Most often it was Matthew McConaughey. There were entire movies made just so that he could appear without a shirt. All of his talent was centered on his chest and abs as far as Kai was concerned. As he was turning the pages of a copy several weeks old, the door across the waiting room opened and Dr. Roth called out, "Kai" in a low calm voice.

Kai closed the magazine immediately and acknowledged the doctor's summons with a cool lift of his chin and a look in the eye that tried to communicate that he was pleased to see the man, but not overpleased; distressed but coping; and he was definitely not going to be a difficult fifteen-minute session. Kai had a lot to say in the short time he had with his psychiatrist. He had a lot of ground to cover fast. Dr. Roth was not a therapist; his sessions were strictly about facts and medications. Kai stood and walked to the door which Dr. Roth stepped back to admit him through,.

With Kai's folder in hand, Dr. Roth waved him to the pair of deep leather chairs opposite his desk while he strolled around the desk and sat in his chair at the helm. "Good morning, Kai. How have you been doing?" Dr Roth began as he opened Kai's thick file on his desk and began to read his notes from their last session.

Kai sat anxiously about half way between the edge of the seat and its welcoming back. He wanted to seem comfortable, but not too comfortable. "I'm doing okay, Doctor," he said in a measured tone. "I'm back on the meds for three weeks now and I can really tell the difference. I'm doing pretty good. I don't feel like I'm me watching myself on TV anymore. I feel I'm back into my life, you know?"

Dr. Roth looked at him and gave him a knowing smile. "Tell me again exactly why you went off the meds. Last time, you said you just wanted to take a break. That's not unusual in patients who are on long-term medications in cases such as yours. But, you know, Kai, I got the impression you weren't being completely honest with me about everything. Can you tell me exactly why you went off your meds a year ago?"

Kai thought about the ready excuses he had, but he'd used them last time. If he repeated them now and the doctor was unconvinced, he might refuse to refill his prescriptions. He decided to take a calculated risk and tell the full truth. "When I came to see you last time I was hooked on painkillers and I had been for over a year. That's really why I went off my meds. When I came to see you, I had decided to go off them, cold turkey, and get started back on my psych drugs. That's exactly what I've done. I've been clean for the past three weeks and three days, counting today. I'll pee in a cup if you want me to. Right now," he offered.

"I could have prescribed you something if you'd told me then, Kai. You didn't have to go through withdrawal," Dr. Roth told him.

"I know." Kai said nervously. "I've done my homework. I was just so scared you wouldn't put me back on my regular regimen if I was on anything else, and I really needed to go back on the meds that work. I mean I really *needed* to. I was pretty out of control. I'd turned my whole life upside down and moved back to my mom's house, for God's sake. I needed the Risperdal badly. I couldn't shut off all the voices in my head and they were all arguing constantly. I hadn't had a full night's sleep in weeks and I knew I had to get off the painkillers. I mean I wasn't really addicted. I had just been chipping, you know."

Dr. Roth nodded and said, "Why did you let yourself get hooked on the opiates anyway, Kai? That wasn't a very rational decision. I've known you for many years now, and you've never been afraid to experiment with street drugs, but you've always maintained your psychiatric meds while you experimented. I still don't know why you went off your meds to begin with."

Kai didn't want to answer the question because it didn't square with what he thought the doctor wanted to hear, or the way he wanted to present himself to the doctor. But he didn't have time to think out a dodge. Brazenly, he again decided to tell the full truth. "I quit because I was happy. I was in love for the first time in my life, and for the first time in my life, I was happy and not *crazy* happy. My dopamine levels were high or something, I don't know. I started fooling around with the painkillers when I was on my meds, but being high was an extension of my personal happiness. I got to the point where I thought I didn't need my psych drugs. I was sleeping. I was working and I could concentrate. Everything was so good for me. I just decided maybe I had become normal or something. Like, I really wasn't bipolar anymore. I was so happy, Dr. Roth. It was what I thought normal people felt like. So I quit."

Dr. Roth leveled a cool look over him from across the table and said, "Part of that was the opiates, the other part . . . I don't know, tell me more."

"I met this guy named Robin at work one day," Kai explained calmly, though his right knee was pistoning up and down as he repeatedly bounced his leg with excess energy. "We started going out, started having sex, and all of a sudden I fell in love with him. I moved in and we lived together for a year before I fucked everything up."

"And how did you do that?" Dr. Roth pressed.

"I started dating this girl named Linda. She had a line on the painkillers and I started sleeping with her partly because I could get the drug from her and partly because I freaked out about how deeply I cared about Robin," Kai admitted. "I never let anyone get to know me as well as he did. I really connected with him and it freaked me out. I wanted him to hate me so he'd go away and leave me alone. I tried to control how he felt to keep him from getting in so deep with me."

"I take it you weren't successful."

"No," Kai said despondently. "Robin kept on loving me, despite the fact I treated him so bad and the fact I was letting the painkillers get out of control. I couldn't take it, so I packed up everything and moved back down here to get away from him and everything else up there. I *had* to. I knew I had to get off them and I had to get away from that whole scene. I needed some time to get my head straight. I've been doing a lot of thinking . . . about the future and stuff."

"So you told me the last time you were here. Of course, you didn't go into so much detail. You did talk about Robin, do you recall?" Dr. Roth asked him searchingly.

"Yeah, I remember," Kai answered. "I remember you were very interested in Robin."

"Well, I wasn't interested in Robin, *per se*. I was more interested in the depth of the feelings you expressed for him. It's not like you to form such deep emotional attachments," Dr. Roth explained.

"Yeah, I can see why you'd be interested," Kai said with a forced laugh. "It's totally not like me to fall in love with anybody. I was always so shut down emotionally. Besides, it never seemed to be such a good idea to get so connected to anyone before. I've thought about that, too," Kai said.

"Do you feel you're thinking clearly now that you're off painkillers and back on the appropriate medications again?" Dr. Roth asked seriously.

Kai nodded yes and bent his forehead to cover his eyes with his right hand for a moment. He felt vulnerable, naked, and exposed.

"Tell me what you've been thinking about, for the future," Dr. Roth suggested kindly.

Kai looked up at his doctor and sighed. He slid back into the chair and sat up. He thought for a moment, trying to think of where to begin. Finally, he said, "All the while I was going through detox, I was thinking about being gay. I'd been fighting against the idea for as long as I could remember, but I realized that loving and needing Robin the way I do, it must mean I'm gay. Do you understand?"

"I can see your line of reasoning, yes," Dr. Roth said and leaned back in his chair as well. "Go on," he encouraged.

"Well, once I got my head around the idea of admitting I was gay, I realized that's the only way I could hold on to Robin. I mean, he's always been ready to commit to me, but I couldn't ever commit to him, even though I know I love him. I've talked to him regularly since I've been down here. We both want to work this thing out. He's even coming down here to spend Thanksgiving with me and my Mom." Kai stopped and tried to figure out how to proceed; how to communicate the struggle he had been going through over the past few weeks. He looked into Dr. Roth's concerned eyes, took a breath and released it slowly, then continued, "I plan to ask Robin to move down here and live with me. I want us to start over, down here, away from the bad things I created between us up on the Banks. I want to be away from who I was when I was there. I don't want to be addicted and alone anymore. I want to have a real life, with Robin in it."

Dr. Roth nodded sympathetically but said, "What are you going to do if Robin doesn't see things happening the way you do? It's a lot to ask of him, to take you back, and to move down here. He might say no. What will you do then? Let's face it, Kai, you are a master manipulator. You've managed to avoid getting close to anybody by controlling every aspect of your behavior and others'. You're big on control."

"I know that, Dr. Roth," Kai admitted sincerely. "We've talked about this before. Damaged people have to keep a tight reign on themselves so they don't get hurt any more than they have to. I realize that.

But I'm tired of being damaged. With Robin, I'm not frightened that I'll be hurt. I trust him."

"All the more reason for you to consider what you're going to do if he doesn't want to rearrange his life to accommodate your perception of how the future could be," Dr. Roth cautioned.

Kai turned his head and stared out the window on his right. The blinds were open enough so that he could see the landscaping outside. He didn't have any answer to the situation the way his psychiatrist had presented it. Deep inside, he felt as if he could talk Robin into moving down to be with him. "I don't know," he answered honestly. "If I had to, I'd go back north to live with him there, I guess. I just know that, in my mind and heart, I'm ready to commit myself to Robin. I don't care if that makes me gay. I just want things to work out between us."

Dr. Roth smiled and leaned forward once more to reach for his prescription pad. "You have been doing a lot of thinking," he said. As he began to write, he continued, "It's a pretty big breakthrough for you to admit you're gay. That's a big head start. I want you to think about how you can make things work between you and Robin, even if it means meeting him halfway."

Kai watched him as he wrote and tore off the prescriptions one by one from the pad. "Dr. Roth, one more thing. My sleeping . . . I'm having a lot of trouble sleeping all night. I have nightmares and racing thoughts, still."

Dr. Roth tore the final prescription from the pad and neatly stacked the sheets of blue paper together. "You have a great deal on your mind right now. I'd suggest you don't nap during the day and try to go to bed later, after you've taken your medication at night. Tell me again what you take before bed," he said as he looked at Kai with a clinical eye.

"I take the Risperdal, Zoloft, and a lorazepam about nine o'clock. That way, I'm asleep by about ten. I only take my Strattera in the mornings," Kai told him. "But I'm sick and tired of waking up at three in the morning and being unable to do anything but sit up and chase the thoughts in my head or try to outrun my nightmares."

"I'm reluctant to put you on any sleeping medication, Kai," the doctor told him. "Your sleeplessness is historical, and introducing opiates into the works could have contributed to the problem. Even after you've been off them after a long period of use, your moods and sleep could take months to sort themselves out. I'd suggest if you can't sleep, try reading or take another lorazepam. Sooner or later, you'll work it out. Remember, you've only been back on your meds for three weeks. It takes longer than that for them to become fully effective."

"Okay, whatever," Kai responded bleakly. He reached across the desk to accept the prescriptions the doctor proffered.

Dr. Roth stood, signaling the end of the session. "I've given you only a month's worth of meds. I want to see you again in three weeks to check on how you're doing. Don't hesitate to call me if you get in over your head before then, okay?"

Kai stood and nodded as Dr. Roth took his folder from the desktop and walked toward the door. Before he could open it, Kai asked, "Am I doing alright? I mean, does all of this make any sense or do I have my head up my ass?"

Dr. Roth gave him a concerned look and hesitated a moment before he responded. "Getting addicted to painkillers and going off your meds was not a wise decision. But, realizing you had a problem and coming in to get help was the smart move. You're doing a lot of growing right now and that's rough. Just remember, I'm here if you need me. I really wish you would go back into therapy for awhile. I think it could be a big help for you to talk with someone as you find your way through this."

"I'm sorry, Dr. Roth, but I really can't afford therapy right now. I have no medical insurance and I'm still trying to get work on a steady basis. But I will promise you to consider it when I can pay for it," Kai told him as he stood.

"Well, if things become more difficult for you emotionally, we could see what we could work out in terms of payment," Dr. Roth offered. "I don't want to see you in trouble. Think about it and stay off the painkillers. Call me if you need me before our next visit." With that, he opened the door and waited for Kai to leave his office.

"Thanks," Kai murmured, then walked out of his doctor's office. With the doctor following along behind him, he went to the receptionist's desk and waited while the doctor handed over Kai's file and told her to schedule him for another appointment in three weeks. Clutching his prescriptions, Kai waited for the receptionist to suggest a day and time while the doctor turned and walked back down the hall. Except for the security of the prescriptions in his hand, Kai felt no better leaving than he had coming in.

After he received his appointment on a little reminder card, Kai made his way outside to his truck. Once he got inside, he tucked his prescriptions under the sun visor and sat for a moment in the warm car. He liked the parking lot of Dr. Roth's office complex. It was in old Plantation where the trees were all fully mature and shady. He'd been coming to this same place since Dr. Roth had moved here when Kai was twelve. When he stopped to think of it, it had been eighteen years since he'd started seeing Dr. Roth. That was longer than he could claim any friend. He was the doctor Maura had found when Kai got out of the hospital after his suicide attempt when he was nine. After all the years that followed, Kai had a deep respect for his doctor, though he had long ago come to the realization that the doctor could never make him well—all he could do was keep him relatively sane.

It was that faith in Dr. Roth that gave Kai pause just now. He had brought up the possibility that Robin might not want to move south. Kai hadn't gotten there yet. In his mind, everything would be easy if people would just listen to him. He never considered that Robin might say no. Kai knew Robin was as in love with him as he was with Robin, if not more so. After all, Robin told him he was, every time they talked. Yet, Dr. Roth had presented the notion of conflict into Kai's well-considered plans.

Kai felt panic clutch at him and his heart rate escalated. He lit a cigarette while he powered up his cell phone. Once it had established its familiar screen, he waited a second or two to see if it would tell him he had any new messages. After a full minute, no change appeared on the static screen. Kai speed dialed Robin's cell number, hoping he was free. After several rings, Robin answered in his bright, cheerful professional tone.

"Hey. What are you doing?" Kai asked, relieved just by the sound of Robin's voice.

"Just answering some emails," Robin told him easily. "Sending a few out too, since I won't be here next week. What are you up to this morning?"

"I just got out of my shrink's office," Kai said forcing his voice to remain calm. "I just wanted to let you know I was being a good dog, trying to stay sane and shit. I don't want you to think I'm going off the deep end or anything."

Robin laughed and said, "I didn't think you were going off the deep end. You've been pretty even keeled since you . . . well, you know, got clean. What does the shrink think?"

"He refilled my meds," Kai told him and then paused before he said, "I think he's a little concerned how I'd react if things went south with you and me."

Robin didn't respond for a moment, then he said, "You're not playing fair, Kai. You make it sound like you'll go nuts if I don't do something. I don't know what you want me to do. I'm coming down there and you said we'd work it out. What makes you think we won't?"

Kai flicked his cigarette out the window impatiently and said, "I didn't mean anything like that, honest. Forgive me, I'm just nervous about you coming I guess."

"Well, don't be," Robin told him. "I haven't had a vacation in a long time and I plan to enjoy every minute I'm with you. I plan on working this out too. Okay?"

"Okay," Kai breathed and sighed with relief. "Okay, I hear you, baby."

"I got a call from your former girlfriend last night after we talked," Robin told him. "She's been in touch with your dad as well."

"Oh hell! What does she want?" Kai asked. "I thought she was in jail."

"She is, but they have pay phones in jail," Robin told him. "She actually called me to tell me congratulations for winning. She had spoken with your dad and he told her you had moved back to Florida. She thinks I convinced you to. Thus, I win . . . in her world at least."

"That's fucked up," Kai told him. "You didn't have anything to do with convincing me to leave. That's all on me. I'm the one who fucked up in the first place, even getting with her."

"Don't worry about it, Kai," Robin said consolingly. "I told her neither one of us won. You aren't a carnival prize. You have a mind of your own and you decided the hell with both of us."

"No Robin. It's not like that," Kai pleaded.

"Oh, I know that, but she doesn't," Robin replied evenly. "Her trial's next week. I guess she just wanted to take her frustrations out on somebody. I was the easiest target. By the time she hung up, I had her feeling sorry for both of us, believe me. I just played you for the asshole you can be sometimes."

"Okay, that's fair," Kai said with a grimace and took a hit off hit off his cigarette. To change the subject away from himself, he said, "You don't have to put up with her shit, Robin," and he flicked the remainder of his cigarette out into the parking lot. "You don't deserve that."

"Like I said, don't worry about it," Robin told him easily. "Look, I got to go. You just take care and have a good day, okay? I'll be there the day after tomorrow and I can't wait."

"Promise?" Kai asked huskily.

"I swear," Robin replied sincerely. "I got to go. I love you. Call me tonight."

"Okay. I love you too," Kai told him and hung up. He turned off his cell phone and dropped it into his pants pocket. He was more than a little disconcerted by the fact that Linda had called Robin. "Jealous bitch," he muttered aloud as he cranked the truck. Linda had long since given up trying to contact him. He'd spoken to her exactly once since she'd been arrested. She had assured him he was safe from the cops and that was all he needed to hear from her. After that, he had tried his best to forget she ever existed. He totally discounted her emotional investment in him. As far as he was concerned, she was done, finished.

Kai had always possessed the ability to write people off completely. If he felt threatened or hurt by someone's actions, he simply removed himself from that person's life with a sudden finality that made him appear totally uncaring and cold-hearted. The truth was, Kai lacked the fundamental ability to care about other people's feelings. He had always taken care of himself first with an instinct for survival that was almost animalistic. Besides his mother, his dogs and now Robin, he basically lived untouched by others' emotions or needs. That was why Robin's admission to his limited pantheon of emotional connection was so significant.

As he drove home, he thought about what he would do if Robin did, in fact, refuse to move south to live with him. For the first time, he considered moving back north to live with Robin again in his neat little cottage in Kill Devil Hills. The idea wasn't unattractive in itself. He had made a firm decision to join his future with Robin's and he had no intention of going back on it. Making that decision had taken him so long, and was fraught with so much anxiety, that he didn't want to waste the effort. No. As soon as possible, he intended to get back together with Robin and damn the consequences. He thought about all the familiar faces who would now read him as gay and they seemed far less important than they had previously.

The problem was that he had expended so much energy to move back south. On the way home, Kai looked around the familiar streets and he felt at ease and comfortable. In its own way, the great sprawling metropolis that ran through Palm Beach, Broward, and Dade counties was big enough to get lost in as easily as the relative emptiness of the Outer Banks was. Kai really didn't want to leave South Florida this time. He felt like he was making a positive new start here. His most recent stint of two years up on the Outer Banks, and the mistakes and gifts it had brought, seemed to be far away. He was done with the place as easily as he was done with Linda. The way he saw it, his future was here, in South Florida amid the easy lilting Spanish, the palm trees and the sunshine. He thought of the windswept beach grass and sand of the Outer Banks and saw only desolation there now. He just hoped to God that Robin could fall in love with Sunrise and Broward County the way he had with Kai.

When he returned home, he thought about the long day that was left to run through with no work and no worries. Fortunately, Bill Kellogg's job had added to his nest egg, and money wasn't a concern at the moment. All he was left with was time to relax and prepare for Robin's visit. Heidi even seemed laid back and uninterested in more than a quick pee in the back yard and a prompt return to her spot on the sofa next to the sunny window. As she led him back into the living room, she jumped on the sofa, turned around three times and settled herself into the cushion with an audible sigh and a dismissive look in his direction.

It was as he closed the sliding glass door in the living room that Kai thought of the stash of pills he had hidden in his dresser drawer. A day like that particular Friday was what Kai had in mind, when he'd saved his last hoard of painkillers rather than sensibly flushing them down the toilet. While he was going through days of detox and withdrawal, he'd resisted the call of the little brown bottle by telling himself he'd have some of the precious pills for special occasions, rather than doing them all up greedily and having no promise of a buzz to look forward to. He'd already talked himself out of treating himself while Robin was visiting, even though it was a holiday. He knew he might be able to fool his mother and Matt if he was high around them, but Robin knew him too well. He'd know in an instant if Kai was high and everything would seem like another lie.

In an instant, Kai smiled and strode to his bedroom. He took the bottle from its hiding place and tipped its contents onto his dresser top. Slowly, carefully, he counted the little spill of pills by two's. There were twenty-three pills left. For just a moment, the torments of withdrawal came back to him. The days of sickness and distracted longing returned, along with a sharp sense of something close to pain. But the feeling passed. He knew if he did a pill today, he wouldn't do up the rest in the days that followed; he had too much at stake in the week to come. But just now he had hours to kill all to himself before his mother and Matt returned home. Patiently, he dropped the pills one by one back into the bottle all but one. He put the cap back on the bottle and returned it to its hiding place before he picked up the little blue pill, quickly put it in his mouth, and crushed it with his back molars. Immediately, the bitter taste filled his mouth, but he swallowed quickly and knew soon he would be floating.

His three-week and three-day fast was broken now. He refused to feel concerned or disappointed in himself. Instead, he turned and walked to the kitchen and made himself a glass of water with a little bit of lemon juice, a dash of his mom's Midori from the liquor cabinet, and a lot of ice. With his cigarettes and ashtray thoughtfully arrayed at ten o'clock and his doctored up water at two o'clock, he opened the windows before he sat down and lit a cigarette. By the time it was done and stubbed out, he felt himself relax. All the ringing noise in his head, kept to a mere murmur by the Risperdal, disappeared. As the drug eased him toward the first rush of his buzz, his mind cleared for the first time in weeks and a precious calm stole over him. Kai smiled.

All he had to do now was think of something pleasant and his thoughts would take off on their own, floating like a butterfly alighting only on a subject or scene briefly before gliding on wherever it wanted as the day turned from morning to afternoon outside the bay window.

Kai's eyes locked on the view outside the window, but after a few moments of appreciating the familiar canal and backs of the houses and yards beyond, he saw nothing. He was looking inward with a force and clarity only the drug opened the door to. He stretched his back and felt it crack comfortably. The sense of overall ease was splendid.

"Oh Robin," he said out loud as his imagination drifted toward the airport on Sunday. Kai could feel himself driving slowly toward the terminal where Robin would be waiting. He could picture Robin standing with his bag, his eyes scanning the oncoming traffic for Kai's truck. Kai felt a visceral swelling in his chest as he imagined the rush of welcome that was to come. Then, just as swiftly, his mind moved on to another pleasant scene, and another, and another.

All the while, Kai felt blissful. His hiatus from the drug intensified its effects. As innately creative and imaginative as he was, the appeal of an opiate drug for Kai was instinctual. It allowed him to focus intently on the embroidery his mind was capable of. He could summon the most elaborately detailed plans and project himself into complex situations and emotions all originating and ending in the comfort of his own mind. When he was high, his mind became a comforting, secure place, free of the insistent nagging noise that its faulty synapses and broken electrical currents could generate. He felt transcendent and joyous, all the while simply sitting still and listening to the jazz station on the radio, with a glass of something to drink and an unending supply of cigarettes close by.

Rationally, Kai knew how dangerous the drug was. He knew he would stay high all of the time if it were possible. It was a rabbit hole he could easily slip into, as he had for nearly a year prior to that Friday. When he'd been using the most, he'd carefully dosed himself so that he could still work and function, yet always have the bliss at hand. Like most manic-depressive people, Kai's moods shifted in cycles, only his was a rare rapid cycling form of the disorder. Instead of high and low cycles alternating in weeks or months, Kai's moods cycled throughout the day. The year he'd spent on painkillers was the most stable he'd ever been in his life. Of course, his relationship with Robin had added the passion and the security that he'd never know with anyone else.

What had finally convinced Kai that he was indeed in love with Robin was the persistence and increase of his feelings for him after he had gone through withdrawal from the drug. It took that wrenching week of torment to prove to himself that what he felt for Robin was genuine. If his need for Robin and his preoccupation with him had diminished with the physical addiction to the drug, Robin would have taken his place along with a score of others Kai had merely slept with and moved on beyond over the years. But Robin remained ascendant even as Kai climbed down from his year-long binge on the drug.

Now, Kai was ready to believe he could have a future with someone else. The terrible loneliness and isolation he felt around other was eased by being close to someone he could communicate with nonverbally and in daily conversation. Kai was anxious to continue on that journey with Robin. He wanted to know if the worn familiarity of the coming years would lessen his delight in Robin's company. He had come to believe it wouldn't. He had finally made up his mind to be a human being and Robin was the reason. With the same inflexible determination with which he could simply dismiss others, he had decided to embrace Robin. From where he sat in his mother's kitchen that Friday, the future looked bright indeed.

Chapter Seventeen

THEIR DINNER had been consumed companionably, but quietly. After the weeks they had all spent together in close quarters, Matt, Maura, and Kai had grown comfortable both with each other's silences and with their garrulous times. Now, the time had come to have the discussion with Kai about moving into Matt's place in Lighthouse Point. Matt gave Maura a significant glance as she cleared away the dinner dishes. Maura suggested coffee to go with the pricey chocolate cake Matt had brought home from the bakery at Doris's Italian Market. Kai nodded agreeably and offered to make the coffee, but Maura placed her hand on his shoulder and urged him back into his seat as she set his cigarettes and ashtray on the table. He'd looked up at her with a grateful smile.

It was the smile that tugged at her heart. For all the worry he gave her, she knew Kai never was intentionally difficult. In fact, he had always been very grateful for her support and care. In a way, she felt she was betraying him by suggesting he move out now. He'd been careful to be on his best behavior since he'd appeared back in Sunrise. She knew what effort he'd put into not asking for any undue attention or making demands. She appreciated that effort. But she knew it was in his best interest, as well as in the best interest of her relationship with Matt, for him to move out on his own. And, to be perfectly honest, she felt as if she had fulfilled her maternal obligations. He'd come home in crisis, but he'd recovered sufficiently now to make some sure steps back out into the world.

"Kai, Matt has a proposition for you," she said as she spooned ground coffee into the coffeemaker's gold mesh filter. "We'd like you to seriously consider what he has to say." There, she'd said it. Without waiting for his response, she took the glass carafe to the faucet and filled it with water.

"Sure," Kai said agreeably. He flicked his cigarette against the side of his ashtray and looked at Matt expectantly.

Matt smiled at him, then earnestly leaned forward with his forearms resting on the table top and began, "You know I own an older house in Lighthouse Point, right?"

"Sure," Kai repeated. "Are you thinking about fixing it up? Maybe something I can do?"

"In a way," Matt said carefully. "Let me explain the circumstances, okay?"

Kai nodded innocently and took a hit off his cigarette before meeting Matt's level look across the table.

"After my divorce became final, I was looking for a place to live that could also serve as an investment. Ideally, I knew I'd want to build my own house in the future, but things were so unsettled in my personal and professional life at the time, I didn't want to tackle a project that big just then. I heard about this house from my CPA. His father was friends with the owners who were elderly and had decided to move back north to be closer to their daughter and grandkids. Long story short, I drove over and took a look at the place and bought it the next day."

"Wow," Kai said admiringly. "I guess it was built back in the sixties, right? Is it on the water?"

Matt's face had grown serious, but now he smiled. "Yes on both counts. It was built in the first wave of development, on a deep water lot. It has a dock, ocean access, the full deal. Back then it was a dream house. This couple retired early and moved down to live that Florida dream. They spent a little money decorating when they bought it and then didn't put a dime more than necessary into it for the next forty-odd years. When I bought it, it was like something in a time warp. I had a crew come in and rip out the kitchen, upgrade the electrical system, put in a new air conditioning system, refinish the terrazzo floors and paint it inside. Other than that, I didn't want to put any money into it because, to be honest, anybody else would buy the place as a teardown and replace it with a McMansion."

"I know, man. And that's a shame," Kai offered sincerely. "The whole tear-down thing was going on right as I moved up to the Banks a couple of years ago. Those old places had a lot of style, even though they were only three-bedroom, two-bath places."

"Well, those deep water lots are worth more than the houses on them," Maura interjected. "Anybody who's going to pay upwards from a million dollars for the place is going to want a modern house with a family room and the works."

"Your mom's right," Matt said. "But the thing was, I really just wanted a simple place for myself. I had a boat at the time that my wife didn't force me to sell in the divorce. I fixed the place up enough so I could live in it and have a dock. My intention all along has been to sell it eventually, but now the market's gone to shit . . ."

"But people with that kind of money are always around, aren't they?" Kai asked.

"It's not just the cost of the land and the construction of a new house," Maura said as she placed the chocolate cake on the table and sat down. "There are the taxes and insurance, which have gone through the roof. Matt and I know a couple who bought a teardown in Lighthouse Point, built a lovely new home on the lot and paid cash for everything. Still, they have a six thousand dollar nut every month to cover the taxes and insurance."

"Ouch," Kai said in disbelief. "Matt, is that what the place is costing you?"

"Not quite," Matt told him with a sly grin. "I bought the place before the market got so hot and that helps with taxes. And, since the house isn't worth what it would cost to rebuild it, I don't have any more insurance than necessary."

Kai nodded appreciatively and put out his cigarette. "So why are you telling me this?" he asked.

Maura stood to gather dessert plates and cutlery saying, "Hold on, hear him out, Kai."

"Well, the point of all this is that now is not a good time for me to get rid of the house in Lighthouse Point," Matt continued easily. "My life has changed in ways I couldn't have foreseen when I bought the place, thanks to your mom. When we started seeing each other, she had just gotten into redoing this house and I wanted to help her out. Now, two years down the road, we've got a baby on the way and your mom is happy here . . ."

"I really don't want to move right now, Kai," Maura said as she placed dessert plates and cutlery on the table. "In fact, I won't really be ready to move for awhile after the baby is born."

"I can understand that," Kai said. "But what does this have to do with me?"

"I'm getting to that," Matt said quietly but firmly. "What I'm proposing is you moving into my house. I don't like it standing vacant for long periods of time and I really need to be with your mother now. If you were to move into my place, you'd be doing me a favor and you'd have your own space."

"Wow," Kai exclaimed, stunned. "That's a fantastic offer, Matt. But there's no way I could afford to pay rent on a place in Lighthouse Point."

"No, you couldn't," Matt said pointedly. "But I'm not asking you to. What you can afford is paying the light bill and cable bill. And you could keep the yard up and do some things around the place, like power spray the roof, patio, and drive, routine maintenance things. I wouldn't charge you rent, but I would ask you for five hundred a month, which I'll put in savings for you. You agree to stay there for one year and we'll readdress the situation then. You'll have six thousand in savings to either get a place of your own, or if we decide to keep the arrangement for another year, you'll have that much more in savings. Meanwhile, you'll have your own place. Your mom and I can fix your room up for the baby and everybody's happy. What do you say?"

"I don't know what to say," Kai admitted honestly. He fumbled getting a cigarette from his pack and lit it distractedly as the notion took root in his mind.

Maura poured the coffee and brought their mugs to the table. As she busily got the half-and-half from the refrigerator and located the sweeteners everyone preferred, she said, "Matt and I want you to know, we're not unhappy having you here, but this seems like a good solution for everyone. It was Matt's idea, not mine. While I think he's being unreasonably generous, I agree with him that it's important for you to get on your feet and into your own place as soon as possible. You know you'll always have a home as long as I live, but to be fair to yourself, you need to do this."

"I hear what you're saying," Kai responded without any hint of resentment. "And I'm grateful, God knows. It's more than I deserve. Matt, is this being fair to you? I mean, damn. A house on the water in Lighthouse Point is a pretty nice option for a guy like me, at this stage in my life. I don't want you to think I'm taking advantage . . ."

"No way," Matt interrupted. "This was my idea, remember? I think it's a good idea for all of us. And in a way, it's doing me a lot of good as well. What do you say, Kai? Does it sound like something you'd like to do?"

"Hell yes," Kai said eagerly. "My only question is when do I get to move in? I mean I love you guys and everything, but the thought of having my own place is phenomenal."

Matt looked at Maura and smiled before he extended his hand across the table for Kai to shake. "Sounds like we have a deal, then."

Kai took his hand and grasped it firmly. "I really have to thank you, Matt. This is too much. I mean, I'll take good care of the place for you."

Matt returned his firm grip and then let go. Settling back into his seat, he looked at Kai and said, "I expect to see you by the fifth of every month with your rent. I'll set up a savings account for you first thing on Monday morning. Why don't you go ahead and give me December's rent this weekend and I'll use that to open the savings account. You've gotten paid for the work you've done at Bill Kellogg's place, right?"

"Absolutely," Kai said and started to stand. "I can give you cash right now."

"Not right now, just sometime before Monday morning," Matt said motioning him back into his seat. "As for moving in, why don't we drive over there tomorrow morning after breakfast and I'll show you the place. Then, as far as I'm concerned, you can move in right away."

"Mom?" Kai asked evenly. "Would that be cool with you?"

"Are you that anxious to get out of here?" Maura asked happily. She hadn't anticipated such an enthusiastic response from her son. Of course, she noted wryly, she was over-concerned about his possible negative response. It never occurred to her how anxiously he wanted to be on his own. "You'd move tomorrow?"

"Mom," Kai said solicitously. "You know I'll miss you, but damn . . . a place of my own? I'd leave right now, but Matt hasn't had his cake yet."

Matt chuckled and Maura sighed and shook her head. She picked up the cake knife she'd placed on the table and set about slicing the cake and dividing it between their plates. "I'm a little hurt," she said teasingly. "I never thought you'd be in such a terrible hurry to leave."

"Aww, Mom," Kai said with feigned anguish. "You know it's not like that."

"I know. I'm just playing with you. You'd be an idiot not to take Matt up on his offer. And I think you and I both owe the man a big thanks for doing this," Maura said only partly teasing this time.

"Enough," Matt said as Maura handed him his cake. "You're embarrassing me. Besides, as sudden as this is, we *are* family now."

"Yes. We are family," Kai said seriously. "And I do appreciate this, Matt. In more ways than you know. I really want Robin to move down here. Before you gave me this chance, I really didn't have much to offer him. Now at least I can give him a really nice place to move into."

For a moment, Matt paused and looked at the cake on his plate. Then he said, "I hadn't thought of that, but you're right, Kai. Good luck."

Kai looked stricken. He quickly said, "Matt, I'm sorry. I thought I'd mentioned asking Robin to move down here. I hope you don't think I'm taking advantage."

"No, of course not," Matt said quickly. "It just concerns me that you would have thought of bringing Robin down here before you did have a place of your own. Was he supposed to live here? With us?"

"Only for a week or so," Kai said sincerely. "Even if that. I mean, if he agrees to move down, he'll still have to give up his place up there and work out a notice and everything. I would have gotten us a place before he came down. I mean, I never would have asked Mom to put us both up. No. Of course not."

Knowing Kai would have thought nothing about moving his boyfriend into her house; Maura looked at Matt and let her lips turn up in a warning small smile. "Well, then this is a timely proposition. I just hope Robin is as enthusiastic about the notion as you are."

Matt caught her look and replied with the ghost of a nod. "I don't suppose you've considered going back up north to be with him, have you?"

Kai looked around uncomfortably and tentatively played with his slice of cake. "I have thought about it," he said finally. "But I don't want to move back up to the beach. Except for Robin, there's nothing there for me anymore. I mean, well . . . there's Dad and everything, but I can never be happy there. I want to live here."

Matt gave him a searching look and took another bite of his cake. He chewed thoughtfully for a moment before he swallowed and said, "You don't sound very flexible on the point."

"Christ," Kai said mournfully. "How can I be when everything down here is falling into place for me?"

Maura looked at him and laid her hand on his wrist. "You've said you believe Robin would want to move down. If he loves you, he'll see the sense of it. If he loved enough to let you leave, he probably loves you enough to follow you. I think he's just waiting for the invitation," she said soothingly.

"You know, Dr. Roth asked me what I would do if Robin didn't see the future progressing the way I do. I told him I didn't know. He told me I should consider that. I just know I can't go back to the beach. I can't think about what I'll do if Robin doesn't move down right now."

"Kai . . ." Maura began.

"No, Mom. Don't get all freaked out. I'm not going to get out the razor blades again," Kai said coldly. "I'll be alright, no matter what Robin decides. Of course, I won't be happy if he won't move down. But my head is fucked up enough without entertaining a lot of nega-tive thoughts. No matter what, I'll survive. I'm fucking awesome at just getting by." With that, he put down his fork, gathered up his cig-arettes and lighter and stood.

"Where are you going?" Maura demanded. "You haven't touched your cake."

Matt looked startled. He said, "Kai, I didn't mean to upset you . . ."

"No. No. No, you haven't upset me," Kai said immediately. "I'm just full, that's all. Mom, please just put some Saran Wrap over my cake. Maybe I'll eat it before I go to bed. I forgot I have to call Robin now. Would you guys please excuse me?"

"Kai, sit down and finish your cake," Matt said anxiously. "Let's talk about this. I know my advice isn't always great, but I'm a good listener. So's your mom."

"That's right, baby," Maura pleaded. "There's no need to get all lit up. We're just talking here. Robin won't mind if you call a little late."

Kai hesitated, sniffled, and wiped his nose with the back of his hand. He wavered for a moment, then sat back down. Heidi, confused and concerned at the sudden change of tone in the room, came to stand by Kai's seat, panting heavily. Absently, Kai reached to stroke her head, then, taking her long face between his palms, he bent to kiss the top of her head. "Sorry, Heidi. Good girl gets upset by her crazy daddy."

Heidi licked his face, then backed up two steps and promptly barked.

"Heidi wants a cookie?" Maura said and stood to make her way to the bowl on the counter. Heidi looked from her master to his mother and barked in confusion once more. She turned her head at the ringing tone the porcelain lid made coming off the bowl and sat down in expectation of her treat.

Maura praised her for sitting obediently and gave the dog her cookie before sitting down at the table once more. She watched as Kai nervously lit a cigarette before she said, "Kai, settle down. You're getting yourself into panic mode for no real reason. Robin loves you."

"Yeah? How do you know?" Kai asked miserably.

"Because he told me himself," Maura said gently.

"When did *you* talk to Robin?" Kai asked dejectedly.

"Actually, he called me at the office yesterday morning," Maura said calmly. "He didn't want me to say anything to you. He was concerned that I might not be entirely comfortable with him coming for Thanksgiving. He wanted to give me a chance to reassure him it was okay."

Kai snickered bitterly and said, "That sounds just like him. He wants everybody to be happy and feel good about everything all the time."

"No, he's just been well brought up," Maura countered evenly.

"So, what did he have to say?" Kai said before taking a deep hit off his cigarette and compulsively flicking away the ash.

"Not that much, really. We didn't talk long. But he did say specifically he wanted me to know that he was in love with you and he cared about you very much," Maura repeated.

"Yeah? Well, I *care* about Heidi," Kai said peevishly.

"Kai, the boy admitted he was in love with you, to me, your mother. I think that takes a fair amount of conviction, don't you?" Maura asked reasonably.

"Man, that's tough," Matt interjected. "I think he has guts to just be so up front about it to your mother, who he hasn't even met."

Kai sat silently for a moment, and then nodded agreeably. Finally he said, "Why does loving somebody have to hurt like this?"

Matt glanced at Maura who gave him a significant look in return before she said, "Kai. Being in love brings some pretty intense emotions. What you're feeling right now is what most people feel for the first time when they're fourteen or so. You never went through this as a kid, but everybody has to go through it at least once. You need to buck up. What you're feeling is perfectly natural. The apprehension, the anxiety, the loneliness and uncertainty, those are very adolescent responses to being in love."

"So, I'm retarded is what you're saying," Kai replied sullenly.

"I don't think that's what your mother is saying at all, Kai," Matt said calmly. "What she's trying to tell you is to not to be so hard on yourself."

Kai nodded and said, "Nobody beats me up better than I do. I'm sorry for being so fucked up."

"You aren't fucked up," Matt said and laughed gently. "No more than anybody else in love. It kind of sucks, doesn't it?"

"Yeah," Kai replied and grinned despite himself. "It kind of does suck."

"Well, it won't forever," Maura said firmly. "Long-distance relationships are a bitch to begin with, and it's not like you don't have other things on your plate."

"Like more work," Kai said evenly.

"More work?" Matt asked curiously.

"For who?" Maura demanded.

Kai took another hit off his cigarette and looked at his mother. "I got a call this afternoon from this interior designer that I met with. Her name is Rachel Weiss. She does a lot of high-end work on the east side. She has a project in old Boca that's all about redoing a formal dining room. She wants me go with her to take a look at it on Tuesday. She wants pilasters and boiseries and shit. It sounds pretty intense."

"That's fantastic, Kai," Matt said heartily. "Challenging, creative, what more could you ask for? I've heard of Rachel Weiss. She did some work for a guy who used to work for me. His wife spent a fortune on their house after we finished building it. I remember the guy bitching about the hundred-dollar-a-yard fabrics."

"Did it look nice when she finished?" Maura asked, eager to take the conversation in this new, positive direction.

"Yeah, really high-end. They had a big party to celebrate when it was all finished. My ex got some wild ideas about doing the same thing," Matt said.

"I told her I'd be happy to go up there with her," Kai told them eagerly. "It's the kind of thing I'd like to get a reputation for doing really well. Now, with my own place, a garage and shit, I'll have a place to do some work off-site if I need to. Staining and priming, shit like that."

"Look, Kai. You were right, things down here are going well for you. You have every reason to believe everything's going to work out for a change," Matt said confidently.

"You see?" Maura seconded. "I bet you Robin spends Christmas moving to Lighthouse Point."

Kai gave her a tight smile and picked up his fork. After a moment, he looked at Matt and said, "This cake is pretty fucking awesome."

"Isn't it? Maura, how about cutting me another piece? I feel like splurging a little," Matt said happily.

Maura picked up his cake plate and held it while she sliced another piece of the chocolate treat. Expertly, she maneuvered the slice onto the plate single-handedly and set it back down before him. She knew Kai was a bit volatile, but overall, his anxiety was more about the possibility of moving out than about Robin. With Kai, nothing was as it seemed. She knew life was throwing a lot of good things at him and that was as disconcerting as a run of bad luck could be in Kai's case. But he could handle it, moving out and moving on. For the first time in weeks, she knew that for sure.

"Kai, I'm going to ask you a question and I want you to think about your answer," Matt said carefully.

Kai swallowed a forkful of cake and said, "Okay. Shoot."

"I know we've really only known each other for a short amount of time," Matt began thoughtfully. "I admit, I was a little wary of you and how you'd react to my relationship with your mother—"

"I was worried you'd think I was a total fuck up," Kai admitted with a smile. "I mean, just showing up and moving in on you guys. So don't feel bad about wondering how I'd act about you and Mom. I've had a chance to get to know you over the past few weeks and I can see how much you love her. I want you to know I have no problem with you, or you and Mom, or whatever."

Matt smiled and nodded as he said, "I appreciate that, Kai. I really do. And I want you to know I don't think you're a fuck up at all. I've never had any experience with anyone with your set of circumstances, so I suppose I've been watching you a little. But you've shown me you really are trying to get your life together down here. That's why I'm so willing to do what I can to help you."

"And I appreciate that, Matt. I really do," Kai said sincerely.

Matt once again nodded understandingly before he shifted in his seat uncomfortably and said, "I just want you to understand the spirit of my question then."

Kai looked at his mother's lover warily and said, "Okay. Go on."

"I am a little concerned about your relationship with Robin. It's not that I have any objections to it, I don't. That's not the issue." Matt said plainly. "What's making me nervous giving me agita is wondering how you'll react if things go south with you two. I have to ask you, do you feel stable enough to take whatever his answer is? I mean, I'm a little concerned you might pack up and take off or something. And to be frank, your mother doesn't need the stress, especially in her condition. Can you tell me you feel good enough to really make a commitment to moving ahead with your future down here, alone if necessary?"

Kai put down his fork and compulsively reached for his pack of cigarettes. In the silence following Matt's concern, he took his time getting the cigarette lit and inhaling a long hit, then let it go. When he spoke, it was with a high degree of confidence. "Matt, I don't have a crystal ball. But I can tell you I'm making every effort to stay level. I'm taking my meds. I'm actively pursuing work. Now, thanks to you, I'm going to move out and take some responsibility for living on my own. All I can say is, I understand how much Mom's needs right now outweigh mine. I will promise you I'll keep that in mind before I do anything that seems like it might be irrational."

Maura watched this exchange between the two men in her life dispassionately. Each was demonstrating to her their individual strengths. She felt proud of both of them, but held her tongue. She didn't want to interject anything. This conversation was between the two of them.

Matt raised his hands and opened them in a gesture of acquiescence. "That's as good a reply as I'd hoped for, Kai," he said gently. "I'm not your father, so you really don't have anything to prove to me. But as your friend, I hope you'll talk to me if you feel like bouncing off the walls, or packing up and taking off. Could you consider me that kind of friend?"

"I'd like that, very much," Kai said humbly. "I'm not the greatest person in the world for a friend. I'm moody and selfish. I'm difficult in a lot of ways. But what I'm not is a child anymore. And I really want to . . . I don't know . . . ," Kai said and hesitated, searching for the right words. "I want to be the kind of person you'd like to have as a friend."

Matt looked at him and smiled. "You already are."

Kai nodded and took another nervous hit off his cigarette before meeting Matt's eyes and nodding once more. Finally, he said, "Cool. Thanks."

Maura let the moment spool itself out before she said brightly, "You're going to really like Matt's house. It's a little Spartan, but the furniture he has there is really nice. He chose the best pieces from some of his model homes, and you know how much effort builders put into the décor of those McMansions."

"Oh it's not that great," Matt said dismissively. "Like I told you, Kai, it's really just a place for me to sleep. I don't even think there's any art on the walls."

"I can fix that," Kai said confidently. "All I need is a trip to Pearl's Art Supply store and a little time. I've been wanting to paint. God, it's going to be so nice to have the space to do that again."

"What would you do paintings of?" Matt asked curiously. "Your Mom's showed me some of your old sketch books. I had no idea you could draw so well."

As Kai answered, Maura cut herself another sliver of chocolate cake, telling herself it was for the baby. Remarkably, after the tension that had passed over their heads like sudden rain clouds, the atmosphere in the kitchen was quite clear and relaxed. She licked the icing off her fingers and picked up her fork, thinking how so much of her stress was self-made. Kai was stronger than she thought. He always had been.

For the moment, at least, she could turn her attention to the tiny lit-tle boy growing inside her. "Have some cake, Junebug," she thought. "I can't wait for you to get here. There're so many things I want to share with you." Happily, she savored the taste of the dark, rich choco-late and smiled privately. It was the baby she wanted to focus on now. She was starting to feel like she could.

Chapter Eighteen

VERY EARLY ON Wednesday morning, Heidi woke him by
jumping off the bed and trotting across the bedroom to the sliding
glass doors that looked out over the patio to the water beyond. She
whined sharply and waited for him to respond. Groggily, he looked
first at the digital clock in the trim little stereo that lived on the bed-
side table. It wasn't yet six, but this close to the ocean, the sky outside had already begun to divide from the water. Heidi's sleek gray
fur was luminous in the meager light, making her a sketch in the room.
She whined once more, and rather than risk the dog waking Robin,
Kai threw off the sheet and stood quickly. Heidi responded by taking
off for the kitchen at the other end of the house.

Naked, Kai followed her to the sliding glass doors in the kitchen
and let her out into the dawn. Matt's backyard was bordered by both
a chain-link fence and a ficus hedge to camouflage it, so Kai had no fears
of his dog wandering off if left alone to take care of her pressing need
to relieve herself. Sleepily, he turned on the bank of lights under the
cabinets and started coffee. By the time it started to brew, Heidi presented herself back inside, ready for her breakfast. Kai picked up her
stainless steel bowl and let himself into the garage by the door in the
kitchen. He kept the large bag of dry dog food in the garage to prevent
roaches from finding it in the kitchen. As he put her customary cupful
of food into the bowl, he thought of how his orderly routine had as-
serted itself in Matt's house. It felt good.

He returned to the kitchen with an expectant Heidi on his heels and let a little water spill over her food from the tap. He swirled it a few times to make a thin gravy before setting the bowl on the floor by the door. While Heidi munched away happily, Kai found his cigarettes next to the coffeemaker and lit the first one of the day. Easy in his nakedness, he made his way around the counter to the small table by the sliding glass doors and sat comfortably in one of the cushioned wicker chairs.

For the moment, he appreciated being alone. Robin had been there for three days, and now, the day before Thanksgiving, they had grown used to each other again. It all seemed so easy and comfortable, almost from the time Robin had climbed into his truck after getting off the plane. At first, they had been a little wary of each other. Robin hadn't said anything, but his own hurt had held him at a remove as Kai's natural reserve had held him. It was only after they'd come straight to Matt's house and Kai showed him around that the strangeness between them began to dissipate.

Robin was impressed by the house. True to his mother's description, it was Spartan. But the pieces of furniture Matt had selected from his model homes were uniformly contemporary, comfortable and nice. That the soft, personable furniture had sat in impersonal rooms of bare white walls and shiny, pale terrazzo floors didn't bother Matt. Kai pointedly told Robin how much nicer it would look with Robin's collection of Oriental rugs on the floors, but other than that, he didn't bring up anything more on the subject of Robin's moving down. Kai had only given a few other hints in that direction over the days they'd spent together—days spent talking and making love in every room of the house. For those few days, it was as if they had met in some fabulous bungalow in a private resort.

They hadn't left the house since Robin had arrived, except to take Heidi for walks around the neighborhood. While there were many things to do and see, especially on Robin's first trip to Florida, neither of them wanted to move from the safe haven of Matt's house. And there really was no reason for them to. Kai had stocked the house with groceries for the meals he knew Robin enjoyed. With Bill Kellogg's tip of a hundred dollars and another hundred of his own, Kai had gone to a wine store and carefully selected bottles of effervescent prosecco and peppery shiraz, rich cabernets and sunny chardonnays. They had spent their days drinking wine and eating when the mood struck them between bouts of lovemaking that were in turn thoughtful and passionate.

This morning, Kai felt both sated and sensually alive. It was as if the weeks and months that had gone before were a desert, and he'd now brought Robin to an oasis of sensual calm. His anxiety and confusion before he left the Outer Banks had unfolded into a tight corridor of recovery and overcoming once he'd arrived back in Florida. Now, he felt like he was pleasantly moored between a harsh chill sea and a sunny sail over warmer waters. Robin's visit had been so right, so timely, that Kai almost felt as he did when he took the painkillers he loved. However, the brown plastic bottle had moved unopened from the chest of drawers at this mother's house to the one in Matt's. Kai hadn't treated himself since the day he'd come home from Dr. Roth's office chasing the idea that Robin could refuse to join him in the world he was making for himself.

The coffeemaker let out a plaintive beep. Kai put out his cigarette and strolled around the counter once more to make himself a cup. Heidi, finished with her breakfast, walked to the counter that held the Blue Willow bowl from Maura's kitchen containing her cookies. Kai opened the old lid and picked up a treat. She took it from his fingers gently and then proceeded to chew it while looking up at him gratefully. Kai spontaneously leaned over and kissed the top of his dog's head. She seemed happy in her new home, adjusting quickly by finding the best places to catch a snooze in the sun at different times of day.

Kai replaced the lid on the Blue Willow bowl and looked at it contentedly. Maura had offered it to him as a token of continuity from one home to another. Kai had accepted it gratefully. It was a happy tie to his past, one without the sting of memory that so many other things from his childhood brought him. He actually had so few possessions of his own that he treasured his mother's gift. In reality, this was his first home. Since he'd left his mother's house at eighteen, he'd always lived in others' houses. While Matt's place wasn't exactly his, he felt a connection to it as if it was.

His first day there, he'd rearranged the few pieces of furniture to suit himself. He really had everything he needed in terms of housewares and accessories. While it might have been Matt's crash pad, Matt hadn't spared himself any necessities or a man's favorite toys. There was a Yamaha stereo system and a fifty-inch plasma screen television mounted to a wall in the living room, and a smaller version of the same television on the wall of the master bedroom. Kai appreciated the amenities, without a doubt, but he wanted to make his own mark on the house so he had gone to the art supply store as he'd told Matt he might.

In a fit of creativity, he'd first painted a four foot by six foot painting of Heidi standing on the lot's seawall framed by the bright reach of water and sky beyond. That painting done, he rifled through his sketch book and came up with the idea of painting a grid of nine, sixteen-inch square paintings, each a portrait of Robin in a different mood. He'd managed to find time to make simple frames from 1 x 4's and cove molding for them all, which he then gilded with gold leaf, and had mounted on the walls by the time Robin arrived. The portrait of Heidi had pride of place on the wall in the dining area, while those of Robin dominated a wall in the living room.

When he first arrived at the house that day, Robin hadn't noticed his portraits right away. He was too enthralled by the view of the water from the bank of sliding glass doors on the living room's back wall. Robin had left Kai with his suitcase at the front door and walked immediately to the opposite side of the room to stand and peer out. It was a nice view. There were a cluster of mature coconut palms on each corner of the lot book-ending the dock that lay directly opposite the doors. Kai had wordlessly walked on to the bedroom with Robin's suitcase, letting the house do its own selling.

It wasn't until late that afternoon that Kai had found Robin in front of the bank of his portraits in the living room. They had been sitting outside on the patio drinking wine when Robin had excused himself to go inside to visit the bathroom. When he hadn't come back out in several minutes, Kai went in looking for him. Robin stood before the nine versions of himself with tears in his eyes. When Kai walked up behind him and laid his hand on his shoulder it startled Robin. He awkwardly wiped at his eyes as Kai explained his technique and new style of painting exhibited in the portraits, which were indeed looser and less photorealistic than most of his earlier work.

Again, Kai left the opportunity to sell the idea of Robin moving down. He simply explained the work from a technical viewpoint and let the obvious emotions of the pieces speak for themselves. Robin's response had been muted, but Kai knew he was deeply moved.

Now, in the pre-dawn hours of Wenseday morning, as he made his coffee, Kai savored that moment again. Once his coffee was doctored the way he liked it, he returned to the table and lit another cigarette. There was another painting Robin hadn't seen. Kai had worked on it last. In the bare bedroom on the opposite side of the house from the master bedroom, he had set up his studio. He'd splurged on a nice easel on casters and went to a restaurant salvage company to purchase a stainless steel commercial kitchen prep table large enough to hold all the various brushes, palettes, and tubes of paint he bought new and found stored at his mother's house. Laboring alone there for a late couple of nights, he stared into the cheap dressing mirror he picked up at Kmart and transferred the image of himself, dressed in only a pair of baggy cargo shorts, onto a twenty-four by thirty-six inch canvas. Working quickly in acrylics, he did it in the same new style as the one he'd used for the portraits of Robin. He'd framed it along with the rest. It waited now, hidden in the closet in his bedroom studio to make its own case as a reason for Robin to move down. Regardless, the painting was Robin's. Kai couldn't have cared less for a self-portrait. But, if Robin did move down, it would look good in the living room near his own portraits. If he didn't, Kai intended it as a continuing argument on his behalf in Robin's house in Wrights Shores.

Kai sipped his coffee and smiled at the thought of showing the portrait to Robin. As he pondered the power of his work's ability to move Robin eight hundred miles south, Heidi appeared in the kitchen with something in her mouth. She was a mischievous dog, never more so than in the early mornings when she was full of energy and good humor. Quietly, Kai called her, coaxing her closer so he could take away whatever she'd found to play keep away with. Eyeing him warily, Heidi walked toward him hesitantly. When she came to within arm's reach, she quickly bounded away and placed the bit of cloth on the kitchen floor, daring him to come after it.

Kai smiled. The dog had come close enough for him to ascertain she had sneaked back into the master bedroom and retrieved Robin's boxer shorts from the floor where they'd gotten tossed the night before. Kai decided to ignore her. He knew he could get up and bribe the underpants away from her with a cookie, but she'd only make another trip to the bedroom to find another errant item of clothing to repeat the process with. When Kai remained motionless, Heidi bent her head quickly and snatched the boxers from the floor where she'd dropped them in hopes of getting Kai to play her favorite game. Seeing he was unwilling to play, she held her head high and took off out of the kitchen at a trot, daring him to follow.

Kai smiled and looked out over the pink streaks of dawn painted on the water outside. Matt's house was an enchanting place to live.

He felt lucky knowing his residence here would last a year at least. But he knew his tenure here would leave him spoiled. It would take him many years to be able to afford to live in this neighborhood on his own. But for the next twelve months, he'd enjoy every minute of living like a millionaire.

He looked up to find Robin standing naked at the kitchen counter taking a cookie from the old Blue Willow bowl. "Come here, you sneaky hussy," he said to Heidi, who'd slunk in after Robin. Warily, she made her way to stand in front of him, his underwear still clasped in her mouth. Robin extended the cookie with one hand and reached for his boxers with the other. Heidi eyed the treat and decided to make the trade. She dropped the boxers into Robin's waiting hand and took the cookie from his other hand.

Robin bunched the underwear in his hands and looked up at Kai with exasperation. "They're wet. Dog slobber," he said in a scratchy, early morning voice still rough with sleep.

"Leave them off," Kai suggested. "You look better with your clothes off anyway."

Robin shrugged and turned his back to Kai to drape the boxers over the handle of the oven door to dry. Kai watched him find a coffee mug for himself and fill it from the pot. He strolled to the refrigerator and took out a carton of half-and-half before returning to his cup to pour. Kai enjoyed following his neat movements and sighed with the simple satisfaction of knowing the flesh standing in the kitchen was his. He knew he possessed it utterly and that gave him a profound sense of confidence.

Ignoring Kai's frank stare, Robin came to the table and sat down opposite him. He raised his eyes to return Kai's look as he sipped his coffee and smiled fetchingly. "Good morning," he said evenly.

Kai jerked his chin toward the sliding glass doors at the end of the table and said, "Look at that sunrise. Isn't it incredible?"

"Hmmm," Robin murmured appreciatively. "I could get used to waking up like this."

Kai nodded and put out his cigarette before lighting another one. He blew away the smoke and looked at Robin with a half smile on his face. When Robin returned his smile, he said, "You can get used to it, if you want to. There's every reason for you to just stay here."

Robin sipped his coffee thoughtfully and nodded. "I was wondering when you'd bring it up. You haven't pressured me, but I know that's what you want."

Kai didn't answer him. Instead he stood, seductively revealing the long bare length of his body across the table before he picked up his cup, stuck his cigarette between his lips and walked back to the kitchen to refill his mug.

Robin turned to watch him walk away but turned his attention back to his own mug of coffee before Kai could look his way again. Absently, he took Kai's pack of cigarettes and lit one for himself. He sat smoking in silence until Kai returned to the table and eased his lanky form back into his seat. Finally, Robin said, "You make it hard to go home. And face it Kai, home for me is up on the Banks."

"It is now," Kai said evenly. "But in the amount of time it would take to work a notice and roll up those rugs of yours, you could be down here with me. Look at this place. Look at me. We're waiting for you and nobody else, Robin. What do I have to do to convince you?"

Robin sipped his coffee and mimicked Kai with a decisive flick of his cigarette. "What if I move down here and six months later you decide you want a girlfriend, Kai? It's happened before. I don't think I could take it again, especially if I've rearranged my whole life to be with you."

Kai regarded him levelly, and said, "I know you don't have any reason to trust me. I know I've fucked up in the past. But I'm not that guy anymore, Robin."

"Really?" Robin asked warily.

"No. I'm not," Kai said with certainty and reached across the table to take Robin's forearm in his grasp. "I've been fighting . . . I've been going over this again and again in my mind ever since I left the Banks. Down here things are different. Down here we can make any kind of life we want for ourselves."

Robin looked at Kai's hand on his arm pointedly and Kai reluctantly let him go. He looked at Robin pleadingly and Robin responded, "You don't know how much I want to believe you. I know I'm crazy for even considering it. Goddamn it, Kai. You know what this means to me. I just don't know if you mean it now, and I'm afriad you'll take it all back just when I'm feeling safe again."

"Robin, I love you." Kai said in frustration. "Haven't I shown you every way I know how these past few days? How about the weeks we've been apart? Every goddamned day, I've called you and told you how I feel. You think you don't feel safe? What about me? I've been happier with you since Sunday afternoon when you got here than I have been ever since I met you. Nearly losing you showed me just how much I want and need you in my life. I don't have any way to prove that to you other than to show you. I swear to God, give me this chance and I'll prove it to you that I'm in this for the long haul this time."

Robin looked away and took a long drag off his diminishing cigarette. He looked out the window and stared out at the water without saying anything for several long minutes—minutes Kai filled by smoking and staring out the window along with him.

Finally, Robin turned away from the view and stubbed out his cigarette. He met Kai's eyes and said, "How long did you say you have this place for?"

Kai looked at him searchingly, then said, "Matt told me our deal was for a year. That's how long he wanted me to commit. Then, he said he might be open to me staying on another year after that. It depends on how the market rebounds out of this slump. In any event, he asked me for a year's commitment."

Robin nodded and sighed. "I haven't told you yet, but your timing is good for convincing me to make a change. My boss cut my draw against commissions starting December first. It actually won't be enough to live off of and I'll have to go into my savings to get through the winter."

"That sucks," Kai said sympathetically.

Robin looked at him coldly for a flash of a second and then his eyes and mouth softened. He drummed his fingers on the table absently and sighed once more.

"What are you thinking, baby?" Kai pleaded quietly.

Robin cocked his head and said, "I'm thinking sometimes you have to invest in yourself and take a chance on getting it right. I moved to Kill Devil Hills on a whim, did you know that? I came down to stay in that house for a week and ended up staying for a year and a half now. And I did pretty well just by following my instincts. I sold a lot of real estate. I've got nearly ninety thousand dollars in savings thanks to selling beach houses. And I met and fell in love with a big, crazy asshole who strolled in and changed my life once, and now again, I guess."

"What are you saying?" Kai asked warily.

"I'm saying yes," Robin said quietly. "God help us."

"Really?" Kai asked carefully.

"Yeah, really," Robin replied without a smile.

"When?" Kai demanded.

"As soon as possible, I suppose." Robin admitted. "I don't owe that bastard at work anything. I'll give up my security deposit on the house; it'll actually save me money not sticking around during December. I'd say I'll be back by the fifth of next month. I want to spend a few days with my mom and dad before I move down."

Kai reached across the table once more and put his hand on the back of Robin's neck and pulled him toward him. Leaning across the table to meet his lips, he kissed Robin before leaning his forehead to rest on his lover's. "You won't be sorry, I swear," he said gruffly.

"We'll see," Robin said tonelessly. "We'll see."

Kai kissed him once more and then leaned back in his chair, looking at Robin with a serious mien. "I want you to be as excited about this as I am, Robin. You sound like I'm luring you down here only to shit on you."

Robin sighed and ran his fingers through his lank blonde hair to clear it away from his eyes. He gave Kai a shy smile and said, "Why don't you tell me how you see things unfolding once I get down here, then? I want to hear your plans for the future. From the hints you've given me, and things you've told me, it does seem like you've been spending a lot of time thinking."

Kai nodded seriously and took a sip of his coffee before putting out his cigarette. "To tell you the truth, I've mostly been thinking about getting you down here. I was scared you wouldn't say yes."

"Really?" Robin asked openly. "All I really wanted was an invitation."

Kai laughed and said, "That's what Mom told me. I don't know. I was just concerned I'd pushed you too far, acting the way I did the last few months we were together. I honestly didn't know what you'd do if I asked you to marry me. And, in a way, that's the level of commitment I'm thinking about, here. Do you want to be married to me?"

"God yes," Robin replied decisively. "I mean, I really want to be with you. It's more than the sex . . ."

"Though the sex is pretty fucking awesome, wouldn't you say?" Kai teased him with a hint of insecurity lurking amid the light tone.

"Shut up," Robin said easily. "You should know better than to even have to ask about that part of us together. I never thought it would keep on getting better and better. But it's more than that. When I'm with you, I feel whole, you know? In a way, being with you is like being alone only amplified and better somehow. Am I making any sense?"

"That's exactly the way I feel about you," Kai admitted. "You know, even from the time I was little, I didn't feel like there was any-body who got me. Like, really saw me, not just reacted to the way I was on the outside. That Kai is just a big front. Until I met you, I was doing alright, but I was lonely in a way I can't describe. I was just this ghost, you know? Even I didn't think I was real half the time. I looked at myself the way other people watch television. Just being me was hurting all the time or being so empty it was like having a whistling wind and a mile of railroad tracks for a heart. Then I met you. Every-thing was so different. Can you blame me for wanting that all the time?"

Robin shook his head, stunned by the admission Kai had made. It was unusual for him to be so forthcoming about himself. Robin knew some of the demons that had chased Kai since he was small, but he didn't know the full extent of them. Kai had given him a glimpse of the emptiness he lived with and it made Robin's heart ache for him. "Well, you don't ever have to be lonely anymore. I'm going to be on you like white on rice," Robin said. "If I make this commitment, you better be prepared for the full deal, is all I can say. Once you got me, you got me for life."

Kai stared across the table at him for a moment before he said, "I just can't understand why someone as beautiful as you are would want me. I mean, you have your shit together. You're smart. You're success-ful. What do you see in somebody as fucked up as I am?"

"I don't see you as fucked up at all," Robin told him confidently. "I know how your head makes you act crazy sometimes, but that doesn't scare me. You don't scare me at all, now."

Kai laughed and said, "I did at first though, right?"

Robin snorted, "Damn right. Somehow I knew, before the first time we slept together, I was in for a world of hurt. There was just some-thing about you that was dangerous—it was like I was telling myself, 'be careful what you ask for.'"

"You got all that on the first date?" Kai asked incredulously.

"Absolutely. I told you. Remember?" Robin said quietly.

"Yeah, you did. I was thinking about that a few weeks ago, actually," Kai admitted. "When I first saw you, I wasn't thinking about anything other than getting you into bed."

"I know," Robin said with a smile. "You were pretty intense."

"Yeah, intense. That's my deal. I don't do anything half-assed. That's why you should be excited about moving down here. I mean, damn, Robin. Look at what I got us as a place to live. You just stick with me. Things are going to be great, I swear," Kai said seriously.

Robin stood and walked across the kitchen to make himself another cup of coffee. He ignored Kai's watchful stare all the while and finally returned to the table saying, "It'll probably take me awhile to find a job. Are you going to making enough to support us? I don't want to spend any more of my savings than I have to, you know, for car payments and insurance. I want to use that money to put down on a house someday."

Kai tilted his chair back and scratched his chest thoughtfully. "I have a great new job lined up. It's going to bring in about five grand. If we don't go crazy, we'll be alright."

"And your little pill problem is totally under control?" Robin asked pointedly.

"Let me ask you, for one minute, or one second, since you've been here, have I appeared high to you?" Kai asked in a hurt tone.

Robin shook his head and said, "No. And your dick doesn't lie. If you were high you wouldn't have been hard like you have been. Christ, does it ever go down?"

Kai laughed and leaned forward on his forearms. "It would be worse if I wasn't on so much psych medication. I'm a stud. You know that better than anybody."

Robin snickered and gave him a certain shared look of intimacy. Then he took a sip of his coffee thoughtfully. He looked at Kai and said firmly, "I want you to swear you're going to stay on your psych drugs.

If you go off them, you can kiss my ass goodbye. That's a non-negotiable term for my moving in with you. Can you swear that?"

Kai lit another cigarette and eyed Robin all the while. He didn't want to lie, but he wasn't sure he could promise that. His relationship with his meds was far longer and older than his relationship with Robin. He knew the facts of his existence. He knew he'd have to be on something as long as he lived. He just hated admitting it to anyone, even Robin. Finally he said, "I promise I won't do anything that will jeopardize my commitment to you. If going off my meds means I'm going to fuck up this thing between us, I swear I won't do it."

Robin looked at him searchingly before he looked away and took another sip of his warm coffee. At last, he nodded. "Okay. I can accept that. But I warn you. If you fuck around on me one more time, and I find out, I'll be gone so fast you'll never see me moving. This is your last chance on that. Do you understand me?"

Kai nodded and took a hit off his cigarette. "Understood," was all he said.

"Good. Because I'm serious, Kai. Guy or girl, I won't play second anymore. You better think before you answer because you're staking everything on living up to it," Robin said firmly.

"Yes. I get it," Kai said peevishly. "Christ, no need to nail it to my forehead."

Robin watched him as he smoked nervously and wouldn't meet his eyes. When the silence finally became loud, Kai did look at him and Robin returned his look levely.

Robin's look was all Kai needed to convince him of the seriousness of his intent. To answer, he reached across the table and gently stroked Robin's cheek with the back of his fingers without breaking his gaze into his eyes. He prayed the earnestness of his own gaze would convince Robin that he got the message.

Robin responded to his caress by closing his eyes and leaning in to his touch. Kai watched his face as it moved from remembered pain, to resolve, to simple surrender. For the first time he felt the weight of responsibility he had for Robin. Just as forcefully as the knowledge of his total possession of Robin's flesh came the fact of his ability to inflict pain on the one he loved. It was the first time in his life that he saw something as an adult. It humbled Kai and strengthened him in a way that was more real than his ability to provide pleasure. That physical act of love was easily accomplished. Living up to this new responsibility for another person would come hard. And he accepted it as fact. "We're going to be fine, Robin, you and I. I'll take care of you, I swear," he whispered.

Robin lifted his head and gave him a small smile. There was a hint of disbelief in his eyes that Kai knew only time would eradicate. Knowing it would take time and more time spent proving himself, Kai thought how he bitterly resented his nature for making that a necessity. Still, he felt up to the commitment. He had changed in the weeks since he'd come back home. He felt this new strength and purpose rising in him like some strong sap. Kai had accepted his faults and made a serious effort to conform to others' expectations of him, something he'd never cared to do before. He returned Robin's shy smile with a genuine one of his own and said, "Welcome home, Robin."

Chapter Nineteen

A FEELING OF holiday permissiveness pervaded the office from the beginning of the day and Maura was not immune. Though there was work that deserved her attention, she found it hard to care. In the back of everyone's mind was the knowledge that Bill Kellogg would make a relaxed round of the offices, cubicles, and the drafting bullpen at about two-thirty, cheerfully telling everyone to pack it in, that the office was closing early. After all, the next day was Thanksgiving and everyone had someplace to be or something to be done. Bill had long endeared himself to Maura for this tradition of his. She teased him, calling him Old Fezziwig after the benevolent boss in Dickens' *A Christmas Carol*.

True to form, Bill appeared at Maura's office door as she was finishing up a discussion of revisions to a set of construction drawings with a junior draftsman. "You guys button it up," Bill told them at two-forty that afternoon. "I'm kicking everyone out at three today. There are turkeys waiting to be cooked and cans of cranberry sauce to be opened," he announced cheerfully.

As Maura's young drafter excused himself; Bill came into Maura's office and settled into one of the chairs opposite her desk. "And what are your plans, Maura? Are you going to be cooking for Matt, Kai, and Kai's friend . . . what's his name? Robbie?"

"No, it's Robin," Maura corrected him good-naturedly as she sat at her desk across from him. "And no, I'm not cooking. Kai has taken the whole epic fest on himself."

"Ah, that's good," Bill said, smiling. "You've said he was a good cook. Is he up to fulfilling the expectations everyone brings to Thanksgiving?"

"Probably better than I am," Maura said. "We're having a small free-range turkey he ordered from Williams Sonoma, stuffed with lemons and onions, with oyster dressing, corn cooked with baby lima beans, Brussels sprouts braised with bacon, rice, and giblet gravy. I'm pretty sure that's what he told me."

"Sounds good," Bill said admiringly. "Is he doing the desserts as well?"

"No, that's on me," Maura said easily. "I always make my grand-mother's recipe for pecan pie. It's a southern thing. What about you? What are you doing this year?"

Bill's face clouded momentarily but he said cheerfully enough, "I'll probably make myself a grilled cheese sandwich and open a can of tomato soup. This is my first year without . . . ," he winced sharply re-calling his loss, then continued. "This year won't be anything special. I plan to spend the day getting moved into my new library and drink-ing a nice old Scotch I've been saving."

"Oh Bill, I hate to hear you're going to be alone," Maura said with concern. "Why don't you join us? We're going to have the big dinner at Matt's place in Lighthouse Point. Kai moved in there a couple of weeks ago. We can sit outside and enjoy the view while Kai takes care of cooking."

"Sounds tempting," Bill admitted. "I've turned down all my other invitations, but now that the day's almost here, I'm not so sure I want to be alone."

"Then come eat with us," Maura said firmly.

"I don't know," Bill said. "I hate to intrude at this late date, and I'll be a fifth wheel."

"Nonsense," Maura said dismissively. "They'll be plenty of food, that's no problem. And, as for being a fifth wheel, I'd appreciate your

company and so would Matt. It will make meeting Robin less awkward."

"You're just meeting him tomorrow?" Bill asked incredulously.
"Hasn't he been here since last weekend?"

"Yes, he has," Maura said with a bit of wry humor in her voice. "Kai
hasn't let him out of the house. Those two have been holed up together
since Sunday afternoon. Matt wanted to take us all out to dinner one
night, but Kai declined politely. Evidently this reunion is going well."

"Evidently," Bill commented dryly.

"No, it's a good thing. Kai was going to ask Robin to move down
here to live with him. I gather he's said yes. If he hadn't, I'm sure Kai
would have wanted some backup from me," Maura said smugly.

"Backup?" Bill asked curiously.

"Oh sure," Maura said easily. "Along the lines of showing Robin
how cool Matt and I are with the idea. Talking Kai up, that sort of
thing."

Bill nodded knowingly and said, "He's very lucky you and Matt are
so supportive. In all the years Jack and I we lived together, my parents
never recognized my partner for what he really was."

"That's so sad," Maura said. "Look at what they cheated themselves
out of—a whole part of your life, really."

Bill pursed his lips and rolled his eyes in reply.

"Say you'll come," Maura pleaded. "I'm sure it will be a lot better
than unpacking books and listening to old songs alone."

Bill stood, and Maura watched the argument he was having with
himself revealed by the slight changes on his face as he clenched and unclenched his jaw. Finally, Bill said, "If you swear I won't be in the way."

"I swear," Maura said easily as she picked up a pen and wrote on a sheet
of notepaper, then handed the paper to Bill, saying, "Here's the address
of Matt's place. You can look up directions on MapQuest, right?"

"Sure," Bill said as he glanced at the note. "What time should I
show up?"

"We're eating at three, Kai says. Why don't you plan on getting there between one-thirty and two o'clock? That way you can enjoy some wine or a drink with us before the feast."

Bill smiled and said, "Sounds good. I really didn't want to spend the day alone, no matter how brave I intended to be. I appreciate this, Maura."

Maura rose from her desk chair and walked to stand close enough to her boss and friend to lay her hand lightly on his shoulder. "I'm delighted you've said yes."

"I have to admit, I am curious about Kai's friend," Bill said mischievously. "Kai's quite a looker, if you don't mind my saying so. Though I'm past it, I still enjoy observing young lovers."

Maura laughed and said, "I'm anxious to meet Robin myself. Kai has never been so enthralled before. This kid must be something special, but I guess we'll see."

Bill left after that and Maura quickly put her office to bed for the long weekend. After she left the office, she stopped at Publix on the way home to pick up the supplies for her pecan pies and then hurried along home, eager to get the chore behind her.

Once she was home, she changed and went straight to work on her baking. As she moved around her familiar kitchen, she was flooded with memories of Thanksgiving preparations of the past. For many years, her mother and father had made the trip south for the holiday. They spent Christmas visiting Maura's siblings' homes. As she rolled out pastry dough made from scratch, she recalled conversations with her mother in that kitchen and in her childhood home. Now, she missed them. She felt the absence of her father in the living room drowsing while the television played on, unwatched. She thought of Kai as a youngster, settled in his room drawing, with his dog for company, while she cooked with her mother. It had been a parade of years spent happily enough for all the challenges and loneliness. There were less pleasant memories of the holidays she and Rhett had lived together in the small cottage in Avalon Beach. Still, she thought as she poured the filling carefully into the browned pie shells, for what it was, it wasn't so bad.

When she at last had the pies in the oven, she made a short pot of decaffeinated coffee and sat at her kitchen table to wait for Matt to return home. Instinctively, her hands found the slight swell of her belly and she stroked her new baby through the protective layer of skin, muscle, and clothing that covered him. "Oh Junebug," she sighed aloud. "You're going to be a lucky little fellow. Your mama knows how to be a mama, and your daddy knows how to be a daddy. We can't wait for you to get here, Junebug."

When the coffeemaker beeped, she rose slowly and made a cup of coffee. She really was pleased to be pregnant once more. It seemed less like she was being sentenced to decades more responsibility than she was continuing with something she enjoyed. Her circumstances this time were certainly different. Importantly, there were financial resources now that there weren't when Kai was born. The teeth-gritting effort it took to keep the rent paid, the house warm, and food on the table wasn't as onerous as it had been then. Also, the nagging self-doubt inherent in doing it all for the first time was gone. Maura knew she wouldn't be constantly asking herself if every little thing she did was right this time. No. This time around, she was relaxed and happy.

She was still concerned the baby would be another manic-depressive. For as long as she lived, she would feel the responsibility for Kai's challenges the way she did. Superstitiously, she had wracked her brain thinking of things she'd done before she got pregnant with Kai that she wasn't repeating with this baby. For one, she wasn't getting high. When she was twenty-two, she was no stranger to Rhett's bong. While she might be fifty, she was not a pot head at this point in her life. In fact, since she'd learned she was pregnant this time, she'd carefully cut out drinking, smoking, caffeinated beverages and avoided anything she felt vaguely could be tainted chemically. She'd slipped up a few times, smoking, having a drink, drinking a Coke, eating commercially produced chicken, but she felt she was doing a good job trying to cut out any external things that might affect her Junebug.

What nagged her, when she allowed herself to think about it, was the mysterious, unseen thread of DNA that held the chemical code for bipoloar disorder. She visualized herself, her fingers tangled in an endless multi-colored skein of chemical coding searching for the tiny single knot that held the aberrant node. She pictured herself plucking it out and flicking it away as easily as she might find and get rid of a flea on Heidi's back.

Maura sipped her coffee and played that image in her mind ritualistically. Holding her coffee mug clasped in her hands before her face, she stared out the bay window of the kitchen and said firmly, "Junebug, you're going to be a happy little boy. The world for you is going to be bright and fascinating. Every day, you're going to look at only blue skies and bowing daffodils in a warm breeze. You're going to get so much pleasure from being here with me and your daddy. You're going to laugh and laugh and laugh. I promise you, Mama swears to you, you're going to be so happy."

She concentrated on her message and internalized it. She willed it to zing along in her blood vessels and infuse her unborn infant with soft colors and soothing sensations. She could almost feel her positivity and conviction nourishing him inside, suffusing him with peace just as the warm coffee stole into the cold self-doubt she had hidden in a knot in her stomach. She wanted this baby to be free of Kai's torments and she willed it so, viscerally.

"Maura?" came Matt's voice, reaching her even as his hands grasped her shoulders and gently pulled her back from her reverie. "Are you okay?" he asked worriedly.

Maura set her coffee mug on the table and tilted her head back to

P. 259 / 260

look up into her baby's daddy's face. She smiled and said, "I'm fine. I'm having a silent conversation with our baby."

Matt leaned down to find her lips for a quick kiss. "You were really zoned. You didn't even hear me come in."

"Yeah," Maura admitted distractedly. She didn't want Matt to know of her intent or concern for the baby. It was something he couldn't understand. "How was your day?" She asked.

"Good, good," Matt said as he slumped into his chair at the table. "You must have gotten home early. Something smells terrific."

Maura smiled and told him, "Bill let all of us go at three. He does that before every holiday. He always has."

"I used to do it too," Matt said. "But now I have to answer to corporate. I'm just one more division president since I sold the company. And, corporate doesn't believe in letting staff off early unless there's a hurricane."

"Not your fault, then," Maura said. "You look tired."

Matt ran his hand over his face and sighed. "I am tired. I'm glad we have tomorrow off. I plan on sleeping until the parade comes on. Then you and I will curl up in the living room with our coffee and watch the balloons come to Macy's."

"Sounds good to me," Maura told him. "I'm glad Kai's in charge of the big dinner. I'm looking forward to simply showing up and eating like a hog."

"Have you talked to him?" Matt asked casually.

"Not today," Maura said. "We spoke briefly yesterday afternoon. Everything seems to be going well over there. He sounded good."

"No word yet on whether or not he's popped the big question?" Matt asked with a smile.

Maura shook her head. "He didn't say. It's kind of maddening isn't it? I'm afraid I've bought in totally to this notion that everything will be fine with him if Robin just moves down."

"You and me both," Matt said and sighed. "It's our own little soap opera. I'm not used to being so involved with another guy's love life."

Maura laughed and reached to pat Matt's hand. "That's because your daughters haven't gotten started yet. You forget, romance rules their world for years. Finding Mr. Right . . ."

"Keeping Mr. Right is the hard part," Matt said wryly. "Well, I guess we'll find out everything tomorrow, won't we?"

"I'll know when Kai answers the door," Maura said. "All I have to do is look at him. I can read his emotional temperature like a thermometer."

"That's a mother thing," Matt said and rolled his eyes. "My mother can do it too. She can take one look at me and know exactly what's going on in my mind. My dad doesn't have a clue unless I tell him."

"It's comes along with the uterus," Maura said and laughed.

"Evidently," Matt said as he looked Maura over carefully. "How are you doing? Are you feeling alright?"

"Yes. Fine," Maura told him. "I was nauseated again this morning, but it passes quickly. The truth is, I feel great. Why? Do I seem out of sorts?"

"No, not at all," Matt answered quickly. "I just have to keep an eye on you is all. After all, you're carrying a pretty special cargo in there."

"I'm good, Matt," Maura assured him. "Would you like some coffee? It's decaf, but it's fresh. Or I could pour you a glass of wine."

Matt thought a moment as he regarded the coffeepot. Finally he stood and said, "I can pour myself a glass of wine. You sit tight."

Maura watched him as he made his drink, enjoying his strong economical movements. She enjoyed knowing he was hers. There was a definite pride of ownership in her view of the relationship. As he returned to the table and sat down, she said, "You're a good-looking man, you know that?"

Matt looked at her and raised his eyebrows questioningly. "What brought that on?" he asked before he took a sip of his wine.

Maura shrugged and said, "I don't know. I just felt like saying it. It's true. I think we're going to make a handsome baby."

"You have a pretty good track record," Matt said easily. "Kai's a nice-looking guy. Tall. I never really thought about my having any influence over what the kid would look like."

"That's because your ex-wife is Latina and you're fair," Maura said reasonably. "The girls look more like their mother. You and I are Anglos. There's every reason in the world to believe the baby could take after you than me. Look at Kai. He has his father's build, hair, and eyes. The only thing he got from me was his height. My side of the family is tall."

Matt nodded and seemed to ponder the idea for several moments. Finally, he looked at Maura and smiled. "I hope our little boy is all you. You may think I'm nice looking, but I think I'm just average. If he looks like you, he'll be a handsome boy. Life is easier for nice looking people, I think."

"Oh I don't know about that," Maura said sagely. "I just want him to be happy and good natured. I'm just concerned that he'll—"

"Maura don't worry, about that," Matt interrupted. "I know what you're getting at. Our baby's going to be fine. There's no problem with any depression on my side of the family. We're just a bunch of boringly good-natured English peasants. Our baby will be healthy, happy, and wise."

Maura smiled in reply and stood slowly. "I think my pies must be about ready to take out. I can't believe the timer hasn't gone off yet."

"They smell delicious, Maura," Matt said hungrily. "What do you want to do about dinner tonight?"

The timer on the stove went off before Maura could answer. She picked up two clean dish towels and opened the door to take the pies out. As the blast of hot air rushed past her face, Maura breathed in the rich scent of her handiwork. The pies had browned nicely. As she set them on the cooling rack, she felt a rush of happiness overtake her as certainly as the oven's blast had. It felt very good to be standing in her kitchen with her baby's daddy settled nearby and her son presumably happy a few miles away. She turned to Matt with a smile and said, "To tell you the truth, there are three pies here and I'd be perfectly happy with a slice of pie and a cold glass of milk. Did you have lunch?"

"Actually, I had a big lunch," Matt admitted. "I'd be satisfied with a sandwich a little later and a piece of pie, if you're going to cut it."

Maura smiled as she refilled her coffee mug with fresh coffee from the pot. "God, you're so easy."

Matt watched her as she sat back down at the table and took a sip of her coffee. "So are you, sweetheart. You're so easy to live with. It's taken me some getting used to."

Maura gave him a meaningful look and said, "Sometimes it takes half a lifetime to find Mr. Right. That's something you can tell your girls."

Matt nodded and sipped his wine.

"Oh! I forgot to tell you," Maura said suddenly.

"Tell me what?" Matt said carefully.

"I invited Bill Kellogg to share our Thanksgiving dinner. He was going to spend it alone with a grilled cheese sandwich and a bottle of scotch."

Matt grimaced involuntarily and said, "God, that's bleak. I remember spending Thanksgiving alone when my wife and I separated. I took the boat out and tried to make myself happy by fishing and drinking beer. It didn't work. Did Bill say he'd come?"

"Yes," Maura said. "I hope you don't mind that I asked him. I know it's spur of the moment. I just couldn't stand the thought of him alone this year. It's so soon after his partner's death."

"No, it's perfectly all right," Mat said quickly. "You did the right thing. I'm glad you invited him. I've always liked him, even before I met you, though I didn't know him all that well."

"He's been a great boss and a good friend over the years," Maura said. "He was really supportive, and being a single mother I needed all the support I could get, believe me."

"Have you told Kai he's coming?" Matt asked.

"Not yet," Maura said. "I guess I should call him. I know there'll be enough food. I'm pretty sure he won't mind. He seems to like Bill."

"Yeah, but this is also the first time we'll all be meeting Kai's boyfriend," Matt pointed out needlessly. "Don't you think that's stressful enough?"

"I don't see anything stressful about inviting a holiday orphan to the feast," Maura said. "Besides, I'm glad Bill's going to be there. That way, if things are uncomfortable with Robin, there will be every reason to be polite around company."

"Do you think things will be uncomfortable around Robin, Maura?" Matt asked carefully.

"Not on my part," Maura said automatically. Then she paused before saying, "I don't know, honestly. Maybe I subconsciously want a buffer of some kind, just in case."

Matt nodded agreeably. "Maybe. It will give us all somebody else to talk to if the conversation lags or something. Anyway, just relax. Bill's coming and we're going to meet Robin regardless. Everything's going to be fine."

Maura sighed and said, "You're right. I suppose I should call Kai and let him know."

"Definitely," Matt said.

"I'll call him after I finish this cup of coffee," Maura promised. In truth, she wanted to savor her time alone with Matt in the sweet scent of her kitchen a little longer. The day had been so good so far, she didn't want a sour note to intrude on it. She smiled, sipped her coffee, and wondered about what the following day would bring.

In Maura's fondest hopes, Robin would prove to be charming and someone she could have a warm relationship with. She'd never given much thought to the possibility of Kai's mate. She had not had the best of relationships with Rhett's parents. His mother was not an easy woman to know. She was distant and unyielding to any of the effort Maura put forth to win her over. Maura hoped she wouldn't give Robin that kind of impression of her. She hoped he'd be friendly, maybe even the type of person she could meet for lunch now and again.

However, at this point she admitted her hopes were premature. She didn't know whether Robin was here only for a longish farewell, or if he was here for a shorter hello before moving down to South Florida and into all of their lives. She sipped her coffee and unwittingly crossed her fingers under the table. Then she stood and walked to the counter for the phone. Most of her answers were a phone call away.

Chapter Twenty

THE CLOCK IN THE stereo by the bed refused to click off more than a couple of minutes at a time, No matter how many times Kai closed his eyes and willed himself back to sleep, his mind would not turn off. Over and over again, he was plagued by the amount of money he had spent on art supplies, groceries, and wine in the past two weeks. He had spent over a thousand dollars from his precious savings on his little manic creative outburst, producing and framing eleven canvases in ten days. Of course, that was the form the demons took. The actual things that were tormenting him had more to do with the decisions he'd made regarding the house he was in, and the boy-man who lay sleeping by his side. The clock read three-twenty-three when he'd been trying to sleep for an hour and a half. Defeated, he sat up and looked over his shoulder at the bed.

Heidi lay curled into a warm doughnut of grey fur at the lower end of the mattress. Robin lay on his side with his shins against Heidi's soft back. He slept on peacefully, unaware of the turmoil that had disturbed Kai's rest. Kai fought the urge he felt to kiss him tenderly. He resisted this spontaneous affection because he wanted to remain alone in the night. Kai's dark three a.m. desert was calling him and he felt more comfortable in it by himself.

Kai stood and walked quietly to the dresser, debating plundering it for the comfort he knew it held. He really didn't want Robin to know he had slipped back into the brown bottle. So much rested on him staying strong and stable in Robin's eyes just now, but he wanted a pill badly. He glanced back at the bed, peering through the darkness to see if Robin had surfaced from his own sleep, but he lay still, his lips parted, his breathing light and slow. Satisfied, Kai slid the drawer open gently, cursing the sound of the wood as it moved against wood. He opened the drawer just enough to snake his hand and wrist inside to clutch the bottle hidden under layers of boxer shorts. Once he had it in his grasp, he took it out and slid the drawer home slowly. Robin slept on. Heidi did, too.

Kai palmed the bottle and left the bedroom to pad softly down the hall to the kitchen. Naked, he had no place to hide the bottle save in the flat of his hand, so he stood in the dark at the sink under the window to open the bottle and extract a lovely blue pill. Once he'd chewed and swallowed it, he opened the cabinet by the sink and hid the bottle high on a shelf he was tall enough to reach comfortably, but too high for Robin to reach. Only after he was satisfied that the bottle was out of sight did he turn on the lights under the cabinets and start a pot of coffee.

Taking his cigarettes and lighter to the kitchen table, he sat and lit one shakily as he looked out over the lawn to the dark water beyond. His eyes were gritty and the smoke from his cigarette burned them. He felt tears well in his eyes, but he rubbed them away. He was scared to let tears start. If they did, he was frightened he wouldn't be able to stop crying. At that moment, alone, naked and vulnerable in the dark, he was no longer a lanky twenty-seven year old with ropy muscles in his arms and calves. He was a scared and vulnerable six year old, scrawny and tired, so very tired, yet electrically awake in the night.

Though this was a new kitchen and a new view out the window, the interior landscape of Kai's mind was very familiar. He knew this place well. It was a plain without pity. He wiped his eyes once more and sat up straight in his chair. Soon, the pill would kick in and he'd be okay. He would be able to reach the other side of this dark place in the night. Kai forced himself to take regular breaths between hits on his cigarette and slowly he calmed a bit. By the time the coffeemaker beeped, he felt the panic begin to melt like fog in bright sunlight. He stood and strode back to the counter to make his coffee, concentrating every movement as though it was a lifeline back to sense and sanity. The familiar collection of activities settled him somewhat as he tore open the Splenda packet and emptied it into his mug, poured the coffee, and added the cream. The tiny ringing sound his spoon made against the side of the mug centered him and by the time he returned to the table, he was breathing normally once more.

As he sat and smoked in the dim kitchen, he reminded himself of all of the good things that were going to happen as the day drew on. There were the turkey and vegetables to be cooked. Wine to be chilled, and a table to be set—those were normal activities free of pain or fear. As the painkiller eased into his blood stream, urged on by the soothing coffee and nicotine, he grew comfortable and sighed with obvious ease. At last, he started to believe everything would be okay. As his buzz pulled him along, his jaw unclenched and he began to smile. His relief was amplified by the amount of time that passed since he'd been in the brown bottle. At last, he felt safe. At last the demon voices stilled and the jazz station he'd turned on out of habit after he flicked on the lights began to sing in his mind. He felt the high sustained notes of the saxophone like fingers dragging slowly across his skin, and the beat of the bass and drums became a secondary, soothing heartbeat.

Before he'd even finished his first cup of coffee, he heard Heidi's claws along the bare terrazzo on her way to the kitchen. She appeared, followed by Robin who sleepily searched the kitchen looking for Kai. More modest than Kai, he'd blindly groped the floor in the dark for underwear and had found Kai's first. The larger boxers billowed out from the elastic clenching his waist, giving him the endearing look of a small child. He found Kai sitting at the table on the other side of the counter and wandered toward him wordlessly. He came to stand by Kai's chair and placed his arm on Kai's shoulder to hug him briefly before he returned to the other side of the table and drew out a chair. As he sat, he said, "Bad dreams, baby?"

"Yeah," Kai replied softly, "but I'm okay now. You should go back to bed."

"No. I've missed this, getting up with you when you can't sleep," Robin said lovingly.

Kai's painkiller opened a sluice of emotion from his brain to his heart and he felt a rush of love for the slight, blond man sitting across from him. He said, "Baby, it's going to be a long day today. You should enjoy your sleep. I'll wake you about seven. Go back to bed."

"You come too," Robin said, only half-awake.

"I can't, baby." Kai said as he stood and walked to the other side of the table. "I can't go back to sleep. Let me do my thing and you rest," he said as he placed his hands under Robin's armpits and lifted him firmly.

Robin obediently stood and leaned his head on Kai's shoulder. Kai hugged him before taking his hand and leading him back down the hall to the bedroom. When they got to the bed, Robin sank down on it and curled on his side. Kai stroked his hair and said, "Sleep now. I'll wake you at seven, okay?"

Robin nodded contentedly and slipped back into sleep before Kai turned and went back into the kitchen. Heidi couldn't be so easily put back to bed. She was too used to keeping her master company on these predawn vigils. Kai took her bowl to the garage for her dog food and made her gravy before setting the bowl down for her to eat.

Once Heidi was tended, Kai walked back to the kitchen cabinet and found the brown bottle once more. Without any reproof from his subconscious, he took another pill and reheated his coffee. He returned to his chair at the table knowing he now had three hours to himself to sit and dream the day into being. He felt like the wizard in the old story who conjured a castle from thin air. His demons were now silenced, the jazz played on the radio, and Kai began his day.

From this rocky start, the hours unfolded and tasks began to be accomplished. Heidi got walked, showers were taken, food was prepared, and as Kai sorted through an unpacked box full of his CDs looking for Christmas music, the front door bell sounded. Robin walked into the living room from the kitchen dressed in a pair of worn white jeans and one of Kai's cotton sweaters. He looked at Kai expectantly and Kai gave him a smile. "Here we go, Robin," he said as he put down the box and started for the door.

Robin joined him in the foyer. Kai gave him another significant look and shushed an excited Heidi before he opened the door to his mother and Matt. "Happy Thanksgiving," Kai said, nearly shouting in his nervous excitement. "Hey, Happy Thanksgiving back," Matt said. His mother leaned in for a kiss, made awkward by the pecan pies she was juggling. "Happy Thanksgiving!" Kai said excitedly as he watched his mother and Matt lift hands occupied with pecan pies in greeting.

Heidi whined and danced among their legs as Matt and Maura came into the house. Robin stood shyly to one side and grinned while Kai casually introduced him, leading their guests to the kitchen to put down their desserts. Once they had free hands, Maura hugged her son and Matt reached to shake Robin's hand. As Robin shook hands with Matt, Maura looked around the kitchen and out into the living and dining room beyond. "You've rearranged," she said approvingly. "And I see some new art on the walls. I want to check it out once I've given Robin a hug," she said as she took two steps to enfold Robin in her arms in a sincere embrace. "Let me look at you," she said as she took him by the shoulders and gently pushed him back a step. "I can't believe I'm finally getting to meet you. You're as cute as a bug's ear!"

Robin blushed becomingly and looked at his feet, saying, "It's good to meet you. You're as lovely as Kai said you were."

"Sounds like they already have a fan club going, Kai," Matt said drolly.

"Yes, it does," Kai replied as he patted Matt's shoulder and passed him to take a bottle of Champagne from the refrigerator. "We're going to go ahead and open this," he said as he wrapped a clean white dish towel around the bottle and began tearing at the foil covering the cork.

"Shouldn't we wait for Bill?" Maura asked gently as she continued to look Robin over.

Kai twisted the cork free of the bottle with a resulting pop and said, "We'll just pour him a glass when he gets here. Robin, give everyone a glass."

Robin turned to the counter behind him and passed Matt and Maura tulip-shaped glasses which Kai then eagerly filled.

"Champagne? What are we celebrating?" Matt asked curiously.

"Well, Thanksgiving for one," Maura answered happily. "We always had Champagne at our house on Thanksgiving. My parents love a mimosa and we would start with them as the Macy's parade came on. We're actually starting late for us."

Kai took his glass from Robin and filled it two-thirds full before setting the bottle on the counter and laying his arm over Robin's shoulder. "We also have something else to celebrate," Kai announced. Maura and Matt exchanged a quick glance before looking at him expectantly. "Mom, Matt. I've asked Robin to move down to live with me and he's very generously said yes. Lift your glass to toast all my dreams coming true."

"Here, here," seconded Matt and clinked his glass against Kai's.

"To new beginnings!" Maura said as she clinked her glass against Robin's and Kai's in turn.

Kai tightened his embrace of Robin's shoulder briefly and looked at him significantly before sipping his Champagne.

Robin returned his look, and, somewhat embarrassed, saluted him with his glass before taking his own sip.

"So, Robin, when are you going to move down?" Maura asked pleasantly.

Robin looked around the small circle of faces waiting for his answer and said shyly, "Soon. Within a couple of weeks. I'll need to give my boss notice, but most likely he'll be happy to see me go. One less mouth to feed over the winter."

"So it's slow up your way as well?" Matt asked.

"Well, it always is in the winter," Robin replied. "But this year, it's especially slow."

"Tell me about it," Matt said. "Last month we only had four closings. This time last year we had forty-three."

"That's enough about business," Maura said calmly. "Today is a happy day. Kai, where are we sitting?"

"How about the living room until Bill comes," Kai suggested. "That way you can check out the new paintings."

As a group, they moved from the kitchen into the great room that held the dining and living areas in the house's central space. As Kai and Robin sat on one end of the generous leather sectional, Maura and Matt strayed to look first at the picture of Heidi, and then on to the grid of Robin's portraits. Heidi nosed them along, herding them toward the sofa.

"These are really good, Kai," Matt commented, obviously impressed. "I don't know anything about art, but these were obviously done by someone with a lot of talent."

"It's a new style for you," Maura commented as she perched on the edge of the sofa and reached to pet Heidi who laid down at her feet. "Were you just in a hurry to finish them, or were you trying a new technique? I mean they obviously look finished, but your usual style is much tighter, less brushy than these."

"I was trying something new, Mom," Kai said seriously. "The ideas were coming hot and fast. It felt really good to be painting again."

"Where did you find those frames?" Matt asked as he sat next to Maura at the other end of the sofa.

"I made them," Kai answered simply. "It's just 1 x 4s with a little bit of trim and some gold leaf."

"They're incredible," Matt said admiringly. "You know your way around a compound miter saw, I'll give you that."

"Thanks," Kai said easily.

"Robin, what do you think of your portraits? It's really something to be all over a wall like that," Matt teased.

"It's pretty intense, actually," Robin admitted. "I mean, I got used to Kai drawing me when we lived up on the beach. I had no idea all those sketches would become paintings. I was really humbled to see them all together like that. It's like I'm an obsession or something."

"No. You're a muse," Maura said seriously. "Isn't that what you call it, Kai?"

"Yes," Kai agreed. "I guess I was just missing the real thing," he said as he lifted his hand from Robin's shoulder and rubbed the back of his head teasingly.

"Stop," Robin protested mildly. "Jeez . . ."

"So Robin, tell us about yourself," Maura said and took a sip of Champagne.

"Oh, I'm not that interesting," Robin demurred. "I grew up in Charlotte. I have four brothers and sisters—I'm the baby in the family. They're all married and have kids of their own. My family all live within a few miles of one another. I'm the one who struck out and left town."

"How did you come to live in Kill Devil Hills?" Maura asked curiously.

"While I was a senior at Carolina, I got my real estate license. When I graduated, I went to work for a realtor in Raleigh. This couple who were my clients got transferred to Fort Worth. I was handling the sale of their house in Raleigh. Anyway, they also own a house in Kill Devil Hills and offered me the key to visit one weekend a couple of springs ago. Long story short, I fell in love with the Outer Banks and ended up getting a job and renting their beach house."

"I see," Maura said evenly. "And now, my son has convinced you to move down here. It's a pretty big move for you."

Robin looked her directly in the eye and said, "Not really. It's the logical next move. Kai and I lived together for a year on the beach. The way I feel about him, it makes sense to take this next step."

"Of course," Maura said quickly. "I just meant it's a whole change of climate, lifestyle, everything—moving to Florida, that is."

"Well, I'm not quite twenty-five. If I'm ever going to make a bold move like this, now's the time to do it," Robin said easily. "Plus, I pretty much know I want to be with Kai, regardless. I'm just glad he's from Florida and not someplace like Oklahoma or Idaho."

Matt laughed and said, "Yeah, you lucked out on that score. Fort Lauderdale isn't exactly a hard-luck place to be."

Robin smiled and nodded.

"So where has Kai taken you since you've been down?" Maura asked with interest. "Have you been over to the beach or on Las Olas Boulevard? That's such a nice part of town, and not far from here, really."

Robin blushed and looked at Kai.

Kai laughed and said, "About all of Fort Lauderdale Robin's seen is in a four block radius from where we're sitting. We've been getting reacquainted; I think that's the best way to put it."

Matt snickered, which he tried to cover by pretending he had coughed instead. Maura rolled her eyes and shook her head. "Kai, you could have at least taken the poor boy for a drive on A1A. You haven't been fair. You've got him moving down here and he hasn't even seen the city. Shame on you."

Kai laughed and said, "There will be plenty of time for that once he gets down here."

"Do you have to fly back tomorrow, Robin?" Maura asked gently. "Couldn't you stay for a few more days, and I'll make sure my son shows you around the place you'll be living."

"Umm ... no. I can't," Robin said quietly. "I have this couple who've been looking at beach houses since last spring. They're coming down for the holiday and have sworn to me that they're going to buy a house during this visit. To be perfectly honest, if they do, the money will come in handy while I'm getting on my feet down here."

"What will you do if they do buy a house? Fly up in thirty days for the closing?" Matt asked practically.

"Yes. I'd do that for sure," Robin said. "Both of the places they're looking at are oceanfront. I'm not bragging, but my commission would be pretty significant."

"I'd imagine so," Maura said encouragingly. "Do you intend to stay in real estate once you move down here?"

"I'd like to very much," Robin told her. "I enjoy the business a lot. Of course, I know the market down here is as slow as in the rest of the country, but I have some money in savings. I'm sure I'll land on my feet."

"I can see why you'd be good at selling houses," Matt observed. "Once you get your Florida Real Estate License, you're welcome to use me as a resource. I always hear of people looking for someone sharp. I'd hire you myself, but you wouldn't be happy selling what I'm building right now."

"Matt's company is building affordable townhouses," Maura explained.

"I see," Robin said. "I'll really appreciate your advice once I get down here. It's a whole new market to learn."

"We'll take good care of you, don't worry," Maura promised him.

"Look! I think Bill Kellogg is pulling up right now," Matt said.

Everyone looked out the generous windows lining the living room wall that faced the street to watch the last guest park and get out of his car carrying a bottle of wine. Unaware he was being watched; Bill locked his car and made his way to the front door.

"You guys sit," Kai said as he stood. "I'll let him in." With that, he moved quickly to the front door along with Heidi who followed him. Before Bill could knock, Kai had the front door open. "Welcome,

Bill. Happy Thanksgiving," he said as he stepped out of the way to let Bill in.

"Happy Thanksgiving to you," Bill said with a smile. "I really appreciate your invitation."

As he closed the door, Kai said, "We're happy to have you. Come in, everybody's in the living room. Can I get you a glass of Champagne?"

"Champagne? That would be great," Bill said as he extended the bottle of wine in his hand to Kai. "This is my contribution to the feast. It's Graves. It's excellent with turkey."

"Thanks," Kai said as he took the bottle and examined the label. "Do I need to chill it?"

"Couldn't hurt," Bill said shyly as he peered around Kai to look into the living room. "Hello, everybody. Happy Thanksgiving!"

"Go in and sit down," Kai urged him. "I'll pop this in the fridge and get you that glass of Champagne."

"Robin, this is my boss and good friend, Bill Kellogg," Maura said as Bill entered the area bound by the sectional sofa.

"Nice to meet you," Bill said and he extended his hand to Robin.

"Nice to meet you," Robin said as he shook his hand. "Kai recently did some work for you, didn't he?"

"He sure did," Bill said happily. "Beautiful work. To tell you the truth, I almost hate to clutter the shelves with all my books. I've put the stereo in its place and have the CDs shelved, but to tell you the truth, I've enjoyed just sitting in my new library and looking at it." Bill turned from Robin and said, "Matt Jenkins, good to see you," as he extended his hand to Matt.

"Bill," Matt acknowledged him as he shook his hand. "Good to see you. I was delighted when Maura said she'd invited you. You're like a member of the family after all the years you two have worked together."

"I feel like an uncle, at least," Bill said as Kai walked back into the living room with his glass of Champagne. He took the glass from Kai with a nod, and said, "I've known this one since he was not quite six, I believe."

"God, that's a long time," Kai said as he sat down next to Robin and placed his arm across the back of the sofa behind his shoulders. "Robin, this man used to let me sit at the drafting table in his office and play with his Rapidograph pens. I remember thinking all I ever wanted to do when I grew up was sit at a desk like that and draw all day."

"You were very good," Bill said genuinely. "You were so careful with those delicate pens. I couldn't believe how neatly you worked on that mylar. Not even seven years old and you could lay down a line my drafters would be envious of."

"I've always loved tedious, detailed work," Kai said easily. "Thanks for all the faith you put in me back then—and since I've gotten back," he said as he lifted his glass of Champagne to Bill.

Bill tipped Kai's glass with his own and took a sip of Champagne as he looked around the large room at the brightly colored art work on the walls. "The art you have in here is impressive. You have great taste in paintings."

"They're his work," Maura said proudly. "The dog is Heidi here, and the ones in the Warhol-esque stack are all Robin. Did you notice that?"

Bill peered at the paintings myopically and then looked at Robin, who smiled shyly. "My God, they are! Kai you really are gifted. I didn't know you did painting like this. I'm almost embarrassed I asked you to paint my walls."

Kai laughed and said, "I make more money painting walls and bookcases than I ever have off my artwork."

"He built those frames too," Matt added proudly.

"No way," Bill said with true admiration. "I'll have to commission you to do something for my place. Have you ever considered doing portraits?"

Kai shrugged and said, "I've never really thought about it. But it is something I can do. We'll talk about it later if you like. Now, how would everyone like to go sit out back? Robin and I cleaned up out there and there's plenty of shade. It's too pretty a day to sit in the house."

"That's a great idea," Matt said and looked at Maura. "Wouldn't you enjoy being outside?"

"Absolutely," she said and stood.

Everyone else stood along with her and the group moved across the room and out the open French doors onto the patio. When he had everyone settled outside, Kai said, "Dinner's going to be ready about three. I've made some appetizers. Would anyone care for some bruschetta, pears, and gorgonzola? A little more Champagne?"

"Oh hell yes," Matt said eagerly. "We skipped breakfast knowing how good dinner will be. I could use something to nibble on, Kai."

"Let me give you a hand," Maura said and started to stand.

"Nope," Kai said as he put a hand on his mother's shoulder and pressed her gently back into her chair. "After all the years you waited on me, this year all you have to do is sit back and be treated like a queen."

"They told me this day would come," Maura said happily.

"Robin, give me a hand, will you?" Kai asked.

Robin stood immediately and said, "Is Champagne okay or can I get anyone anything else?"

"More Champagne is good for me," Bill said.

"What the hell, it's a holiday," Matt told him. "Why don't you just bring out another bottle?"

"I need to switch to something else if I'm going to have a glass with dinner," Maura said disappointedly. "I can't get little Matt in here drunk," she joked as she patted her stomach.

"Papaya iced tea?" Robin suggested. "It's fresh."

"Thanks, Robin. That sounds perfect," Maura said with a genuine smile.

"C'mon, Robin," Kai said as he stepped back inside the French doors.

Robin followed him into the kitchen where Kai quickly kissed him and whispered, "Well, what do you think?"

"You didn't tell me your mom was so pretty," Robin said back in a low voice. "You also didn't tell me she's pregnant."

"Oh yeah, duh," Kai said as he took the plastic cling film off a plat-ter holding toasted slices of baguette arranged around a bowl of freshly chopped tomato, basil, garlic, and olive oil. "She and Matt, they're like a couple of twenty-year-olds having their first kid. What do you think of them?"

"They're really nice," Robin said as he opened another bottle of Champagne. "I mean, you told me they were cool about us, but they're really great. I feel totally comfortable around them."

Kai picked up a clean pear and began slicing it into neat wedges. "Bill Kellogg is gay."

"No way," Robin said incredulously. "How do you know?"

"Jeez, Robin. I've known the guy since I was six. He had a partner for almost thirty years, but he died not too long ago. Of a stroke. It was really sad," Kai told him.

"Thirty years? My God. Things must have been a lot tougher for them than they are for us. We're pretty lucky, don't you think?" Robin asked.

"You're lucky you're here and not up on the Banks. Why do you think I want to be down here? You and me together here is no big deal. Up on the beach, it would be total bullshit all the time," Kai said firmly.

"Oh it wouldn't have been all that bad," Robin said evenly. "We did live together up there for a year, Kai."

"Yeah? And you didn't catch any shit for it. I did," Kai said as he arranged pear slices around a wedge of gorgonzola. "I hate it up there. I can't live like that anymore."

"Well, you don't have to now," Robin said as he came to stand close beside him. "I understand how you feel. If being with you means I have to leave a place I love, I will. You gotta do what you gotta do, I guess."

Kai distractedly turned his head to peck Robin on the cheek before finishing the plate. "Don't think I don't know what it's costing you to be with me, baby. I appreciate it."

Robin patted Kai's back possessively and said, "That goes both ways, Kai. I know you never wanted to admit you were gay. I understand what a big step you're taking with me. I can't get over how relaxed you are around your folks. God knows—"

"Let's don't talk about that now," Kai said gently. "Let's just enjoy all the goodwill coming our way and get started off on the right foot this time, okay?"

"Okay," Robin agreed. "You want me to take out the bruschetta?"

"No. I'll bring it," Kai said with a smile. "You go refresh their drinks. I'll be out in a second. I have to check on the turkey."

Robin nodded as he took the bottle of Champagne and Maura's iced tea and went back outside. Kai stepped to the sink under the kitchen window. As he washed his hands, he watched Robin as he neatly served everyone and sat down. Kai smiled contentedly and picked up a clean dish cloth to wipe his hands. Everyone looked so happy sitting out in the breeze. The gnawing fear and dread he'd had at three a.m. was gone. He'd managed to out run it with the help of the painkillers. Briefly, he considered taking another one now. It was ten hours since he'd had the last one, but he decided against it. Another glass or two of Champagne would put him where he needed to be for the moment. Without another thought, he picked up his turkey baster and opened the oven door.

The rest of the afternoon passed contentedly. Everyone enjoyed the food, and unlike other holidays in the past, there was not an excessive amount of food left over. Kai had planned well, and with the exception of the leftover braised Brussels sprouts and a respectable turkey carcass, there wasn't much to package up when everyone began to say their goodbyes as darkness fell. Bill Kellogg was the first to depart. He thanked Kai sincerely and brought up the question of a possible portrait once more. There was a photograph of him and his partner together, twenty years ago on the beach in St. Barts, which he longed to have turned into a painting. Kai could hardly say no. They agreed to talk again after Bill found the picture in the shoebox where it was stored. He departed, not drunk, but in considerably good spirits. Matt and Maura lingered for a second cup of coffee and another piece of pecan pie before, they too, decided to head home to settle in for the night.

Maura hugged Robin once more and wished him a safe trip back up to the Outer Banks. Matt complimented Kai on how well he'd already fixed up the place by power cleaning the sidewalk, patio, and roof. Maura interrupted him to hug her son goodbye and whisper that she'd call him the following afternoon.

Once they were in the car, and had waved farewell to Kai and Robin once more, Maura said, "Matt, if you don't mind, can we drive home by way of A1A? I feel like being close to the beach tonight."

"It's kind of out of the way," Matt groused gently, "but if you really want to . . ."

"Please," said Maura and then fell silent. Matt turned the car out of Lighthouse Point and made his way to the coast. Sensing Maura wanted to ride in silence; he turned on an old Steely Dan CD and listened to it as they made their way down the motel-strewn remains of Fort Lauderdale's beach. Maura stayed quiet until Matt turned off A1A at Oakland Park Boulevard to head straight west toward home.

"What are you thinking about, sweetheart?" he asked Maura with concern. "Didn't you have a good time today?"

"Oh, I had an excellent time," Maura said easily. "I think Bill really had a nice time, don't you?"

"Oh yeah," Matt said and chuckled. "He really seemed fascinated by Kai and Robin, you know, as a couple. I guess the world has come a long way since he was their age."

"Yes, it sure has," Maura said quietly. "When I think of how I was taught to respond to gay people, never mind a gay couple, when I was a kid . . . I don't know. I think it's a good thing overall."

"I agree," Matt said. "My attitudes have sure changed. When I was Robin's age I wouldn't have been caught dead in the same room as a gay couple. Now I have one as an in-law, or something. Still, seeing them together was no big deal. It was kind of normal in a way."

"Kai seems so happy," Maura observed. "And I think I'm going to really love Robin. He was a bit reserved, but I would have been, too, if I was in the same situation."

"He seems like a good, steady kind of guy. If you ask me, that's exactly what Kai needs," Matt reasoned.

"You know, with Kai, I'm always waiting for the other shoe to drop," Maura said sadly. "I wish I could trust the happy picture he showed us today. I've just known him too long. I can't shake the feeling there are new, fresh disasters just waiting for him now that he seems to have gotten his shit together."

"The other shoe doesn't have to drop, Maura," Matt said firmly.

"What do you mean?" Maura asked defensively.

"I'm just saying sooner or later, everybody gets their shit together. Why shouldn't Kai? He boomeranged back down here a month ago and you put him up, but look at what he's gotten accomplished. He's back on his meds. He's working. He's got a place to live, and now he's gotten things settled with his love life. Maybe from here on out, there won't be any drama," Matt concluded optimistically.

"God, I hope you're right," Maura sighed. "Maybe there are happy endings."

"Maybe happy endings are ongoing," Matt suggested easily. "Look at you and I. Neither one of us had a clue we'd find a soulmate at this late date. Now, we've had that happy ending and we're starting out a whole new book with our baby. Happy endings are what you have to hope for, Maura."

"Maybe you're right," Maura said and smiled. "Maybe my boomerang kid has finally found a place out in the big wide world."

"Yes, let's hope so," Matt said evenly. "You've seen enough drama out of Kai to last you a lifetime. But life isn't about drama. Life is just a combination of little, small moments, like this afternoon, where things settle into place and you can breathe a sigh of relief. That's what you ought to be thankful for."

Maura reached across the seat and took Matt's free hand. Squeezing it, she thought about what he said. She'd had her share of knocks, but she was happy, she thought. Happiness could surprise anyone, even a bipolar kid who struggled with himself and the world he lived in. Kai had found someone worthy of his best intentions, Maura was sure of that. She settled a little deeper into the comfortable leather seat of Matt's car and enjoyed the feeling of speed as they headed west into what was left of the sunset. And, somewhere in suburban Oakland Park Boulevard's flash of neon and streetlights, she finally let go of her first born son.